THE GREATEST NOVEL
EVER WRITTEN

THE GREATEST NOVEL EVER WRITTEN

Howard Camner

Library of Congress Control Number:		2021921800
ISBN:	Hardcover	978-1-6641-9668-1
	Softcover	978-1-6641-9667-4
	eBook	978-1-6641-9669-8

Print information available on the last page.

Rev. date: 10/25/2021

To order additional copies of this book, contact:
Xlibris
844-714-8691
www.Xlibris.com
Orders@Xlibris.com
836292

INTRODUCTION

Since the beginning of the written word some 5,500 years ago in Mesopotamia, which is present-day Iraq, writers have dreamt of writing the greatest novel in literary history. Throughout the ages many have tried and have failed miserably. Hemingway couldn't do it. Dickens couldn't do it. Fitzgerald, Austen, Proust, Melville, Tolstoy, Faulkner, couldn't do it. Updike couldn't do it. Wells couldn't do it. Steinbeck, Vonnegut, Woolf, Joyce, Christie, Doyle, Hardy, Salinger, London, Rand, none of them could do it. It just couldn't be done... until now. Late one night, in a trailer in the small redneckish town of Interlachen, Florida, where thinking isn't a very popular sport, a scruffy reclusive me put down my beer, picked up a pen, and put it to paper to empty my already half-empty head. I didn't for one moment think that I was about to write the greatest novel ever written, but boy, was I wrong... sort of.

Rabbi and author Chaim Potok said that all beginnings are hard. It's not the most difficult statement to make. If a monkey with a second grade education could talk, the monkey could say that too. I don't agree with that statement. *Beginning* to eat a bologna sandwich isn't hard (unless you have no teeth). *Beginning* to watch a movie isn't hard (unless you can't see). *Beginning* to pour orange juice into a glass isn't hard (unless you have no hands to pour with). Potok's statement is both very deep and profound, and yet profoundly shallow and superficial at the same time, which brings me to me. How does one begin the greatest novel ever written? That's a damned good question. Logic tells us that the best place to begin the greatest novel ever written is on an asteroid with some banished intergalactic outlaws staring at each other. And you can't argue with logic. So gather your inner strength and confidence (even though it's hard), pack a few things, and let's head up to Asteroid #9 so we can stare at the outlaws as they stare at each other.

CHAPTER 1

The Outlaws of Asteroid #9 just sat around staring at each other, not saying a word. They were not a pretty bunch and they knew it. Rollo Starguy, their incredible leader, looked down at their home planet Zartov and sneered. "Someday," he said. And they all nodded in agreement, not knowing what he meant. But Rollo Starguy knew exactly what he meant. Three light years before, he and his band of outlaws had been banished from Zartov for various petty crimes and assorted lewd acts against morphological individuals and the outer space version of Mother Nature, known as Mama Jama. Rollo knew that someday they would return to Zartov. Not that Zartov was such a swinging planet, but it was home. The Outlaws watched from Asteroid #9 as the Battle of the Universe was underway. Freedom fighters, supply transports, and spaceships of all kinds exploded with dazzling flashes of blazing blues, rollicking reds, and a greenish color (sort of a tropic green mixed with a neon forest lime kind of green). More attackers continued to surge ahead. There was lots of Sturm und Drang (German for "storm and stress") as five planets and three planetoids fell to the power of The Evil One, and as they died they left no indication that they ever existed, but for a moan of agony. Despite the setbacks, the defending freedom fighters pushed on. More waves of assault ships were beaten back. With one last desperate effort, the freedom fighters attempted to break through The Evil One's defense shield, but the ships turned a gleaming glossy candy apple red from the extreme heat of the entry and exploded. The Evil One was again victorious as the universe fell under his power, planet by planet.

A brilliant beam of glittering Persian blue light penetrated the musty haze which surrounds Asteroid #9 sending the Outlaws scurrying. In the center of the light beam appeared none other than Dweezle Dwindle, the peculiar intergalactic messenger dwarf. Dweezle handed Rollo a telegram, extended his hideous little hand, and waited impatiently for his tip. The Outlaws checked their pockets but no change could be found. Dweezle slapped Rollo and the Outlaws hard and then vanished into the darkness as quickly as he appeared. Rollo placed his reading glasses on the tip of his nose and read the telegram silently to himself moving his lips like some people do. After a moment, he addressed his outlaws like the great leader that he was. The news was grim.

"Boys, The Evil One has overthrown the Cosmos Command, has taken control of Zartov, and is planning total domination over all the galaxies in the universe. Can we allow this to happen?"

"NO!" came the collective answer sending shivers up Rollo's spine. He was proud of his boycotted boys. Rollo's right-hand man, Sluggo, raised his right hand to signal an inquiry. Rollo called on him.

Sluggo inquired, "Rollo, why should we help save Zartov when they banished us?"

"Who knows the answer?" Rollo asked like a teacher who was cornered and didn't know the answer. Effron knew, but refused to tell, so Alfie told.

"This is our big chance!" Alfie proclaimed like Knute Rockne with two seconds left in the game, a fourth and goal staring him in the face. "If we can save Zartov, then we'll be able to go home again! And I think I know where The Evil One is. Don't you get it?"

And they all nodded in agreement not knowing what they got. "Prepare to dematerialize!" Rollo ordered. And The Outlaws of Asteroid #9 stood up, straightened their outlaw costumes, which were sort of like a cross between Robin Hood's Merry Men and the cast of *Les Miserables*, and prepared to dematerialize. "Prepare all emergency procedures for hostile action," Rollo ordered. "Load stun torpedoes. Set to full power, reserve capacity to maximum!"

"We don't have any stun torpedoes," came the collective response making Rollo look ridiculous.

"Just do it!" Rollo snapped.

Bulbous space junk storm clouds hovered on the horizon. Eggnog colored lightning flashed with a roar followed by stinging harlequin hail. Rollo had miscalculated their landing site and was soon leading the Outlaws through a tangled mass of groping nagging jungle vegetation that copped feels and criticized every step they took on the planet Bogone in the third solar system. It was like being with every woman I've ever known, except for the groping part. For safety's sake they stayed in the shadow of Bogone's moon, but that precaution did little to keep them from danger. For as soon as they found their way free from the groping nagging jungle vegetation, they found themselves face to face with Bowser, the hostile three-headed dragon-tailed psychologically damaged puppy dog that was twice the size of Brooklyn and almost as mean. Well…the truth is that two of Bowser's three heads were fake and held on with duct tape. So was his dragon tail. And he wasn't really twice the size of Brooklyn. He was more the size of Buford, Wyoming, a town with only one permanent resident, Mr. Sammons, who runs the Buford Trading Post. Bowser's idol was Cerberus who guards the entrance to Hades in Greek mythology, so he tried to look like him. We'll meet Cerberus later. The Outlaws were terrified but acted cool because they had a reputation to uphold. "Anybody got a doggy biscuit?" Rollo asked without moving his lips which he was able to do because he had once taken a correspondence course on how to be a ventriloquist. That was kind of weird actually. He moves his lips when he reads silently to himself and yet he can throw his voice without moving his lips. I stopped understanding things long ago. Sluggo, who happened to be nibbling on a turkey-flavored doggy biscuit right when Rollo asked the question, quickly swallowed the doggy biscuit and almost choked to death, but didn't. Not one of the Outlaws moved to help him as he was choking. They pretended not to notice, which wasn't nice. Rollo quickly accessed the situation with Bowser and concluded that he and his boys were in deep dire danger, which was true. Effron, who had once taken a class in auto mechanics but dropped out, pointed his pointer finger at Bowser and commanded, "Roll over and play dead, Boy!" But Bowser did not obey. Instead, he ate Effron, much to the dismay of the other outlaws. Rollo's right-hand man Sluggo raised his right hand to signal another inquiry. Rollo called on him.

Sluggo asked, "Why don't we just dematerialize our tushies outta here?"

"We can't do it so soon after we just did it," explained Alfie. "It's got something to do with the weakening of our molecular structure, I think. It's sort of like sex."

The Outlaws all stared at Alfie. They had never had sex. They had heard about it, but never had it. Sluggo had a cousin who had sex with himself once and almost died. Bowser showed his tremendous fangs, let out a bloodcurdling growl and crouched, ready to pounce on the Outlaws.

3

He was crazed with bloodlust and hungry for a snack. Like the agile leader that he was, Rollo Starguy spun around, did a backward flip, whipped out his laser gun, and blasted the pup to smithereens. When the smoke cleared and the applause died down, an aged farmer climbed over the remains of Bowser and introduced himself to the Outlaws. He had been exiled from another colony. Condemned for having an intimate relationship with his plow horse's harness, he had been sent to work the grain fields of Bogone forever. He expressed his gratitude to the Outlaws for destroying Bowser since Bowser was a bad doggy and always messed up the grain fields. The farmer claimed that it was indeed The Evil One who put Bowser on Bogone to terrorize him.

"What does The Evil One want and why?" Sluggo inquired, forgetting to raise his hand and getting slapped hard by Rollo. The old farmer looked at the Outlaws grimly and said, "Power. He wants raw naked power. He will never be defeated."

"Don't bet on it, Mr. Green Jeans," winked Rollo with the confidence of a thousand confident men. "We'll give that dingus the what-for."

To show his appreciation to the Outlaws for knocking off Bowser, the old farmer gave them an old model ZX-12 Celestial Renegade Astro Pod that he never used because its girth reminded him of his first wife Helga, and he didn't want to enter it because once inside it's not easy getting out, which also reminded him of Helga. The ZX-12 would get them from place to place without risking the weakening of the molecular structure which so often occurs with continuous dematerialization and is sort of like sex that they never had. The Outlaws thanked him for his kindness and took off to find The Evil One.

The next stop would be the evil planet Shlump, the last known headquarters of The Evil One where he had set up a fighter squadron support base eons ago. The blastoff, the vault into hyperspace, and the journey to Shlump seemed to take less time than expected, although there was time lost dodging the advances of a Cyclon Pirate Cruiser. On the way to Shlump they were pulled over for speeding by an outer space traffic control officer. Rollo insisted that they weren't speeding, but that the street was going too slow. The officer explained that there are no streets in outer space and let them off with a warning, since they were infamous legends. When I tried that "I wasn't speeding, the street was going too slow" line, I got a ticket, because even though I'm infamous, I'm not a legend yet. I will be soon, but not yet. Just as they arrived on the perimeter of Shlump's atmosphere, Alfie pointed out a nebula on the pod's scanner that was not supposed to be on their course. Red lights on the console flashed on and warning buzzers started screaming. Suddenly the particles and gases of the nebula surrounded them. There was also meteorite debris dead ahead. They attempted some evasive maneuvers, but overall it was useless. Their gravity generators and life support systems blinked on and off hinting at possible power failure. Rollo looked up from the scanner and called for a full-range screen presentation and the whole array of stars and galaxies appeared. Suddenly there it was, Gigantis-Singe! Gigantis-Singe was a giant star twelve times the size of Earth's sun, and it was directly in their path! The Outlaws of Asteroid #9 slipped on their shades and began to sweat.

The tremendous gravitational pull of Gigantis-Singe was extremely dangerous, so the ZX-12 Celestial Renegade Astro Pod attempted a wide orbit around Gigantis-Singe, and at the proper moment with all heat deflection shields, antimatter reflectors, and dematerialization gear operative, it broke orbit and dashed for the star. It was sheer insanity, but Rollo, who knew it was insanity, realized it too late. It's one thing to know something. It's another thing to realize it. It was futile, and totally in vain, when suddenly a heavy meteor shower blasted down and tossed the small space pod around like a marble in a bag of marbles in the pocket of a fat kid running. The Outlaws looked through the portholes as the ZX-12 began to tumble in a maze of colors and shapes. They saw stars born and they saw stars die. They saw planets twirl off into space, comets come and go, supernovas exploding, and they saw a huge cave worm defending her underground nest from an egg eater. Just as suddenly as the meteor shower fell, it was over. The warning lights stopped, the distress signal shut off, the console blinked with crackling energy, and the navigation systems said GO. The Outlaws removed their shades and exchanged relieved glances as Gigantis-Singe mysteriously disappeared into the cold darkness of outer space. Not an easy trick for a star that size.

"Where did Gigantis-Singe go?" Alfie asked fearing this was a ridiculous question. "All I see is a big black hole where Gigantis-Singe used to be."

The Outlaws exchanged terrified glances at Alfie's observation. They did not expect to find black holes on their journey to Shlump. No preparation had been made for this type of problem. In desperation Rollo ordered deployment of the full-propulsion booster. With a whining grinding whirling sound the pod shifted courses and the engines strained like a midget trying to lift a truck. Warning lights screamed on. Within seconds the booster was quickly exhausted. No cigar. They looked at each other, horrified at the thought that what they were looking at might be the last thing they ever saw. You live your whole life, and the last thing you see is the ugly mug of some fictional outer space outlaw? No thanks. And so they drifted helplessly in outer space locked in an orbit just beyond the reach of the black hole.

The danger is that once near the gravitational field of the black hole there is no possible escape and they all knew it. The Outlaws stared at Rollo Starguy, their phenomenal leader, for some kind of answer, some hint of leadership, as the pod was violently wrenched from its orbit and continued to move toward the massive black hole which was obscuring more and more stars as it loomed larger and larger. Those who have been trapped by black holes have never returned. Black holes in space are there because the mass of the star is so great that nothing can escape its gravity field. Rollo knew that. He also knew that he had a decision to make, but he didn't know what it was. There's a difference between having to make a decision and knowing what the decision is.

"This may get hairy, Boys!" Rollo warned his brave band of bandits. "Switch on the undetectable electromagnetic shielding!"

The Outlaws exchanged glances. "We don't have any undetectable electromagnetic shielding," Alfie said, making Rollo look like…Rollo.

"Just do it!" Rollo snapped.

With a shudder, the tiny space pod was grasped by the tremendous pull of the black hole and The Outlaws of Asteroid #9 found themselves hurtling into a tunnel-like void of darkness.

With a sudden jerk the pod came to an abrupt stop and the Outlaws felt themselves being reeled out of the black hole like a 6-ounce mullet on a 30-pound test line. They were drawn by a tractor beam into the receiving bay of a giant space station. It resembled a mile-long sponge cake, but it had lights, portholes, projection screens, computers, lab equipment, living quarters, and unfamiliar markings that most sponge cakes don't have. Rollo wondered if the aliens who manned the space station were hostile. Did they understand friendship? Did they know how to play chess or how to find the hood latch on a 1957 Chevy Bel Air? Did they know what hot dogs were really made of or what the hell bologna was? The Outlaws would soon find out. Rollo Starguy and The Outlaws of Asteroid #9 climbed out of the pod and were greeted by a group of creatures who before their eyes transformed into different things: toaster ovens, number two pencils, throw pillows, doodads, roulette wheels, widgets and more. They were in fact the survivors, or rather what survived of the survivors of the Cosmos Command; the most powerful governing body in existence. The same Cosmos Command that banished The Outlaws to Asteroid #9 three light years before. They explained to the Outlaws that there is a dominant solar drain throughout all the galaxies in the universe. There is a closing down of all quadrants. The universe was in dire danger and The Evil One was responsible. Simply put, he was destroying all the planets one by one.

Rollo eyed the lousy remains of the Cosmos Command suspiciously and asked, "Why are you telling us all this? You weren't so crazy about us when you banished us to that floating rock."

"Now's your chance to make good," said the Cosmos Command Commander. "If you can stop The Evil One, then you can return to Zartov and live happily ever after. What do you say?"

"We'll think about it," Rollo said while thinking about it.

The Cosmos Command Commander went on to say that The Evil One had made life on Zartov and the other planets absolutely intolerable. There was no food, so they had to eat each other. The film industry was faltering. Verbal communication was forbidden. And wet T-shirt contests were no longer permitted. Rollo was stunned.

"Wet T-shirt contests no longer permitted?! The Evil One is evil! We'll stop him if it's the last thing we ever do!" Rollo proclaimed, realizing that it probably would be the last thing they ever did.

It was decided that those factions opposing The Evil One's reign of terror would meet in secret on Saturn's moon, Titan, the following night. And so it was that on the following night the meeting took place. The Great Hall of Titan was filled with the babble of many different tongues as delegates from all over the multi-galactic system yammered away about the evilness of The Evil One. The Congressional leader, Sven Rosenfelt, took his place before the Multi-Galactic Congress and addressed them as a Congressional leader of a Multi-Galactic Congress should.

"Folks, we must have the courage of our convictions. I implore you. The Evil One is as good as his word, which isn't good at all. He has attacked and annihilated most of the space colonies, and he will obliterate those that remain unless we can get to him first. Our fate now rests in the hands of Rollo Starguy and his band of Outlaws. Although it is true that they were banished to Asteroid #9 for doing really nasty things, it is also true that they are a clever bunch who has a way of doing things that, although unorthodox and unacceptable, gets things done."

Every member of the Congress stared blankly, not understanding one word that Sven Rosenfelt had just said. Sven continued, "I have absolute confidence that the Outlaws will join us and save us from The Evil One or die trying. And now, without further ado, I give you Rollo Starguy!"

Rollo leapt to his feet and stood before the Multi-Galactic Congress (who did not applaud) applauding himself with a smirk on his face. He reveled in the irony of it all. Now it was he, Rollo Starguy, who held the fate of the universe in his sticky palms. It was he, Rollo Starguy, who was their only hope. Rollo addressed the Congress.

"On behalf of me and the Outlaws, and with a nod to Groucho, we would never join any Multi-Galactic Congress that would have us as members. But we will do all we can to stop The Evil One. We have a pretty good idea of where he is, so now we can go about the business of deciding what to do with him."

After much discussion and debate and arguing and bitching and moaning amongst the members of the Multi-Galactic Congress, The Evil One's fate was narrowed down to three options: either he would be destroyed and the rule of the universe would be returned to the Cosmos Command (what's left of them), or two other options that I forgot. Oh yeah, a list of demands would be drawn up and presented to The Evil One in the name of justice, goodness, and compassion. This of course depended on The Evil One cooperating with the congress, and the chances of that happening were somewhere between "It won't ever happen" and "It will never happen". And there was a third option, but I have no idea what it was. A message was written out for The Evil One and Dweezle Dwindle, the peculiar intergalactic messenger dwarf, was summoned to deliver it. The multi-galactic system comprises a handful of galaxies including major planets, secondary planets, satellites, stars, anagalactic nebulae, and all the constellations, including Scutum, the Shield of Sobieski, Fornax, the Furnace, and Puppis, the Poop. Puppis, the Poop is a real constellation. I'm not kidding. Look it up. Under the authority of the Cosmos Command, the multi-galactic system had rendered assurance and liberty for all its members. However, liberty costs, and it had incited the rage and resentment of those planets refused membership in the system. Many of them were rejected because the Cosmos Command believed they had a greater inclination for vicious foul wickedness than for nice virtuous niceness. Those rotten low-down good-for-nothing planets banded together under the leadership of the supreme repugnant pain-in-the-ass entity, a real bad banana...*The Evil One.*

The Evil One sat at the head of the dinette table that doubled as the captain's table addressing the generals of his droid armies (and their spouses and some hookers) toasting his near-completed takeover of the entire universe. On the wall behind him was a multi-galactic map which should have been in front of him, blocking everyone's view of him, because he was a ghastly unsightly sight to behold: part donkey, part jellyfish, part salamander, and only half an inch tall. He was gruesome.

"We've got them running, don't we?" The Evil One snickered, rubbing his slimy gross jackass ears together. "The Cosmos Command will surrender to me, and the universe will be mine. All mine!"

And then he let go this long stupid laugh that was supposed to sound wicked and sinister but sounded more like those Earthlings who suck in when they laugh and sound like they're dying. Like when you're trying to have a nice quiet dinner at a restaurant and at the table next to you Nancy is trying to make Biff think he's the funniest guy in the world, so she forces laughter at everything he says, but it sounds like she swallowed a cup of sawdust. Anyway, the celebration feast consisted of delicacies from every conquered planet, including cold cuts from Cetus, Squish from Saturn, and the most popular dish, fleh from Fleh (a sort of meatloafy moose mousse thing). Maggots would turn it down. To make his guests feel more at ease, The Evil One thought he would try out some new material for his stand-up routine and attempted a little levity concerning those who had perished during his blitz on the universe.

"It doesn't take anyone on any of the planets I conquered to screw in a light bulb, because they're all dead!"

Not wishing to perish themselves before dessert, all the guests forced hysterical laughter to placate The Evil One who snorted and brayed at his own lousy joke. There was one general who hated his job, didn't think the joke was amusing, and refused to be intimidated into laughing. The Evil One noticed that the general didn't laugh and agreed with the general that just because he was about to become the supreme ruler of the entire universe and was, in fact, the cruelest most sadistic SOB ever, that should in no way influence the general into laughing at a joke that he didn't find funny. He then had the general escorted out and tortured, in hopes that he would regain his sense of humor. Covered with blood, his spleen hanging out, and half-dead, the general was dragged back into the room and thrown into his seat.

"The general doth protest too much, methinks. I hope you've regained your sense of humor, General," The Evil One snarled. "Here's a joke especially for you…why do flies have wings?"

The general, in agony, whispered, "I don't know. Why?"

The Evil One answered, "So they can beat the Cosmos Command to the garbage cans where they will go to visit the remains of their loved ones."

All the guests started to laugh, but The Evil One motioned for them to stop abruptly so he could hear the general, who forced a false hysterical howl.

The Evil One grinned, "You don't have to overdo it, General. As long as I know you're trying."

As The Evil One rudely reached for a bowl of Pluto Pudding, that crazy brilliant beam of glittering Persian blue light flashed across the dinette table that doubled as the captain's table illuminating the bowl of Pluto Pudding, and Dweezle Dwindle the peculiar intergalactic messenger dwarf, slid down the light beam and landed with a SPLAT! tushy-first in the pudding bowl, splattering Pluto Pudding all over The Evil One. The general who was tortured and beaten half to death looked at The Evil One and broke out laughing. This time it was a real laugh, a genuine laugh, a really real laugh, a soulful laugh.

"Something amuses you, General?" asked the unamused Evil One.

"You look funny with that pudding all over you," commented the half-dead anyway general.

"Do I?" sneered The Evil One. "Well, let's see how funny you look without a head. Take him away!"

And as the droids dragged the screaming general away, Dweezle Dwindle handed The Evil One a telegram. He then extended his hideous little hand toward the more hideous Evil One and waited impatiently for his tip. None came and he didn't press it, knowing how evil The Evil One actually was. However, he did sit down to lick the remainder of the Pluto Pudding from the bowl and from The Evil One who read the telegram letting go that obnoxious jackass-esque bray of his. He addressed his guests.

"It's from The Outlaws of Asteroid #9. It seems they wish to meet with me at the second void when Venus next rises. But it doesn't say why. It might be amusing to hear what those low-life scumbag criminals have to say. Besides, it says there's a reception afterwards and a buffet. Free food is free food."

He turned to Dweezle Dwindle with a scowl: "You tell Starguy and his band of filth that I will meet with them. And I'm bringing a date. I can get dates, you know."

"Yeah," smirked Dweezle, "and I'm in the greatest novel ever written."

The dwarf vanished as quickly as he appeared, wondering what broad in her right mind would want to get near that jackass slime. The Evil One noticed the lovely star maiden Zelda Borealis passing by the dinette table that doubled as the captain's table on her way to bathe, and needing a date for his meeting with the Outlaws, he approached her demanding that she accompany him to the meeting. She turned him down flat. In a fit of rage The Evil One pointed at one of his droids and zapped the droid to bits, leaving nothing but smoldering ash. "I live for gratuitous gore. It's my hobby," The Evil One proclaimed evilly. He then threatened to destroy Zelda in the exact same fashion if she refused him again. Zelda, who had once won a pie eating contest at a Masonic lodge picnic, didn't like to be pushed and let her feelings be known.

"Just the sight of you makes me sick," she snarled. "The sound of your voice gives me the creeps, and the thought of your slimy disgusting touch makes me wish I was dead so I couldn't feel it. You're the lowest form of life there is, walking scum, talking garbage. I couldn't warm up to you if we were cremated together. Whenever I eat something I shouldn't eat and I want to puke I think of your face. When you stole this authority, it turned your head, you nauseating nutcase. It's too bad it didn't wring your neck, you foul freak!"

"So will you be my date to the meeting?" The Evil One asked as Zelda Borealis stormed away, like star maidens do when they're upset. "To quote the Bard, 'The course of true love never did run smooth'," The Evil One said, quoting the Bard.

At the next rising of Venus The Evil One and several henchmen droids waited impatiently for the Outlaws at the second void, so called because there was nothing there. There was no ground, no sky, no restaurants, no bargain outlets, no life, absolutely nothing. It had always been regarded as an uncertain region. Voids were often considered dangerous because they were unplotted. *But if there's nothing there to plot, what's to fear?* Rollo thought, as he and his Outlaws hurried through the universe late for their meeting with The Evil One because Sluggo wanted to rent a tux for the occasion, which made them late. The traffic in that particular sector of the solar system was always horrendous, so they took an alternate route, the truck route, you might say. Defensive screens were deployed. All weapons were energized. The tiny space pod was going so fast that objects outside the portholes began to blur as the ZX-12 merged into the emptiness which was the entrance to the void. Drifting through the void, searching for The Evil One, the Outlaws felt the pod suddenly tumble out of control. The dials on the command console reversed back to zero readings. The tiny pod spun end over end as a light stream, cold and harsh, encompassed the pod taking hold of the ship and locking it into place. A vaguely familiar sinister voice pierced the silence with a cackle:

"WELCOME ROLLO STARGUY AND YOUR BAND OF IDIOTS! I DIDN'T THINK YOU'D BE FOOLISH ENOUGH TO CONFRONT ME. YOU HAVE MY ADMIRATION AS WELL AS MY SYMPATHY FOR YOUR LOVED ONES. I'M SURE YOU WILL BE MISSED. I WAS GOING TO BRING A DATE TONIGHT, BUT SHE'S BUSY BEING DEAD RIGHT NOW. I CAN GET DATES, YOU KNOW."

An eerie sensation swept over the ZX-12. The Outlaws felt numb. Paralysis set in. They could not move. They struggled violently to free themselves from whatever had its grip on them, but it was useless. They couldn't even blink. The Evil One materialized as a hologram in front of them.

"IT IS USELESS, OUTLAWS, TO STRUGGLE AGAINST ME. FOR I, THE EVIL ONE, THE ULTIMATE POWER, AM INVINCEBLE!" And with that he let go that stupid braying laugh of his and winked out.

"Is he dramatic, or what?" asked Rollo rhetorically, not really looking for an answer. "He's such a negative character. I bet he was raised by telemarketers. Maybe this meeting wasn't such a hot idea. What do you say Boys, should we head back to our rock?"

The fact that not one of them could move didn't faze Rollo Starguy.

———

He just liked believing that he had the option of going back to Asteroid #9 if he wanted to. The pod came to a stop and The Evil One's henchmen opened the hatch and pulled the Outlaws out into the void. A cloud of putrid smoke billowed, and out of the bottom of the cloud stepped a life form; part donkey, part jellyfish, part salamander, all asshole (and only half an inch tall)...The Evil One. *Gag me with a spoon*! Rollo thought to himself. *This guy's ugly*!

"What do you want from me?" spat The Evil One hitting Rollo's right space boot.

"We have business we'd like to discuss with you," spat Rollo hitting his left space boot.

The Evil One glared, "I don't do business with the dead, and you're all about to die. To quote the Bard, 'Cowards like The Outlaws of Asteroid #9 die many times before their deaths; The Evil One shall never taste of death but once.' And maybe not even then, maybe I'll just keep coming back, because it's in my contract."

At The Evil One's signal, the henchmen droids pulled out their laser guns. But before they could fire, the remains of the Cosmos Command descended upon The Evil One and his henchmen, melting together into a large jumbled mass trapping them in a slimier slime than his own slime. He tried to break free, but for the moment he was trapped. Rollo Starguy paced before him like an irate mommy deciding what to do with her bad kid.

"Evil One," Rollo said, having more to say, "I know we can't hold you like this forever. Your goons will come looking for you. Just listen."

Rollo went on to explain that the Multi-Galactic Congress did not approve of the way The Evil One was destroying everything and everyone, and yet they realized his power and could possibly accept him as some sort of ruler if he would change his ways and abide by certain laws and limitations set forth in a written declaration known as the Remus Opus. Rollo further explained that the Remus Opus guaranteed certain rights to all creatures in the universe, justice to all free beings no matter how many eyes, legs, or arms they have, the right to habeas corpus, and the limitation of power (in case of abuse thereof) over all inhabitants of the universe. It guaranteed no taxation without representation, and proclaimed that no being shall be imprisoned, or exiled, or destroyed, except by the lawful and fair judgment of his or her or its peers and what remained of the Cosmos Command. No creature in this universe could be imprisoned or dispossessed without a fair trial. No one could be sold, refused, or delayed right or justice. Rollo went on to discuss sixty-three articles in all, limiting The Evil One's power and giving what remained of the Cosmos Command power over him. The Evil One laughed that stupid braying laugh of his in Rollo's direction saying he would never agree to limit his own power. Rollo laughed back in The Evil One's yucky face threatening an uprising, a revolution, and a force of abdication, and strongly suggesting that The Evil One would indeed be overthrown since no one liked him. And he added, "I understand that you hurt, Evil One. It's been no bed of roses. You're part donkey, part jellyfish, part salamander, you're only half an inch tall, and your breath could capsize a cruise ship. So you lash out and you want to hurt others. But that's the wrong thing to do. You're better than that."

For some strange reason The Evil One was touched by Rollo's words, and emotionally so. With a lump in his part donkey, part jellyfish, part salamander, all asshole throat, he told this heartbreaking tale (and I am quoting verbatim):

"Let me tell you the story of a young lad who struggled with a crippling illness and traveled through blinding meteor showers to work his part donkey, part jellyfish, part salamander claws to stumps in a disgusting filthy zakon-infested Martian sweatshop so that his family and all who depended on him might have food to eat and star particles for warmth. Let me tell you how this young lad compromised himself and sold his yucky body and soul so that he and the sickly that depended on him might have medication and care to survive through yet another solar day. Let me tell you how he slept on rusty satellites, survived on scraps of rotten zeedreck which he fought scavengers for, and sacrificed himself for others. Let me tell you how this young lad gave up all his dreams, ambitions, and hopes because he had to work like a common kremlipper from solar rising to lunar eclipse to support not only his family, but countless orphans who came to him for help. Yes, it's all true, every word of it. This young lad gave up everything so that he might help others. And yet, he was scorned and ridiculed and hated and strongly disliked and despised his whole life!"

A heartfelt hush fell over everyone, and they all started sobbing for this young lad for whom fate had dealt such an unforgiving hand. The remains of the Cosmos Command released their hold on The Evil One and started weeping, even feeling compassion toward him. They wanted to hold him in a different way now, in a comforting way. Rollo's right-hand man, Sluggo, raised his right hand to inquire softly between sobs: "Are you that young lad, Evil One?"

"Certainly not," The Evil One scowled. "He was a loser!" Then turning to his henchmen he snapped, "Let's make like a banana and leave. These fools bore me."

"We demand your seal on the Remus Opus!" demanded Rollo Starguy, "Or there will be big trouble, Eeyore!"

The Evil One and his henchmen were almost outside the void when he turned back around to face the Outlaws and the remains of the Cosmos Command.

"Ambitious but incompetent; I like that about you Starguy. Therefore I will make you an offer. There is a certain object which I value greatly. It is known as the Golden Fleece of the Argonauts. It is very old and very valuable, and I want you to find it for me and bring it to me."

"Where is it?" Rollo asked like someone who didn't know where it was.

"If I knew where it was I wouldn't need you to find it, now would I?" snapped The Evil One making Rollo look like a weenie. "What goes on in that muddled mess of mishigas that is your brain?"

Alfie was once a student of ancient civilizations with a minor in theater. He was also a stage-door Johnny infatuated with Angela Lansbury and knew the history of the Golden Fleece. He explained it to the Outlaws as best he could recollect. "It seems that in mythological times Jason and the Argonauts set out on a quest for the Golden Fleece because a Greek king got tired of his wife, put her away, and married another. But the first wife was afraid for her son because she thought the second wife would try to kill him so that the second wife's son would inherit the kingdom and she was right to think that. The second wife got possession of all the seed-corn and purposely parched it so there would be no harvest. She was a real bitch. When the king sent a man to ask the oracle what he should do, the oracle, who was paid off, declared that the corn would not grow unless the first wife's son was sacrificed. Like that's gonna make corn grow. An amazing thing happened. When the boy was taken to the altar to be sacrificed, a wondrous ram with a fleece of gold snatched him up and saved his life. The boy later sacrificed the ram that saved him in gratitude for being saved. Let that one soak in for a minute. He then gave the Golden Fleece to the king. Jason's cousin Pelias took the kingdom from Jason's father so Jason needed the Golden Fleece to reclaim his kingdom. Get it?"

Unfortunately, no one got it. In fact, no one understood a single word Alfie said. For not only was the tale boring as death and difficult to follow, but Alfie had a lisp and hardly ever paused, as though there was very little punctuation in the story.

The Evil One stared defiantly at Rollo and recapped his deal: "Bring me back that Golden Fleece, Starguy, and I'll put my seal on your Remus Opus. If you return without it, I will totally annihilate the universe. Get it?"

Rollo got it. *That puts us under some pressure*, Rollo thought to himself as he watched The Evil One exit the void in a dramatic cloud of putrid smoke. When the smoke cleared, there stood the Festersmit, a vicious creature with nine heads, one uglier than the next. Rollo suspected right then and there that this journey would not be a piece of cake.

The battle began. With a horrifying shriek, the Festersmit pounced on the Outlaws. Alfie, who had been on the wrestling team in high school before he dropped out to join the Outlaws, had two of the heads in headlocks while Sluggo kept raising his hand, poking out eyes right and left. Alfie relinquished the heads he had and shoved the monstrosity away from him, adding a well-placed kick for good measure. Then with his laser blaster at the ready, took aim and fired. ZAP! The beam stabbed the void and found its mark. The heads dropped off, but four more grew in their place! Suddenly, in a surprise move, the Festersmit spun around and cornered Sluggo and Alfie. Just as it looked hopeless, just as it looked like Sluggo and Alfie had met their doom, their well-groomed leader who had once screwed a 60-watt bulb into a 40-watt socket, Rollo Starguy, dropped to a crouch and advanced on the Festersmit. Then, with the finesse of a cat, Rollo jumped on the Festersmit, wrestled most of the Festersmit's heads to the bottom of the void which was like trying to hold down a bunch of helium-filled party balloons and delivered a paralyzing blow to the base of the main skull. Unfortunately the only thing paralyzed was Rollo's hand from the force of delivering the blow. All that happened was that the Festersmit's skull popped off and six more grew in its place. The Festersmit kicked Rollo around and then reached out a long scaly tentacle exposing sharp menacing talons. "Hail to The Evil One!" the Festersmit gurgled. It then took a swipe at Rollo, drawing blood. Rollo wouldn't have minded if it was someone else's blood, but it was *his* blood, so he minded. Alfie and Sluggo, who had managed to escape harm while Rollo was getting his butt kicked, backed the ZX-12 space pod into the battle area, and hovered just above their dashing and debonair leader. They quickly pulled him into the pod through the belly hatch just as the Festersmit was about to take another swipe. The monster moved menacingly toward the pod, and now there were more of them than could be counted; zillions of Festersmits in all shapes and sizes! They invaded the tiny pod through seams and cracks where they seemed to melt like cheap processed imitation mozzarella cheese all over the control board. The navigation and communication systems were instantly crippled. Alfie attempted to send distress signals, but to no avail. The Outlaws knew they had no choice but to fight for their lives. Alfie reached for the emergency energy switch. Just as he did, 185 Festersmits surrounded him and melted together into a large jiggling form unlike cheap processed imitation mozzarella cheese, but very much like a very large lime Jello mold that someone's spinster aunt brought to a family dinner that no one wanted to eat. To be clear, no one wanted to eat the large lime Jello mold, the dinner, or the spinster aunt.

With great difficulty The Outlaws of Asteroid #9 escaped the gooey sticky yucky mass that held them. Trusty laser gun in hand (the other hand that wasn't paralyzed), Rollo Starguy released the safety, took dead center aim, and fired at the center (which makes sense) of the jiggling mass of gunk. The mass shriveled, changed colors from lime green to a marmalade orange, faded slightly, turned bright fuchsia, smoldered, shook violently, and then regenerated! The Outlaws kept firing. Strange sounds filled the air and even places where there was no air. Sounds never heard before; sounds that root vegetables might make if root vegetables made sounds. The more the Outlaws fired, the louder the sounds got. Unnoticed by the Outlaws, the laser beams hit the control panel destroying major portions of its circuitry. The Outlaws continued blasting away: *WAP! ZORK! SQUARSH!* etc. The mass shriveled completely and vanished. There was silence. The Outlaws had won the battle, but a bitter victory it was. The space pod control console was demolished. The Outlaws got out, said bad words like they were raised in a sewer, and pushed the pod to the only service hangar they could find outside the void. It was operated by Manny "The Wrench" Sanchez who did some time years before for having an affair with a judge's shoe while court was in session. Manny charged an arm and a leg to repair the pod, but he was, after all, the best grease monkey for millions of miles, and the only one at that, so what could they do? The idea of the great adventure (finding the Golden Fleece, remember that?) enticed Rollo. He warned the Outlaws that this would be an extremely dangerous voyage for only the mightiest of men, and chances were pretty good that they would be killed somewhere along the way. It was Rollo's mother, Enid, who kindled in her son the desire not to live a life without peril, and he hated her for it.

CHAPTER 2

Meanwhile on a movie set on location in Barstow, California, things were hectic and tempers were flaring. Lights, cameras, and cables were being adjusted. People with script copies, clipboards, and walkie-talkies were running around. Actors were rehearsing their lines. Extras were meandering about as extras do. Here in Barstow with the sun blazing hot and the humidity uncommonly high in this derelict desert town, the unrelenting heat had ignited film director Syd Singer's fuse, making it shorter than usual, which was usually pretty short anyway. His lead actor was nowhere to be found, and Singer wasn't happy. He mopped sweat from his forehead, glanced at his watch which was given to him by his maternal grandfather who became a transvestite lounge singer sparking his grandson's interest in show business, and snarled. His assistant, Aston, who had nightly fantasies about the director, rushed over in a futile attempt at damage control.

"What'll we do, shoot around him?"

"Take dead center aim," Singer snapped. "Where is that bastard? His call time was an hour ago. I have a movie to make. I wanna get this done and get out of this damned place. It's an oven! Aliens wouldn't land here!"

Aston reminded the director that movie star Nick Nero would cross the desert by car, as he didn't like to fly. Singer said, "Listen. I know this guy. We're five minutes by puddle-hopper. He likes his 24-karat ass in a limo. He likes the entrance. But here's his exit. Get Mike on the phone and call Smitty. Get me another lead, right now."

"Like who?" Aston asked.

"De Niro, Pacino, Bugs Bunny, the man in the moon, I don't care. I want someone who knows how to show up."

"Syd, just getting out of L.A. could take five hours."

Singer shrugged, "His problem, not mine."

Someone handed Singer a bottle of water and he sucked it in. Aston's cell phone rang. He talked for a few moments as he and Singer walked together. Then he ended the call.

"Nero's going berserk. He just fired his agent and his manager."

"I'm not interested in his prima-donna shit. I need that son of a bitch on set *now*!" Singer looked around. "And fire my location scout."

"I was the one who found this place," Aston said. "I thought it was perfect."

"If I was making a film about Hell, you'd be right. But I'm not, so you're wrong. Fire yourself."

An over-the-top flamboyant wardrobe assistant wheeling a cart full of costumes passed by and beamed, "Can't you just feel the love?"

One place where no one could feel the love was on Nick Nero's face. He was miles past livid. Nero sat on a throne-like chair he had custom made to look throne-like just glaring at a clock on the wall of his mansion. The tick-tock of the clock became progressively louder, so Nero did what anyone would do; he pulled out a handgun and aimed it at the clock. Elvis shot televisions, Nero shot clocks. Nero was about to kill the clock when the annoying tick-tock was suddenly shattered by the sound of a car screeching to a stop. Nero looked out the window and saw a black stretch limousine. He sat back in his throne-like chair that he had custom made to look throne-like, waiting. For four full minutes nothing happened. That's a long time. Just sit there for four full minutes not doing anything and see how you like it. It was like a strange chess game with each player deciding their next move and not moving. And then there was a long blast on the horn. Nero was angry, then disgusted, then angry again. He heard the door to the limo open and then slam shut. He heard stomping coming toward the mansion, and then pounding on the front door. Nero's harried housekeeper, Margot Dankworth who had slaughtered her family and needed a job when she got out of prison, rushed to answer it, but Nero sharply waved her back with the handgun. He got up and opened the door himself; gun in hand. On the other side of the door was Izzy, a short plump woman wearing a too-tight chauffeur's uniform and cap, smacking chewing gum, and looking down at an index card.

"Nick Nero. I'm looking for a Nick Nero going to Barstow to see a movie. Why in Hell would anyone go across a desert to see a movie?"

She looked up from the card and kept looking up. Nero was a big guy, a big guy who wasn't overly thrilled with her.

"Holy crap! You eat furniture?" she asked, sort of rudely.

Nero just glared.

"Are you Nick Nero, or what?" she asked sort of rudely, again.

Nero couldn't believe this person, or anyone for that matter, didn't know who he was.

"I'm Nero," he sneered, disgusted that she didn't know.

"Are you deaf, Nero?" Izzy sneered back. "I blew the horn for a week. Lose the heat, grab your bag, and let's go. I'm Isabella (she paused) *Barone*, but you call me Izzy. I'm your driver and that's where it ends. I don't do sexual favors, especially for someone who looks like world wars were fought on their face. I speak seven languages in case you don't understand English. Now move it, you're wasting my time."

Somehow, stunned, Nero did what he was told. They went out to the limo and stood there, each waiting for the other to open the car door. After three full minutes, which is a long time standing there waiting for someone to open a door, though not as long as four full minutes, Izzy, still smacking her gum, snapped, "Hey Mr. Manners, open the door for a lady."

Again, somehow Nero did what he was told. He then got into the back of the limo and it peeled away, soon turning onto I-10 East, heading for Barstow. Inside the limousine things were just as tense as they were outside the limousine.

"You're two hours late!" Nero pointed out in a manner that didn't make things better.

"No, I'm on time," Izzy pointed out in a manner that didn't make things better either. "Your original driver's late because she didn't want to be your driver no more. It says on your card and in your file that as a client you're a known pain in the ass. Yesterday your original driver walked into an exotic fish store and purposely drowned herself while being eaten alive in a piranha tank so she wouldn't have to drive you anymore. What does that say about you? *She's* two hours late. Me, I'm on time."

"Lucky me," Nero mumbled.

Izzy slammed on the brakes sending Nero crashing into the back of the front seat and bringing the limo to a screeching stop in the middle of the freeway and setting off a chain reaction of instant mayhem. Horns blared, cars swerved around them, people cursed, several cars ran into each other. It was total chaos. However, Nero and Izzy were too wrapped up in their own melee to notice or care. "You can walk to Barstow! Get out!" Izzy snarled.

"I'm not getting out!" Nero snapped.

Accidents and pile-ups continued all around them.

"GET OUT!" Izzy screamed.

"I am *NOT* getting out of this car!" Nero sneered like someone who had no plans to get out of the car.

Sirens approached as angry commuters got out of their vehicles and ran toward the limo. Izzy scowled with a scowl.

"Say you're sorry, you pompous ass!"

"For what?!" Nero inquired like a pompous ass.

Izzy said, "Alright. When the cops get here I'll tell them that you tried to force your affections on me."

Nero quickly got out of the limo. As he did, an angry commuter ran up to slug him. Nero cracked the man's head into the door of the limo and tossed him aside without even blinking. We sense that he's done this before. A woman who had once won third place in a Tic-Tac-Toe tournament noticed that the reason for all this road rage was none other than big deal celebrity movie star Nick Nero and pointed him out to the wild crowd: "OH MY GOD! IT'S NICK NERO!" she hollered. At that the angry commuters quickly became adoring fans and rushed Nero for autographs. He jumped back into the limo and locked the door.

"I'm sorry, I apologize, forgive me. Let's go!"

Izzy stepped on the gas and they were back on the road.

"So you're famous, huh? For what, being an asshole?" she inquired like someone who wasn't impressed.

Nero smiled slightly. "You really don't know who I am?"

"Not a clue," Izzy said, like someone who didn't have a clue.

"You don't go to the movies?" Nero asked, pretending to care about the response.

"I'd rather have ten root canals," Izzy said, seriously preferring to have ten root canals than go to the movies. "Are you a famous usher or the candy guy? When I was a kid, before my entire family was wiped out in a movie theater when space junk crashed through the roof killing them, I used to like those chocolate covered raisins. In fact, I was at the concession stand buying those things when my family was killed. Do you sell those?"

Nero was silent for a moment taking in what she had said.

"No. I'm an actor."

Again Izzy slammed on the brakes and Nero flew into the back of the front seat. The limo came to a screeching stop in the middle of the freeway setting off a chain reaction of more pandemonium. All Hell broke loose all around them, again. Izzy spun around seething, "GET OUT! I hate actors!"

Nero snapped, "You're crazy! I've known some nutty broads in my day, but you win first prize!"

Izzy smirked, "That's funny, an actor telling someone they're crazy."

"Listen honey, I gotta get to the set," Nero said, trying not to lose it. "I'm the star. I have to be there. We're very late."

"I'm not late, you are," Izzy pointed out. "And don't call me 'honey', moron."

Furious commuters stopped being adoring fans and charged the limo.

"May we please go now?" Nero asked sarcastically sweetly.

"Yes, we may," Izzy answered sarcastically sweetly back.

She stepped on the gas and the limo took off. Several angry people had to dive out of the way to keep from being hit. They were in front of the limo because people are stupid and I guess they thought they could stop a ten-ton car with their bare hands. Speaking of stupid, the same guy who Nero previously introduced to the limo door, held on to the rear bumper for a short distance and then flew off.

"I-10 East to I-15 North," Nero said.

Izzy had other ideas.

"I know a shortcut. We'll get there on time."

"*You'll* get there on time," Nero said. "I was late long ago."

Unnoticed by Nero, Izzy spoke quickly and vaguely into a small walkie-talkie radiophone and then turned the limo toward the exit ramp. As she did so, she saw a giant billboard with her passenger's smiling face on it. He looked ridiculous dressed in costume as Shakespeare's Hamlet, smoking a huge cigar with actual smoke rings coming out of the cigar, and holding a smoked ham in the famous theatrical pose of Hamlet holding Yorick's skull. The billboard read:

"NICK NERO KNOWS
HAMLET'S SMOKED HAM TASTES TERRIFIC!"

Izzy shook her head and said, "Wow! Look at that! I know what the ham represents, but what about the cigar?"

The limo exited the freeway and turned onto a side street.

"Where the hell are you going?" Nero asked.

"Shortcut," she said. "I told you fifty times."

"We're going to Barstow," Nero frowned. "It's in the desert. How many shortcuts could there be?"

"Just one and I know it," she said. "Trust me."

"How could I not?" Nero mumbled. "So why do you hate actors?"

After a few moments of tense tenseness Izzy said, "Not that it's any of your business, but in Palermo in 1846 my sainted grandmother was defiled and deflowered by a troupe of traveling actors just passing through. Actors are self-righteous anal sphincters who don't accomplish anything. If you'll notice, Mr. Big Shot, the only awards they get are the ones they give themselves. Me, I'm a sphincter mover. I move sphincters like you from point A to point B."

"You shouldn't have a job where you deal with people," Nero said. "You have a really bad attitude."

"Screw you! I have a great attitude," Izzy sneered as she turned the limo down a dirt road. Nero took hard notice but kept his mouth shut. He removed a small black address book from his inside coat pocket, tapped it against his palm, and slipped it back where it came from. Izzy noticed the book in the rear-view mirror, but said nothing. There was a long uneasy silence between them as Nero watched the scenery change. Finally Izzy asked, "So why'd you get into acting? Couldn't find work?"

Nero took a deep breath and kept looking out the window. The ride started to get bumpy. He said, "I didn't want to stay in the family business." He didn't volunteer more. Izzy glanced in the rear-view mirror again and saw him looking in the backseat vanity mirror and primping.

"And what's the family business, dog grooming?"

Nero looked up into the rear-view mirror and they made "eye contact," "Problem solving, smartass, problem solving."

He looked back out the window and drifted away into his memory, as we go right along with him into several flashback scenes.

Ten years earlier a helicopter hovered over the Hollywood Sign on Mount Lee in the Hollywood Hills of the Santa Monica Mountains. The same Hollywood Sign where frustrated actress Peg Entwistle jumped to her demise from on top of the 45-foot letter *H* on September 16th of 1932. At that time it was the "Hollywoodland" sign. But at this time three men were bound and gagged with cinder blocks tied to their ankles. One man was on top of the letter *H*. Another man was on top of the letter *O* (which Alice Cooper purchased in honor of his dear friend Groucho Marx). And the third man was bound and gagged on top of the first *L*. All three were wide-eyed and terrified. A younger Nick Nero was hanging from the chopper by a rope, a harness attached to his waist. He was lowered onto the top of the letter *H* where he addressed the first man. He bent down to secure the cinder blocks, and yelled over the noise of the chopper, "This is our best selling shoe, Al. I would show you something in a green pump, but we're out of stock. These shoes look great on you!" Nero pulled an old beat-up index card out of his pocket and read from it, giving a quick history lesson to anyone who cared. And trust me, no one did. "The Hollywood Sign was first erected in 1923 as a real-estate advertisement. Each letter is 45 feet tall. Wow, that's tall. In 1932 a depressed actress took a dive from right where you're standing." Nero stopped reading. He said, "Let me see you walk in your new shoes, Al. And tell that actress I said to cheer up." Nero shoved Al off the *H* and called after him as he dropped, "AND TELL YOUR FRIENDS NOT TO BORROW MONEY THEY CAN'T PAY BACK!" Nero gave the thumbs up, and the helicopter lifted him up and carried him over to the letter *O* to victim #2 who had the hell beat out of him. Nero smirked, "Joey, you look unhealthy. You were the best hard-on with a briefcase we ever had, but you screwed up. This is only business, Joey. Don't take it personally." Nero looked at Joey's terrified face and grabbed it affectionately. "You always look so serious, like you're going to a funeral. Smile for once. You'll find that life is better when you smile." He shoved Joey off the *O* and called after him, "HEY JOEY, WHILE YOU'RE DOWN THERE MAKE SURE AL DOESN'T TRY TO GET AWAY. IF HE TRIES ANYTHING STUPID, WHACK HIM FOR ME!" The chopper carried Nero over to the giant *L* and victim number three who Nero wagged a finger at. "And you, you cut me off in traffic. That's rude. I could blame it on your car, but I'd look pretty silly talking to a car and then pushing it off of a giant letter. See if they have a driving school down there, fuckhead." He shoved #3 off the *L* and watched him drop.

Outside of a heavily guarded MAFIA fortress, a goon in a black suit signaled for the front iron gates to open, allowing a black limo to pass through. Security cameras followed every movement. A few more goons in black business suits patrolled the grounds. They were armed to the teeth.

"I gave flying lessons just about every day," Nero told Izzy. "It got old. My heart wasn't in it. I guess my old man figured that out and invited me in for a little father and son chat."

Inside the private office of Noldo Neroni, the most powerful don on the West Coast, two goons, Angelo and Toto, neckless apes in suits, "escorted" Nero into the office and forcefully sat him in a chair across from his father's desk.

Angelo growled, "Keep your ass in the chair, Superstar."

"Fuck off!" Nero growled back.

Noldo Neroni glared at his son.

"This isn't that birds and bees speech is it?" Nero asked.

Angelo drew his hand back to slap Nero, but the don motioned for him not to. Neroni was in his twilight years. He was somewhat frail, but still ran the family and all family matters with great authority. He sat in an ornate almost throne-like wooden chair, tapping his fingers on a small black address book that Nero was well aware of. The don spoke with a thick Italian accent. His delivery was stern and strong, but the discord between father and son was much stronger. Don Neroni explained to his son that he whacked the wrong people. He was livid, but restrained. Had it been anyone else but his flesh and blood, there would have been a lot of blood.

"I don't want substitutes, Nicolo. I want the ones that don't pay their debts: the rats, the canaries, the deadbeats. I don't want some nothing that cuts you off in traffic! I want anyone disloyal to me! *And what about Joey?!* I took him out of the gutter and put him through law school like Marlon Brando did for Robert Duvall, and you burn him for nothing!"

Nero shrugged, "He was a fucking lawyer."

The don fumed. He tapped the black address book on his desk, his nerves on edge. His son kept a steady eye on the book.

"Did you do any cleaning after your brilliant show of force?" Neroni asked, wiping sweat from his forehead.

"No one saw me," Nero said.

"That's not what I asked!" Neroni snapped. "When you break an egg you clean it up. Capisce?! You're sloppy. You don't care about your position or your work here."

"So fire me," Nero said. "I don't belong here anymore. I'm an actor."

Neroni shook his head. "Yeah, I know all about your brilliant acting career. Five directors disappeared and were never heard from again."

Nero shrugged, "We had creative differences."

Neroni leaned in close and menacingly, "What a coincidence, so do *we*. I let you have your fun in Tinsel Town. Now it's time to grow up."

Angelo snickered, "Poor Superstar couldn't make it in Hollywood."

Toto snickered too, "And it's only three miles away."

"Fuck both of you apes!" Nero sneered.

Don Neroni with the shakes popped a pill and motioned to Toto who quickly brought him a glass of water to down it with. The don looked at his son and tried a different approach.

"Nicolo...someday soon you may have to...take over here. But that takes life experience, and you don't really have that. You say you're an actor. Pretending to be other people is not life experience. Act like you understand that you are heir to the most powerful borgata outside of the east coast." The don strained to rise. Angelo and Toto rushed to help him but he shooed them away, using his ever-present walking stick to steady himself. The walking stick was hand-carved from a tree branch that snapped off when angry villagers in Dozza tried to lynch his Uncle Lorenzo for attempting to copulate with an Apennine shrew and ordering a cappuccino after 11 P.M. Two things that are deeply offensive in Dozza. "I have people in my pocket you can't imagine," he told his son. He got loud and passionate, pounding his palm into his chest, "And when we were in New York...*CAPO DI TUTTI CAPI!*" For those unfamiliar with MAFIA terminology, that means *Boss of the strongest of the families.* The don continued passionately. If this were a movie he'd win Best Supporting Actor for this speech alone. He raised his fist in the air and yelled, "No Gambino! No Genovese! No Lucchese! No Colombo! No Bonanno! ME! NOLDO NERONI! *CAPO DI TUTTI CAPI!*" He started to cough, weakened by his outburst, and sat back down. There were a few moments of silence as the don composed himself. "I clawed my way to the top, Nicolo. You had everything handed to you. I blame your mother for that; too soft." Both father and son grew quiet. They both missed her terribly. It's probably the only thing they had in common. "I've arranged for you to acquire some real life experience quickly, my son," Neroni said. "Another problem we have, Nicolo, is that you use too much profanity, 'fuck this and fuck that'. You have no class, like some two-bit gunsel. You talk like you crawled out of a sewer. Your vocabulary needs lots of work. So I've also arranged for you to have a vocabulary tutor, and you're not gonna like it. Strip him."

The goons savagely tore Nero's clothes off of him and slammed him back in the chair. The don nodded to Angelo and Toto. Angelo quickly left the room. Toto pulled rubber gloves out of his coat pocket and put them on. The don flicked a toggle switch at his desk and automatic restraining cuffs sprung from the arms of the chair Nero was sitting on and bound his wrists so he couldn't move his arms.

"What the fuck?!" Nero seethed.

His father shook his head in disgust. Angelo returned with an Odyssey PC680 car battery, which is a really powerful battery. It really is powerful. Look it up. (We can pause here for you to look it up or we can keep going. I think we'll just keep going and you catch up to us when you can.) So anyway, Angelo returned with the Odyssey PC680 with attached jumper cables. He connected a wire from the battery to another toggle switch on the don's desk. Nero looked on in horror and inquired most uncalmly, "What the fuck is that?!" To which his daddy the don replied, "To most people it would be a car battery, a very powerful one, an Odyssey PC680. You can look it up. But to you, it's your vocabulary tutor, Miss Comare."

Toto nudged Nero, "Hey Superstar, she's single. Ask her out."

"Fuck you, Palooka!" Nero seethed again.

Toto socked him on the side of the head, "That ain't polite, Superstar. And watch your language. That's why this tutor lady is here in the first place. Now put your fuckin' feet together."

Toto squatted down and forcefully shackled Nero's ankles. The don gave the word, "Hook him up." Angelo doused Nero with Perrier as Toto moved the booster clamps over Nero's body. Nero was terrified.

Toto asked, "Is positive black or red? I always get that mixed up."

Angelo said, "Red is positive. Black goes to the engine ground, a part that don't move. In this case, even though it moves sometimes, we'll use the rectum."

Toto said, "Then red should go here."

He attached the large serrated alligator clamp to Nero's balls and Nero screamed in agony. Don Neroni attempted to console his son by telling him that things were about to get much worse. With that, he threw the toggle switch, sending a searing jolt into Nero's beanbag. Nero went through the roof. He also let out a bloodcurdling scream. Don Neroni turned the switch off and complimented his son on the fact that he screamed but did not say any bad words while screaming, which meant he was learning.

"What the fuck are you talking about?!" Nero seethed for the third time.

The don threw the switch again. Nero jerked violently, shrieking in agony.

"You see, Nicolo, this is a vocabulary crash course. In case you haven't caught on, every time you say the word 'fuck', I'm gonna shock the fuck outta you, until you learn not to say the word 'fuck'."

"You just said it!" Nero seethed for the fourth time.

"Said what?" asked his father, knowing damn well what.

"It went on forever," Nero told Izzy. "My father was like some crazy teacher who would kill you so you would learn what it's like to be killed."

"You don't sound too bright in this story," Izzy said.

"Hey, I need to be on that set. Step on it, please."

"Hold on to your shorts, Mr. Olivier. We'll get there. Continue with your somewhat amusing tale of tragedy."

Nero looked back out the window at the desert sand.

"My father was as fed up as I was. He said, "Since you say 'fuck' so much, tell me what it means."

"It's when you do a broad or when the Salami Brothers over here do each other," Nero answered.

Angelo didn't like the response and socked Nero on the opposite side of the head of where Toto socked him.

"You deserved that, Nicolo. You offended them. 'FUCK' is an acronym, which means that each letter stands for a word. In the old days even married couples could not fornicate without permission from the king."

"What the fuck is fornicate?" Nero asked.

The don just stared at him. Even the goons couldn't believe it. Angelo asked the don's permission to shock Nero, and permission was granted. He puckered a kiss at Nero, savored the moment, flipped the toggle switch, and fried Nero's eggs. As Nero was screaming in absolute agony, his father continued.

"The king gave married couples a sign that they put on their door. The sign said 'FUCK'."

"Fuck"?! Nero asked.

Don Neroni lunged across his desk, but couldn't reach his son. The goons tilted Nero's chair forward and Don Neroni hit him on the head with his walking stick. "I'm trying to teach you something and your stupidity keeps interrupting. 'Fuck' meant, and still means, 'Fornication Under Consent of the King'. *F, U, C, K.* So you see it's not really a bad word. It just sounds bad when *you* say it."

"What do you want me to do?" Nero, physically destroyed, asked his loving father.

Don Neroni moved in close to his son. "I'm glad you asked that question, but I already answered it. You're gonna work. I set up some situations for you, and you're going to learn how to be responsible, how to be a man. I can't have an idiot taking over this family. They call this 'organized crime'. You couldn't organize a closet. Angelo and Toto will be with you at all times, just to make sure you do what's right."

Angelo smirked, "We'll have fun, Superstar."

Nero started to say something that wouldn't have ended well, and Angelo saved him, "Easy, Superstar. I'd shut my head if I was you."

Don Neroni nodded to Toto, "Give my son his graduation present." Toto bent down in front of Nero and attached a stun bracelet to Nero's ankle. Don Neroni explained, "Since Angelo and Toto are going to watch over my precious offspring, and knowing how my precious offspring acts, I thought they could use a leash. Angelo has the remote."

Angelo held up the remote for Nero to see and grinned. The don continued. "If you screw up, or try to get away-" He nodded to Angelo who pressed a button on the remote and Nero shrieked in pain. "Don't screw up. You'll try different things, and hopefully you'll learn. Your first job begins tomorrow at 9:00 A.M. sharp. Go get some sleep Nicolo. You look like you had a rough day."

The next morning, Nero, Angelo, and Toto were looking up at a huge mural of a nude baby boy wearing a police officer's cap, an exaggerated scowl, and looking down at them, pointing at them, like they were under arrest. All three of them were disgusted. Under the mural was a sign that said "Kidland Photos." Toto gave Nero a shove toward the door and they entered the building. There was a flurry of activity preparing for the day's photo shoots. Lights were being adjusted, film slapped into cameras, tripods adjusted, picture backdrops lowered, props being arranged such as alphabet stacking blocks, stuffed animals, etc. and kids being primped.

"That job brought me back to my acting roots," Nero told Izzy. "It allowed me to stretch as an actor. I was able to reach an audience who could really appreciate my work. I didn't have much of a choice. Big Daddy got off humiliating me and stun boy had his thumb on the trigger."

A little girl was placed on a platform in front of the camera as some other children waited their turn with their parents. The photographer quickly arranged the props, patted the kid's hair, and moved over to the camera, ready to snap away. The little girl sat there, expressionless. You could just tell that her life was meaningless, dull, and a waste of time at the age of five. It was very sad. The photographer, who had slept with his first cousin 18 times, dropped out of high school just to say he was a high school dropout, and was currently living with a drunken bitch that was 23 years older than he was, said, "I need a smile, sweetie." The little girl refused to smile, and why would she, given that she was a waste of oxygen? The photographer, already out of patience, spoke loudly as a cue, "WELL I KNOW SOMEONE WHO COULD PUT A BEAUTIFUL SMILE ON THAT PRETTY FACE! GUESS WHO IT IS!" Nero half-assed hopped over to the platform in a white bunny costume. He wasn't happy. Angelo turned to Toto and said, "I know who it is. It's a hopping asshole."

"That was my guess too," Toto said.

The photographer announced that it was Peter Rabbit. It wasn't. Nero as the bunny got in the little girl's face and said, "How ya doin' kid? Smile, *NOW!*" The little girl, whose future involved a stripping pole, single dollar bills, and lots of Japanese guys with cameras, seemed very disturbed by the big bunny. Nero put his thumbs in his bunny ears and made faces at her to get her to smile. He was getting annoyed. "Smile Toots!" he growled. The little girl frowned and was on the verge of tears. The goons exchanged glances and shook their heads at how pathetic Nero was. The little girl's "father" who wasn't really her father (but didn't know it) came over to her and tried to coax a smile.

"Look sweetie! It's Bugs Bunny! Daddy knows you like Bugs Bunny!" Then he turned to Nero and unwisely said, "What's up, Doc?"

Nero said, "I'm not Bugs Bunny, you dickhead. You're gonna be saying 'What's up, Doc?' in the emergency room."

Things started getting very heated between the little girl's "daddy" and the big angry bunny. As all hell started to break loose, Toto said to Angelo, "I like Bugs Bunny. You know he's from Brooklyn, like me. Same neighborhood I think."

Angelo said, "No shit? They got rabbits in Brooklyn?"

Right in front of the goons, the big bunny grabbed the little girl's "father's" face and planted the kiss of death on him. This is usually reserved for members of the crime family who were marked to meet their maker, but Nero didn't care. After the kiss, he pulled a gun on the girl's "father" sparking pandemonium. Everyone started running and screaming. Nero let the girl's "father" go. He just wanted to scare the hell out of him. And it worked. The little girl and her mother, who had slept with 376 men not counting the entire cast of her high school's horribly bad production of *Hair*, stayed put, determined to get that picture taken. The goons were a little baffled by the sudden commotion. Angelo asked, "Where'd Cottontail get the bean-shooter?" Toto explained that Nero had lifted it off a kid who was dressed like a cowboy when they came in, and that the gun wasn't real. The little girl's mother (whose vagina had more visitors than Grand Central Station between the hours of 2 to 6 P.M.) approached her daughter and bent over to tell her something. She was one sexy broad. She alone kept the antibiotic business in business. Nero and the goons were all staring at her ass. Nero commented, "I'd like to hop on that and drive it around the bunny trail." The little girl's mother who's had more screws than every hardware store on the planet combined, spun around feigning horror and slapped the big bunny. Angelo shook his head in disgust and commented, "Very rude rabbit." He hit the button on the remote for Nero's ankle bracelet and the big bunny hit the floor shrieking in pain. The little girl broke out into a huge smile, the photographer snapped the picture, and it was time to try another job.

Izzy took another turn and Nero saw a coyote chasing a roadrunner. I'm not kidding. Most cartoons are based on reality. "The bunny hop didn't work out," Nero told Izzy. "But next was a role that launched the careers of many great actors. It was a chance for me to try some of Strasberg's method acting techniques. That's where you don't act but you just be yourself so your performance comes off real."

The next day in an upscale shopping mall there was a long line of excited kids waiting to see Nick Nero. It wasn't actually Nero they were waiting to see. It was Santa Claus. Nero just happened to be dressed the part and was sitting on Santa's throne surrounded by tacky North Pole scenery, stuffed reindeer, and a couple of elves or midgets or dwarfs or whatever the hell they were. I didn't really care. I was watching the goons who were close by. They didn't seem too impressed with Santa Claus. Toto said to Angelo, "You know Santa Claus was real. He was a bishop in Asia Minor in the fourth century. He didn't fly around with reindeer, but he was good with kids in the neighborhood. He'd buy them Hot Wheels and Silly Putty and Barbie dolls and stuff like that. It really pisses me off when people say there's no Santa Claus. I accidentally killed 38 people who said that to me. Not all at once."

"No kiddin'?" Angelo said. "Do they really got rabbits in Brooklyn?"

An elf escorted a little girl up to "Santa" who lifted her up and sat her on his knee. "Santa" looked at the little girl and said, "You're gonna be a cute little number when you get older. But don't be a Ho Ho Ho." Angelo shook his head in disgust. Then he laid on the remote, sending Santa a package of pain. Santa was on the floor writhing in agony.

Toto said, "He sure is a great actor."

Angelo nodded, "Yeah, he's the best. He's really good at playing people in pain. Maybe he'll get typecast."

The following day they took Nero to the Graceful Garden Retirement Home to help him with his social skills. Outside, old folks were being walked and pushed around in wheelchairs by nurses, aides, and visiting relatives. Some were reading. Some were sitting. Some were staring into space. Some were talking to their hands and yelling at their shoes. Inside, in the "Sunshine Feel-Good Room" which was dedicated to the Graceful Garden Retirement Home by the Dankworth family in honor of their great Uncle Sheldon P. Dankworth who co-created the two-headed Q-tip but never received any money or credit for it, a Bingo game was in process. The Bingo balls spun around the crank cage and toppled over each other. The hand turning the crank stopped cranking. The balls came to a stop and the caller reached into the cage and pulled a ball out. The caller was Nick Nero. There were 15 residents of the home playing the game. Some were in wheelchairs. Some were on rolling cots. Some sat at card tables. A few nurses were there as well. Angelo and Toto sat in the back of the room, glaring at their charge. All the residents had Bingo cards and markers in front of them. Izzy glanced in the rear-view mirror and said, "I can't imagine you running a Bingo game in an old age home. You're more the back alley 'If you shoot his right ear off I'll give you a buck' type. That had to be something to see."

Nero shook his head and continued the tale. "So I looked at the ball and call B39! B39!" In the Sunshine Feel-Good Room Nero was suddenly attacked by an old woman who tried to ram her walker right up his ass. She was absolutely livid and screaming at Nero, as Angelo and Toto watched in disbelief, loving every minute of it. The old woman (who knew who the real biological father was of the little girl in the story where Nero played the bunny rabbit and the mother turned more tricks than every magician on Earth combined) screamed, "I CAN'T BE 39! I'M 102, YOU DUMB BASTARD!" She let out an attack yell, and all the old people jumped on Nero beating the crap out of him with their canes and walkers. Angelo and Toto just looked at each other and shrugged. Nero survived the thrashing, but vowed he would never call a Bingo game again. Angelo and Toto were proud of him for not defending himself against the old and frail and bought him lunch on the way to his next gig.

"There was one more job my old man set up for me that week," he told Izzy who had slowed the limo down to let a Gila monster pass in front of the car. She thought about the 1959 cult classic *The Giant Gila Monster* that was produced by Ken Curtis who was a really good singer and played "Festus Haggen" on *Gunsmoke* which ran from 1955 to 1975 starring James Arness whose brother was Peter Graves from *Mission Impossible* fame and also starred in the sci-fi cult film *Killers from Space* where the aliens had Ping Pong balls for eyes.

"I was supposed to be an "Odor Judge" for a company that made antiperspirant and cat litter. My old man was a funny guy. Tweedle Dum and Tweedle Dee said they had a stop to make on the way to my career sniffing armpits and cat crap. The journey to the stop wasn't fun."

Angelo was driving. Toto was in the passenger seat jotting something down in a pocket-sized notepad. Nero was in the back, serious and silent. Angelo glanced in the rear-view mirror at him. "You enjoying your first week of real work, Superstar?"

Nero sneered, "When I'm head of this family, you two are gonna be the ass cheeks."

Angelo shook his head and said, "Very rude." He then explained to Toto that he was driving, which required his full attention, and asked Toto if he would mind doing the honors. Toto activated the stun remote and Nero screamed in agony. Angelo said, "You scream like a broad, Superstar."

Toto agreed, "Just like a broad."

Angelo said, "Hey ain't that a Bob Dylan song, "Just Like a Broad"? And it says, 'Nobody feels any pain'. But I think our little Superstar would disagree."

With that, Toto shocked Nero again, and Nero hit the floorboard of the car. Livid, he growled, "You motherfuc-". Angelo cut him off. "Watch your grammar, Superstar. We can do this all day."

Toto corrected him, "That ain't grammar, that's vocabulary. Two different things."

Angelo chuckled, "Mr. Night School over here. I went to Night School for a week, but after my teacher gave me a bad grade in conduct he accidentally fell down three flights of stairs after stabbing himself in the back six times with my switchblade." He glanced at Toto who was writing in his pocket-sized notepad. "What are you doin', takin' notes?"

Toto said, "No, I'm writin' poetry. I'm a poet."

"I didn't know you was a poet. Ain't poetry for broads and guys who want to be broads?"

Toto said, "Nah...Anyone can write poetry: Joe "The Animal" Barboza, Charlie Sheen, Clyde of Bonnie and Clyde, Henry the Eighth, even one of those blue midget Smurfs is a poet. He's pretty good too."

Angelo was amazed. "No kiddin'? Let me hear your poetry."

Toto beamed, "Alright. This one here is called "The Look.""

Angelo said, "I like it so far. It sounds like something Shakespeare would say. Go ahead."

Toto cleared his throat and got dramatic, reciting from his pocket-sized notepad.

"The Look...
Hey, what the fuck are you lookin' at?
I'll blow your fuckin' brains out
like split cavatappi pasta in sweet basil marinara sauce
all over your mother's floor.
You can look at that...*asshole!*"

Angelo nodded, "Hey, not bad. All kinds of hidden meanings and shit like that." He looked in the rear-view mirror at Nero. "Hey Superstar, we got fuckin' Shakespeare over here." He pointed out a house up ahead. "Is that it, Shakespeare, the blue house? I'd call you 'Longfellow' but I've seen it."

Nero mumbled, "I'll bet you have."

Angelo glanced in the rear-view. "Don't get cute, tough guy. So, is this the place, Poetry Boy?"

Toto nodded, "That's it."

The car rolled to a stop. Angelo and Toto went to the back of the car, opened the trunk, and looked inside. Toto slipped a 12" x 6" paper cover

over the license plate that read "Stolen Tag." Angelo said, "I think we got everything." He leaned into the car window addressing Nero and said, "Pay attention, Superstar. This is how you do a job. Don't move."

Toto rang the doorbell. A minute later, an old man answered the door and opened it fully. Toto was immediately mesmerized by the spectacular collection of baseball memorabilia on display: a framed and autographed picture of Babe Ruth's famous called shot, more signed photos of famous baseball players past and present, signed gloves, an amazing collection of signed baseballs, many with their cork guts hanging out, jerseys, caps, trading cards, game programs, team pennants, you name it. The collection seemed to go on forever. Toto himself had put on a Dodgers jersey with the number 13. He was also wearing a phony grin and a cap for the occasion. He was holding a clipboard with some paper on it and a bag of peanuts which he handed to the old man. He said, "Good afternoon, Mr. Hill. I'm doin' a survey about the great American pastime, known as baseball. Do you enjoy the sport of baseball, Mr. Hill?"

The old man said, "Look around. It's my passion. I was a batboy for the Yankees when I was a kid. I knew all the greats. I see you're wearing number 13. It's not real popular in the park. Branca wore it when he pitched Thomson's 'Shot heard 'round the world'; most famous home run in baseball history. Bad luck that 13. Valentine wore it and had all kinds of hell. He busted his leg so bad he never played again."

"Terrible," Toto said, not caring.

The old man wouldn't shut up. "Did you know, in 1907 Alfred Lawson, the manager of the Philly team, they were called the 'Reading Red Roses' at that time, was the first to give numbers to his players so the fans could identify them. But he skipped number 13 because he was superstitious. Yeah, 13 is bad news."

Toto scribbled on his "survey" paper as he said the words out loud, "BAAAD NEEEWS." He looked at the old man. "Do you sometimes bet on games, Mr. Hill?"

The old man started getting a little nervous, and rightly so. "Sometimes, who did you say you were?"

Toto said, "Congratulations Mr. Hill! Being that you love baseball so much, it is with great pleasure that I inform you of the fact that you won the Grand Prize!"

The old man got excited, "The Grand Prize? That's great! What is it?"

Toto immediately dropped straight down and Angelo was standing there with a baseball bat cocked back. Angelo said, "It's the original Louisville Slugger. It was made in the mid-1890s in Louisville. And it works like this."

Angelo swung the bat as hard as he could. Nero was waiting in the backseat of the car as Mr. Hill's decapitated head landed face-first on the front windshield. Its mouth opened as though screaming, eyes wide with fright. The head slid slowly down the windshield leaving a trail of blood and other matter. Nero stumbled out of the car and lost his lunch.

Nero told Izzy, "I couldn't stomach anymore. I decided to leave the Neroni Hotel."

That night around 2:00 A.M. as it appeared that everyone was asleep, Nero snuck into his father's office and made his way to the desk. He straightened a paper clip and started to pick the lock of the top desk drawer when he realized that it had been left unlocked. He quietly opened it and removed his father's black address book. Inside the book was an envelope. He opened it and found a wad of cash. He hesitated with a sad smile, shoved the book and envelope in his pocket, and climbed out the window. Don Neroni watched silently in the dark as his son left. The goons started to go after Nero, but the don quickly motioned them to stop. As Nero fled into the night he looked up at the Heavens and wondered what was going on up there.

CHAPTER 3

The space pod repaired, The Outlaws of Asteroid #9 were soon on their way in search of the Golden Fleece. They put in first on Dykon, a strange planet inhabited by fierce vicious cruel women who were lousy cooks and had risen up against the men on Dykon when it was called "Mencon" and had killed them all except the old king, Solomon Creole, who was known for his ability to cut people in half while singing popular jazz tunes. He was really good at singing Ella Fitzgerald and Cab Calloway songs. After passing through radiation storms, bouncing around asteroid belts, smashing through threatening ice clouds and other fun hazards of space, the pod landed on the dark side of Dykon and the Outlaws followed their fearless leader exploring the place. They climbed up on a lunar crest and saw below them none other than King Creole himself sitting on his throne (too many thrones in this book) appearing extremely frail and looking very forlorn. Perhaps King Creole could point them in the direction of the Golden Fleece, Rollo considered. They would ask him. If he didn't know, or refused to tell, they would slap him around and beat him to a pulp to prove that they were stronger and tougher than any little old frail skinny king. As the Outlaws turned to descend the crest, several of the fierce vicious cruel women who were lousy cooks appeared and jabbed primitive spearheads into the Outlaws' power packs. In a high-pitched somewhat nervous almost soprano voice, Rollo Starguy instructed his outlaws to remain calm in this stressful situation. He strongly suggested that they not try any heroic funny stuff unless they desired to have their eggs poached. The Outlaws were brought before King Creole who was singing Cab Calloway's "Everybody Eats When They Come to My House" while cutting a Martian in half. They politely waited for him to finish both the song and the murder before explaining their quest for the Golden Fleece. The king, who was a nice guy despite having just murdered a Martian, agreed to help the Outlaws in their quest if they performed an act of valor. None of them had any idea what the word "valor" meant, but they agreed anyway. The king told the Outlaws that every time he prepared to dine he was savagely attacked by the Flookies, which were frightful flying creatures with hooked beaks and claws and dragon tails and no respect for personal property. The Flookies were sent to terrorize him because he opposed The Evil One. In fact, The Evil One was the one who sent them. To demonstrate, King Creole beckoned a fierce vicious cruel woman who was a lousy cook but was good at bringing him things, to bring him an Earth apple. As he raised the Earth apple to his mouth, the Flookies darted down from behind a giant chaise lounge in the sky. I have no idea how it got there. I know as much as you do about it, which isn't much. The Flookies attacked the king, took the Earth apple, and left behind an intolerable stench, sickening to all living creatures. Keeled over and holding their noses, the Outlaws agreed to rid Dykon of the Flookies if the king gave them information about the Golden Fleece. At first the king refused until the Flookies were gone, but when the Outlaws started to walk, he started to talk. King Creole told the Outlaws that the Golden Fleece was on the square planet Digby in the possession of the great space warrior and leader, Emperor Zee, who among other things was famous for sitting on a rocking chair instead of a throne and that they were three solar revolutions away from Digby. He warned that to get there the space pod must first pass through the Mashing Moons of Molotov. They mash against one another while the Boiling Sea of Tobor boils up around them and tries to boil them. He said that many space explorers had lost their lives attempting to pass through without knowing the secret. At first King Creole refused to tell the secret and started singing Ella Fitzgerald's "Can't Help Lovin' Dat Man" while cutting a public defender in half, but after suffering a severe groin injury, he spilled the beans. The way to pass through the Mashing Moons of Molotov is first to make trial with a zanzibat which is sort of like a blind pigeon with four wings. If it passes through safely, then the chances of the Outlaws passing through unharmed were slim to none. But if the zanzibat is mashed, then the Outlaws must turn back and give up their quest for the Golden Fleece, or the ZX-12 would be destroyed and The Outlaws of Asteroid #9 would surely perish.

Keeping their end of the bargain, the Outlaws devised an ingenious elaborate plan to rid Dykon of the Flookies once and for all by having their own stench kill them. The king was placed on his throne under a huge crate which was propped up in front with a stick. Everyone else hid in the surrounding brush which was really just poster board with brush painted on it to look real because I couldn't afford real brush for this scene. The Outlaws were close by holding one end of a string. The other end of the string was tied to the stick. At Rollo's signal King Creole raised a lightly toasted cinnamon raisin bagel with a schmear of strawberry cream cheese to his mouth. I don't know where he got it. I didn't see any delis there. Suddenly the Flookies swooped down from behind the giant chaise lounge and attacked the king. After several minutes of watching the king being tortured by the Flookies, Rollo gave the command and the Outlaws jerked the string which caused the stick to fall and the crate to slam down over the Flookies and the king. Everyone came out of hiding and rejoiced. They were high-fiving each other, dancing around, and celebrating. The horrible Flookies had been defeated so that the king could now eat in peace. Sluggo approached Rollo and raised his hand with an inquiry. Rollo called on him.

Sluggo said, "Rollo, I understood the whole plan about catching the Flookies in the big box and letting their own smell kill them so the king could eat his food, but were we supposed to catch the king too?"

There was a long uncomfortable silence as Rollo pondered Sluggo's question. Finally he answered, "No. But sometimes in life we must sacrifice one thing in order to get something else. In this case we had to sacrifice the king in order to catch the Flookies."

"So they wouldn't bother the king?" Sluggo asked.

"Now you're catching on," Rollo said, patting Sluggo on the back. He was proud of his boys. He watched them having a grand time being thrown around, taunted, emasculated, and forced to eat terribly-cooked meals by the fierce vicious cruel women of Dykon, and then he interrupted the celebration to say this, "Boys, have a good time tonight with these lovely ladies, but remember that tomorrow we must attempt to pass through the Mashing Moons of Molotov and we could die a very gruesome death. So we have a big day ahead of us. I want to see you boys bright-eyed and bushy-tailed in the space pod at O-700. And don't fall in love, it's too expensive."

And so it was, that at 0-701, the ZX-12 took off and was soon within sight of the menacing merciless Mashing Moons of Molotov. All about them were remnants of wrecked spaceships and starships and skeletal remains of those who had dared to pass through and were squashed to death. On either side of the Mashing Moons was nothing but calm open space with clear passage. The Outlaws of Asteroid #9 took in the awesome sight, and it was some sight to see. Alfie pointed out that there was no way in tarnation that they could make it through the Mashing Moons of Molotov, and asked why they couldn't simply go *around* the Mashing Moons. Why should they risk their lives when they didn't have to? It was a good question and one that deserved an answer.

There was a long uncomfortable silence as Rollo pondered the question and then responded, "There is an easy way to do things and a hard way to do things. We do things the hard way."

The Outlaws looked at each other. Then Alfie asked, "Why do we do things the hard way if we can do things the easy way?"

Again Rollo pondered. It was another good question and he was getting annoyed with all these good questions. He said, "We do things the hard way because we can."

"But what if we can't this time and we die to death?" Alfie asked.

Rollo said, "Your death is none of your business." With that he picked up a small cage and removed a zanzibat. He explained that he was about to release the creature. If it made it through the Mashing Moons then they might have not much of a chance, but if it got mashed, then it was all over and the journey thus far had been for nothing. He told his outlaws to watch the zanzibat carefully and to follow her every move, as their very lives depended on it. With a wish of "Godspeed" Rollo released the zanzibat and the Outlaws simultaneously moved their heads in unison like synchronized swimming only not swimming, following the zanzibat's spastic flight as it went every which way but through the Mashing Moons of Molotov. It unloaded some zanzibat caca on Rollo's head and flew in the opposite direction never to be seen again. Rollo Starguy spoke to his outlaws in a tone they hadn't heard in years. He spoke like a man on a mission, a man with true grit. And I don't mean the John Wayne movie or the remake with Jeff Bridges. He spoke with spirit, with fire, and with something else that I can't think of right now. He was a great leader who had just been crapped on by a misguided zanzibat with very little education.

"Boys," he said with zanzibat caca on his head, "What you have just witnessed was a cowardly act by a flying wimp. But *we* are not flying wimps. We are The Outlaws of Asteroid #9! We are legends! We are heroes! And we must prove it every day of our rotten lives! Prepare to go through the Mashing Moons of Molotov!"

The Outlaws nervously awaited Rollo's command. The Mashing Moons seemed to invite death. They were hungry for it. They were salivating for it. They wanted it. The Outlaws (all except for Rollo) had a very quick meeting which included lots of uncontrollable sobbing, and decided that they really wanted to return to Asteroid #9 and skip the whole "let's die today" thing. But Rollo was determined, and he called the shots. He gave the command and the Outlaws reluctantly sprang into action. Sluggo threw the tiny space pod into overdrive and with a SWOOSH and a prayer, accelerated beyond the VNTE line. For those unfamiliar with space technology vocabulary and stuff like that, VNTE stands for "Velocity Not To Exceed" (whatever that means). Anyway, they continued accelerating and there appeared to be no end to their speed. That can of beans was really moving. Then it all became a blur as the Mashing Moons of Molotov struck together with a tremendous "MASH!" which sent the tiny space pod tumbling end over end through space. Then everything went black. There was nothing, only darkness. Alfie was the first to regain consciousness, awakening from a dream about a cave worm defending its underground nest from an egg eater while he was busy playing nude Egyptian Rat Screw with two girls he knew in high school. Sluggo and Rollo came to shortly after, rubbing their noggins, dazed, with the feeling like they'd been stone drunk and hit by a herd of wild gassxders which were sort of like geese only very different. Apparently they had made it through the Mashing Moons of Molotov, but the sound and vibration of the "MASH!" was so powerful that it sent them hurtling through a space warp, which was not a pleasant experience. It's like when you're fooling around with a girl and you reach into her change purse and you discover that she's not a girl. You know what I mean? We've all had that little mind-numbing experience. Well, let's get back to our story. And then, almost mystically, a beautiful enchanting song filled the ZX-12. It was a song so soothing, so comforting, that all unpleasantness was forgotten, like that crazy tale I made up out of my wild fertile imagination about the guy who is fooling around with the girl and finds out she's not a girl. Anyway...where was I? Oh yeah, only beauty existed. There was only serenity and pleasure. The Outlaws were drawn to the source of the song (the song's singers) like paper clips to a magnet. Suddenly Rollo remembered hearing about these singers from his mother's brother, Uncle Alfred, who was an unemployed satellite polisher who warned him about the Sonny Mann Singers (the singers of the song that was sung). Their enchanting voices make a man forget all else, and their songs steal his life away. Don't ask me how, because I don't know. You don't need to know how everything works. "DO NOT LISTEN TO THEIR SONG, IT IS CERTAIN DEATH!" Rollo Starguy yelled to his outlaws who were two feet in front of him. A strange glow seemed to surround Rollo Starguy as he himself got so caught up in the melody, that he himself (Rollo Starguy) started humming along with the Sonny Mann Singers. Soon The Outlaws of Asteroid #9 were all glowing and humming along with the Sonny Mann Singers as the ZX-12 seemed to land under its own power on Mermonia where the singers of the song sang.

The beautiful enticing Sonny Mann Singers were wearing revealing nighties and perched on heart-shaped beds singing their latest intergalactic cover hit "Maneater" first recorded by Hall & Oates and released in 1982 on their H20 album. I was never a big fan of theirs. Some of their stuff was okay, but I wouldn't go out of my way to listen. The Sonny Mann Singers were surrounded by piles of moldering skeletons of those space explorers who had been lured to their death. Slowly the Outlaws' life functions began to slow down (as opposed to "*Quickly* the Outlaws' life functions began to slow down"). Their breathing rate dropped to four breaths per minute. Their pulse rates dropped to three beats per minute. Although their bodies were not in the best shape at this point, their minds were clearer than ever before. They were fully aware that they were suspended in time and space, unable to struggle. Just as the Outlaws were about to meet their demise, Mr. Green Jeans, the old farmer who had given them the ZX-12, rode up on a space tractor, pulled out a shotgun, and blasted the Sonny Mann Singers to Kingdom Come.

"I hate that kinda singin'," spat the old farmer. "I don't see what the big attraction is. They sound outta tune to me. Now, Little Jimmy Dickens, he could sing. Tiny little guy, dressed weird, but lots of talent."

Gradually the Outlaws' strength returned and they continued on to the square planet Digby. *Outer space is pretty big* thought Rollo Starguy as he looked down on the Milky Way galaxy. It was eight hundred million billion miles long and ten times as deep. And there are millions of known galaxies bigger than the Milky Way. Makes you want to stop paying your bills, don't it? While Rollo was imagining how much whipped cream it would take to fill up the universe, Sluggo picked up an emergency distress signal from an odd little uncharted planet known only as "Edwina" on the fringe of Gamma Four out in the frozen reaches of space at the tip of the spiral nebula. It was a bitch and a half to get to. At Rollo's command Alfie slammed down the clutch and shifted the ZX-12 to supralight warp speed and they were on their way to Gamma Four. As they began their approach to Edwina, they quickly ducked the pod behind some space junk comprised of rockets' empty core stages (whatever that means), dead satellites, old refrigerators, and several copies of the movie *The Underachievers* which I played a scumbag gang leader in. The movie sucked, but I was great and should have won an Oscar. The Cyclon Pirate Cruiser they first saw on Shlump's perimeter was hovering over Edwina's rocky terrain while the pirate scavengers were looting the planet. They were stealing anything they could find: Chevy hubcaps, guacamole bowls, a glow-in-the-dark Frisbee, a collection of horror and sci-fi movies from the 1950s including *Monster on the Campus*, *The She-Creature*, *The Brain Eaters*, *Daughter of Dr. Jekyll*, *Attack of the Giant Leeches* starring Yvette Vickers playing a backwoods slut who in real life died a horrible death which I won't go into here, but it involved becoming a mummy and being eaten by her own dogs, *The Killer Shrews*, *Bride of the Monster* which was an Ed Wood classic of ineptitude starring a strung-out Bela Lugosi on his way out, and *The Giant Gila Monster* which, as I mentioned to you before and am repeating again so you don't forget, was produced by Ken Curtis who played Festus on *Gunsmoke* and would say things like "It's hotter than a jug full of red ants." And "You got enough money to burn a wet elephant with." Mr. Curtis also starred in the aforementioned *The Killer Shrews* as the bad guy. They also stole a signed 8 x 10 glossy headshot of Gene Hackman who let Dustin Hoffman stay with him in his apartment when they were first starting their acting careers in New York. The pirate scavengers planned to sell the things they stole on the black market or eBay to make their alimony payments. The planet was apparently uninhabited, which was understandable because its surface was so rocky that no one or no creature could walk there. The scavenger pirates, who were obviously in alliance with The Evil One's regime, easily loaded the stolen goods into the cruiser while the Outlaws looked on curiously while hidden behind the space junk. And then a very strange thing started to happen. The planet's rocky surface seemed to move around the Cyclon Pirate Cruiser. The rocks started wobbling and rolling toward the pirates who dropped the goods they were carrying and freaked. Do you all still use that expression? I don't know and I don't really care. The rocks started blurting out Leonard Cohen lyrics and hurling themselves at the pirates. The pirates took refuge inside the cruiser and the rocks smashed against the hull.

After a time, the rocks stopped their attack and fell asleep, as rocks tend to do after lots of excitement. There usually isn't any excitement on Edwina. The last exciting thing that happened there was a cover band from Uranus ended up there and wanted to play their own hits, but because they were a cover band they didn't have their own hits, so there was just silence. The band just stood there on stage doing nothing for almost two hours. Quietly, so as not to awaken the sleeping rocks, out of the top dome of the cruiser emerged the diabolical Stellar Converter, one of the most powerful weapons in the spiral nebula. The ruthless weapon, which was a converted anti-gravity ray beam cannon used to change the configurations of constellations but certainly capable of destroying a crummy little planet where you can't even walk, trained on the hub of Edwina and was triggered and set to blow it to bits. Alfie whipped out his slingshot from his back pocket, picked up a tiny little baby rock, pulled back as hard as he could, and launched it at the Stellar Converter, lodging the baby rock in the firing mechanism, jamming the weapon so it couldn't fire. Yes, the tiny little baby rock screamed and cried and its mommy and daddy and older brother never saw it again and all that noise, but I have to move on. Lodging the little miserable rock into the firing mechanism was a smart move because the Outlaws also would have been blown to bits had the weapon fired. But it didn't, so they weren't. A powerful gust of solar wind shoved the space junk away and the Outlaws were exposed. The cruiser shot back into space and fired a photon torpedo at the Outlaws who now all had their slingshots out shooting tiny little screaming baby rocks at the cruiser. It was a nasty little skirmish, if I do say so, and I do say so. I've seen several skirmishes. Some were nasty and some weren't, but this one was definitely nasty. Alfie turned around and tried a backward over-the-shoulder shot. It was a masterpiece, striking the torpedo in mid-flight and exploding it. The blast was so close to the Cyclon Pirate Cruiser that it ripped a hole in the hull (that's the main body of the cruiser, including the bottom, the sides, and the deck, in case you didn't know) sucking the pirates out of the cruiser and flinging them out into the infinite universe where they would never annoy anyone again. The living rocks of the planet Edwina on the fringe of Gamma Four out in the frozen reaches of space at the tip of the spiral nebula cheered The Outlaws of Asteroid #9 who had saved their planet from total annihilation. They were the happiest bunch of rocks ever except for the little baby rocks who were sacrificed and their families who would never see them again. But the rest of the rocks were rocks and didn't have any arms, but they wanted to wave goodbye to the Outlaws who got into the ZX-12 and took off. Even though they didn't have any arms to wave goodbye to their heroes with, the rocks waved goodbye in their rock heads. Alfie set the space pod on cruise control and the Outlaws sailed through the starlit universe singing bad Iron Butterfly songs and reading Archie comic books aloud to each other while exchanging warped fantasies involving Betty, Veronica, and sometimes Miss Grundy, the English teacher at Riverdale. A sudden jolt sent the Outlaws crashing around the cabin. It felt as though a giant hand had reached up and snagged them. Rollo looked out a porthole and saw that the pod wasn't moving. They were suspended in mid-flight; caught like rats in a trap. At Rollo's command Alfie shifted into overdrive, but the space pod wouldn't even budge. Rollo slipped on his 3-D infrared galactic goggles that he used to watch William Castle films with, and saw that they were indeed caught in some sort of massive spider web. It appeared to be a complex network of impenetrable strands, possibly pulverizing to anything it catches, yet invisible to the naked eye.

Like the quick-thinking courageous leader that he was, Rollo Starguy bravely volunteered his favorite right-hand man Sluggo Saperstein to climb out on the web and cut loose the strands holding the ZX-12. He rented Sluggo his 3-D infrared galactic goggles that he used to watch William Castle films with and insisted that they be returned unharmed because he wanted to watch *13 Ghosts* again. He also rented Sluggo a pair of hedging shears at a generous discount, and sent him out of the pod to get to work. Sluggo cautiously and nervously crept out on the web and tried to cut the strands, but he couldn't make a scratch. As he headed back to the pod to tell the Outlaws that they were in big trouble, something pounced across the web and plastered itself to Sluggo's face. All Sluggo saw was blackness. It was an eerie blackness. It was the kind of blackness one sees when something weird is plastered to one's face. The Outlaws, however, saw something quite different. They saw a weird spider-beast clinging to Sluggo's face like it had found its long-lost mate and wanted to make up for lost time in the romance department. Don't think *Alien* because this is a whole different creature and a whole different story. Rollo and Alfie quickly pulled their companion back into the cabin and tried everything they could to get the spider-beast off his face. First they tried prying it off with soupspoons, but that didn't work because the spoons got all bent out of shape. They each had lubricant that they could have tried, but they didn't bring out the lubricant because then they would ask each other why they had lubricant and that could be really embarrassing. Next they tried lying to it, claiming that there was a nude female spider-beast named Sophie Sweetbuns waiting for it just outside the pod. But that didn't cut it either because as far as *this* spider-beast was concerned, Sluggo's face would do just dandy, thank you. Nothing they tried did the job. When finally they accepted the fact that Sluggo would always have the spider-beast attached to his face, which quite frankly was an improvement, Alfie took a red crayon from his arts and crafts box and drew a picture of Sluggo's face on the back of the spider-beast so he would have a face to look at when conversing with Sluggo. Well, miraculously, that did the trick. Sluggo was allergic to the red color dye in the crayon. I know that most of you think that crayons grow the color that they are, but that's not true, dyes are used to create the color. I think. I haven't looked it up, and I'm not going to, but that's what I think. So Sluggo, being allergic to the dye, sneezed, sending the spider-beast flying out of the porthole and into the mouth of a hungry Yoob who was crawling across the web toward the pod and it wasn't to make friends. The Yoob put its big slobbering mouth over the porthole and sucked out the Outlaws into its big icky cheeks. It carried them over to where it resided, which was a dying planet on the tail end of the tail of Canis Minor, and spit them out onto a tremendous ping-pong table. Those crazy slobbering Yoobs just loved ping-pong. They were the self-proclaimed ping-pong champions of the universe. The Yoobs rolled the Outlaws into a ball and started a championship match. But the Outlaws as a ball would not bounce. The Yoobs got mad and threw the ball of Outlaws down into the pit where they kept their other ping-pong balls. Now, their other ping-pong balls, called "whiff-whaff" balls were actually Eebs who were actually a race of little round bouncing creatures who were captured by the Yoobs at the beginning of The Evil One's blitz. They were held captive in their pitiful pit and only allowed out when the Yoobs used them in their tournaments. The pit was very uncomfortable because it was formed when a meteor crashed through the planet's surface, and the meteor was still at the bottom of the pit and still very hot from its entry into the atmosphere. Therefore, the Eebs couldn't keep their little feet down for more than a second or else they'd get very badly burned, so they had to keep dancing all the time. A Yoob reached into the pit and felt around for a nice plump ball to play with. It pulled out Grandma Esther Eeb, smacked her with a paddle on the rump, and the tournament began. It lasted an eternity because it kept ending in tie games. Tie games that could not be broken. Finally, when one of the Yoobs was too pooped to ping, he accused his opponent of cheating. That did it. A fight almost broke out but was soon stopped by the other Yoobs who suggested a rematch with a different ball. Hearing this, the Outlaws and the Eebs quickly tunneled under the meteor and pushed it up toward the surface so that when the Yoob reached down for another ball it picked up the meteor. It looked a little different than their usual balls because it was five miles wide and weighed several million tons, but to a Yoob, a ping-pong ball is a ping-pong ball. A Yoob prepared to serve, tossed the meteor into the air, and when it came down he slammed it with his ping-pong paddle. The paddle broke into a thousand splinters. Well, maybe not a thousand, I didn't care enough to count them. All the Yoobs went wild with anger because they only had two paddles and now there would be no more ping-pong. The only joy they ever knew was gone. They all jumped on the Yoob who broke the paddle and massive mayhem ensued. While the Yoobs were busy attacking the poor Yoob who broke the paddle, the Outlaws and the Eebs helped each other out of the pit and quickly climbed up the web to the pod to make good their escape. Because the Eebs were always well groomed, they had their nail clippers with them and immediately got to work cutting the web to free the ZX-12. Now I know you're asking yourself how nail clippers cut the impenetrable strands when the hedging shears couldn't even scratch them. That's a good question. So anyway the Outlaws and the Eebs climbed into the pod and they zipped away in search of a new home for the Eebs. The Outlaws looked everywhere (well, not "everywhere") for a place to put the Eebs but the Eebs couldn't afford first, last, and security, so the pickings were slim. The Outlaws eventually grew tired of looking, so they passed out hats and harmonicas and dumped the Eebs in Asteroid Alley which is like Skid Row only in outer space, and continued on to Digby. As the ZX-12 headed toward Digby, Rollo Starguy looked out of a porthole and caught a glimpse of the giant Felix the Cat balloon float from the 1927 Macy's Thanksgiving Day Parade as it floated by the pod. Earth always amused Rollo, and he wondered what was going on down there.

Chapter 4

As if obeying the don's command to his goons not to pursue Nero, there was a sudden violent jolt and lurch followed by a loud grinding noise as the limo basically fell apart coming to a very definite and abrupt stop. After a moment or two, Nero and Izzy got out. They were both frazzled and dazed. Izzy staggered, about to collapse. "Loved the decapitated head story, I think I'm gonna puke." She leaned over with her hands on her knees and tried not to. Suddenly there was a high-pitched giggling which stopped as quickly as it started.

Nero snarled, "Did you land on a witch?"

"Yeah, me and your old man," Izzy snarled back.

Neither one of them was overly happy at the moment. Nero looked around and asked no one, "Where in hell are we?" There was a sudden gust of wind and a bunch of large tumbleweeds rolled away revealing an odd assortment of shanty-like structures in various cartoonish colors and sizes. It looked like a bizarre carnival had broken down years ago and the carnies just settled there. Set off some distance from the shanties was an area called "Hog Heaven" as proclaimed by a rotted wooden handwritten sign stuck in the desert sand. Hog Heaven included a pig-farrowing barn and several hoop structures which are "greenhouses" for pigs. A brown flag with a black crescent moon waved overhead on a rusty pole. There were charred pieces of a large executive bus scattered here and there like it exploded, some abandoned kitchen appliances, a few old rusted cars, skids of empty vials, huge spools of thin tubing, and stacks of old tires. The one road Izzy and Nero were on ran through the center of town. To one side was an odd wooded area that appeared man-made and in stark contrast

48

to this one-horse town with no horse. There were, however, plenty of pigs meandering about. Izzy saw more handwritten signs and read them out loud: "*Zoo…Mayor's Office…Car Repairs…Welcome to Percy! Pig Semen Capital of the World! Population 24*…Terrific, you live your whole life and end up here."

Again they heard the sound of high-pitched giggling as two young boys both dressed as Pippi Longstocking popped out from behind a rusted-out 1957 Chevy Nomad and approached them. One of the boys was carrying a small pot-bellied pig dressed up like Pipi's monkey Mr. Nilsson. The boy holding the pig dressed as Mr. Nilsson the monkey stared up at Nero and asked, "Are you a giant Martian?"

Nero snarled, "Yeah. Now take me to your leader before I put my foot up Uranus. I need my flying limo fixed and I need to get out of this… place."

Izzy looked at him. "Aren't you gonna look under the hood and pretend you know what you're looking at?"

"I don't need to look. It's broken, and it's your fault," Nero said. Then he addressed the boys, "Let's go."

The boys led Nero and Izzy into town, which was about another twenty feet. When they got there, all the good people of Percy came out of doors and windows and from behind fake one-dimensional trees and bushes to stare. They were an odd lot indeed. In a way they appeared as simple country folk, like on a 1950s postcard of rural America, but something was a little off in a major way. Something just wasn't right in the town of Percy. The boys then led Nero and Izzy to the town mechanic, a schlub in overalls with a deep passion for chewing tobacco and all the loveliness that comes with it.

The boy not holding the pig said, "This here's Percy. Best mechanic in town."

The boy holding the pig added, "*Only* mechanic in town."

Nero said, "I thought the name of the town is Percy."

The mechanic spit a big glob of yucky disgusting brown chewing tobacco spit and said, "It is. My name's Percy too. But me and the town ain't related. That would be stupid to be related to a town. That'd be like havin' a really big cousin with all kinds of little people livin' inside of him."

Nero and Izzy stared at Percy as though he had just said something that would make them stare at him. Then Percy said, "Hell, I see you're confused. Just call me *Mister* Percy. That way you won't mix up me and the town."

Izzy said, "Mr. Percy, our limo broke down and we need it fixed fast."

Mr. Percy said, "I don't do that. Repairin' and fixin' is two different things. Fixin' means you cut off its privates so it can't have no kids, or if you want it to sing high notes. A limo is a car and cars ain't got no privates. Cars don't have kids. And they can't sing worth a damn."

Izzy started to get mad. "Can you *repair* the car or not?"

Mr. Percy said, "I don't *repair* cars, I *work* on 'em. If I repaired 'em they'd break down again eventually and I'd just have to repair 'em again, so what's the point of repairin' 'em in the first place? So I just work on 'em. Y'all must be from the city, 'cause you ain't the brightest tools in the shed, if you know what I mean."

Nero saw some old cars for sale next to the mechanic's shop and pulled out a wad of cash. "I'll buy a car."

"You can buy all the cars you want, mister, but they don't work. Like my brother-in-law, he don't work neither. You can buy him too."

At that a huge obese man wearing only torn faded flowered boxer shorts waddled by drinking a beer. Mr. Percy said, "There he go. Five bucks cash, he's all yours."

Nero said, "You keep your brother-in-law. I want that limo repaired, *now*. The faster you repair it, the more money you get." He stuffed a few bills in Mr. Percy's pocket.

Mr. Percy said, "You're in luck, I have parts for a 1972 Dodge Swinger."

Izzy said, "It's not a Dodge Swinger. It's a Lincoln Town Car Limousine."

Nero shoved more cash in Percy's pocket.

"I'll do what I can," Percy said, "but it could take a few months."

Nero started losing it. "I want it fixed or repaired or whatever you call it, *now*, or I'll fix *you* so you'll *talk* in high notes. Got it?"

A long-time annoying resident of Percy, Milo Mabbitt, ran up and interrupted the conversation. "Mayor, is I interrupting anything?"

"No, Milo," Percy said.

"Then I'll come back later," Milo said, and ran off.

Izzy looked at Percy, "Mayor"?

Percy spat some more yucky brown disgusting chewing tobacco spit and said, "Yep. I'm the mayor too. There's no money in bein' a car mechanic in a town with cars that don't work."

Izzy glanced around and saw a strange building with a handwritten sign that said *HOUSE OF THE CHOKING CHICKEN.* "Look, there's a chicken restaurant. I'm hungry. Let's eat while he gets to work."

Mr. Percy said, "No Mam, that ain't no chicken restaurant. That's our brothel. We ain't got no hookers 'cause they all went to Nevada and Hollywood, but we got some animals and cold cuts that don't put up much of a fight anymore. There's four rooms in there. In one room is a monkey. In another room there's a chicken. There's also bologna and a weasel. You pay your five bucks admission fee at the door, choose your room, get a firm grip on the occupant, and do your business. You can spank it, choke it, bop it, or whack it. The choice is yours, free of charge."

Nero said, "You just said it was five bucks. Not that I care."

"*Admission* is five bucks. The choice is free. Listen with both ears, young man."

Milo Mabbitt ran over and said, "We also got that movie of Lester's Aunt Eugenia and her dog Romeo. Nasty stuff, that is! And it's a double feature with *The Really Dirty Dozen!*"

Percy said, "Heel Romeo!"

Milo said, "Roll over Romeo!"

And they both broke up laughing at their terrific inside joke. It was, in fact, the most popular joke in Percy (the town, not the mechanic/mayor). Nero and Izzy looked over at The House of the Choking Chicken and watched as a line of men and boys entered and exited. Entering, they had lots of energy and looked as well as someone in Percy can look. Exiting, they were exhausted and disheveled.

As Mr. Percy continued talking to Nero and Izzy, a boom mic dangled over his head. It took a few seconds for Nero to notice it. He spun around and saw a 16mm production camera aimed right at them, a documentary film crew, and finally renowned documentary director Nigel Daw at the helm. Daw was British, arrogant, and serious about his work. Nero and Daw knew each other, and it wasn't love. The boom mic accidentally smacked Percy on the head and Daw exploded.

"You're incompetent!"

The boom mic operator said, "Sorry, slipped. I had bologna for lunch and it was greasy."

"If you can't be professional, I'll get someone else. One call is all it takes," Daw warned, waving his cell phone.

Milo Mabbitt ran over to Daw, snatched the cell phone out of his hand, and tossed it high up in the air. Mr. Percy whipped out a sawed-off shotgun and blew the cell phone to bits. Daw didn't allow his crew to have cell phones on a shoot, so that was the only one they had. He instructed his camera operator to stay on Percy (the mechanic/mayor, not the town) who snarled, "No fancy talkin' machines allowed in Percy! Work of the devil!" Mr. Percy frisked Nero who allowed it only because he needed the limo repaired, took his cell phone, tossed it to Milo who tossed it up high, and shot it to pieces. He then moved to pat down Izzy who knocked his hands away.

"Hands off a lady, Goober!" she snapped.

Nero shook his head and Percy wagged his finger at Daw, "You people's like gnats! We can't live normal lives with outside peoples up our nose and buzzin' 'round our heads all the time! If the world sees this here movie you're makin', everyone'll wanna visit Percy to see how nice and peaceful is Percy. We'll have tourists up the cornhole! Next thing you know we'll have a giant black anthropomorphic rat in red shorts runnin' around squeakin', "Welcome to Percy!" We'll have a talkin' duck that you can't hardly understand that don't wear no trousers!" He broke down sobbing. "Don't take my Percy! I love Percy!" he sobbed, like a man who believed he might never have Percy again. Nero walked over, put his arm around Percy (the mechanic/mayor, not the town), and moved him out of the others' earshot for a private talk.

"Let's make a deal," Nero said.

Mr. Percy was emotional. Drying his eyes he said, "I loved that show, especially the mule with the straw hat behind door number three. And that Carol Merrill. She sure was a honey."

Nero said, "I'll get rid of these gnats if you get that limo running pronto."

Percy agreed, "Okay, I ain't no Injun but that's a deal. I got a third cousin twice removed west of here that knows a guy who eats in a diner off the pike every other Thursday between 7:00 P.M. and 8:00 P.M. That guy knows a trucker named Karl that brings the parts you need down from Seattle. So you're in luck."

"I don't think we're in luck. I think we're in Percy," Izzy said.

"How do you know the limo needs parts? You haven't even looked at it," Nero said.

Percy glanced over at the limo from where he stood. "You busted the right spindle and the rear axle. I can tell by the way she's sittin'."

Nero glanced at the limo which looked like it'd been through a war, then he stormed over to the documentary crew and got in Daw's face, "You're done. Goodbye."

Daw didn't flinch. "Well, if it isn't the great Nick Nero, a legend in his own mind."

Nero was seething, "Loved your documentary on organized crime, Daw. You're lucky you're alive. You have no idea how many button men wanted you gone. My old man stopped them, which I was against. I'm happy to remedy that, right here and now."

Daw ignored the threat. "What brings you to the uncharted quaint little town of Percy, Mr. Nero? Did your car break down?"

"Go climb up your thumb, Daw," Nero snarled.

Daw said, "I'm sorry, Mr. Nero. I don't speak your back alley thug lingo."

Nero snapped, "It means get lost."

Daw said, "Even if I wanted to 'get lost', which I don't, my crew and I travel by bus, and the good gentleman you've been hobnobbing with over there, decided to blow it up. It seems that buses and many other things look like phallic symbols to him. And that's not allowed in Percy. Ironic, isn't it? No phallic symbols in Percy. You would think that a place called Percy would be wide open to phallic symbols."

Nero growled, "Daw, they don't want you here. I don't care if you skip back to your mud hole, just leave."

"Save your Cosa Nostra persona for the screen, Mr. Nero."

Nero grabbed Daw's face with both hands and kissed him full on the mouth delivering the Mafia kiss of death just like he did to that little girl's "father" when he was a bunny at Kidland Photos. "That's usually reserved for family members who betray the code, as you know, but I'm making an exception here. Leave or I'll kill you," Nero sneered, wiping his mouth.

"And a breath mint wouldn't kill *you*, Mr. Nero," Daw said, not wiping his mouth. Nero stormed over to the movie camera, popped open the magazine, and pulled out the film which he ripped to shreds.

Daw smirked, "That was new film, hardly anything on it. We have lots more. This is a documentary, Mr. Nero. It's about a strange place with strange people. This isn't one of your crappy Hollywood merchandise pimps you call 'movies'."

Nero returned to where Izzy was standing. He whispered, "I need to scare them off or we'll never get out of here."

Izzy said, "That lip-lock would have scared anyone. I think he liked it. He was looking at your ass when you turned around. Why don't you just use your irresistible charm and nicely ask him to leave?"

Nero said, "Percy blew up their bus, so they'd have to walk. Besides, documentary filmmakers hate movie stars."

"I understand completely," Izzy said. "So do I."

Izzy noticed Mr. Percy rubbing his forehead like he was in pain. "Are you alright there, Mr. Percy? Looks like you have a headache like I've had ever since I met Mr. Nero."

"If I don't eat a frozen dinner at least once a week, my head will explode. And this here bein' the desert, there ain't no frozen dinners, so my head explodes once a week, and it's that time again."

Rubbing his throbbing head, Mr. Percy ran off. Nero and Izzy started aimlessly wandering around town. Percy residents continued to watch them suspiciously from cracked doors and windows and from behind one-dimensional trees and bushes and parts of blown-up vehicles. As they watched another line form to enter The House of the Choking Chicken, they heard a loud bell ring. The line quickly scattered. All the townspeople ran outside, frantically running into each other, and then all simultaneously running from one shanty to another. They were bounced around and turned away at each place they tried to enter. As the frustrated townspeople started frantically running around each other, a boy riding a pig galloped by Izzy and she grabbed him to get some answers.

"Where's everyone goin'?"

"It's another saint-sighting!" the boy said breathlessly and excitedly. "We got lots of saints here in Percy. They show up in coffee grounds, our stop sign, our outhouse, and even one time in my sock drawer! The whole town came to see! Folks was passin' out right and left!"

Suddenly Big Al the dwarf, who owned "Big Al's Instant Java Hut" and was a very distant cousin of Dweezle Dwindle, ran outside of his small instant coffee shop and waved everybody in. The boy said, "It's Big Al! The saint must be in his place! Come on!" Inside Big Al's place the crowd had swollen like a cheap whoopee cushion ready to pop. They were all struggling to look inside a standard eight ounce coffee cup. Big Al himself was shoved to the back where he was jumping up and down no higher than four inches trying to get a look inside the cup, but to no avail. He couldn't see higher than anyone's tushies. Fortunately for everyone, Percy's most famous couple, Camila Fernsby and Randy Relish, who were famous for being able to breathe backwards at the same time, wiggled free from the crowd, and were able to look into the cup. Randy Relish started pointing inside the cup, frantically overwhelmed with excitement. "There's his chin! And there's his nose!"

Miss Fernsby looked at what Randy was pointing at and said, "That ain't his nose! That's his weenie!"

Randy exclaimed, "Saints don't have weenies!"

Big Al, from the back and unseen, yelled, "I THINK THAT'S SAINT LEWIS, THE PATRON SAINT OF DIFFERENT PLACES!"

Randy Relish asked, "Where in Hell, Michigan, are you Al?"

Suddenly Big Al came hurling toward the front, because he was hurled. He slammed into the coffee cup and it crashed to the floor where it shattered, sending the saintly coffee grounds everywhere. Several people in the crowd started screaming and weeping and cursing Big Al for killing Saint Lewis.

The town carpenter, Hansel Hill, who kept his in-laws in a beautiful wooden cage that he made by hand from stolen Ponderosa pine pointed out, "And that's why dwarf-tossin' was outlawed, because bad things happen, like saints in coffee cups are murdered. If Big Al didn't have the best instant coffee in Percy, I would never come back."

As the population of Percy spilled out of Big Al's Java Hut, an old woman went up to Nero and Izzy who were waiting just outside and said, "It's too bad you folks weren't here when dwarf-tossin' was legal. When they outlawed it, this town turned to shit."

As Nero and Izzy were walking away, Big Al limped over with two cups of his homemade instant coffee for them. He said, "Here's some Joe for the road. You seem like nice people."

Izzy said, "I am. Thanks."

Al said, "If you find any saints in your coffee you can keep 'em."

Nero said, "I will. Thanks."

Izzy noticed a strange-looking yellow toad hopping by in front of them and pointed it out. "You don't see that every day."

As Big Al turned to look, both Izzy and Nero took a sip of his homemade instant coffee and immediately spit it out. Big Al said, "Oh, that there's Mr. Nowicki. He's-"

"Not from around here, Mr. Nowicki is a foreigner," blurted out Ivan Kash, resident Percy historian, who knew quite a lot about very little and thought very highly of himself. Kash continued. "He's from Central

Europe. Don't speak English, that one. Technically he's what you call a yellow-bellied toad. The Latinos call him 'Bombina Variegata'. His kind likes to be around water, so what he's doin' here, I don't know. I've asked him 328 times but he can't tell me 'cause he don't speak English. He's been here a while."

Mr. Nowicki started making loud popping sounds. Mr Kash commented. "Their call is really more of a musical 'POOP POOP POOP', but this fella pops instead of poops. I mean, he poops, but that's a different kinda poop. I think he's sick, poor yellow hoppin' poppin' bastard. He's probably lonely too. Their matin' season's from April to August, and there ain't no one around here's gonna do the nasty with Mr. Nowicki...except maybe Old Man Perkin's daughter Molly. She's everybody's parking space if you know what I mean."

The two boys dressed like Pippi Longstocking held hands and skipped behind Mr. Nowicki while over a crackling public address system came the announcement: "LADIES AND GENTLEMEN! BOYS AND GIRLS! IT'S SHOWTIME!" The residents of Percy, also known as "the Percy People," all excitedly ran in the same direction that Mr. Nowicki was hopping as best he could, since he was sick.

Nero asked, "What's this, a stupidity stampede?"

Big Al said, "They're all going to see *the Barry Slinger Show*. It's the only show we got, other than the stand-up comedy show at the Percy Comedy Club, and it's great. Mr. Nowicki goes to every one."

Izzy asked, "And how do we get there?"

Big Al said, "Follow the yellow sick toad."

In the center of town was a large raised platform which was used as a stage of sorts. At the front of the platform was the ravaged shell of a 1961 Magnavox television set. Through the empty TV shell where the picture screen should be, the platform behind the TV was set up like a talk show. Seated on stage were the guests of the day: Brunella Gubb, her husband Calvin, and Percy's resident romantic, Edmond Stout. Throughout the show the townspeople (the Percy People) were transfixed on the shell of the television. Not once did any of them look up or acknowledge that the action was actually happening on the platform right in front of them. The show's host, Barry Slinger, took the stage to wild applause and cheers. He was handed a microphone. An audience response prompter held up cards which instructed the audience how to react. Barry Slinger spoke into the microphone, "Thank you for that warm welcome! I love being in Percy!"

The prompter held up a card that said, "CHEER" and they did. Slinger mopped his brow and said, "It's so hot here!"

Again the prompter held up the "CHEER" card and they did. Slinger pointed out the yellow sick toad in the audience and announced, "MR. NOWICKI IS IN THE HOUSE!" and the crowd went wild. Mr. Nowicki popped with pride. Slinger said, "I had frog legs for lunch today, Mr. Nowicki."

The crowd booed. Slinger said, "What? I kid Mr. Nowicki. I had chicken, but it *tasted* like frog legs!"

The prompter held up the "LAUGH" card. The audience laughed. He put the card down and they stopped abruptly. Mr. Nowicki didn't find it funny. Slinger said, "Today we have secret confessions that our guests have come here to reveal to their friends, families, and lovers."

The prompter held up the "OOH AND AAH" card, and the audience oohed and aahed. Slinger paced the platform. He said, "Let's meet our guests. First is Brunella Gubb. You all know her. Some of you have known her more than once, if you know what I mean. Right, Mr. Nowicki? Brunella is an unemployed oyster shucker. Brunella, are there many oysters here in the Mohave Desert?"

The prompter raised the "LAUGH" card. The audience laughed. She didn't. He put the card down and they stopped abruptly. Slinger continued. "When Brunella was a kid she used to put her nasty chewed up, wadded up, chewing gum on our Percy stop sign. It's been 22 years and we still can't get it off! Many years ago, as you know, a midget sanitation worker on vacation flew out of a dune buggy, hit the stop sign, got stuck on the gum, and died of thirst. If that midget hadn't died, he'd be alive today."

The crowd went wild cursing, hissing, booing, and tossing things at Brunella who leapt to her feet and yelled at the audience, "Y'ALL JUST JEALOUS! NO ONE SHUCKS LIKE ME!"

Slinger said, "I do hear you're a great shucker. Right, Mr. Nowicki?"

The audience went wild with no prompt cards needed. Brunella whipped them into a frenzy yelling at them: "Y'ALL CAN'T SHUCK AND YOU UGLY TOO! CAN'T SHUCK N' UGLY! CAN'T SHUCK N' UGLY!"

Slinger said, "Brunella, you and your husband Calvin here have been married for 22 years. I believe you got married right after the gum incident that killed the midget who had a very short life."

Brunella dried crocodile tears and said, "That's right, Barry. My darling Calvin was the only one who stood by me in my darkest hour of despair and heartache."

Slinger said sort of curtly, "So you married him. Couldn't you have just thanked him?"

Brunella replied sort of defensively, "I guess I could have just thanked him, but that didn't occur to me. I can't have every thought in my head, Barry. There are hundreds of thoughts in the world and my head ain't as big as the world."

Slinger shot back: "That's just *one* thought, Brunella. For 22 years you've been keeping a deep dark secret from your husband. The moment is here. Tell him what that secret is."

Brunella looked at Calvin, blotted some more bullshit tears, and confessed, "Calvin...I cannot keep this a secret any longer...Calvin, my love, I am...*a man*. My real name is Enoch Berrycloth and I'm not an oyster shucker. I'm a dice quality control inspector. I make sure dice meet strict specifications. It's hard work because you have to check on the dice through the entire manufacturing process."

The prompter held up the "OOH AND AAH" card and the audience oohed and aahed again. Slinger said, "Shocking! Calvin, your reaction?"

"That ain't nuthin'," Calvin said. "I am a *woman*! And I love havin' sex with myself 'cause I like women!"

The prompter started flipping through his cards for the best audience response, but he got frustrated and threw them down. The audience laughed. Edmond Stout, the third guest, leapt to his feet and announced, "So what?! I did it with a pig! Best lovin' I ever had!"

Brunella continued working the crowd into a frenzy confessing, "I did it with a *married* pig!"

Slinger asked, "What was this married pig's name?"

Both Brunella and Edmond answered at the same time: "Roger!" They stared at each other in total horror and then lunged, rolling around on the platform stage clawing at each other.

Slinger said, "Let's bring the pig out. Here's Roger."

A pig wearing only a purple Speedo and a matching bow tie came out on stage and the audience booed him and threw paper airplanes at him. The audience started chanting, "PIG WHORE! PIG WHORE! PIG

WHORE!" During the chanting Slinger noticed Izzy and Nero looking directly at him and not through the TV shell like everyone else was doing. He flashed them a dirty look. Edmond scrambled away from the brawl, got down on one knee before Roger, and presented Roger the two-timing pig whore with an engagement ring. The audience immediately stopped chanting because they wanted to experience this tender moment. Edmond was emotional before his beloved and said, "Roger, my beloved love, I love you. We have our differences-"

Under his breath but still purposely audible, Slinger said, "Not many."

Edmond continued, "We can work things out. Will you be my bride?"

Slinger interrupted the tender moment. He said, "You understand, Edmond, Roger can't be your bride because he's a guy. And he can't answer you because he's a pig."

Edmond said, "Love is blind, Barry. Love is blind."

Slinger nodded, "Well said, Edmond. Well said." He then moved over to the TV set and poked his head through the hole where the screen should be and addressed the audience directly: "I want to thank all my guests and I wish them all the best. Love isn't a toy or a game. Keeping secrets is bad for any relationship. So be who you are, not the opposite sex. And if you're a dice quality control inspector, don't pretend to be an oyster shucker in the desert where there are no oysters. And whatever you do, don't be a two-timing pig whore. Until next time…"

The audience applauded wildly and Mr. Nowicki popped. Nero and Izzy continued on and came to the stand-up comedy show at the Percy Comedy Club that Big Al had mentioned. The Evil One's true goal in life, other than the total annihilation of the entire universe, was to perform at the Percy Comedy Club. Nero and Izzy looked at each other, shrugged, and went inside along with many of the Percy People who attended the Slinger show. On stage was the only stand-up comedian in Percy. He was nothing more than a giant mouth with one arm, one eye, one leg, and a bowler hat. He stepped into the spotlight and up to the microphone. He tapped on it to see if it was working. It was. He pointed out a woman in the front row and said, "You could be very attractive if you were someone else."

Nobody laughed.

"Let me ask you a question because I'm intrigued by ignorance," he said. "Anyone know the difference between 'lay' and 'lie'? I didn't get laid last night and that's not a lie."

He laughed. No one else did. Then he told the story of a guy named Sadler who didn't bother to knock on the door of his boss's office and just barged on in.

"You wanted to see me?" Sadler asked.

"No, but I want to talk to you," said his boss. "Don't bother sitting down, I'll be brief."

Sadler sat down.

"I told you not to bother sitting down!" the boss snapped.

"It's no bother," Sadler said.

"I'll get right to it, Sadler. You have a bad attitude and you contribute nothing to the progress of this company. Therefore, I'm terminating your employment here effective immediately."

"What am I a dictionary?" Sadler asked. "What does 'terminating your employment effective immediately', mean? Am I getting a raise?"

"If you were a dictionary you'd be useful," replied the boss, "but you're not, so you're fired."

"Could you stop beating around the bush?" Sadler said. "I have things to pretend to do. What are you trying to say?"

The boss turned as red as a sunburned tomato painted candy apple red and said, "You're fired! Goodbye! Scram! Get out!"

Sadler fired back, "Oh really? Maybe *you're* the one who's fired!"

"This is *my* company, Mr. Sadler. I'm the boss!" snapped the boss.

"You *were* the boss," Sadler said to the boss. "Now *I'm* the boss."

"*Get out of here Mr. Sadler,*" sneered the real boss to Sadler who thought he was the boss. Sadler, who thought he was the boss, looked at the real boss and said, "I'm afraid I'm going to have to let you go. Clean out your desk and leave, or I'll have security throw you out."

The boss, the real boss who wasn't Sadler, picked up his phone and demanded, "*Get security in here now!*"

But before security could get there, a meteor from outer space with a lovely note attached that said "Bye Bye" and was signed "Warmly, The Evil One" smashed into the office and everyone died, except Sadler.

There was no response from the audience. Five people got up and walked out. The comic called after them, "You losers walking out didn't invent stupidity, you're just taking it to a higher level!" The last guy walking out shot the comic a bird. The comic yelled, "You remind me of my daughter. She said, 'Dad, can we make a deal?' and I said, 'I don't negotiate with terrorists'. My wife said, 'Sometimes I think I'm crazy.' I said, 'It's not you, it's them. And by 'them' I mean you.'"

The comic tapped on the microphone again to see if it was working. It was. The comic pressed on. "One time when me and my 28 brothers and sisters were in our pool, my father put down his booze, came out and said, 'It's starting to rain. Get out of the pool before you get wet.'"

One person chuckled. The comic nodded to him and said, "Thank you. You're a great audience, but only you. So I said to my father-in-law, 'Tell me the truth. At night when your wife is sleeping, do you ever stand over her with a meat cleaver?' Speaking of meat cleavers, a scumbag...no, not you sir...you'll have your fifteen minutes but this isn't it...a scumbag is sitting in a restaurant and has his foot up on the table. The waitress tells him to remove his foot. He tells her to screw off. She goes in the back and tells the chef. The chef comes out with a meat cleaver, slams it down, and chops off the scumbag's foot. The scumbag screams in agony. Blood shoots everywhere. The foot is still on the table. Speaking of restaurants, you know how when you see someone out of context in a place you're not used to seeing them, that you might not recognize them, or you know the face but you can't place it? Well, one night I was in a restroom of a restaurant I had never been in before, and I saw my reflection in the mirror and I had no idea who I was."

There were a few scattered chuckles. "And then one time I saved an elephant from being eaten by a raccoon, and someone called me a hero. I said, 'I'm no hero. I'm just someone who did something extraordinary that other people would not have done.'" The comic lifted his bowler hat off his head and tossed it up in the air. He missed it coming down and it dropped on the stage floor. He picked it up with his one arm and flipped it back on his head which was really just a giant mouth with an eye on top of it. He looked at the audience with that one eye and said, "Anyone here believe in Creation and the Garden of Eden and that you didn't crawl out of a swamp or evolve from monkeys?"

Several people woke up and clapped. The comic said, "Adam and Eve had two sons." There was a long extremely uncomfortable silence. The people that clapped for Creation got up and left. The comic said, "Those people that walked out are really stupid. They're so stupid that they don't know that they're stupid. That's how stupid they are. The things they don't know could fill warehouses. I'm trying to expand your horizon. The comic stared down at his one beat up shoe trying to remember his next bit. After four minutes of silence he said, "A woman says to a writer, 'Have I read anything that you've written?' The writer says, 'How the hell do I know what you've read?' A guy goes to the funeral of another guy who owed him money. The widow says, 'Thank you for coming.' The guy says, 'My pleasure. I've been looking forward to this for a long time.' A young man proposes to a young lady. He says, 'Honey, marry me. I've searched everywhere for someone as pure, innocent, and virginal as you.' She says, '*Virginal?!* I've slept with hundreds of guys, lots of farm animals, and everyone in Hooker, Oklahoma. I made 357 adult films and won the Golden Dildo Lifetime Achievement Award for my performances!' He says, 'That's okay. You just slept with them, it's not like you had sex with them. Congratulations on the award. I won a ribbon for winning a three-legged race by myself when I was in seventh grade.' So they get married. A few years later the same young man is sitting on a park bench talking to an old man. He says, 'I'm so good in bed my wife screams.' The old man says, 'My wife screams too, but that's a different thing.' I took a road trip with my mother. She said, 'Isn't this better than being alone?' I said, 'When I'm alone I don't criticize myself for seven hours straight.'"

That was enough of that. Nero and Izzy walked out of the Percy Comedy Club and came to a large enclosed dilapidated dirty white canvas flat-topped tent one might find at a bad carnival, with a sign that said "THE WORLD FAMOUS PERCY ZOO." Izzy wondered aloud, "I wonder what's in there."

"I don't know," Nero said. "Freshly ground saints...transsexual pig lovers...let's go see."

They cautiously entered the Percy zoo. There was a long metal gray snap-leg table upon which was a flimsy cage, a fish tank, and some other cages and containers. The air inside the dirty white tent was very dusty which was evident in the occasional ray of light jutting through open seams in the canvas, but the overall atmosphere was somewhat dark and shadowy. The floor was desert sand strewn with straw and debris. The only sound was the occasional squeak of a turning wheel. There was a bucket on the table with a handwritten sign that said "admission $5.00". Nero looked into a cage and saw a hamster running on a wheel, which was the source of the squeak. A sign on the cage said "Domesticus Mus." Nero said, "Man, this place stinks! What the hell's a domesticus mus?" Izzy said, "I think they're trying to be fancy. It's Latin for house rat." They both looked into a fish tank. There was no water, just desert sand, a miniature seesaw, and a small tightrope setup with a miniature rusted red bicycle on the tightrope. As Nero and Izzy looked on, the seesaw began to move up and down and the bicycle began to pedal back and forth on the tightrope. Izzy read a sign on the tank. "'Canis Pulex. Real live French Poodle fleas'. Wow. You can't beat that." Nero corrected her, "Yes, you can." He was staring at something that had him amazed. Izzy looked with him. She, too, was a bit stunned as she read the sign for what they were looking at, "'Putridus Monstrum'...Disgusting Monster...Holy crap! That's *The Creature from Gruesome Gulch!*"

They were looking at a monster costume. Nero, still staring at the costume, said, "I thought you didn't go to the movies."

"Not anymore. I used to go when they were good. *Gruesome Gulch* wasn't good. It stunk worse than this place. But the monster was...I don't know. I felt sorry for him. He didn't bother nobody. The humans showed up and harassed him. He wiped out the town, but he was defending himself. I was probably the only one in the audience that was on his side." Izzy looked at a sign at the foot of the costume that said "Do Not Feed." "They don't want you to feed the costume."

Nero patted the belly of the costume and then his own belly. "You're right. He was just defending himself. The humans were the real monsters."

"You don't seem like the type that would see *The Creature from Gruesome Gulch*. You really saw that movie?"

Nero smiled sort of sadly. "I *was* that movie."

Izzy was floored. "You're yankin' me. You were the monster?! Okay, now I'm impressed."

"It was my very first part. We shot it in three days. It was non-union. We didn't have permits. We were running from the cops every ten minutes."

Izzy looked at Nero looking at the costume and thinking loudly. "I see this comin' down the block. You wanna wear this to scare off that film crew. If that director saw the movie he'll know it's you."

"Nigel Daw would never see a movie like that. His nose is too far up his ass."

Izzy glared at Nero, "So only low-class scum like me would see a movie like that."

Nero shot back: "I didn't say that! *You* said that! You really love trouble, don't you?"

"Keep telling yourself that if it'll help you sleep better," Izzy fumed. She spun around to leave and smacked her head into a sign hanging above an enclosed pen. She staggered back, grabbed her forehead, winced, and read the sign. "Warning: Pig Boy – Do Not Feed or Touch!" She looked down into the dark pen, let out a scream, and bolted out of the zoo tent almost knocking Nero down. From the dark pen came horrible sounds which included snorts, squeals, and the words "come play," "blue ball", "hungry me" and more snorts and squeals. Nero carefully looked into the pen. Within two seconds he was more than ready to heave in Technicolor. A strange man appeared. He seemed very out of place in Percy, which had more of a dumb redneckish tilt. This guy looked like someone you might see slithering around in an old Hammer horror film. He smiled at the look of sheer queasiness on Nero's face. He said, "I see you've met our beloved Pig Boy. He is the result of a 9 minute passionate union between our blue-ribbon sow, Frieda, and 12 of our fun-loving native sons. We affectionately refer to them as 'The Dirty Dozen'." He let go an extremely long and bizarre laugh. It was weird. It should have won an award for long bizarre laughs. He continued, "It was an excellent film, *The Dirty Dozen*, not the film of the boys having their way with Frieda, that we have showing at The House of the Choking Chicken as a double bill with the film of Lester's Aunt Eugenia with her dog Romeo; nasty stuff, by the way. That one's called *The Really Dirty Dozen*. I'm referring to *The Dirty Dozen* starring Lee Marvin, Charles Bronson, and Ernest Borgnine...great cast. Robert Aldrich directed, 1967, MGM. It ran two and a half hours. It was long, but good, as some things are." He let go that long bizarre laugh again. It was creepy, but much better than The Evil One's long stupid slimy donkey laugh. "I am Reginald Radcliff, the Percy Zoo Curator. I admired you admiring our original creature costume from the epic motion picture *The Creature from Gruesome Gulch*. That was *not* a good film. I don't know how long it was, but if it ran 90 minutes, that was 90 minutes too long. That film sucked like a starving vampiric whore vacuuming in a black hole in space." Again, he let go his long weird creepy bizarre laugh. The curator, who looked and sounded more like a crypt keeper than a zookeeper, then reached into a rusted bucket, scooped some brown chunky slop out of it, and flung it into Pig Boy's pen. There was intense snorting, squealing, and slobbering, followed by a very loud belch and an orgasmic "OH YEAH!" Nero looked and felt sicker than ever. The curator looked down at Pig Boy sympathetically and explained, "He was a twin. His brother Marvin committed suicide by throwing himself on the grill at our annual Masonic barbeque. He was immediately consumed by hungry Shriners. It was horrible!" Nero, who was just about green, gasped, "Listen...I want to buy that monster costume from you."

"Yes, I overheard you talking to your associate. You can have the costume, with my apologies for saying that *The Creature from Gruesome Gulch* bit the big cinematic weenie. But it really was a waste of money, time, and celluloid. You must know that."

Nero nodded, "Yeah...I know."

The curator said, "I know you're quite ill at the moment, but since I'm giving you the costume, do the growl for me. That's the only part of the movie I liked." Nero did an extremely half-assed sickly monster growl. The curator jumped up and down, clapping his hands with joy. "Fabulous! You scared the willies out of me! I was horrified! Now, you don't have to worry about me telling anyone about your devious little plan to drive away that awful Nigel Daw and his film crew. I'll be having dessert with Mr. Reaper later this evening because I've had too much Percy, and enough is enough." He put on his black overcoat and bowler hat and stuffed a few things in a briefcase. He then looked at Nero's mid-section and said, "It's been some time since *Gruesome Gulch* came out, and not to be rude, but you may have put on a few pounds since then. If the costume needs alterations go see Madam Mancowitz. She's an odd duck, but a damned good seamstress. Ta-ta." The curator took his leave. Nero looked at the costume, plotting how to scare off Daw. Pig Boy was making his disgusting Pig Boy noises, and four hours and two minutes away in Los Angeles, Angelo and Toto were getting ready to bust into the office of a very unlucky dentist, without an appointment.

Chapter 5

Inside the dental office of Dr. Richard Munson, the good doctor was just finishing up with a patient. He said, "You're all done, Bucko. Scrub those gums and I'll see you in six months for a checkup."

"My mouth really hurts, Doc. I think something's wrong. I'm in a lot of pain," the patient said painfully.

"If you can feel pain that means that you're alive because your nerves are sending messages to your brain that tells it to tell you to feel pain. Just don't listen to your brain and you'll be fine. Have a nice day." Just as the patient left, Lana Holliday slinked in. She was strikingly gorgeous and knew it. "I know I don't have an appointment, Doctor, but I need to see you desperately," she said sultry-...sultrai-...really sultrily.

"Do you do binding?"

"You mean *bonding*. Do you need to be worked on? I fill cavities too," stated Dr. Munson like all that time in dental school had just paid off.

"I'll bet you do," Lana winked. "How 'bout you bond me with lots of floss so I can't put up a fight. And you can fill my cavities while you're at it."

Dr. Munson corrected her, "You mean *bind* you with lots of floss. *Bond* is past tense for 'bind' and the name of a fictional British secret agent created by Ian Fleming in 1953 who was himself an intelligence agent during World War Two. He also wrote *Chitty-Chitty-Bang-Bang* which most people don't know or care about. Sean Connery was the best Bond. I know that because I minored in English." Dr. Munson started rummaging wildly through a drawer full of dental floss as Lana sat back seductively in the dental chair. Dr. Munson called out frantically, "Extra fine, regular, or wide-strip?!"

"I want wide-strip and waxed because un-waxed shreds. I hate that! I really like alpine mint if you got it. Please hurry!" Lana said breathlessly. Munson rushed to her with lots of floss. "Put the lights out. I like surprises," Lana said seductively like the slut that she was. Munson turned off the lights and the room went completely dark. There was passionate moaning and then Dr. Munson, sounding a bit startled said, "What are doing, Lana?!"

Lana sizzled, "I feel like taking charge."

Munson purred, "I like it!"

One door opened, another closed, and there was silence.

Munson was in the dark in several ways. "Lana? Lana? Where are you?!"

Suddenly the lights went on. The dentist was tied to his dental chair with miles of dental floss. And Angelo and Toto were standing there. Angelo said, "Lana had to leave. She said to tell you goodbye."

Toto said, "But before we tell you goodbye we want the dental X-rays of The Chinaman."

A shaken Munson said, "I don't recall ever having a patient by that name."

Angelo said, "Well, maybe we can jog your memory." He picked up the dental drill and revved it. "I always wanted to do this to a dentist." Toto held Munson's nose closed, Munson opened his mouth, and in went the drill. Munson screamed like a man whose nerves were sending lots of urgent messages to his brain. He was a man having a very very bad day.

The name of the detective agency on the pebbled glass of the outer office door was "DANGER and Moore – Private Detective Agency." Behind that door, Secretary Irma Finkelstein was sitting at her desk, snapping gum between her teeth, filing her nails, and babbling on the phone. "Listen to me, darling. I had a third cousin who used guacamole salsa mixed with melted caramel once to enhance her moment of ultimate pleasure. She was in a coma for two weeks. Plus, you would never get it out. It'd be like peppermint chewing gum that some high school dropout spit on a sidewalk stuck to your shoe."

Private Detective Sheldon Danger entered the office. He appeared to be the stereotypical straight out of a 1940s film noir flicker detective. He wore a trench coat which he never removed, a fedora, shades, the whole bit. But there was one thing that separated Sheldon Danger from all the others. He had an ego larger than the universe that The Evil One was bent on annihilating. He considered himself to be the greatest private detective in history, real or fictional, and he wasn't shy about saying so. He was a self-idolizing egomaniac beyond comprehension, and yet he did have a certain charismatic charm that was hard to pin down. Irma said into the phone, "I gotta go. Mr. Wonderful just swaggered in." She hung up and addressed Danger. "The President of the United States called. He wants to honor you at the White House as "Detective of the Year." After the award ceremony there will be a lovely reception in your honor in the White House Rose Garden which was established in 1913 by Woodrow Wilson's wife. Also, as an added surprise and you're not supposed to know this, they're changing the name of Pennsylvania Avenue to Danger Avenue."

"Really?!" Sheldon asked excitedly.

"No. Not really," Irma answered unexcitedly. She handed him his mail. "Here's your *Detective Magazine*, lots of overdue bills, and the usual death threats. Most of them are from me."

Sheldon read the cover story aloud as he looked at the magazine. "I was a Sex Slave for Seven Dwarfs."

"If I had any money I'd bet it all. There's some skank in your office. She won't tell me her name. Says she'll only talk to you. Why anyone would want to talk to you is beyond me."

"Looks are beyond you too. Is Max in yet?"

"Mr. Moore phoned. He'll be a little late because a meteorite hit his dog this morning and he took her to the vet."

"He overslept. He doesn't have a dog," Sheldon said as he entered his private office where inside Lana Holliday was perched seductively on his desk. "Are you Private Detective Sheldon Danger?" she asked, trying to sound like a cross between Marilyn Monroe and Betty Boop.

"No, I just hang out here 'cause I like his name," Sheldon zinged.

"I'm Lana Holliday," she said.

"And I'm working. Get to the point," Sheldon responded with lightning comedic speed which he had learned from watching the comic handling hecklers at the Percy Comedy Club. Lana got emotional. She said emotionally, "Friday night my fiancé Dr. Richard Munson was murdered because he refused to turn over dental X-rays of a criminal called The Chinaman to some thugs who drilled him to death."

"I heard about that murder. How do you know about the X-rays?"

Stalling, Lana picked up a framed photo of Bogart as Sam Spade from

Sheldon's desk. "Did you know him?" she asked in her annoying Marilyn Monroe/Betty Boopish voice.

"I was his idol. You didn't answer my question, cupcake."

Lana fumbled with her answer. "I was there, hiding in the closet next to some rubber dental dams and cheap fake designer discount clothes," she shuddered in disgust. "It all happened so fast, but in a very slow way. It was like a terrible nightmare!"

Sheldon mulled. "This was no amateur hour. Call it woman's intuition, but it sounds to me like it was a professional hit. The Chinaman broke jail last week. It was all over the news."

"He needed emergency work done on his teeth and he came to Richard because Richard never turned anyone away, even escaped criminals. Richard was very kind and sweet and giving and generous. He was a good man, Sheldon."

"Call me Mr. Danger. When I see some green we'll skip the formalities," Sheldon...I mean, Mr. Danger, said.

Maximus Moore entered. Max was a roly-poly butterball at Sheldon Danger's command. He would do anything for Danger, whom he worshipped, and yet it was clearly obvious that Max was humoring Danger in his role as the sidekick, as he was by far the brains of the two. Max wore a black trench coat, greased-back hair, a goatee, and shades on occasion. I mention that in case this ever becomes a feature film and they need physical traits. Sheldon sneered when he saw Max. "Where have you been, you walking planet?"

"Please Boss, no fat jokes. I'm sensitive about it."

"Alright Mr. Hindenburg, this is Lana Holliday. She was hooked up with that dead dentist who died Friday night when he died. She says he was whacked because he refused to turn over the dental X-rays of The Chinaman. Brief me."

Max responded like a lightning-fast rapid-fire encyclopedia without taking a breath or having any regard for punctuation "The Chinaman alias Ching Dang Nip was incarcerated in 1973 for allegedly single-handedly purloining the priceless Peking Duck statuette from the Ming Dynasty exhibition which traveled throughout the United States in that very year which was the same year that Nathaniel Wyeth received a patent for shatter-proof bottles and it was quite obvious that The Chinaman alias Ching Dang Nip could not have possibly worked alone as the intricate network security system protecting the Peking Duck was much too complex for one individual to have penetrated so the priceless statuette was never recovered and neither were The Chinaman's accomplices in this immoral transgression."

There were several beats of drawn heavy silence as Sheldon glared at Max with a look of total annoyance on his face. He was thoroughly confused by Max's explanation and made that very clear...in his own way of course.

"Miss Holliday looks a little confused, Funk n' Wagnalls. Try again, using smaller words, and ease up on the gas."

Max said, "He stole the duck. He went to jail. End of story."

"That's better."

Lana said, "I understood him before."

"Sure you did," Sheldon winked, "and Max has sex, why would someone want dental X-rays, Max?"

"Sometimes they're the only way of identifying a body," Max explained, "Especially if it's been burned beyond recognition, or something like that."

Sheldon removed his ever-present *Creature from Gruesome Gulch* PEZ dispenser from the pocket of his trench coat. He took a PEZ for himself, and then offered one to Lana who refused it claiming that she was trying to cut down. Max reached for one and Sheldon quickly shoved the dispenser back in his pocket. He looked at Lana's legs and said, "So what do you want from us, Miss Holliday?"

"Find the creeps who murdered Richard. We were supposed to get married, but now that he's dead that probably won't happen."

"Congratulations!" Sheldon said.

"Mazel tov!" Max added. "I know a good caterer."

Sheldon said, "Maybe it's a good thing he croaked. He'd probably be a dud in the sack and you'd be passing yourself around like cheap booze in the Bowery."

Lana went to slap Sheldon. He ducked and she knocked over a lamp. He said, "You're paying for that. That lamp was from the Ming Dynasty, just like the Peking Duck. You owe me a bundle."

Lana shifted gears and sensuously caressed Sheldon's face. "Are you involved with anyone, Mr. Danger?"

Irma laughed from the outer office. Sheldon sneered in her direction and said, "Not at the moment, Miss Holliday. I was in a relationship, but she squeaked when we were in the sack and I didn't like it, so I dumped her."

"Squeaked"? Lana asked.

"Yeah, squeaked," Sheldon said, "like a doggie toy. It drove me nuts, so I got rid of her."

"Maybe the mattress squeaked, Boss," Max suggested. "Sometimes loose screws or bad springs could cause that."

Sheldon glared at Max with the longest glare that ever happened in the history of glares and said, "*You* have a screw loose, Max. Do you have a theory pertaining to the case of the dead dentist who died and the missing priceless Peking Duck statuette, instead of wasting my time with your ridiculous squeak excuses?"

Max said, "I have a theory, Boss. Suppose when The Chinaman broke jail he stole the Peking Duck from his partners. They caught up to him and knocked him off. Then they went back to every place he'd been and got rid of every piece of evidence that could prove he was ever there. That way he could never be found. Then they stole his dental X-rays so no one could ID the body if it was in bad shape."

"Or maybe he's still alive," Sheldon added. "Maybe his partners didn't get to him yet. But if they stole his X-rays, you can bet they'll smoke him soon."

"Or maybe not," Lana interjected, "Maybe he has the Peking Duck in his possession and left the country hoping to start a new life. Maybe he'll settle down, start a family, and become a responsible citizen."

"Shut the hell up!" Sheldon snapped. "I'm the detective, not you! You're just an ad for ceftriaxone and doxycycline."

Max interrupted. "Getting back to your theory, Boss, if you're right, we should try to get to The Chinaman before his partners do."

Sheldon turned to Lana. "You said The Chinaman needed emergency work done. Why?"

Max answered, "Maybe he had cavities that were really hurting."

Sheldon glared at Max. "I wasn't talking to you."

"Mr. Moore is right. He had bad cavities. I know that because Richard always told me about his day. Sharing was the foundation of our love."

"That guy sounds so boring," Sheldon said. "Maybe he was always dead and you just didn't know it."

Lana started for the door. "You're not the only private detective in the world, Mr. Danger!"

Sheldon grabbed her by the arm, stopping her. "But I *am* the greatest. Didn't mean to get you all hot and bothered, sugar. I just need to know who I'm dealing with. We're talking about murder, and that can be serious. Fill me in on cavities, Max."

Again Max reeled off a lightning-fast explanation that annoyed Sheldon from start to finish. "Too many sweets can cause decay which implies gradual deterioration from a normal or sound condition resulting in a hole or hollow place within the tooth. Certain types of bacteria found in almost everyone's saliva use sucrose which is glucose and fructose to make themselves a protective coating. This coating, that I just mentioned not long ago, helps them cling to our teeth like wet socks cling to feet as sticky stuff called dental plaque. These organisms known throughout the dental world as streptococci multiply very quickly and produce large amounts of acids and enzymes and poisons which drip on or between our teeth which damage the enamel and irritate the gums-"

Max stopped dead and panicked when he noticed Sheldon glaring at him and loading his gun.

Sheldon asked, "Max, do the acids and enzymes and poisons irritate the gums as much as you irritate me?"

"You asked me!" Max said nervously.

Sheldon frowned. "Remind me never to ask you anything again. What's sweet that can cause cavities, Max?"

"PEZ?"

"Be more specific," Sheldon said.

Max thought for a moment and said, "Candy?"

"Bingo!" Sheldon nodded, gloating and basking in some unknown glory. Lana was stunned. She said, "Wow! You two are just like Sherlock Holmes and Dr. Watson! You're amazing!" She handed Sheldon an 8 x 10 glossy headshot of The Chinaman. Sheldon said, "Sherlock Holmes was a jerk, especially when he played Basil Rathbone in the movies. But at least he looked better than this guy. Pack a piece, Max. We're going duck hunting."

Inside the Confection Connection Candy Store on Santa Monica's 3rd Street, meek bespectacled proprietor "Uncle Buddy" was serving a group of children who awaited their turn in line at the candy counter. Uncle Buddy yelled his jovial catchphrase:

"HERE IT COMES LIKE A BOOMERANG,
WHO'S YOUR FAVORITE UNCLE, GANG?!"

All the kids yelled back, "UNCLE BUDDY!"

Uncle Buddy grinned from ear to ear. "And you're my best pals! Now who's my next little sweetheart?"

Suddenly the kids went flying through the air right and left being tossed aside to clear a path as Sheldon Danger and Maximus Moore carrying a boom box on his shoulder stormed to the front of the line. Sheldon said, "That would be me, Milk Dud. Sheldon Danger, Private Detective."

Max pressed "play" on the boom box and Henry Mancini's "Theme from Peter Gunn" filled the air. Sheldon snapped his fingers and the music stopped abruptly. All the kids were staring up at Maximus Moore in his black trench coat and shades. Max never acknowledged them at all. Besides, he was too busy munching on candy and filling the pockets of his trench coat to really notice. Sheldon showed the photo of The Chinaman to Uncle Buddy. "Ever see this geek before, Pops? Not the sow behind me, the one in the picture. Give me the straight goods."

Uncle Buddy very nervously said, "He's been in here a few times. Why?"

Sheldon leaned on him, "Recently?"

Uncle Buddy swallowed hard, "A few days ago. Why?"

Sheldon sneered. "I'll ask the questions, not you. Did you take the Philo Vance Private Detective Correspondence Course and graduate with honors for only another twenty-five bucks?"

"No," Uncle Buddy shamefully publicly admitted.

"So shut up!" Sheldon snapped. "Was The Chinaman alone?"

"He usually has a pretty girl with him," Uncle Buddy revealed.

Max paused the sucking of a Jolly Rancher and asked, "Was she inflatable?"

Sheldon spun around and glared at Max. "Your doll's not two-timing you, Max. Keep sucking that rancher." He turned his attention back to Uncle Buddy. "Where does The Chinaman hang out?"

Uncle Buddy hesitated. Sheldon snapped, "Come on, Pops. I wanna get out of here before Mr. Hindenburg explodes again."

"I have no clue where he hangs out," Uncle Buddy lied.

Sheldon reached across the counter and grabbed Uncle Buddy. He yanked him in close. "What was that? I couldn't hear your answer because a plane was flying by overhead, right Max?"

Max scooped up a hand full of Candy Corn and said, "Right Boss. I believe it was a Boeing 747 kept aloft by the aerodynamic forces of air upon its wings driven forward by jet propulsion with a wingspan of 211 feet, length of 232 feet, and a top speed of 614 miles per hour. Cruising speed is 580 miles per hour."

Sheldon pulled out his gun and fired at Max, startling him. Candy Corn went flying in every direction. Uncle Buddy was rattled and changed his tune. "The Chinaman hangs out at Madame Wong's. I've seen him there a few times with that girl."

Sheldon released Uncle Buddy who he was throttling with one hand while he shot at Max with the other and said in disbelief, "Madame Wong's?! That's a rough place. *You* go in there and come out alive?"

Uncle Buddy whispered so the kids couldn't hear him, "The bartender there is my boyfriend."

Sheldon said, "No kidding? Does he put a good head on your beer?"

A little girl started sobbing. Uncle Buddy said, "Please go. You're scaring the children. I told you where he frequents. Maybe you can find him there."

Sheldon sat down next to the little girl. He said, "What's your problem, little broad? Did you find out there's no Santa Claus?" A shot rang out as a bullet just missed Sheldon's head and blew apart a Lifesavers display. He looked out the window and saw Toto pointing a gun at him in a way that said you don't deny Santa Claus. All the kids started wailing. Sheldon attempted some fast damage control. "I was kidding, kids. Hey that rhymes! Santa Claus is real. He's a big fat guy like Maximus Moore over there. He wears a red fairy suit like Uncle Buddy without the red suit, and he works at the North Pole making cheap toys from China with a bunch of little boozed-up midgets." He turned to the little girl and said, "When I was your age I used to drive all the little broads wild because I was so handsome and charming and witty and great. Do you think I'm still handsome and charming and witty and great?"

The little girl said, "No, I think you're an asshole."

A little boy said, "And I'm telling my mother on you! She's waiting for me outside!"

"I'm shaking in my shoes, kid. Am I shaking, Max?"

Max bit into a Peppermint Patty and said, "You're shaking like a bowl of lemon-lime Jell-O in a hurricane, and I feel like I'm on a snowy mountain top slow dancing with a polar bear."

Sheldon glared at Max and shook his head. "I don't know anything about polar bears, Max. But I do know that there's an elephant gun with your name on it." He turned to Uncle Buddy and said, "Give these kids some candy on the house."

All the kids cheered except for the little boy who had threatened to tell his mother about Sheldon. Sheldon addressed the kids (except for the little boy who had threatened to tell his mother about him) as someone who truly cared about their well-being. "Kids, you don't want to end up like Maximus Moore over there, so stay in school and eat your vegetables. You boys, stay away from loose women. And you girls stay off the pole." He turned to Max and said, "Let's roll, Tootsie Roll."

Max pressed "play" on his boom box and Mancini's "Peter Gunn" filled the air as they exited the candy store. Max rushed back in, grabbed a handful of malted milk balls, shoved them in the pocket of his trench coat, and rushed back out.

That night Madame Wong's was hopping like the son of a mob boss in a bunny costume. It was smoky, loud, and chaotic. There were violent card games, drunks, biker gangs, roughnecks, pimps and prostitutes. An aquarium with a mean piranha swimming in circles sat on an upside down whiskey crate with a sign that said, "Make a wish, toss in a coin, and then reach in and get it." There were lots of wasted coins and useless hands in that tank. A stripper was grinding it out on stage to lots of wolf whistles and lewd suggestions. This was the roughest bar around, a gathering hole for the dregs and scum of society who looked like they should all be in prison, and most had been many times over. The striptease music stopped. The stripper picked up her wrap and left the stage to some groping hands that she slapped away. The club DJ addressed the crowd through the PA system with as much enthusiasm as a corpse. "Give it up for the lovely Crystal." A few "people" clapped. Several only had one hand to clap with. There were a few whistles of appreciation. But mainly, no one cared. A new stripper took the stage. The DJ said, "I be doin' this a long time and I never seen anyone sexier or hotter than this next vision of loveliness–" Suddenly Mancini's "Peter Gunn" interrupted the DJ as Danger and Moore blasted into Madame Wong's. Sheldon looked like he'd been hit by a truck with bandages on his face, a black eye, and his arm in a sling. A huge thug sitting on a stool grabbed the boom box off of Max's shoulder and slammed it down, smashing it to bits. Both Sheldon and Max started to react but quickly changed their minds when the thug got off the stool and stood up to confront them. He was gigantic. They acted like nothing happened and backed away.

"That kid's mother was almost as big as that guy," Max pointed out to Sheldon who didn't need to be reminded.

"I could've taken her easily, Max, but she came at me from the front. I'm used to being jumped from behind."

Sheldon attempted to swagger up to the bar but could only manage a limp. Every stool was taken. It looked like a rogues' gallery of evil barflies. Sheldon moved in next to a hefty, sexy (if you've reached a level of desperation that can't even be measured) woman who was seated and soon flirting with him. He looked her up and down and asked, "What's a classy beef tomato like you doing in a dump like this?"

"Hooking...wanna date?" she said, like a hooker who was looking to turn a trick and a profit.

"Hit the road, sleaze," Sheldon snarled. "I'm on a hot case."

The hooker woman said, "Drop dead, creep!"

Sheldon snapped his fingers using the hand that was not in the sling and Max knocked the woman off the stool allowing Sheldon to sit down. The woman reached up from the floor and pulled Sheldon off the stool. A vicious fight ensued. The other class acts in the bar were completely oblivious to the fight. The woman and Sheldon rolled around going at it. The woman removed a high heel and slammed Sheldon in the nuts with it. Sheldon howled. She then pulled off one of her earrings, flicked a switch, and it became a dagger. Just as she was about to finish Sheldon off, Max intervened, pulling the woman off of Sheldon and onto himself. Sheldon was on the floor holding his meat cabbage with the hand that was not in the sling and grimacing in pain. The woman got Max in a headlock. Max flipped the woman who landed on her feet. They turned and faced each other. Max struck a kung fu pose. The woman lunged at him with her earring-dagger which Max kicked away. The earring-dagger flew through the air and killed a biker midget at the bar. To clarify, the biker midget was really just sort of a mascot who rode in a sidecar with the Oxnard Outcast Outlaws Motorcycle Gang and was in fact a distant cousin of Percy's Big Al and an even more distant cousin of Dweezle Dwindle, which was weird because midgets and dwarfs are two completely different things. At least dwarfs tried. Max reached into the pocket of his trench coat, pulled out some malted milk balls, and rolled them toward the woman who slipped on them and fell toward the aquarium. The mean piranha jumped up out of the water and sunk its razor-sharp teeth into the woman's groin with no intention of letting go. The woman hit the floor next to Sheldon and they were both writhing and shrieking in agony. Max reached down and pulled the woman's hair which came off in his hand. It was a wig. It was the wig of a woman who was not a woman but a man disguised as a woman. It was Toto in drag. Sheldon, in an extremely high-pitched voice asked, "How did you know she was a man, Max?"

Max explained, "The way he held the dagger, Boss. Men hold it knuckles down, women hold it knuckles up."

Max helped Sheldon back up to the bar and the bartender "Big Mama" moved over to serve them. He was a huge tattooed mountain of a man wearing a bright orange bikini top and a lemon yellow pleated skirt.

"What'll it be?" Big Mama asked.

"Some answers," Sheldon said. He snapped the fingers of his hand that was not in the sling and Max held up the photo of The Chinaman.

"Ever see this palooka before?" Sheldon asked.

Big Mama glanced at Max. "He came in with you."

"Not *that* palooka, the one in the picture. Your boyfriend says he hangs out in this nightmare."

Big Mama became emotional and pulled Sheldon aside. "You saw Buddy? How is he? We had a terrible spat last week about which way to put in a toilet paper roll. He said it should go in backwards and I said it should go in forwards because forwards you can just grab it and use it and backwards it can stick to the wall because of static electricity. Toilet paper experts call it 'The Beard or Mullet Decision.' If toilet paper rolls out from the front, it's the beard way. If it rolls out from the back, it's the mullet way. The beard way is the right way."

After a few moments of deep rumination, Sheldon said, "Thanks. I've been living my life wrong. Buddy's a little shaken up. He really misses you and wants you to be his Valentine on Valentine's Day. Does The Chinaman come here or not?"

Big Mama motioned to a new stripper on stage. "He kills time with Brandy there. She goes on break in a minute."

Danger and Moore sat down at a table at the foot of the stage. The stripper turned her full attention to Max, blowing him kisses and dancing seductively in front of him. She grabbed the pole, did a few gymnastic moves, and locked Max's head in a scissors grip. The spotlight hit Max with his head between the stripper's legs and the crowd cheered. Sheldon said, "I didn't know you were in showbiz, Max. If you don't stop eating you'll never lose weight."

The stripper looked at Sheldon. "Is there a pistol in your pocket or are you just happy to see me?"

"There's a pistol in my pocket," Sheldon said. "Come join us."

The music stopped and the stripper released Max's head. She picked up her wrap, collected tips, and stepped off stage. Sheldon said, "She wants me, Max. Did you see the way she was coming on to me?"

"I couldn't see much," Max admitted.

The stripper came to their table looking for a tip. "Did you like my dancing?"

Sheldon said, "Yeah, you're a regular ballerina. Who'd you study with, Pierre Beauchamp? And save the hurl story about how you're only here to earn money so you can go to medical school and discover the cure for some crazy rare fatal disease that your kid brother has. Just answer a few questions."

"I can't stop and chat unless you mean business. It's fifty bucks for the two of you. Pay Big Mama at the bar or get lost."

Max took out some cash and started counting it. Sheldon snatched it from him and shoved it in his pocket.

"Oh I mean business, sister."

"You cops?" she asked taking a seat.

Sheldon handed her his business card. "We're private detectives. I'm Sheldon Danger, the stuff dreams are made of, and I believe you already encountered the boy who does my laundry, Maximus Moore."

The stripper gazed at Max. "He's a cutie."

Sheldon brushed it off. "Yeah, Max sure is adorable. You don't have to play chess with *me*, honey. Just say the word and I'm yours."

"I'd rather die," the stripper said lovingly.

"Enough chitchat," Sheldon snapped. "Where's The Chinaman? And no green gumballs, I want the truth."

The stripper seemed taken aback, "The Chinaman?! How do you know The Chinaman?"

Sheldon snarled. "I'll ask the questions, not you. Did you win Honorable Mention in the Philip Marlowe Private Detective International Haiku Poetry Contest three years straight?!"

"No," the stripper sheepishly admitted.

"Then put a lid on it!" Sheldon sneered. "I understand you and The Chinaman were making time. True? And don't lie."

"So what if it is true?" she said. "He's in prison *doing* time."

"Save your song and dance for the stage," Sheldon said. "You've been seen with him plenty. Where is he?"

"I don't know. I'm telling you the truth. I never know when he'll show up. It could be in five minutes or a month or never. I was with him yesterday in the candy store. We bought some caramel because sometimes we like to mix melted caramel with guacamole salsa to enhance my moment of ultimate pleasure. I was in a coma for two weeks once because of it."

"That's a great story," Sheldon said. "I'll wait for the feature film. If you care about him at all you'd better come clean. We're trying to get to him before he's wasted. Your boy's attracting buzzards."

Max added, "We think it has something to do with the Peking Duck."

All the chaos in the bar stopped abruptly at the mention of the Peking Duck. Sheldon looked around at everyone staring at them. "You should try mouthwash, Max. That Peking Duck sure is a hot number."

The stripper said quietly, "It's worth millions, maybe more."

"Do you know where it is?" Sheldon asked like a private detective asking a question.

"No," answered the stripper, causing the chaos in the bar to immediately resume. Several people left. The stripper added, "But someone thinks I know where it is 'cause they're trying to kill me."

Sheldon dug deeper. "Why would someone want to kill you?"

"I don't know anyone who *wouldn't* want to kill her," Max remarked.

Sheldon glared at him. "Was I talking to you, Max?"

"Not directly," Max admitted shamefully.

The stripper exploded violently, knocking over the table. "I don't know why anyone would want to kill me, you stupid sleaze bucket!"

Sheldon pulled his gun on her and warned furiously, but not quite violently, "One more crack like that and I'll blow your brains out!" He holstered his weapon and tried again, "Now...nice and easy...why would someone want to kill you?"

The stripper apologized. "Sorry for the outburst. I have IED, Intermittent Explosive Disorder and I'm a Gemini."

"I'm a Capricorn," Max volunteered proudly.

"Now I have *more* reasons to sleep better at night," Sheldon noted. He turned to the stripper. "So what happened?"

The following is a flashback scene. If this were a bad movie or an old television show instead of the greatest novel ever written the screen would get fuzzy and have wavy and squiggly lines as the stripper remembered what happened. Here we go into the flashback... The stripper was in her dressing room at Madame Wong's the previous night. Her best friend, a plush panda named Orson, was propped up next to her vanity. Her first boyfriend Leopold Lipschitz (who died horribly when a bowl of pickled beets exploded and was the second cousin of bit part actor Allen Lipschitz) had won Orson for her at the Putnam County Fair at the balloon-popping booth where you throw darts at balloons to pop them and maybe win a prize. That's the great thing about county fairs and carnivals; you spend a hundred dollars to win a prize that cost two dollars. And then there's the goldfish that die before you get them to the car. But I won't get into that now. It'll push me over the edge. The stripper took that plush panda everywhere with her, except the stage. She didn't want him to know what she did for a living. He thought she was a nun. She removed her show outfit and reached into the closet for a robe. She put it on and sat down at the vanity to remove her makeup. In the vanity mirror she saw the reflection of a figure dressed in black wearing a black ski mask coming up from behind her with a taut G-string. She grabbed her powder case off the vanity and threw powder in the eyeholes of her assailant momentarily blinding the attacker which allowed her to escape.

"Whoever it was probably thinks I know too much about The Chinaman and the Peking Duck. Then later someone took a shot at me when I was getting ready to go to sleep."

As the flashback continued, the stripper got into bed, pulled her large plush panda bear Orson in close to snuggle with, and hugged him as she fell asleep. There was a gunshot and the panda bear bought it right between the eyes. The stripper screamed and the flashback ended. She handed Sheldon a piece of paper. "When I came into work today this message was waiting for me on the mirror in my dressing room."

Sheldon read the message aloud: "'you're dead!'...What do you think it means, Max?" He looked at Max who was staring at the stripper's cleavage. He waved a candy bar in front of Max who snapped out of his trance. "Glad you could join us, Max." He gave Max the candy bar and addressed the stripper again. "You need protection."

Max said, "Safe sex is better than no sex."

Sheldon glared. "I meant police protection, Max, not sex protection.

What do you know about sex anyway? You're the only guy I ever met who gets rejected by his own hand." He looked at the stripper. "Where's The Chinaman? To save you we have to get to him."

"Try Malibu Beach, he unwinds there."

Sheldon nodded. "Yeah, being a psychotic criminal can be stressful." He handed the stripper his card. "We'll try to find him. If you hear from him, call us."

The stripper headed backstage and Angelo approached Sheldon. "You spent too much time with her. I wanted some action."

"How selfish of me," Sheldon smirked. He removed his *Creature from Gruesome Gulch* PEZ dispenser from his trench coat pocket. "Please accept my humble apologies in the form of a PEZ."

Max mumbled to himself: "uh-oh."

Angelo got loud for the crowd: "PEZ! JAMES BOND OFFERED ME A PEZ SO I DON'T KICK HIS ASS! AIN'T THAT SWEET?" Angelo laughed and all the scum at Madame Wong's joined in. Max, nibbling on the candy bar Sheldon gave him, started laughing too. Sheldon took out his gun and shot the candy bar out of Max's hand. Max stopped laughing. Sheldon addressed Angelo. "What's wrong with PEZ, Estelle?"

There was sudden silence as all eyes were on the confrontation. Angelo snarled, "My name ain't Estelle, Maria. And PEZ is for little kids and big sissies like you."

"You don't know what you're talking about, Estelle. PEZ is for *real* men." Sheldon raised the head of the *Creature from Gruesome Gulch* on his PEZ dispenser. He held the dispenser open and coaxed Angelo to take one; as this was going on, Max climbed on top of the bar.

"Go ahead tough guy; take a PEZ, unless you're afraid that all this slime will laugh at you."

"No one laughs at me," Angelo snarled.

"So take one, or are you scared?" Sheldon snarled back.

Angelo reached into the PEZ dispenser to take a PEZ. Sheldon yelled, *"NOW MAX!"* Max jumped off the bar, flew through the air, and slammed the head of the PEZ dispenser down on Angelo's fingers. Angelo shrieked and dropped to the floor holding his hand and writhing in agony. The other patrons cowered in fear as Sheldon slowly paced before them, PEZ dispenser awaiting its next victim.

"Anyone else want a PEZ?" Sheldon asked menacingly. No one did. "I thought not," he said, returning the PEZ dispenser to his trench coat pocket. He turned to Max and said, "Let's roll, Tootsie Roll." At that very moment there was a bloodcurdling scream coming from the stripper's dressing room. Sheldon jumped on the stage and addressed the crowd: "Don't worry folks, crime and women screaming are my business. I live for this."

Danger and Moore rushed backstage. As they did, Big Mama nodded to two sinister-looking dwarfs, the Clutterbuck brothers, who acknowledged his cue and exited through a side door wondering why there are so many dwarfs and midgets in this book. Danger and Moore burst into the stripper's dressing room, guns drawn, to find the stripper and her beloved plush panda Orson both hanged. "Somebody means business, Max," Sheldon said. "Look around." Max searched for clues. He eventually opened the closet door and found Lana Holliday winking at herself in a compact mirror and holding a 4 jewels Russian clock.

"I think I found a clue," Max said like a private detective who had just found a clue.

Sheldon squinted at her. "What are you doing here, princess?"

Lana was flustered. She placed the Russian clock on the stripper's vanity table and rambled off an excuse for being there. "I wanted to find out where strippers buy their stripper clothes because I thought you might want to see me in them and then out of them. Then she died. Her clothes look expensive from a distance, but up close they look cheap. You don't want me to look cheap, do you Sheldon Danger?"

Sheldon shook his head. "You could never look cheap, you dime-store doll. But you do look tired. Go home and get some sleep. You've been around too many murders lately, and I know how exhausting that can be."

Lana blew Sheldon a kiss and left. Sheldon watched her go.

"That's all I need is another groupie hanging around. It's bad enough I have you. Did you find anything else?"

Max picked up the Russian clock, looked it over, and handed it to Sheldon who glanced at it and put it back on the vanity table. "You see that clock, Max? That's a 4 jewels Russian clock, except that clock isn't just a clock. That clock is also a bomb. That's why you're just a sidekick, because you don't know things like that."

"How do you know that's a bomb, Boss?" Max asked.

"Because it's ticking," Sheldon said.

"Maybe it's ticking because it's a clock," Max suggested. "Or maybe it's a dog. Dogs have ticks."

Sheldon glared at his partner/sidekick. "Does that bomb disguised as a clock look like a dog to you, Max?"

Max looked at the clock and admitted, "Not really."

"We probably need to get out of here before the clock that's not a clock or a dog but a bomb, explodes, and kills us," Sheldon strongly suggested. "Look around one more time then let's beat it." Max gently pushed Orson, the hanged plush panda, and let him swing. Something fell out of Orson's rear and Max picked it up.

"I think someone left a calling card, Boss. It's an origami duck. Origami is really Japanese in origin, not Chinese, so I don't know if this makes sense with the plot, if there is a plot. Some people believe the word origami was a direct translation of the German term 'papier falten' brought into Japan with the kindergarten movement of 1880. But the big debate is whether it came from the Muromachi era which began in 1333, or the Heian era which began before that."

"Max, if the bomb doesn't kill you, I will."

Sheldon then gave a slight push to the hanging stripper and an egg fell out from between her swinging legs. Max quickly flipped his fedora upside down and caught it in his hat.

"It's a duck egg! That's three clues in one place! This is like looking at a Beatles album when the whole 'Paul is dead' thing happened."

"Max, this case is really heating up. Defrost your bikini. Tomorrow we play Beach Blanket Bingo."

Danger and Moore made like a banana and got the hell out of there. A few moments later Lana Holliday slipped back in, admired the dangling stripper's stripper shoes, (yes, there's actually shoes called "stripper shoes") stole them, and left, exactly two minutes and 15 seconds before the place exploded.

CHAPTER 6

The explosion of the stripper's dressing room was so big that The Outlaws of Asteroid #9 could see it from the portholes of the ZX-12 space pod. Well, not really, but that doesn't mean it didn't happen. I was ten blocks away in a park pretending to read a book about the history of nutmeg when I was actually looking at little girls imagining what they would look like older, when I heard the explosion and even felt it a little. The truth is that the vibration from the blast knocked my Mountain Dew all over my lap and I left because it just looked wrong and inappropriate. The remainder of the journey to Digby was virtually uneventful except that the Outlaws had a major squabble with another outer space traffic control officer who stopped them for driving erratically and then, ironically, they accidentally drove erratically over the outer space traffic control officer 236 times. But other than that, the journey to Digby was rather boring except for one thing that happened. While reaching for a strip of kangaroo jerky, Rollo Starguy tripped on a Comcast coaxial cable that never worked when they needed it to, and hit his noggin on a bunk ladder. He lost consciousness. It wasn't just because he hit his head, but also because sometimes when traveling through outer space, there is a gas exchange in the lungs. Breathing continues as it tends to do when one is alive, but then all the gases, including oxygen that humans like to inhale now and then, are removed from the bloodstream and after an even dozen seconds the blood without oxygen reaches the brain and it's blackout time. While unconscious, Rollo had a dream. It was a very strange dream, and it went like this…a stormy night was brewing in the post-apocalyptic city of Hazardville, Connecticut, in what was left of the post-apocalyptic

United States, on what was left of the post-apocalyptic planet Earth. The night manager of the Red Robot Restaurant whose name coincidentally happened to be Rollo was closing the place down for the night. He went into the kitchen and found his two busboys ironically named Sluggo and Alfie asleep on the job.

"Wake up you bums!" Rollo the night manager at the Red Robot Restaurant yelled.

Sluggo and Alfie stirred and opened their eyes at half-mast. Alfie said sleepishly (*"sleepishly"*?), "We're tired, Rollo. We've been working seventeen hours a day for fifty cents an hour, and that's not fair. In fact, it's against the law. We checked with my second cousin whose neighbor knows a lawyer."

Rollo warned them: "Unless you two want to be in the unemployment line tomorrow, don't complain! I pay you fools a lot more than you're worth. Now, I'm going home early tonight so I don't get caught in the storm. I want you two to close up. And clean up that salad bar. It's a mess! If you do a good job I won't fire you."

Rollo stormed out so he wouldn't get caught in the storm. Sluggo and Alfie went out front and started cleaning up the salad bar. Sluggo was tossing croutons up in the air and catching them in his mouth. Alfie told him to stop or they'd get in trouble. Sluggo explained that croutons acted as an aphrodisiac for him, and his girlfriend said they make him a better lover. Alfie reminded Sluggo that Sluggo didn't have a girlfriend, and was just about to accuse him of lying, when the conversation was interrupted by the thunderous sound of booming thunder. A bolt of strange chartreuse green lightning shot through the roof of the Red Robot Restaurant and hit the salad bar electrifying it with an odd pulsating glow. Sluggo and Alfie were knocked unconscious, which was weird because Rollo who was having this dream was also unconscious. So an unconscious guy was dreaming that two other guys were unconscious. I don't think that's ever happened in the history of literature before. I'm very proud. So anyway...where was I? Oh yeah...so they're unconscious and there's salad all over their bodies. In their unconscious state and through some unexplainable turn of events that weren't in the dream (which is good because I don't feel like explaining it) Sluggo and Alfie began to undergo a strange and troubling transformation. The lettuce clung to their skin, face, and hair. Tomatoes, onions, mushrooms, carrots, olives, pickled beets (not the exploding kind) and various salad fixings were strewn all over their lettuce-skinned bodies. Slowly they regained consciousness and looked at each other groggily.

That's the word I should have used before instead of "sleepishly," which I made up.

Sluggo said, "Alfie, you're a salad!"

Alfie said, "So are you! Something very strange is going on here. We gotta get help to get back to our original strikingly handsome selves. I got a date tonight with a female woman."

A few minutes later Sluggo and Alfie who were now salad monsters were walking the post-apocalyptic streets of Hazardville. The citizens of Hazardville (some of whom were zombies) who encountered Sluggo and Alfie the salad monsters ran or shambled away screaming which always happens when people of low intellect encounter monsters. I've never been to Hazardville, but what kind of schmuck lives in a place called "Hazardville"? The boys/salad monsters decided to go see the girl Alfie supposedly was supposed to go on a date with. Her name was Sheila and she was the town tramp, sometimes known as "the Hazardville Harlot." Sluggo and Alfie (the salad monsters) entered Sheila's place through an unlocked door. Most people enter Sheila's place through several possible entranceways, but this was the first time through a door. They heard strange moaning sounds and followed the moaning sounds to Sheila's bedroom door, which they pushed open with their salad hands. They found Sheila in the sack with Hazardville's favorite romantic womanizing Romeo, Rex van Gogh. Ironically, Rex van Gogh was related to Rembrandt whose full name was Rembrandt Harmenszoon van Rijn (which you did not know) and not Vincent van Gogh. Rex had picked up Sheila that morning at a blood pressure checking booth at a local hospital exhibition. Picking up Sheila was about as challenging as remembering your name. His pick up line to her was, "My blood pressure was fine before I saw you." I was at the next booth learning about flossing when I overheard it. I almost puked. Anyway, 25 bucks later, they were doing the nasty when the salad monsters burst in. At the sight of them, Sheila screamed. Rex picked up a shoe he had purchased at a Walmart three towns over and prepared to throw it at the monsters. He warned, "Take another step and I'll clobber you! What do you want? What kind of monsters are you?"

Alfie got emotional. He cried, "Sheila! How could you do this to me?! We had a date tonight! I had tickets to a wet T-shirt contest which The Evil One banned!"

Rex looked at Sheila and frowned, "Do you know these salad monsters?"

Sheila shook her head and said, "I don't date salads."

Rex hurled the shoe that he purchased at the Walmart three towns over at Alfie and hit him in the cucumber. Sluggo, who was a carnivorous salad, got mad and ate Rex. Sheila pretended to cry. Alfie told her he never wanted to see her again because he didn't think she was a virgin like his mother was, and the salad monsters left. Later that night they broke into the Hazardville Grocery Store because they needed croutons to stay fresh or they would wilt without them. When Alfie first suggested that they break into the grocery store to find croutons, Sluggo reminded him that they had just murdered and eaten someone and they didn't need to add breaking and entering to their rap sheets. But Alfie reminded Sluggo that they were monsters now, and causing trouble was expected. Throughout the night they broke into several other grocery stores in search of croutons. A short time later every news channel was carrying the story of the salad monsters terrorizing what was left of Hazardville. Here's a wild thought, if you don't want to be terrorized, don't live in a place called "Hazardville." Do I have to do the thinking for everybody? I was in a Walmart three towns over from Hazardville looking at televisions I couldn't afford, and older women imagining what they looked like as little girls, when I saw a news anchor on WTNH out of New Haven reporting: "And so these odd creatures who witnesses say resemble large salads continue their spree of terror, murder, cannibalism, breaking and entering, and petty theft. Sources say that it is believed that croutons are their primary source of nourishment and they must have them to survive."

A few miles outside of Hazardville in a small crumbling cottage, a blind man was nibbling on a Greek salad when there was a knock on the door. "Come in! Come in! All visitors welcome!" he called out joyfully. The salad monsters entered the cottage. They were very weak and in desperate need of croutons. They asked the old man if he had any. The old man told them that he did and instructed them to sit down while he got them. The salad monsters sat down wearily at the table as the old blind man fumbled around searching for croutons. When he finally found a box he headed back to his seat slamming into things along the way. He complained that every time he rearranges the furniture that happens. He opened the box and sprinkled croutons on his salad and then on Alfie's salad arm. He took a bite of his salad and then a bite of Alfie's salad arm that was resting on the table next to the Greek salad. Alfie yelped in pain, killed the old man, Sluggo ate the old man, they both ate some croutons, and they left.

The following day at the Hazardville Town Hall the townspeople were assembled and furious. The mayor, Mayor Marvin Mulligan addressed them: "As mayor of Hazardville, I say enough is enough! These salad monsters have terrorized the good people of Hazardville to no end. Last night, Old Man Smithers who was related to Old Man Perkins was brutally murdered and eaten. We know that because we found his shoes that he purchased at the Walmart three towns over, and he wasn't in them. I say it's time for action! Are you with me?!"

The townspeople cheered because they were with him. He then explained what he had in mind to stop the monstrous salad monsters. I can't tell you what he said because I didn't stick around to hear. I don't like crowds, because crowds can become mobs very quickly, especially crowds with low intellect like those you might find in Hazardville, Connecticut. Hell, I don't even like people individually. Why the hell would I like a crowd of them? That said, a few days later, the salad monsters (formally known as Sluggo and Alfie) were staggering down the street extremely weak and in dire need of croutons.

Alfie said, "Sluggo, if we don't get croutons soon, we're gonna be two dead salads."

Just then Sluggo spotted a poster tacked to a telephone pole. He read it aloud: *"Attention crouton lovers! Come to the opening of Irving's Salad Sanctuary and get free croutons! Right now! All salad monsters welcome!"*

Alfie said, "It's a trap. Salad monsters aren't welcome anywhere. You should know because you're one of them. And I'm the other one of them."

Sluggo said, "But if we don't eat croutons soon, our salad days are over."

Alfie agreed. They crossed the street and entered a building that displayed a temporary banner that said, "Irving's Salad Sanctuary. Salad Monsters Come On In!" The place appeared to be vacant. Sluggo said, "I don't think there's anyone here." Suddenly, and without warning, which is sort of redundant, Mayor Marvin Mulligan and the angry uneducated townspeople of Hazardville popped up and aimed fire hoses at the salad monsters that were really just two busboys that ran into some rotten luck.

"We finally caught you!" Mayor Marvin Mulligan grinned like he was snapping up votes for re-election. "You've terrorized this town long enough. Now it's payback time."

The mayor signaled fire chief Griffin Mulligan who was his son from a 16 minute 25 buck adventure with Sheila the Hazardville Harlot, who using a special pentagonal tool turned counter clockwise slowly and completely, opened two valves on a large vat that the fire hoses were connected to. The hoses slammed 500 gallons per minute of Thousand Island dressing for four full minutes which came to 2,000 gallons all over the salad monsters (formally busboys Sluggo and Alfie). As the salad monsters lay on the floor drenched in Thousand Island dressing and feeling their lives slipping away, Mayor Mulligan introduced the Hazardville Vegetarian Arts Council and informed the salad monsters that the council members had not eaten a thing in three days, were extremely hungry, and were about to consume them. He then asked if the salad monsters had any final words before their demise.

Alfie said, "Yeah, lettuce go. Get it?"

The mayor was the only one who got it. But then, that's Hazardville for you, not exactly the Brain Center of the world.

Mayor Mulligan said, "You're real funny. The comic in Percy is funnier than you, and he's not funny at all. I hope you taste better than you tell jokes."

The mayor gave the signal and the starving Hazardville Vegetarian Arts Council attacked the salad monsters. And as they were being eaten alive, Sluggo whispered, "Mankind has always destroyed what it can't understand."

Rollo Starguy regained consciousness. He looked over and cringed at Sluggo and Alfie who were sleeping on the job. Then he looked out a porthole of the ZX-12 and saw that two interceptors were escorting the tiny space pod toward Digby's docking bay. Rollo shook Alfie awake who quickly reacted by hitting the accelerator instead of the brakes causing the pod to crash into the Digby palace which knocked Digby's ruler Emperor Zee off his rocker. A droid rushed over to Emperor Zee, helped him up, and excitedly announced the arrival of The Outlaws of Asteroid #9. The whole planet was bustling with eager anticipation. They had heard of the infamous Outlaws of Asteroid #9 but had never actually seen them live in person. Many of the Digby teenagers had posters of the Outlaws on their walls and collected issues of *Tiger Beat* that featured them on the cover, so seeing them in person was a real thrill. The Outlaws of Asteroid #9 were similar to The Monkees in that they were a manufactured thrown-together group that became a real group, and a damned good one at that. The Outlaws staggered out of the pod to thunderous applause, signed autographs, posed for photographers, and were immediately ushered into the palace where they were brought before the great Emperor Zee. After some initial denial and razzing, Emperor Zee finally admitted that the Golden Fleece of the Argonauts was indeed in his possession. Then he declared that if Rollo Starguy wanted the Golden Fleece, that he must first prove himself worthy. The trial of his courage to be only what Emperor Zee had to do to gain possession himself. He must first harness savage monstrous Qudrags whose feet are of bronze and whose breath is flaming fire (as opposed to *un*flaming fire) behind razor-sharp fangs, as Zee described them. The Qudrags measured two kilometers across, with scores of dangling tentacles. They also had the ability to change their appearance if they wanted to. With the harnessed Qudrags, Rollo must then plow a field. Then the teeth of a dragon must be planted into the furrows like seed which will spring up at once into a crop of huge armed angry androids, who no doubt will attempt to mutilate and slaughter Rollo. And that was about it.

"Whew!" Rollo sighed with relief, "I was worried that you might try to make it difficult for me, but this'll be a breeze. Anything else you want me to do, like jump over Jupiter or stuff the Milky Way in a Coke bottle?"

"Naah, that'll do it," Emperor Zee grinned. "I have done all this myself and I will give the Golden Fleece to no man less brave than I." He turned to one of his droids and commanded, "Send the orb to the planet Earth right now, and then bring in Marty and Bink."

The Outlaws watched as a large strange round object was brought out to the courtyard on a hand truck by Danny Fishman who was working part-time doing odd jobs at the palace to save up enough money to buy his cousin's 1970 Chevy Impala. Danny and two droids lifted the orb and placed it in the winched-down "launch bucket" of a Ballista which is a larger version of a catapult and was invented around 400 BCE. Emperor Zee was an avid collector of ancient artifacts like the Ballista, old novelty hand buzzers, Chinese finger traps, Matchbox cars, and every Barbie doll that ever existed including all Barbie play sets, dollhouses, clothes and accessories, which was kind of weird, but to each his own. The Outlaws looked on as the droid released the restraining rope on the Ballista which freed the stored tension and energy and sent the orb catapulting into space toward Earth. A few moments later, Marty and Bink, Digby's best location scouts were brought before Emperor Zee who informed them that they were being sent to Earth to see if it was worth conquering before The Evil One gets to it, and more importantly to locate the orb that Emperor Zee had just catapulted to Earth, although the orb sort of had an attitude and a wicked sense of humor and would lead the scouts on a wild ride through the universe before it got to its destination.

Marty said, "Sir, if you don't mind me asking, if the orb was already here, why in hell did you send it to Earth for us to locate it? It was *here!* Not two minutes ago, it was *RIGHT HERE!* Talk about a goyishe kop! With all due respect Emperor Zee, that was a schmucky move. I mean, that was really really dumb. Are you nuts?! I heard you were off your rocker a little while ago, and now I understand."

Emperor Zee had enough. He said, "Marty, you and Bink are my best scouts. Go to Earth, blend in, see if we can conquer it, and find the orb. Bye."

Two droids grabbed Marty and Bink, tossed them in a flying saucer, had Danny Fishman reset the Ballista, lifted the flying saucer into the winched-down launch bucket, and catapulted Marty and Bink toward Earth. Cool as ice and reeking of confidence, Rollo and his outlaws swaggered out of the palace to more thunderous applause. They signed more autographs, posed for some more photographs, and climbed back into the space pod where Rollo Starguy broke down sobbing like a little girl who just had her Barbie doll taken away by Emperor Zee. But a great leader's gotta do what a great leader's gotta do, so Rollo courageously called for two volunteers to get the dragon teeth. Alfie and Sluggo looked at each other and then at Rollo who wished them the best of luck on their suicidal mission. The next thing Alfie and Sluggo knew they were standing outside of a dragon's lair trying to convince themselves and each other that there was nothing to fear because there was no such thing as dragons. Any outer space outlaw knew that. And then they heard it, a hideous snorting growl coming from the lair, which convinced them otherwise. Alfie and Sluggo pulled their laser guns and nervously entered the lair. Suddenly there was nothing under their feet. They slid down a slippery slope into a dark dank damned smelly pit. It was shrouded in darkness and frightening. Reminds me of a girl I knew in New York. They trudged slowly through the muck and mire, eyes wide and lasers at the ready. They stepped cautiously toward the hideous snorting growl which grew ever louder as they drew closer. Soon it was apparent from the sound that the dragon was just around the bend. They held their weapons tightly, prepared to fire, and charged around the corner screaming an attack scream, which I never understood. You've seen this in movies and television shows where the attacker screams as he or she starts to attack, ensuring that the attack*ee* will be warned that they're about to be attacked. It's like when someone falls from a great height and they scream as they're falling. If ever there was a pointless scream, that one wins the big prize. All it does is alert people that someone is falling so people can look over and point and say, "Looky there, that person is in the process of falling. I'm not cleaning that mess up when they hit the ground." The scream can't save the falling person; it's just a ridiculous way to get attention. You want attention? Go run naked through a shopping mall. Speaking of shopping, what Alfie and Sluggo found around the corner was not a dragon, but rather a dragon-themed souvenir shop with an old 78-rpm record album spinning on a 1947 Philco 1256 radio/record player turntable producing the dragon growls courtesy of Eddie "Rochester" Anderson and Mel Blanc. Admittedly Alfie and Sluggo were a little disappointed that there was no real dragon, but what can you do? They looked around the shop and started fondling the dragon souvenirs when the proprietors appeared from the stockroom. They were three purple sisters joined at the hip and withered and weathered from extreme old age. They shared but one eye between them which they took turns seeing with. They would slap it into their foreheads like they forgot to pay the electric bill, and would then hand it to the next sister, and so on. It was a magnificent eye. It was a hypnotic eye. It sparkled like a rare jewel and seemed to see through anything it looked at. There was more to this eye than just face value. It was a treasure unto itself. Alfie and Sluggo admired the eye but didn't say anything because they didn't want the purple sisters to get swelled heads and think they were hot or something. From my personal experience, purple women can be tough to take when they think they're lusted after, so I've always treated them like something I stepped in. The Outlaws browsed through the souvenirs while the purple sisters explained that warriors come into the lair to kill a dragon and this way they can just purchase the souvenirs and *say* they killed a dragon without having to go through the trauma of actually having to do it, because most likely a *real* dragon would kill them instead. It was a pretty good gimmick actually. They had dragon scales, dragon tails, marbleized dragon eyes, dragon ears, dragon claws, all kinds of dragon novelty items: dragon lamps, dragon toothbrushes, dragon vibrators (where the eyes lit up glowing red at the moment of ultimate pleasure and the dragon roared), and of course, their most popular item, dragon teeth. They had front fangs, side fangs, bicuspids, molars, and wisdom teeth; whatever you need. Alfie and Sluggo took a dozen of each. They plopped down five bucks and eleven cents, and while it was being rung up they concocted the story they would tell Rollo. All the while they admired the sisters' beautiful eye. The Outlaws being outlaws (that's how they got their name) wanted to steal that beautiful eye, so they quickly devised a scheme. Alfie put Sinatra's "Five Minutes More" which was on Frank's 1958 album "Love is a Kick" on the 1947 Philco, gave it a spin, and shoved Sluggo into the purple sisters. On the record label it says to use only Columbia needles as though no other phonograph needle would work, which is absurd. As they waltzed, Sluggo gazed lovingly into their eye and commented about what a beautiful eye they had. The assumption was that women always fall for that line. The purple sisters passed the eye to one another as they danced, slapping it on their foreheads, and gazing lovingly at Sluggo.

"We think we love you," cooed the sisters.

"Yuck!" Sluggo replied like a jerk.

"That means he absolutely adores you," piped up Alfie attempting damage control. "He can't wait for you to meet his folks. This looks serious to me."

As the eye changed hands again, Sluggo snatched it away and tossed it to Alfie who shoved it in his pocket.

"WE CAN'T SEE! WE'RE BLIND!" screamed the purple sisters, more than a little distressed.

"We have your eye, ladies," confessed Alfie. "Sorry to leave you like this, but we're professional well-known intergalactic outlaws, and your eye is quite a treasure. See you around."

As they turned to leave the souvenir shop they heard another hideous snort and growl. *That's a neat record* Alfie thought to himself as he spun around to steal it, but alas, it wasn't a record at all, for in a blind rage the purple sisters transformed into terrifying Gorgon mutations. Like their infamous maternal ancestor Medusa, they were dreadful creatures with tremendous creepy wings and horrid bodies covered with purple scales and unconditioned hair which was in fact an orgy of twisting hissing serpents. It was really yucky. Petrified, terrified, and horrified, Alfie and Sluggo backed away from the sisters and tripped on the power cord to the 1947 Philco. The eye flew out of Alfie's pocket and landed smack in the middle of the forehead of the middle sister. Now able to see, the sisters jumped on the Outlaws and beat the living daylights out of them. The sisters attempted to turn Alfie and Sluggo to stone by staring at them real hard, but all they managed was a cluster headache because they didn't have the power that Grandma Medusa had in her prime. It sort of faded through the centuries one supposes, and by the time it got to the purple sisters, they inherited the looks, but that's about it. Still, as a precaution against the remote possibility of being turned into a couple of garden gnomes, Alfie and Sluggo slipped on some mirrored shades to protect themselves. When the sisters saw their reflection in the mirrored shades they were so embarrassed, humiliated, disgusted, embarrassed again, and totally grossed out, that they immediately changed back to their original form, which as we know, wasn't exactly an improvement. I completely forgot what their original form was and had to go back and find it. Where was I? Oh yeah, so Alfie and Sluggo staggered out of the lair, badly beaten and taken down a few notches. The purple sisters plugged in the Philco and played Sinatra's version of Bing Crosby's "I Don't Stand a Ghost of a Chance with You" which was released March 4th, 1946 on Columbia's "The Voice of Frank Sinatra" and re-recorded for the 1959 Capitol album "No One Cares." As they listened to the song they realized that true love may have just passed them by, and a tear fell from their lovely eye.

Rollo Starguy was pretending to be spellbound listening to Alfie and Sluggo tell of their great adventure. Alfie explained how Sluggo held the dragon's mouth open with his bare hands while he (Alfie) reached in and just ripped the dragon's teeth out with needle nose pliers. They were afraid of nothing, fearing no danger, thinking not of their own safety, but of their mission and the vital role they were playing in saving the universe for us all. They were concerned only with the betterment and survival of mankind and other kinds and the destruction of The Evil One like the true heroic heroes that they were. Rollo was proud of his boys. But now it was time for the contest for the Golden Fleece to commence. The Outlaws climbed out of the space pod and headed out to the arena behind the palace. When they arrived and found no one there Rollo expressed his disappointment that the extremely dangerous contest had been called off, because he was looking forward to fighting an army of huge angry androids all by himself. As the Outlaws quickly turned to leave, lots of Digbians flocked into the arena. Not as many as attended Rod Stewart's 1994 New Year's Eve performance at Copacabana Beach which brought in 4.2 million of them, but damned near close. Emperor Zee approached Rollo.

"Greetings Starguy. I must admit I am surprised that you and your

Outlaws showed up to attempt such an impossible task. I admire you for your stupidity. Are you ready to begin the contest?"

"No," replied Rollo.

"Splendid," said Emperor Zee slapping Rollo too hard on the back. "Enter the Field of Death."

Emperor Zee had Angelo and Toto toss Rollo into the Field of Death and the spectators gathered around the galvanized chain link fence. Then Emperor Zee smiled, and it was clear that he brushed his teeth once a month at the most.

"I am about to give the order to release the Qudrags. They will kill you, Starguy. Good luck."

Rollo started feeling a little uneasy about the whole thing, like maybe being attacked by brutal uncultured Qudrags whose appearance changed since Emperor Zee first described them, wasn't such a wonderful idea. They were now like huge naked mole-rats with venomous fangs and 12 foot tentacles and 48 inch claws and the ability to spit fire. Nothing you'd want to tangle with. Just as he was looking for a way out, Emperor Zee gave the command and the Qudrags rushed out of their lair and charged directly at Rollo who was paralyzed with fear like the paralyzed undaunted leader that he was. On the sidelines a young lady quickly tossed the Outlaws a vial of potion and instructed them to give it to Rollo at once before the Qudrags got to him, which didn't leave a whole heck of a lot of time. Frightened to death in the Field of Death and facing death, Rollo was unable to move. It was not a great situation. Frozen with fear he just stared at the brutal uncultured Qudrags as they thundered toward him and thought to himself *there are things that I should have done that I didn't do that I wish I did but didn't.* Suddenly there was a blinding blur as Mercury from mythology fame snatched the vial from the Outlaws, got to Rollo, pinched Rollo's nose shut forcing his mouth open, dumped in the potion, and split with blinding speed with sparks flying from his winged sneakers. It turns out that the young lady who provided the potion was none other than Zelda Borealis, the star maiden, who escaped to Digby to get away from The Evil One. She was one smart chick. As you know, The Evil One proclaimed that the star maiden was dead earlier in this book when she refused to be his date at the meeting with the Outlaws, but the guy was a half inch halfwit, part donkey, part salamander, part jellyfish nutcase, and you can't always believe what they say.

"What does that stuff do?" asked Sluggo, again forgetting to raise his hand and getting kneed good by the lovely yet temperamental star maiden.

"See for yourself," winked the star maiden motioning toward Rollo. Where Rollo stood there was a swirling glittering golden cloud with a magenta fringe. When the cloud cleared, Rollo was standing there dressed to the nines with a gold sequined dinner jacket, a silver ascot, gold chains, slick-backed hair, an unlit cigarette in one hand, a dirty martini in the other, and an aura of coolness not to be believed. Just as the Qudrags were upon him, Rollo motioned them to stop.

"Cool it."

The Qudrags came to a screeching halt. Rollo addressed them. "Now listen to me, babes. You cats don't know me and I don't know you, so why bicker? You do me right and the next time you're on Asteroid #9 we'll do lunch. Light me."

The lead Qudrag spit fire and lit the cigarette. Rollo harnessed the Qudrags and they pulled a plow while he nonchalantly tossed the dragon teeth into the furrows. Every so often he paused at a female spectator, handed her an autographed headshot, and allowed her the thrill of touching him. He was simply too hip for the Field of Death. After all the dragon teeth were planted, the crop of mean vicious weapon-wielding android warriors sprang up from the ground and rushed to attack Rollo. He motioned them to stop and they did. He shook his head disapprovingly.

"Gentlemen, violence is totally uncool. Throw down your weapons, change your attitude, and let's do lunch."

The android warriors weren't impressed and charged again, and again he motioned them to stop and they did, again. Rollo, who had taken a psychology course on procrastination but never made it to class on time and always waited till the last minute to turn in assignments, tried psychology to get out of his predicament. He spoke to the android warriors like the epitome of groovy cool personified.

"I just want to mention very briefly that the cats on my right told me that the mothers of the cats on my left wear army boots. And the cats on my left strongly suggested that those on my right have absolutely no conception at all of who their biological fathers are. Dig it."

The android warriors and the Qudrags turned on each other and slaughtered each other as Rollo Starguy took a slow drag on his unfiltered menthol Kool and watched. Victorious, he crushed the Kool under his heel and calmly strolled out of the arena changing back into his "normal" self as the potion wore off. The Outlaws cheered their amazing leader and Emperor Zee slinked away sulking like a wimpy little girl who just had her Chatty Cathy decapitated and cooked in her Easy Bake Oven. A peon droid approached the Outlaws and handed them the Golden Fleece along with a message from Emperor Zee which I dare not repeat, for not only did the message violate every obscenity law in the history of obscenity, but the grammar and punctuation was atrocious. Later that night there was a swinging five-keg bash to celebrate the Outlaws' victory and the end of their quest for the Golden Fleece of the Argonauts. After the party broke up because Mrs. Trevino across the street called the cops, Rollo Starguy and Zelda Borealis were a short distance away from the space pod gazing lovingly at each other.

"You saved my phenomenal hiney with that potion of yours, sweet thang. How can I repay you?" asked Rollo trying to sound sincere, but really just wanting to jump her bones.

"I'll think about it," answered the star maiden pretending to think about it but not really thinking about it, really just wanting Rollo to jump her bones. She got caught up in the drama and romance of the moment and walked away from Rollo to gaze up into the sky like women do in those old flicks from the forties, hoping that he would follow her into the darkness and they would do the nasty until they went blind just like our Aunt Goldies warned us about when they walked into the kitchen unannounced and caught us auditioning the finger puppets. Remember that? You don't? Well...I do. The star maiden was followed into the dark alright, but not by Rollo. A moment later she was gone. Rollo became concerned when he couldn't find her and had the Outlaws search the area. In the darkness they were jumped. There was a slight struggle but the Outlaws finally managed to be overtaken and bound together by The Evil One's Droid Pursuit Unit. A bomb was set between Rollo's legs to blow the Outlaws apart, starting with Rollo's favorite part. Just as the bomb was about to be activated, Alfie, who had once coached a Pop Warner football team called "Heaven's Devils", called for a time out so the droids could recharge, because droids have to recharge now and then. They bought the ploy and Rollo whispered aside to Alfie, "What's the idea?"

"To stall," whispered Alfie.

"Stall for what?" asked Sluggo.

"Stall for time so we can think up a plan of escape before they blow us up," responded Alfie.

The Outlaws all thought silently for two full minutes (which is actually a long time to think silently) then Rollo gave in.

"I can't think of anything, can you guys?"

"Nope," came the collective answer sending chills up Rollo's spine. He was ashamed of his boys. The droids finished recharging, activated the bomb, and hit the road with the star maiden in tow. The Outlaws struggled to free themselves but could not. Just as they finished saying their final farewells to each other, and telling each other what they really thought about each other, which was quite unpleasant, and just as the bomb was about to blow for real, in a much debated and extremely contrived appearance, the old farmer who Rollo rudely called "Mr. Green Jeans" in honor of the character portrayed by Hugh Brannum on the Captain Kangaroo show which ran for 6,090 episodes from 1955 to 1984, arrived on the scene riding an old hog English style, reached between Rollo's legs and quickly defused the bomb by...well, pulling the fuse out. In other words, he saved their keisters. The old farmer confirmed that The Evil One still had his headquarters on Shlump. The Outlaws decided to take Shlump via a different route than before, the back door so to speak, thereby avoiding the perils of Gigantis-Singe and the black hole.

CHAPTER 7

As The Outlaws of Asteroid #9 took off for Shlump, Don Neroni's limousine pulled up to the front entrance of his estate. The security cameras automatically followed every motion as one of the goons in the black suits guarding the entrance gate approached the car. He opened the back door and helped Don Neroni out of the limo. Angelo and Toto stepped outside of the limo and stood next to the car respectfully as the don slowly walked over to a rose bush that was surrounded by a small white picket fence and removed an old sheet of newspaper that was tangled in the thorns. He handed the paper to Angelo who folded it and put it in his pocket. Don Neroni spoke to Angelo and Toto who had heard this a thousand times, but remained silent and respectful.

"My Rosie planted this rose bush herself. She said she wanted a little beauty in my world." He choked up. "*She* was my beauty, but she never understood that."

Lost in his thoughts, Don Neroni caressed a rose. As he did, his hand brushed against a thorn which pricked his finger. He drew his hand back, brought his finger to his mouth, and tasted his own blood.

"She still punishes me," he said. "Even the rose has thorns to protect itself against those who would do it harm. She never understood that either."

Suddenly the squeal of tires from a speeding car cracked the calm as a black sedan tore around the corner. A gunman hung out the passenger window of the sedan with a MAC-10 and opened fire on Don Neroni. As he did, an army of goons in dark suits popped up from the front wall of Neroni's fortress with sub-machine guns and pumped the sedan so full of holes that it was virtually obliterated. When the trigger talk was over, Don

Neroni was still standing, unharmed. He turned to his army and nodded approvingly. They immediately disappeared behind the wall. The don then looked at the rose bush that did not fare so well. This was very upsetting to him, but he did not react. Angelo and Toto holstered their weapons and rushed to his side. He motioned that he was okay, and they walked him over to what was left of the sedan, which wasn't much. The don poked at something with his walking stick.

"I can tell by the tiny brain in the ashtray, this was one of Musetti's jobs; cheap hoods." He turned to Angelo. "I want a sit-down with Musetti, today."

"After what he done?" Angelo snarled. "Let's whack 'em."

"No wars," Don Neroni declared. "We sit. I don't like violence."

Toto noticed something in the street. "That must be what's left of the driver. Ain't that his mouth?"

"Yeah, it's frowning," Angelo pointed out. "It ain't too happy."

Don Neroni poked at the mouth with his walking stick. "That's understandable. He's having a bad day. Get me inside."

Later that afternoon in Don Neroni's office, he and Don Musetti had their sit-down. Musetti was significantly younger and a known hothead. That said, he did have great admiration for Don Neroni. They each had two goons with them who were on opposite sides of the room glaring at each other. Angelo and Toto were Neroni's. The don frowned at Musetti. "As you can see Musetti, your triggerman had bad aim."

"What makes you think-" Musseti began.

"No no. Don't even try," Don Neroni sneered, cutting him off. "I was running the East Coast when you were crapping fruit loops in your diapers. This is about the casino property."

Musetti started getting angry. "You undercut us! We were set to buy that fucking land and you muscled in. That's fucking disrespectful, and *nobody* disrespects me!"

Angelo and Toto exchanged glances. Musetti's goons glared at them. Don Neroni pointed his walking stick at Musetti. "Trying to kill me is disrespectful too. Business is business. You know what I can do to you now."

Musetti turned to his goons. "Leave us."

Don Neroni nodded to Angelo and Toto as well and all four goons left the room. Musetti spoke with respect.

"I always admired you, Don Neroni. Your climb to the top is legendary.

But I think the top is starting to teeter. I see no fucking underboss. Something's wrong here. Where's your son?"

"My son goes his own way. That's none of your concern."

"Maybe not or maybe it is," Musetti said.

Don Neroni looked at a photo of his beloved Rose, thought for a few moments, and said, "I have a proposal. What if we partner for the casino?"

Musetti was taken aback. "Two families?! Unheard of."

"So we lead the way," Neroni said. "We make a marriage for this one project and see how it goes."

Musetti turned insolent, which was nothing new. "Maybe your proposal is because you're afraid you're losing power."

Don Neroni leaned into Musetti's face and snarled, "Go outside and ask the pieces of your failed hitman and driver if they think I'm losing power. What happened to them can happen to anyone, capisce? To begin with, I'm not crazy about the location for the casino. We need room. I want to build a tremendous complex; a class act; no dives, no clip joints. I want something that will last long after I'm gone; a legacy."

Musetti smirked, "Fuckin' Neroni World."

The don smiled, "Why not? You know, Musetti, you say 'fuck' too much. Since you say it so much (he leaned in menacingly) tell me what it means."

Meanwhile in the odd wooded area of Percy, Nero and Izzy were grunting and groaning, frustrated and straining, trying desperately to squeeze Nero into the body suit of *The Creature from Gruesome Gulch* monster costume, but it just wasn't happening. Izzy was aggravated. "Forget it! It's like trying to cram a planet into a Dixie cup. You're not a skinny monster anymore."

There was a gunshot and then a heavy thud like the sound of the body of a strange zoo curator hitting the floor. They ignored it, but it did spark an idea in Nero's mind. He strongly suggested, "Let's go see Madam Mancowitz. I hear she's an odd duck, but a damned good seamstress."

Izzy looked up at Nero and asked, "Who?"

"Hoo-hoo-hooooo" screeched a great-horned owl on a limb of a dead tree in a dark, spooky, creepy, and forbidding part of the woods as Nero (carrying the monster costume) and Izzy, made their way through the twisted trees and brush under a full spooky moon. Millions of miles above, the Digby orb zoomed through the universe with Marty and Bink in their flying saucer in hot pursuit. Marty and Bink were unaware that far below them, mob underboss turned bad actor, Nick Nero, was in front of his chauffeur clearing the way through spooky woods toward Madam Mancowitz's place, and doing a pretty good job, although some limbs did snap back and smack Izzy in the kisser. She wasn't overly happy. "Do me a favor, Tarzan. Next time you need a limo, make sure I'm not the driver."

Nero spun around and snapped, "*You* got us into this with your great shortcut to Barstow. I'm trying to get us out."

"You're doing a terrific job," Izzy replied, most likely probably sarcastically. Nero growled as they came upon four arrow-shaped wooden signposts one after another and a few feet apart that said the following:

"I'D TURN BACK IF I WERE YOU!"
"ALTERATIONS GUARANTEED FOR LIFE!"
"MAKE ROOM FOR DOOM!"
"LOOK PROUD IN YOUR SHROUD!"

Izzy turned around to leave and Nero stopped her. "Oh no, it wouldn't be the same without you." He pushed aside one more tree branch and there before them was a small eerie cottage with a sign on the door reading:

"MADAM MANCOWITZ - THE BLIND SEAMSTRESS
(& part-time visionary) WELCOMES YOU!
clothing alterations, fortunes told, curses cast and lifted"

"If flying monkeys rip you apart, I'm not doing a damned thing," Izzy mumbled. As they approached the front door it opened by itself with a foreboding creak and they nervously stepped inside. They looked around the place and tried to take it all in. There were cobwebs everywhere, human skulls and bones, a bubbling cauldron, measuring tape, scissors, spools of thread of various sizes and colors, crystal balls, a broom, a black cape hanging on a hook, books of magic and spells in Braille, lit candles, slithering snakes in an aquarium, live toads in bottles, bats hanging upside down from the rafters, a few meandering rats, bells, feathers, assorted bottles and vials, pentagrams, and a stuffed taxidermied black cat, fangs and claws exposed, poised to pounce.

"Nice place," Izzy commented, probably sarcastically.

Suddenly a creepy old woman dressed in a black vintage gothic gown that had seen better days entered through a red velvet curtain leading to an adjoining room. She mumbled to herself and turned a few things such as candles, beakers, a few skulls both human and otherwise that were on their sides, right-side-up, and then just stood motionless in the center of the room, like she was waiting for pigeons to land on her. And they did. After a few very awkward moments, Nero asked, "Are you Madam Mancowitz?"

"Do I look like I would live in a dump like this?" asked the creepy old woman.

There was no answer. But we all know the answer.

"I'm the maid," said the old creepy woman. "I come once a week to tidy up."

"You do good work," Izzy said.

The old creepy maid snapped, "She's blind! What in Blue Balls, Pennsylvania, does she care? Have a swell day."

The old creepy maid exited with a sinister hacking cackling laugh just as Madam Mancowitz entered. She looked *exactly* like the creepy old maid who had just left, except she was wearing dark Cat-Eye Sunglasses and felt her way around, knocking over the exact same objects that the creepy old maid had just turned right-side-up.

"Madam Mancowitz?" Izzy asked.

"Most likely," Madam Mancowitz who was really Madam Mancowitz answered. "And you are the anal-retentive chauffeur with a personality like extra coarse 50-grit sandpaper. And I also sense a bad actor with Mafia connections in my presence."

Nero gritted his teeth but said nothing. Madam Mancowitz pointed to the red velvet curtain and said, "Step into my parlor, my children."

Izzy pretended to be puzzled. "I thought you were blind. How do you know where the parlor is?"

"Because I've lived here for 187 years," Madam Mancowitz muttered. "You get to know your way around."

They all went behind the red velvet curtain into the adjoining room and then quickly returned with strange looks on their faces. "I didn't know people could bend in those positions," Izzy commented. Madam Mancowitz pointed in the opposite direction. "Maybe it's over there. My husband and his dog are usually in the parlor."

The parlor was a smaller version of the outer room, much in the same way that a second bedroom is a smaller version of a master bedroom. It was also darker, very shadowy, and contained several of the same things as the outer room. One particular thing it contained that the outer room did not contain, had Nero and Izzy staring and startled. In a corner of the room, seated at a small table, was the skeleton of a man with a pipe in its mouth. The skeleton was holding an old yellowed newspaper as though he is (or rather *was*) reading it. The skeleton of a sitting dog was at the man's skeletal feet. In front of the man's skeleton was an empty plate covered with cobwebs. In front of the skeleton of the dog were two empty bowls, also covered with cobwebs. This was a moment frozen in time that had Nero and Izzy frozen with fear. Madam Mancowitz piped up. "From the silence and smell of sheer bewilderment and horror, I can tell you have met my unfaithful hubby Frank and his unfaithful dog, Scooter." She got suddenly excited and addressed the dog's skeleton. "Roll over Scooter! Heel boy! Play dead!"

"He's great at that one," Izzy remarked.

Madam Mancowitz sighed, "They're still dead aren't they?"

"Looks that way," Izzy said, feeling a little queasy.

"You know why they're dead, sweetie?" Madam Mancowitz asked rhetorically. "'Cause I stopped feeding those two bastards 37 years ago. Men are shit, and stupid too. No offense to the bad actor with Mafia connections."

Izzy smirked at Nero who smirked back.

"I need some clothes altered," Nero said.

"Don't bullshit me, Mafia Boy! I don't call a monster costume 'clothes'."

"How do you know it's a monster costume if you're blind?" Izzy asked.

Madam Mancowitz ignored her and addressed Nero.

"Remove your shoes."

Nero hesitated.

"*Today*, Goombah!"

Annoyed, Nero removed his shoes.

"Now place a twenty dollar bill face up inside of each shoe," she instructed.

"Why?" Nero asked, getting more annoyed than just regular annoyed.

"So the money will smell nice," Madam Mancowitz mumbled, probably sarcastically.

Nero put a one-dollar bill in each shoe and Madam Mancowitz blasted him. "Don't fuck with me, Meatball!"

Nero, steaming, pulled out two twenties and shoved them in the shoes. Madam Mancowitz held up a stolen beat-up hubcap with both hands extended before her and spoke in a mystical commanding tone. "Now you shall place both shoes upon the Mystical Platter of the Voyager."

"What happened to the other three mystical platters of the Voyager?" Izzy asked.

Again, ignoring Izzy, Madam Mancowitz turned Nero's shoes upside down, quickly shoved the forty bucks down the front of her black vintage gothic gown, and started sniffing the soles of Nero's shoes, making disgusted faces as she sniffed.

"You have walked many roads in your lifetime," she choked, yet sniffed again. "Your journey has not been an easy one," she choked, yet sniffed again. "You have suffered in ways that no child should suffer," she choked, yet sniffed again.

Nero nodded, teary-eyed. Izzy mumbled something about him throwing people off the Hollywood Sign, but no one heard.

Madam Mancowitz sniffed more sole and said, "And you have stepped bravely into werewolf pooh-pooh." She lowered the shoes from her nose and addressed Nero. "My advice, dear boy, is to watch where you're going in life, and to start going now." She picked up the hubcap and Nero's shoes and turned to leave. Nero stopped her.

"And where are *you* going?"

"Show's over; scram!" Madam Mancowitz muttered.

Nero went from zero to 120 real quick. "I want my shoes and my money back *NOW!*"

"You can have your shoes back for ten bucks each," Madam Mancowitz croaked. "If you want your money back, that will cost you two hundred dollars."

"I gave you forty bucks," Nero grumbled.

"That's right, you *gave* me forty."

Nero started to steam. "*Gimme my shoes, Witch!*"

"Don't get personal, tough guy," she said. "Say 'please'."

Nero was boiling. "*Please.*"

"Forget it!" she croaked again.

Nero picked up *The Encyclopedia of Witchcraft and Demonology* by Rossell Hope Robbins (1959) and hurled it across the room knocking Frank's skeleton on his skeletal ass.

"YOU KILLED MY HUSBAND!" Madam Mancowitz screamed.

"Give me my shoes and money back or you're next!"

"Finders keepers," she snarled.

"You didn't *find* them, Shrew, I *gave* them to you!"

"What a poet," Izzy mumbled, but no one heard.

"That's right; you *gave* them to me," Madam Mancowitz maintained. "Now get lost!"

"I *am* lost," Nero said, getting misty.

This is probably the most sensitive moment in this whole book. It even shook *me* up, and I was the one who wrote it. I actually needed a few minutes to compose myself after I wrote it. Madam Mancowitz handed Nero back his shoes but kept the dough.

"You remind me of my son," she said. "He was a snot-nosed little prick, so I turned him into a toad. He's in one of these jars here somewhere. Enough chitchat, let's fix your…clothes."

Some time later Nero was once again struggling like mad to squeeze into the bottom half of the creature costume as Madam Mancowitz and Izzy looked on.

"Somebody's been eating sequoia trees since they last wore this costume," Madam Mancowitz pointed out. Izzy nodded.

"I thought you were blind," Nero pointed out back. (Not that he pointed out something in the back, but that he made a point in return. You know what I mean.)

"When you lose one sense, your other senses grow stronger," said the witch. "I can smell pork fifty miles away. Now hold still."

Madam Mancowitz made a few adjustments which caused the costume to loosen, but too much.

"Better?" she asked.

"Too big," he answered.

"Oh crap. Alright, time for the big guns," she said. "Get down to your birthday suit."

He hesitated. "Here?"

"No, Peculiar, Missouri."

Not overly thrilled, Nero started taking everything off. Izzy hung her head. Madam Mancowitz felt her way over to some wooden crates. She removed several large vials from the crates and felt her way back to Nero who was now nude. She grabbed for his one-eyed wonder weasel and he whacked her hand away. She held up a vial.

"This here is my secret sauce. It will make the costume fit perfectly. But ya gotta leave the costume on a spell for it to metabolize to your body."

"What does that mean?" Nero asked, overly concerned.

"I don't know," admitted the witch.

She started smearing the contents of the vials, a milky gray-white sticky substance somewhere between rancid skim milk and Elmer's glue, all over Nero's body. He moaned and groaned now and then as she smeared away. He went from total disgust to the strain of trying to avoid a woody (as the kids say, if they still say that). It was a rollercoaster of physical emotions. I think I just made that up, "physical emotions." When she got to his weenie, she spoke to it, "Well, hello there little fella! Are you happy to see me?" With no desire to watch the penis pageant, Izzy wandered around looking at the odd assortment of witch things here and there as Madam Mancowitz cooed and made baby talk noises to Nero's weenie. Izzy made her way over to the wooden crates from which the old witch removed the vials. If this were a movie, this scene would be severe and extremely jolting. Izzy looked over the crates and stifled a scream when she saw stenciled on their hidden sides:

"PIG SEMEN
EXPORT ONLY
PERCY, CA."

She quickly looked over at Nero as the old witch smeared more of her "secret sauce" all over his body. Suddenly there was a loud clap of thunder followed by cheering outside. Izzy ran to the window, brushed away cobwebs, and took a look. The town was visible through the trees. It was starting to drizzle and several of the people of Percy, the Percy People, were all screaming bloody murder and running for cover. Izzy noticed the mayor coming *out* of a building, raising his arms to the sky, and dancing a wild jig. He was in ecstasy, something Nero was trying very hard to avoid.

"Why is everybody running and screaming?" Izzy asked.

"You heard the thunder, honey. It's rainin' ain't it?" Madam Mancowitz muttered. "Well, to *you* it's rainin'. And to *me* and this Mafia guy, it's rainin'. Even his little tiny fella knows it's rainin'." She grabbed Nero's weenie and Nero shrieked. "But those loonies out there think somethin' else. They think that the thunder is the man upstairs bowlin' and makin' strikes. So they get all excited, like he's got a bowlin' alley up there." She let go a sinister hacking cackling laugh which was very similar to the sinister hacking cackling laugh that her maid demonstrated not long ago. "How the hell's a bowlin' alley gonna float in the sky?"

"Are you done?" Nero asked, really annoyed.

107

"Cool yer jets, Mafia Boy! I gotta stitch up this part right here. There's a big hole in it."

"That's my ass!" Nero screeched.

"And you're mine," said the old witch. "Now shut up and don't move. I'll install a poopy flap so you can do your business."

She "accidentally" pricked him with pins.

"OW! You're sticking me!" he screeched again.

"I'm blind, you moron!" the old witch pointed out. "Now quit movin' around you crybaby with your wah wah wah."

From the outer room the maid called out, "I'm back again, Madam Mancowitz! Hope you had a good week!"

Nero and Izzy both quickly turned to see the maid standing in the doorway. Again, she looked exactly like the old witch but without the dark glasses. They both quickly turned back to look at Madam Mancowitz and she was gone. Izzy looked at the maid. "I thought you came here once a week. It's been twenty minutes."

"A week, twenty minutes, what difference does it make? To finish her story, which you two keep interrupting, a few years ago the town of Percy tried to have Madam Mancowitz hung because Mr. Mancowitz wasn't." Nero and Izzy glanced over at Frank's skeleton, but it was a wasted glance. The maid continued. "Then they tried to burn her at the stake, but it rained, and that screwed that."

"Why did they want to kill her?" Izzy asked.

"They accused the poor dear of practicing black magic, which was a load of crap, so she cast an evil spell on the town. Now when it rains, they think the Almighty is takin' a leak. Madam wants you to go now."

"That's not true, my dear," said Madam Mancowitz from somewhere. Nero and Izzy looked to where the old witch was before and saw that she was back. Then they looked to see if the maid was gone and she was. Madam Mancowitz muttered, "I'd be happy to let you children stay here, but you don't match the furniture, so you're out. Bye-bye. You can have some waffles and latkes before you go. There's some syrup for the waffles in the cupboard."

"How do you know we don't match the furniture?" Izzy asked.

Madam Mancowitz muttered madly, "You clash with everything, my dear. The only hotel we have is the Caribou Inn down a ways. Percy ain't exactly a tourist trap, although it is a trap." She addressed Nero. "You, my dear, cannot go out like that in your monster costume. The whole town will think you're in a bad B-movie: *Attack of the Bad Actor with Mafia Connections.*" She let go her sinister hacking cackling laugh and then felt her way to a small closet. She opened the closet door and several bats flew out screeching. "There goes lunch," she said. She felt around and pulled out an old trench coat and a beat-up fedora which she gave to Nero. "These were Frank's. He dressed up like that private detective Sheldon Danger every year for Halloween. You take them."

"Frank might not be using them for a while, being dead and all," Izzy pointed out rudely.

The old witch wagged her bony hideous witch-like finger at Izzy. "That was rude my dear. Frank may have been a filthy cocksucking piece of shit whoremonging loser, but he was still my hubby, so have respect."

"You're right. I'm sorry," Izzy said apologetically.

"No, I'm sorry," Madam Mancowitz mumbled morosely. "I never should have married that filthy cocksucking piece of shit whoremonging loser. But I did." She turned to Nero. "You should also wear dark glasses to help hide your monster face. Do you have any?"

"He's an actor," Izzy reminded the old witch. "They all have dark glasses."

Madam Mancowitz started to leave, stopped, and turned back to Nero. "You bring that tiny little fella back some time to see me. I'll knit a sweater for him."

Some time later Nero and Izzy were standing in front of a wooden sign with antlers sticking out of it that said:

"THE CARIBOU INN
Better than the Bates Motel"

They looked over at the small one room freestanding building which looked similar to a tiny cheap car rental agency that might have three crappy cars to rent out. This was the most eye-catching building in Percy. It was painted magenta-purple and had a pair of gigantic antlers as large as the inn itself coming out of the tiny roof. It looked as though the inn would topple over from their absurd size and weight. Sort of like when Fred Flintstone gets the brontosaurus ribs at the drive-in and the car tips over. In fact, the back part of the building was several inches off the ground as the tremendous weight of the antlers was pulling it forward. Nero and Izzy were both entranced by the sheer elegance lacking from the Caribou Inn. They entered the "lobby" which was stark white and consisted of a small service counter, a plastic pink flamingo propped up on one leg against the wall, a potted rubber cactus plant, the mounted head of a mouse, and a sign:

"WELCOME TO PERCY
PIG SEMEN CAPITAL OF THE WORLD
Population 26"

The desk clerk spun around to greet them, and it was none other than Mr. Percy wearing a very bad blond toupee. Nero attempted to keep his monstrous face hidden during this exchange. Izzy asked, sort of rudely, "Is our limo repaired, Mr. Percy?"

"I'm the Caribou Inn desk clerk now. I will only reply to Caribou Inn desk clerk inquiries. But I'll give you a hint…no. That Nigel Daw movie gnat is still buzzin' my rectum. Now I have a question." He looked at Nero. "Are you a spy?"

"He's just a bad actor with Mafia connections," Izzy said.

"Then why the devil is he wearing a trench coat in the desert? Only spies wear trench coats, and that detective Sheldon Danger and his partner over there in Los Angeles. Temperature-wise we're set on broil here."

"It rained earlier," Nero mumbled, trying to hide his face.

"Not bad, and without a script," Izzy said rudely. Nero sneered at her and Mr. Percy shook his head.

"I can tell you're not from here. It don't rain in Percy. The good lord takes a leak here. Percy is the good lord's outhouse, not me, the town. I ain't no outhouse. I have lots of jobs, but outhouse ain't one of 'em. I think He leaks a lot 'cause He drinks a lot of coffee. Coffee makes me tinkle like mad. How the Hell do you think He made the Heavens and the Earth and all this crap in only six days? Caffeine!" Mr. Percy noticed Izzy transfixed on the mounted mouse head and started boasting. "I took that little bastard myself. He put up a fight and a half, but I nailed him with my 12-guage partner 'Imogen'. Put an end to his reign of terror."

"And what exactly was his 'reign of terror'?" Izzy asked getting steamed.

"Think about it, honey. Walt Disney made friends with a mouse, just like that one there. Next thing you know he's got 50 million people in his yard goin' on rides and singin' stupid songs about the world bein' small.

We don't need that kind of shit in Percy. No Mam! So I put a stop to that right quick, and there's the proof."

Nero could see that Izzy was about to explode and changed the subject, "Any caribou around here?"

"Nope," said Percy as Izzy glared at him wishing she had a 12-guage partner.

"Then why is this place called the Caribou Inn?" Nero asked, and it really was a brilliant question, I'll give him that.

"Do I look like a calendar to you?" asked Mr. Percy. "How do I know?"

At that very moment, Milo Mabbitt, Percy's most annoying resident, popped his head in.

"Hotel clerk, is I interrupting anything?"

"No Milo," Percy said.

"Then I'll come back later," Milo replied. As Milo exited, the hideous monstrous spine-chilling tail from Nero's *Creature from Gruesome Gulch* costume popped out from under the trench coat, and Izzy quickly stuffed it back before Mr. Percy noticed it.

"Do you have any rooms?" Nero mumbled.

"Just one and you're standing in it," Percy pointed out.

Nero was as confused as you are. "Where do people sleep?"

"I don't know. No one's ever stayed here before. You checkin' in?"

"There's no other hotel in town?" Izzy asked using bad grammar.

"Nope, all the rest are somewhere else," Mr. Percy said.

"Then I guess we're staying here," Nero mumbled.

"I heard about you two. Word around town is you're strange. I don't want strange people in my establishment."

Nero and Izzy spent the night lying on the ground just outside the inn under the sign which had been changed to read: "NO VACANCY." The "NO" was handwritten in blue chalk. Both of them were just staring up into space, silently. Izzy turned and looked at the monster next to her on the ground. She then turned back on her back and gazed up at the Percy night sky which happened to be rather beautiful. Suddenly she saw what she thought was a falling star, but was in actuality the Digby orb followed by Marty and Bink in their flying saucer.

The next morning elderly Percy couple Fred and Ginger Tanaka was sitting on their front porch swing on their front porch of their shanty which stood out among the other shanties because their shanty represented the American dream. It had a picket fence and flowerbeds full of aloe plants, brittlebush, and Baja fairy dusters. An American flag flew proudly overhead next to a boom mic. A stuffed cat sat on the windowsill next to a fake apple pie, and a stuffed Rough Collie (think Lassie) sat at Fred's feet. It seems we have been watching this on a video production monitor. Watching along with us, documentary director creep Nigel Daw who instructed his crew, "Alright. Print that. Label it 'psychotic old couple'." And then mumbled to himself, "What a bloody mess."

Suddenly Daw was drenched in blood. Every member of the documentary crew screamed and scattered except for key grip Ethan Griffin who was in an outhouse practicing his key grip. There was a tremendous terrifying growl as two large claws reached down from above Daw's director's chair and pulled Daw straight up out of the chair and hurled him 23 feet through the air. Daw came crashing down on his rear and the monster slowly, menacingly, approached him, swiping ferociously as it moved in for the kill. The Creature from Gruesome Gulch had returned. He was a Skid Row combination of *The Creature from the Black Lagoon, The Horror of Party Beach, The Beast from Haunted Cave, The Creeping Terror, The Beast from 20,000 Fathoms,* and anything else you wouldn't want to wake up next to. He had that hideous monstrous spine-chilling tail that popped out earlier at the inn, frightening claws, and a horn protruding out of his head. It was large enough to scare the devil out of someone and small enough to be covered by a beat-up fedora. The monster drew closer and closer to Daw who was petrified. A trickle of the blood Daw was doused with trailed slowly from his forehead toward his mouth. Just as the Creature from Gruesome Gulch cocked his claw back for the final swipe, sure to take Daw's head off, the trickle of blood slipped into Daw's mouth, and Daw became immediately aware of something strange as he tasted the blood.

"HOLD ON!" Daw yelled. Nero stopped in his tracks. In fact, everything stopped. "*This isn't blood!*" Daw reached up to his head and collected more "blood" to taste. "This is Karo syrup! They used it for blood in lousy low-budget horror films years ago!"

Daw glared at the Creature from Gruesome Gulch who let out a huge growl, knocked down the camera, and ran into the woods. Local loon Milo Mabbitt watched the monster run past. "Someone must've fed the costume," he observed.

Daw's cameraman Walker Adams who was on his ninth wife and was eyeing a tenth, checked the camera.

"Speak!" Daw barked.

"She's okay," Adams said. "The matte box got bashed a bit, but she'll live. We're almost done here anyway, aren't we?"

Nigel Daw ignored the question. He was staring at Percy's strange wooded area. His crew wandered back, awaiting his instructions.

"Did you get any of that?" Daw asked sternly.

"Any of what?" Adams asked.

Daw turned away from the woods and snarled at his cameraman, "Oh, I don't know...*How about the FUCKING MONSTER THAT JUST ATTACKED ME?!* DID YOU GET ANY OF THAT?!"

"Yeah, I got it," Adams said.

"Swell. *He's* our story now," Daw said, "not this psycho town."

"Christ, Nigel, we've been in this armpit for two months! Let's go home," the first assistant director groaned.

"If you wanna go, if *any* of you wanna go, *GO!* I'll do it my bloody self!" Daw snarled. "And let me know how you get out of here. I haven't seen any moving vehicles in a long time."

Adams adjusted the monitor, saw something on it, and looked toward the road. "There's one," he said. He looked through the camera lens at the vehicle and zoomed in. It was a white OB (outside broadcasting) van with broadcast antennas and a satellite dish to transmit video back to the studio. The van came to a dust-up stop some distance away from the documentary crew. On the side of the van were the words "HOLLYWOOD EXPOSED" which was one of those ridiculous tell-all-and-hope-you-don't-get-sued-for-slander exploitation shows.

"*Hollywood Exposed*. They turned me down for a job, but another door opened and I found myself here in paradise," Adams mumbled.

"I forgot about this," Daw said. "They're here to promote the Percy doc. If they see our monster friend they'll say they found him first."

"He's not real, Nigel," Adams said.

Nigel shrugged, "What *is?* They're *all* fake. The Loch Ness Monster was a toy submarine. A bloody gynecologist took blurry pictures of it and conned everyone. Bigfoot's a guy in a hairy suit. We all know that, but we still like the mystique. It's human nature. We love to be fooled, and now's my chance to cash in on human stupidity. I'll make a fortune."

"When I was a kid we used to toss potatoes up in the air and snap blurry pictures of 'em. I told supermarket rags they were flying saucers; sold lots of those," Adams confessed.

"There you go," Nigel said. "If a half-wit can make the public believe that a potato is a flying saucer, imagine what *I* can do with my monster."

"Blow him?" Adams mumbled under his breath.

The assistant director interjected, "*Hollywood Exposed* can't say they found him first if we have timed footage."

"Can it for me quick," Daw demanded. "Finders keepers, I don't trust Hollywood. They rob people *from* a living *for* a living."

Adams looked over at the van. "Do you trust them enough to let them take us home and out of Crazy Town?"

Daw waved goodbye. "I told you, luv. Have a nice trip." Then he turned toward the woods and mumbled to himself, "Where's my monstrous lad?"

In a small clearing in the woods early that evening, Nero was still in costume, of course, and extremely annoyed, of course. "He knows it's me," he growled rhetorically (hurling me into the history books because this is the first time in literary history that any character has ever "growled rhetorically"). Izzy tried to calm him down. "You said yourself that a guy like that would never see *The Creature from Gruesome Gulch*. He doesn't know it's you."

"Well, he knows it's phony," Nero said. He started to attempt to remove the costume, but to no avail. "Help me get this thing off." Both Nero and Izzy tried to remove the monster costume but it wouldn't budge. They were both getting very frustrated, and Nero was heading straight for rage. Izzy, trying to head that off, grabbed on tightly to his tail and with a loud grunt pulled on the costume with such force that she lost her hold and fell back on the ground. The force of the fall caused her small walkie-talkie radiophone to fly out of her pocket. Neither one of them noticed it. Nero was seething. "What'd that witch put this on with, glue?"

"We need to go see her," Izzy said. And that they did. That night in Madam Mancowitz's parlor, Madam Mancowitz told Nick Nero something he didn't want to hear: "It's never coming off." After a very long and dangerous silence, Nero asked the old witch, "What do you mean '*never*'?"

Madam Mancowitz felt and fumbled her way to her old dusty bookshelf. After feeling the Braille lettering on the spines of several books, she finally pulled one off the shelf. She blew off some dust, brushed away some cobwebs, and slowly felt the Braille lettering as she turned some pages. She stopped at a page, trailed her finger halfway down, and read verbatim:

"NE.VER *(adverb)* - at no time: not ever: in any way or degree: not at all under any condition."

She slammed the dictionary shut sending dust everywhere, and said to Nero, "Ain't gonna happen, Toots!"

Nero exploded, and rightfully so. **"WHY DIDN'T YOU TELL ME IT *NEVER COMES OFF?!!!*"**

"Because life is much more interesting when we find out things for ourselves," the old witch explained. "That's how we learn, my dear. And besides, you didn't ask."

At that, Nero went berserk. He let out an enraged howl fitting the Creature from Gruesome Gulch, knocked over a cauldron spilling its green bubbling slimy contents, and smashed through the door, running into the woods.

"He's a method actor. I better go," Izzy said.

The old witch held up a tiny phallic-shaped sweater and a tiny matching cap she knitted for Nero's weenie.

"Look what I made for his little fella, just like I promised!"

"That's lovely," Izzy said. "I'll let him know, and maybe you can put it on his little fella yourself."

Izzy headed out, literally bumping into Madam Mancowitz's maid who was coming in. "Sorry, Madam Mancowitz," Izzy said, mistaking Madam Mancowitz's maid for Madam Mancowitz.

"I'm the maid," said the maid, who pointed to the green bubbling slime from the cauldron on the floor and snapped, "I ain't cleanin' that up! I guarantee you that, missy!"

Izzy ran outside to find Nero. Madam Mancowitz stood next to the maid who was watching Izzy run off.

"Both those kids need to get laid," the old witch said. "All that pent up stress can wear a body out."

The maid nodded her head. "Speaking of which, Witch. I need a raise."

"Well, good luck to you," Madam Mancowitz said. "Bring up a raise again and I'll turn you into that yellow water Johnny Cash talked about at Folsom Prison."

Back on the location set, *Hollywood Exposed* reporter Jerry Juxson, microphone in hand, was being quickly powdered to go on the air. The cameraman counted him down, pointed to him, and Juxson looked into the camera.

"*Hollywood Exposed* has just learned that acclaimed documentary filmmaker Nigel Daw, while shooting a documentary on the small peculiar desert town of Percy, California, has shot some extraordinary footage of a strange creature. Daw describes the creature as half-human and half something else!" *Hollywood Exposed* anchor, Blaze Reed, cut in. "'Something else'? Jerry, is Nigel Daw there?"

"Right here, Blaze."

Nigel Daw stepped into frame in front of the camera. He was still covered with "blood."

"Mr. Daw, I see you cut yourself shaving for this interview."

"Quite humorous, Mr. Reed. I see you're still a Tinsel Town tramp, working Hollywood and Vine, no doubt."

"The viewers should know that Nigel Daw and I go way back and love to kid each other. Tell us what's going on there in Percy, Nigel."

"Yes. We shot some amazing footage of something that I would wager no human being has witnessed before, possibly a mutation of some kind. Perhaps some sort of missing link. I have absolutely stunning footage. As you know, we have been here for several months putting together a magnificent documentary on the town of Percy, something that has never been done before, which I find unfathomable, because this place is bizarre."

Blaze Reed looked at his notes and chimed in. "For those who don't know, and I'm sure many do not, Percy is a very very small town located somewhere east of Victorville. It's not even on most maps. Victorville is where they have the Roy Rogers and Dale Evans Museum. Isn't that right, Mr. Daw?"

"I hope so," Daw replied, not giving a damn. Behind the reporter and Nigel Daw, the townspeople started gathering and looking up at the sky. The Digby orb, followed by Marty and Bink in their saucer, flew by but none of the townspeople cared. They were waiting for something else.

"What's happening there behind you?" Blaze Reed asked.

"Pan over, Lou," Jerry Juxson instructed his cameraman.

The camera panned right so the television audience could see the crowd looking up at the sky. Many in the crowd were pointing at something high above their heads, and it was clear that they were very excited about whatever it was. Blaze Reed addressed Daw. "Nigel, you're probably very familiar with the people of Percy, known as the Percy People, by now. What's going on there?"

"Oh, that's the evening gathering of the Percy Welcoming Committee."

"And who are they welcoming?" Reed asked.

Daw said, "Well, they call him 'Billy'. Your viewers and the rest of the people on this rock who aren't completely insane like these people are, know 'Billy' as the moon. Here in Percy they like being on a first-name basis with planets and stars. It makes them feel special."

Suddenly the Percy Welcoming Committee started cheering wildly, jumping up and down, waving frantically at the sky, and shouting, "HOWDY BILLY! WE LOVE YOU BILLY! WELCOME BACK TO PERCY!" Several of the Percy People were so overwhelmed with emotion at seeing "Billy" that they burst into tears of sheer joy and then fainted. Mr. Percy ran up to the reporter, ecstatic. Mr. Percy looked into the camera and it was quite obvious that he was in total rapture. "BILLY'S HERE! BILLY'S HERE! I AIN'T SEEN THAT SON OF A BITCH ALL DAY!" He let out a hoot and a holler and ran away.

"Interesting place with interesting people," Reed commented. "Now tell us more about your monster, Mr. Daw."

"As you so astutely pointed out earlier, Mr. Reed, I'm a bit bloody. While working on the documentary, we, or rather *I* was brutally and viciously attacked by this creature. They're only flesh wounds, but it was a horrifying ordeal. Horrifying and yet fascinating simultaneously. That means 'at the same time' for your viewers. Therefore, I have decided to follow the road where it leads me, and shall now focus my documentary on this very dangerous and mysterious creature."

Reed addressed his field reporter. "And Jerry, I understand Nigel Daw has consented to let us show our viewers a glimpse of his footage of the… uh…Percy Monster."

"Yes, he has, Blaze. Here we go." He spoke into his microphone to the engineer in the OB van. "Roll that, Abel."

In the home office of his compound, Nick Nero's father, Mafia boss Don Neroni, happened to be watching the show. He leaned in close and menacingly to his television screen watching the few recorded moments of "The Percy Monster" attacking Nigel Daw. The Don knew exactly what and who he was looking at. His fist tightened around his walking stick and he called to Angelo, "Pack my bag and bring the limo around. We're going to Percy."

CHAPTER 8

It was a beautiful sunny day on Malibu Beach. Surfers were surfing, volleyball players were playing volleyball, bathers were bathing, and some guys were pretending to read newspapers with the sports section covering their crotches when in reality they were looking at broads in bikinis and shaking hands with the milkman (if you know what I mean). A group of gorgeous girls in string bikinis were watching a musclehead lifting weights and flexing.

"What a perfect day!" one of the girls said. "The sun isn't shy, great-looking guys, and *more* great-looking guys! Nothing could ruin this day!"

With that, Henry Mancini's "Peter Gunn" disrupted the beach sounds as Private Detectives Sheldon Danger and Maximus Moore stepped onto the sand. Max was struggling to carry two lounger beach chairs, a beach umbrella, a six-pack of beer, Sheldon's *Detective Magazine*, and a brand new boom box which was playing the "Peter Gunn" theme. Sheldon carried nothing. They were both wearing their trench coats and shades, so they stood out like soar thumbs (complete loons) surrounded by lots of flesh and skimpy bathing suits. Danger stopped at the girls. He snapped his fingers. Max dropped everything and pressed a button on the boom box. The music stopped.

"This looks like a nice spot, Max," Sheldon said.

Max set up the beach chairs and shoved the umbrella in the sand. Sheldon lay back in his chair. Max handed him a beer and the *Detective Magazine* which Sheldon opened and read aloud from. "Listen to this one, Max. 'Her well-groomed lover who could play sax, braid hair, communicate with wolves, fix motorcycles, and make things out of wood, thrust his massive throbbing swizzle stick into her quivering womanhood while pieces of her late husband rested quietly on the new ivory shag rug. After the sizzling love session, the pretty bleached-blonde slut queen dragged the remains of her late husband's body out to the shiny new car, and placed them carefully in the spacious trunk next to her brand new jumper cables. Then she went back to get his mangled legs and a cool drink of pink lemonade…'."

"She sounds like a fun date," Max quipped, using up his annual quip. Sheldon tossed Max the magazine. Max flipped through and pulled out a pair of cardboard glasses with red and white spiraled paper lenses. "Look at this, Boss. They give you a free pair of X-ray specs in the magazine!"

"Keep 'em Max."

Max was filled with excitement, "For real, Boss?!"

"For real," Sheldon said, adding to Max's excitement.

"You're the best, Sheldon Danger. And thanks again for the new boom box," Max beamed.

"You earned it, Max," Sheldon said. "I'm deducting the cost of the X-ray specs and the boom box from your salary."

The girls began to converse about the musclehead lifting weights and flexing just behind Danger and Moore. Throughout their conversation, Sheldon thought they were talking about him and reveled in the praise.

"He's gorgeous! Bet he's great in bed!" one girl noted.

Sheldon winked at Max who gave him the thumbs up.

"I'll bet he's great *anywhere*!" another girl said.

Sheldon nodded in agreement. A third girl who wore faculty glasses and was clearly the most intelligent girl on Malibu Beach because she wore faculty glasses said, "You two are so shallow. What about brains and personality?"

The second girl said, "He's got all that in his crotch."

All the girls giggled as both Sheldon and Max stared at Sheldon's crotch. They stared at Sheldon's crotch for seven full minutes which is an extremely long time. Stare at your own crotch for seven full minutes to see how long it is (the time, not the crotch). Your neck will hurt too. I tested it. I personally test everything that goes into this book. You can't write the greatest novel ever written and not test things. Everything has to be accurate and factual. Anyway, Sheldon addressed the girls. "Ladies, I'm overwhelmed that you're overwhelmed by me. It's understandable. I overwhelm myself sometimes. Although I appreciate your compliments,

I'm here on business, not pleasure. Sex on the beach can be fun, but I already got sand in my shoes and it really annoys me. Not as much as Max here annoys me, but damn near close."

Max took off Sheldon's shoes and emptied out the sand as Sheldon continued. "Sweet things, I'm Private Detective Sheldon Danger, and this...this is Maximus Moore, the result of a passionate one night stand between a sloth and a Sea-Monkey. Show 'em the photo, Max."

Max had on the X-ray specs over his shades and was looking at the girls, grinning from ear to ear. He was mesmerized. Sheldon snatched the X-ray specs off Max's face.

"You're embarrassing me, Max. I gave you these hoping it would make you a better person, and you've let me down. I'm very disappointed. Now show these lovely ladies the photo of The Chinaman and redeem yourself."

Max held up the photo of The Chinaman. As he did, Sheldon quickly slipped on the X-ray specs and looked at the girls, grinning ear to ear.

"How come *you* get to wear the X-ray specs, Boss?" Max asked. And it was a damned good question. Sheldon attempted to answer while still wearing the X-ray specs and still fixed on the girls.

"Because I'm on a hot Max, case. I'm the world's private greatest detective, remember?" He took off the X-ray specs and got down to business. "Any of you tempting tomatoes ever see this yak before? The one in the picture, not the one holding it. I have it on the QT he kills time here. And by the way girls, I think we could all use a shower to get this sand off."

The intelligent girl with the faculty glasses answered, "I've seen him here, usually with a girl. She always has a veil or a scarf hiding her face. Like that."

She pointed to an old woman who was wearing a ragged black mourning dress with a veil hiding her face heading toward them. The old woman hobbled over to Sheldon. She spoke with a heavy Chinese accent.

"Do you like Chinese food, Private Detective Sheldon Danger?"

Sheldon scowled, "None of your business, Granny. Get lost!"

The old woman was getting frustrated because the world's greatest detective wasn't getting the message. She said, "Why don't you come to my place and let me cook you my specialty, *PEKING DUCK!*"

Sheldon snarled, "Because Grandma, we'll get to your place and you'll want to use me as your ticket to ecstasy, and frankly, I'd rather take that trip with Max than with you. And the thought of Max squealing like a blue ribbon winner at the Putnam County Fair makes me seasick on dry land. Now beat it before I change my mind."

"I have no idea what you just said, Boss," Max said.

Sheldon shrugged. "I don't know either, Max. I wasn't listening."

Screams pierced the Malibu Beach air. Danger rolled up his *Detective Magazine* into a makeshift telescope and scanned the beach. After a few passes he finally saw frantic bathers fleeing from a shark's fin and whimpered, "It's a shark!"

Danger and Moore whipped out their guns and took wild potshots at the shark, hitting everything but the shark. They hit inner tubes, children's float toys, surfboards, rubber rafts, all kinds of things that weren't meant to get shot. They were sinking bathers right and left. The bathers all turned and glared at the detectives. In response, Sheldon and Max held up their IDs which of course no one could see. "Everything's under control, folks," Sheldon assured them, "you've got Danger and Moore on the case, and we're tickled pink to be here!"

Suddenly the shark emerged from the ocean, sprouted four little legs, and walked up on shore. Sheldon said sort of nervously, "I think you got him mad, Max, and I don't mean the movie. He's looking right at us."

The shark's mouth opened and from inside a maladjusted dwarf with a Napoleon complex and a latex fetish fired a speargun. The old woman started running away. The spear ripped through her mourning dress and flew into the photo of The Chinaman. The old woman disappeared behind a dune and the shark returned to the sea. Sheldon, a bit shaken, asked, "Was that a land shark, Max?"

"No doubt about it, Boss," Max replied. "I could tell by the tough spiny slate-gray skin, the separate lateral gill openings, and the slender rounded body with the mouth on the underside. Most sharks are fish-eaters, but some will attack man. I think the one we just saw is the kind that attacks man."

Sheldon was annoyed. "You just wasted several moments of my life that I'll never get back, Max. Knee yourself in the groin."

Max tried repeatedly to knee himself in the groin but only managed to raise his knee slightly toward his waist. Frustrated, he said, "Sorry Boss, I just can't do it. I think it's physically impossible for someone to knee themselves in the groin." And he was right. Try it. I have.

"Then allow me to help you," Sheldon said, and did. Max hit the sand holding his groin and rethinking the case.

"There doesn't seem to be any opportunity for progress or advancement at this point," he pointed out.

Sheldon was thoroughly confused. "What?"

"We're at a dead end."

"Your brain is at a dead end!" Sheldon snapped. "I'm not. Now grab the gear and let's go."

He started walking away. Max staggered to his feet and called after him. "I thought you said that if I carried the stuff here that you would carry it back."

"I lied," Sheldon admitted publicly. "Besides Max, I'm more important than you are. You're just a sidekick like Robin was to Batman, or Tonto was to the Lone Ranger."

"You right, Kemosabe, me sorry," Max muttered.

Sheldon sneered, "Don't let it happen again. And don't call me Kemosabe; the Lone Ranger was a masked dork."

Sheldon walked away. Max gathered up the stuff and followed him. The old woman peeked out from behind the dune and lifted her veil as she watched them leave. It was The Chinaman.

Later that day at the Danger and Moore Detective Agency, Irma was sitting at her desk, snapping gum between her teeth, doing her nails, and jabbering into the phone: "Alphabet soup, darling. It works wonders. That way you can spell out what you want him to do to you…Messy shmessy! As long as he gets the message." There was a loud knock at the door. "I gotta go. It's Grand Central Station here." She hung up and yelled, "TRY TURNING THE DOORKNOB LIKE THE GENIUS YOU ARE!"

A Chinese delivery boy entered carrying cartons of Chinese food. He set the cartons down and began to rap:

"Delivery for Detective Sheldon Danger,
Chinese food from a perfect stranger"

Irma was not happy. "He's in his office with Mr. Moore. Did they order this without asking me if I wanted something? I'm not a machine, you know. I get hungry too."

She reached for the food and the delivery boy quickly pulled the cartons away from her. He continued rapping:

"Don't lose your cool, go eat from a manger,
I give *only* to Sheldon Danger"

"Whatever blows your Mao suit up," Irma sneered as she shoved the delivery boy into Sheldon's office. Sheldon was moping. Max was reading the new *Detective Magazine*.

"Listen to this one, Boss. Maybe this will cheer you up. 'Not a trace of the A-student could be found anywhere until detectives looked in her biology professor's desk. Inside the top drawer, next to an ink blotter and a Slinky, they found her lovely face, wearing a frown'."

Irma interrupted, "Your Chinese food is here. Don't choke."

Sheldon scowled, "I didn't order any Chinese food. Did you Max?"

Max's head was buried in the magazine: "Nope. I'm on a very strict diet where I can't eat dog."

The delivery boy continued rapping:

"Chinese food is good for you
Listen close and find the clue
chicken chow mein, wonton soup,
pork fried lice, and here's the scoop...
fortune cookies, and just for luck..."

He leaned into Sheldon's face

"a special serving of ***PEKING DUCK!***"

He winked at Sheldon

"Chinese food makes me queasy," Sheldon said. "Take it back."

The delivery boy, Max, and Irma exchanged glances. Once again, the world's greatest detective wasn't getting the message. The delivery boy tried again.

"Don't be a fool! Don't be a schmuck!
I think you should try ***THE PEKING DUCK!***"

"No thanks kid. Chinese food and I don't get along. Don't take it personally."

The delivery boy had enough.

"Do you need a building to fall on you?
Skywriting planes? Rockets too?
Billboards, posters, neon signs?
Open your eyes, man, are you blind?!"

Max suggested, "You should try the Peking Duck, Boss."
Sheldon started getting mad. "I didn't order any of this! I won't pay for it!"

The delivery boy was exasperated.

"It's all paid for. The meal is free.
Just give me a tip and I'm history."

"Who paid for it?" Sheldon asked.
Irma shrugged, "Not me. On my salary I can only afford alphabet soup."
Sheldon said, "Well, I never could pass up a free meal, so what the hell? Even if it does rip my insides apart, free is free. Let's see what we have here... (He started opening the cartons.)...chicken chow mein, wonton soup, pork fried lice, fortune cookies, and Peking-"

It hit him like a ton of bricks and he rushed the delivery boy toward the door speaking frantically: "Thanks for dropping by kid. You're a great delivery boy and I love those Godzilla movies. Here's your tip, never put anything in a hole you can't see into. Here's some money too." He handed the delivery boy some loose change. The boy frowned at the change and rapped a reply.

"Oh wow! Seventeen cents sure is a lot!
I think I'll go and buy a yacht!
It feels so good to be so rich
Drop dead you cheap son of a-"

Sheldon tossed the delivery boy out, slammed the door, and locked it. He rushed back into his office and dumped the food out on the desk.

"I'm not cleaning that up," Irma made very clear.

Sheldon opened the last carton and carefully pulled out The Peking Duck: a magnificent dazzling diamond-encrusted golden statuette of an Asian duck with slanted eyes and a conical rice hat. As he pulled it from the carton, a spectacular resounding choir sang, accompanied by a brilliant blast of Heavenly light from above which shone directly on The Peking Duck. This thing was really a big deal, not as big as this book will be in the history of literature, but pretty damned close. Sheldon, Max, and Irma looked heavenward for the source of all this hoopla, saw nothing, and then gazed, mesmerized, at The Peking Duck. Max marveled mightily.

"Look at all those diamonds, Boss! That thing must be worth a king's ransom!"

Irma shuddered. "I'm not sure, but for the first time in my life I think I'm having an orgasm."

Sheldon quickly moved away from Irma and said, "The fact that we got the duck means The Chinaman's either dead or on his way there."

"How do you know that?" Irma asked.

Sheldon ran his fingers over the statuette. "No one would dump a piece like this unless they were scared."

Max cracked open a fortune cookie. "I love fortune cookies," he said looking at the strip of paper inside. "Mine says I will flirt with fame."

"And fame will reject you, just like everyone else you flirt with," Sheldon smirked.

"What does yours say, Boss?" Max asked Smirking Sheldon. Sheldon shook his head.

"I don't believe in that stuff, Max. You know who writes those fortunes? Little drunken Chinese midgets who just sit in a basement all day, drink themselves blind, and make that crap up for jerks like you who believe it."

"Just try one for fun, Boss."

Sheldon shrugged, "Alright, just for fun, Max. But this is the last time I ever do anything for you. Plus, I'm deducting the cost of my time and trouble from your pay." He cracked open a fortune cookie and read his fortune aloud, "'Meet The Fat Man at Barney's Bathhouse ASAP'...a sap?! Your cookie just called me a sap, Max! No one calls me a sap! Not a man, not a cookie, no one!" He took off his shoe and smashed the fortune cookie to bits with the heel.

"That's *A, S, A, P,* Boss," Max explained. "It means 'as soon as possible'. Meet The Fat Man at Barney's Bathhouse as soon as possible."

Sheldon shuddered, but not like Irma shuddered. "How come there's always some fat guy involved in these things? Irma, take the rest of the day off, and while you're at it stash the duck where no one will ever find it. Your bedroom's a safe bet. Max, go with her, no detours. Go straight to her place. Then I want you to check on Miss Holliday. Try to shake her down a little. She knows more than she's letting on. Take the fire escape, I don't want you seen."

"Right, Boss," Max said. "What will you do?"

Sheldon Danger caught his reflection in his Aunt Penelope's stolen mirror and gave himself a knowing wink.

"I'm expecting company. I got a feeling that duck doesn't travel alone."

"Boss, did you know that Chinese royalty used silver chopsticks to detect poison in their food in case someone was trying to poison them? The poison would turn the silver black, and that's how they knew."

"That's interesting, Max. It's too bad that I don't care. Now get moving."

Priceless Peking Duck in hand, Irma and Max crawled out a window and onto the fire escape. Sheldon leaned back in his chair, propped his feet up on his desk, and thumbed through his *Detective Magazine*. As he expected, he heard glass shattering and Angelo and Toto burst into the office. Sheldon didn't react at all. He just kept looking at the magazine.

"Where is it?" Angelo snarled.

"Down the hall; second door on your right. You gotta flush twice. It doesn't work very well ever since Max unloaded that spicy burrito. And don't leave any souvenirs," Sheldon warned, not taking his eyes off the magazine. Angelo and Toto lifted Sheldon out of his chair and hurled him against the wall. The magazine went flying.

"You made me lose my place! I was reading a story about a dumb Mafia thug who writes crappy poetry."

They lifted Sheldon to his feet and Toto slugged him in the gut. Doubled-over in pain, Sheldon gasped, "Your little tough guy act doesn't impress me, Ladies. The only thing that impresses me is me."

"Where's the duck, Dead Duck?" Toto snarled.

Sheldon looked at Angelo through dancing eyes. "Is your girlfriend threatening me, Maria? If I were you I'd leave right now before I get mad, because if I get mad, somebody's gonna get hurt!"

Toto slugged Sheldon in the jaw and he hit the floor. From the floor, Sheldon warned gasping, "You girls are really beginning to upset me." He clawed his way to the phone and struggled to dial.

"Who do you think you're calling?" Angelo growled.

"An ambulance," Sheldon wheezed, about to collapse. "You and your blushing bride there are gonna need one."

Two hours and eleven minutes later in the waiting area of Southern California Hospital in Culver City, Sheldon's attending doctor walked over to Max and Irma. Max jumped to his feet. Irma did her nails.

"Will he live, Doc?" Max asked, not completely sure of the answer he wanted to hear.

"He's alright," the doctor said, "just badly bruised. Your Mr. Danger is quite the hero, you know. He told me how he beat up those thugs who attacked him and prevented them from taking over the country; very impressive."

"Yeah, we're thrilled. Can we see our hero?" Irma asked while chewing Wrigley's Juicy Fruit gum which was introduced to the world in 1893.

World's greatest private detective (according to him anyway) Sheldon Danger was in his hospital bed, bandaged and bruised, and wearing his trench coat over his hospital gown. An attractive nurse was taking his blood pressure.

"Your blood pressure's a little high, Mr. Danger," she said.

"That's 'cause of you, doll," Sheldon winked. "Let's play doctor when you get off duty."

"With *you?!*" asked the nurse laughing hysterically. Irma and Max entered the room and Sheldon got loud when he saw them. "NO! I will NOT have sex with you no matter how much you pay me! Now go empty some bedpans, *tramp!*"

The nurse stormed out. Irma and Max approached the bed.

"I see your personality escaped injury," Irma grinned.

Sheldon ignored the remark. "Did you stash the duck?"

Max handed Sheldon a magazine. "It's safe and sound. I got you this *Ellery Queen*. There's a great story in it called "Girl in a Dumpster" about a girl who lives in a dumpster and comes out at night to kill and eat transvestite midgets."

Sheldon glanced at the *Ellery Queen*, "Very thoughtful of you, Max. I'm docking you two weeks pay for reading my magazine. After you two left, some thrill-seekers came looking for the duck, like I figured. I taught them not to mess with Sheldon Danger."

Irma looked him over. "I can see that, amongst the bandages and bruises. I'm missing my soap opera." She kissed her palm, slapped him hard on the forehead with it, and left.

Max said, "Boss, I got a tip that The Fat Man is feeling heat from a silent partner, but I don't know who it is. Haven't heard from Miss Holliday either. Not a word."

As if on cue, Lana Holliday rushed into the room and fawned all over Sheldon, "Oh Darling! I rushed right over from shopping when I heard what happened!"

Sheldon turned to Max. "You see that, Max. I can find her just lying here. That's why I'm great and you're not."

As Lana became extremely affectionate with Sheldon, Max picked up the *Ellery Queen* and thumbed through it. In a rare move, Sheldon pushed Lana off of him.

"I don't mean to change the subject, buttercup, but this case is getting a little too rough. People are getting knocked off right and left, so I think it's time to turn the whole mess over to the authorities. Let them handle it. I quit. I'm going to Rio for some downtime."

Hearing that, Max started dancing around the room and singing Peter Allen's 1976 song "I Go to Rio" which hit number one on the charts in Australia according to the Kent Music Report. It only made it to number 30 in Belgium. It most likely hit number one in Australia because Peter Allen was Australian. In that case, this book should make the New York Times best sellers list since I lived in New York from 1979 to 1981. Allen was married to Liza Minnelli from 1967 to 1974. I wasn't, and I'm pretty happy about that. Sheldon interrupted Max's rendition.

"I didn't know you were a singer, Max."

Max explained, "It's just a hobby, Boss. I'm not a professional or anything."

"No kidding," Sheldon said. He turned his attention back to Lana. "Like I was saying, angel cake, I'm off the case. I'm going to Rio."

He removed his gun from under his pillow and glared at Max who started singing "I Go to Rio" again. He aimed the gun at Max who quickly noticed and decided to immediately give up his singing career. Femme fatale Lana Holliday was desperate and made it known.

"Find The Peking Duck and I'll give you a bonus of five hundred thousand dollars. And you can do whatever you want with me. My body will be yours to use any way you want."

"Five hundred thousand dollars?!" Sheldon questioned and exclaimed ignoring the rest of the offer and getting dressed. "Rio can bite me."

"What would you do with all that money, Boss?" Max asked because he really wanted to know. Sheldon Danger answered with a passion and a sensitivity that Maximus Moore, his partner and childhood friend, had never witnessed before.

"Max, everywhere I look I see poverty, misery, suffering, and hunger. I see people sleeping on the streets, wearing rags, and digging through garbage for something to eat. I see people cold and lonely with nowhere to turn. It breaks my heart. I've always wanted to be in a position to do something about it, so I would take that money and buy a nice big house in the country where I wouldn't have to see any of that. Let's go. We got a meeting with The Fat Man."

Lana was startled. "The Fat Man?!"

Sheldon looked at her. "You know him Tootsie Roll? You look like I struck a nerve."

Lana, not hiding it very well, lied through her bonded teeth.

"No, I don't know him. I think I saw him once in a movie where he played Sydney Greenstreet."

Sheldon Danger's private detective senses tingled and he grew very suspicious. "I guess it's my good looks that shake you up, sugar angel. They do it to me too. When I take a shower I can't take my hands off myself." He turned to Max. "Let's lose this joint, Max. We got work to do."

Danger and Moore were walking toward the bathhouse when the dwarfs who were once disguised as a shark started following them, this time disguised as fireplugs.

"We make a great team, don't we, Boss?" Max asked for no reason whatsoever.

"Sure Max," Sheldon said. "We're like Dudley Do-Right and his horse who was so insignificant that his name was 'Horse'. You're the horse named Horse."

"Actually," Max said, "Horse always helped Dudley Do-Right get out of trouble, and Nell loved Horse, not Dudley."

"Maybe in your ridiculous cartoon world, Max, but not mine."

They arrived at the bathhouse and read the sign out front

"BARNEY'S BATHHOUSE
Where the customer always comes first!"

Sheldon Danger's private detective senses tingled again and he had the feeling that things weren't exactly kosher in Denmark. "Let's split up here, Max. I got a funny feeling you're about to walk into a trap, and I don't want to be around when you do." Max took off. A boy who collected root beer bottles as a hobby came by struggling to walk several large dogs on leashes. He worked part time as a dog walker to make extra money because being a male prostitute at his age would have been inappropriate. Sheldon stopped the kid and slipped him five bucks. "Take those dogs over to those fireplugs."

"Sure thing mister!" the boy said. As he headed the dogs toward the fireplugs (which they were eager to get to) he mumbled to himself, "At least he didn't want a blow job."

Sheldon watched as the dogs soaked the fireplugs and the dwarfs within, smiled wickedly, and entered the bathhouse. An attendant handed Sheldon a towel which he wrapped around the waist of his trench coat. The attendant cautioned him sternly, "If you charge anyone for favors I'll throw you out. Sauna's on the right." Sheldon headed down the hall to the sauna. He opened the door and saw that it was full of huge fat men sitting around in opened towels, sweating like pigs, and not hiding their noises. "So this is where Macy's stores the floats," Sheldon remarked rudely, but with good reason. Like the Red Sea, the fat men parted, and The Fat Man stepped forward. "I'll save you a lot of time and trouble Mr. Danger," he said, "I am The Fat Man."

"A skinny little thing like you?" Sheldon asked.

"Take a massage with me, Mr. Danger," The Fat Man insisted. "I'd like to see you in private."

"Who wouldn't?" Sheldon asked rhetorically like a putz.

Inside the massage room The Fat Man and Sheldon were face down on massage tables. Sheldon remained in his trench coat. Angelo and Toto disguised as geisha girls (very big and ugly geisha girls) started massaging The Fat Man. Max, also disguised as a geisha girl and not an overly attractive one, started massaging Sheldon who was unaware that the geisha girl was Max. Sheldon started moaning with pleasure.

"You're pretty good, baby. Your hands feel almost as good as mine on me, my little china doll."

"I thoroughly enjoy a good rubdown. Don't you, Mr. Danger?" The Fat Man asked.

Sheldon got serious. "Let's skip the dinner and dancing and get into the sack. What do you want?"

"The Peking Duck, Mr. Danger. And before we dabble in any dinner and dancing as you so eloquently put it, I know the statuette is in your possession and I will stop at nothing to acquire it. I'm prepared to offer you the generous sum of eight hundred dollars. Certainly a man who dresses like you could use the money."

"No dice, Twiggy. I know what it's worth. And as far as the way I dress, at least I don't have to get my clothes at Circus Tents "R" Us." He turned his attention to Max, his geisha girl. "Alright sexy, work your way down to my stick shift and drive my hot rod."

If this were a movie, Max would look right at us. Luckily (I guess) at that very moment the attendant came into the room and snapped at geisha girl Max. "You got a John waiting at the Hilton, room #708. He's a Republican senator. He likes it rough and to be called 'Little Miss Muffet'."

"But, I'm busy-" said Max in a bad falsetto voice.

"Move it or you're back on the streets!" the attendant snapped.

Max took his leave and Sheldon felt blue. "That doll stiffed me in many ways."

"My apologies, Mr. Danger," The Fat Man said. "Perhaps you'd like one of mine."

Sheldon looked at The Fat Man's geisha girls, Angelo and Toto in drag, and declined. "No offense, but your girls could soften tungsten. Mine was a real dish."

Sheldon got off the massage table and sat in a chair facing The Fat Man. "I have a couple of rejects from Munchkinland shadowing me, yours?"

The Fat Man chuckled sinisterly, "No Sir. You amuse me. Little people don't fill me up. Mr. Danger I have been searching for The Peking Duck for thirty-two years now. My quest has taken me from one end of the globe to the other. I've spent half of my life on airplanes, traveling everywhere, searching for it. Many lives have been lost, armies have clashed, and empires have crumbled because of that statuette. Are you familiar with its history, Mr. Danger?"

Sheldon shook his head, "I'm still trying to figure out how you fit in a plane."

The Fat Man began passionately, "In the year 1644-"

Sheldon mumbled, "Here we go." He pulled the *Ellery Queen* out of his trench coat and started flipping through it. The Fat Man continued, "-a bejeweled statuette of a duck given to the Emperor by the king of Siam-"

** (Listen, the history of The Peking Duck is really long and involved and goes through several centuries. I really don't want to have to write it, so if you're that interested look it up yourself. I'll just cut through this part and pick it up in the 1800s.)

"And the statuette resurfaced and was presented to the Dowager Empress Tzu-hsi as a token of his affection," The Fat Man continued.

"He was porking her," Sheldon interrupted, half asleep.

"Precisely," The Fat Man went on. "The duck was stolen from the Empress by a mysterious bandit in 1874 and its fate remained a mystery until 1957 when it was discovered at a garage sale in New Jersey and returned to Peking where it was placed on permanent exhibition. In 1973 The Chinaman came forward and claimed to be the only surviving descendant of Tzu-hsi. He demanded the statuette. When he was refused, he resorted to stealing the duck from the exhibit and fled to the United States where-"

"LOOK AT THE SIZE OF THAT BUFFET!" Sheldon pointed excitedly. The Fat Man, Angelo, and Toto turned to look and Sheldon made tracks. He was walking away from the bathhouse when Max, still dressed as a geisha, ran up next to him. "Hey, sweet thang," Sheldon winked. "Couldn't get enough of me, huh? Let's find a cheap hotel and see if Tom Bodett left the light on for us."

"It's me, Boss," Max confided.

Sheldon froze in his tracks and stared at Max the geisha girl for the most uncomfortable few moments of his life. Then he shook Max's hand vigorously. "Congratulations Max! You passed the Honey West Private Detective Endurance Test! That's why I called you 'sweet thang', because honey's sweet! And I said those things I said when you were massaging me because I didn't want to blow your cover! I was protecting you, Max, and for that you should be eternally grateful. You're like a sister to me, which reminds me, how was your date at the Hilton you cheap floozy?"

"I made twelve bucks. He's a Republican senator so he wanted me to ride him like a horse and make him drink from the trough. Except there was no trough, there was only-"

Sheldon cut him off, "I get the disgusting picture, Max. Let's get to the office."

Meanwhile, in the office where Danger and Moore were headed to, Irma was tied to her desk with the telephone cord as the dwarfs were ransacking the place.

"You miniature morons are wasting your time," Irma scolded. "There's no duck here; just one hot sexy woman who couldn't put up a fight even if she wanted to. You could run your nasty tiny little hands all over me and there's nothing I could do about it. You think because you have a gorgeous woman in a totally helpless position that you can have your way with me, you tiny little sex-starved bastards."

"It's not here," one dwarf said. "What'll we tell The Fat Man?" The second dwarf thought a minute and said, "We tell him that it's not here. You should have gagged her. I've never been so unhorny in my life. Let's get out of here."

The dwarfs headed out the door. The office was a wreck from the ransacking. Irma called out after them, "I'M NOT CLEANING UP THIS MESS!" A few minutes later Danger and Moore entered the office, completely oblivious to the place being in shambles. They walked right past Irma tied to her desk and into Sheldon's private office. Max started removing his geisha girl outfit and Sheldon sat at his desk, propped his feet up, and opened the *Ellery Queen*. Suddenly they stopped abruptly, looked at each other, and rushed to the outer office. Sheldon looked around at the mess in disbelief and glared at his tied up secretary. "What did you do to this place?!"

"I redecorated," she said, glaring back. "And then I was attacked by a couple of horny dwarfs."

"Dwarfs, huh?" Sheldon muttered. "Things are adding up."

"Before they busted in, the coroner called. He wants to see you in the morgue, and so do I. He said it was urgent."

Sheldon nodded to Max and they rushed out, leaving Irma tied to the desk.

Inside the Los Angeles County Morgue, Max was looking at the corpse of a beautiful woman lying on an embalming table. Sheldon was glaring at him and warned, "If you think one thought that I think you're thinking I'll kill you right here so you won't have to travel far."

The coroner walked in and ushered Sheldon over to a body refrigeration unit. Sheldon returned to Max, grabbed him by the collar, and pulled him along. The coroner explained the situation. "Danger, there was a bad crack-up last night near Malibu. A car went over a cliff and exploded. The body was burned to a crisp. We salvaged what we could and were able to determine from the shape of the facial bones that the victim was Asian. The pelvis was found some distance from the wreckage. It was male."

"What you're saying is that the victim was an Asian male," Sheldon deduced.

"Exactly," the coroner said. Sheldon gloated. Max gave him the thumbs up. The coroner continued. "We weren't able to identify the body until we found the teeth, which were located two miles from the crash site. The castings we took matched the X-rays. No doubt, it's The Chinaman." The coroner pulled open a drawer of the body refrigeration unit. There was a big black burnt toe with a tag on it. Sheldon passed out and Max caught him before he hit the floor. He slowly gained consciousness and groggily looked at Max.

"What happened?"

"You fainted, Boss."

"I didn't faint, Max. I took a quick nap." Sheldon turned to the coroner. "How did you know to contact me?"

"Richard Munson and I went to medical school together. I've known Lana Holliday for years. I don't know anyone who hasn't bumped nasties with her. She told me that she hired you and Mr. Moore to find Richard's killers and I knew they killed Richard for The Chinaman's X-rays. Anything I can do, I will."

At that very moment, as if someone was writing it, Lana Holliday slinked in and sensuously caressed Sheldon's still-bruised face. She air-kissed Max and the coroner like some girls used to do in ancient Greece.

"I'm getting a little jealous of the Grim Reaper, cupcake. You spend more time with him than you do with me," Sheldon said sardonically, suspiciously, and skeptically, sort of.

"Very cute, Sheldon Danger," Lana grinned, swatting him on the tushy. "I came to see what's left of The Chinaman for myself."

"There's nothing to see, Lana," the coroner said. "The body's in such bad shape there wasn't anything left for the insects."

"I know what he's talking about," Max interjected, "and it's not pretty."

The coroner added, "Not to us, Mr. Moore, but we can't be so presumptuous as to say how the insects feel. They wouldn't do it if they didn't enjoy it."

"Do *what?* Enjoy *what?* What are you two talking about?" Sheldon asked, getting aggravated.

The coroner explained, "You see, Mr. Danger, when someone dies outdoors as parts of The Chinaman did, within ten minutes flies lay thousands of eggs in their eyes, nose, ears, and mouth; every orifice of the head. Twelve hours after that, the eggs hatch, and maggots start eating the tissue. Twelve hours later beetles arrive and consume the dry skin. Within forty-eight hours spiders, millipedes, and mites show up to consume the maggots and the beetles. It's all quite grotesque, like a nauseating ballet of horror."

Sheldon went white. Max was looking over at the attractive woman on the embalming table and failed to catch Sheldon as he hit the floor with a heavy thud. Lana slapped Max who snapped out of it, reached down, and picked Sheldon up off the floor. "You okay, Boss? You fainted again."

"I didn't faint, Max," Sheldon said groggily. "I was formulating an amazing plan to flush out The Chinaman's partners. I know what we'll do. Let's wrap this up."

The following night the world's greatest private detective (according to him anyway) Sheldon Danger put his plan to flush out The Chinaman's partners into action. With permission from CEO Jeffrey David Pasternak who was great at playing Mexican Train (and once had a fling with an inflatable passion doll named Roxanne) to use a room at Southern California Hospital in Culver City, Maximus Moore was propped up in bed with his entire body wrapped in bandages over his trench coat. Lana was finishing up wrapping his head as Sheldon Danger looked on.

"Can I listen to my boom box? I think "Peter Gunn" is playing," Max asked.

"Not now," Sheldon said. "It's quiet time. I spread the word with a few of your street rats that The Chinaman survived the crash and is here. Whoever knocked him off that cliff will want to finish the job."

"That means they'll kill me, Boss," Max said, a little concerned and rightfully so.

"Are you The Chinaman, Max?"

"No, but if they think I am-"

Sheldon cut him off and snapped at Lana, "Why does it take ten years to cover his mouth?!"

Lana quickly wrapped Max's mouth and continued to bandage his head until he was completely wrapped head-to-toe. Sheldon turned out the lights and hid in the closet with Lana. Moments later The Fat Man disguised as a doctor, Angelo and Toto as orderlies and the dwarfs as tiny female nurses snuck into the room. Sheldon peeked out of the closet and then turned his attention to Lana. "As long as we're here, why don't you try to find my pretend pocket watch?"

The Fat Man, Angelo, and Toto were around Max looking down at him menacingly. The dwarfs were looking *up* at him menacingly. "I don't know how he survived, Fat Man," Angelo said bewildered. "That car went off like the Fourth of July. We made sure of it."

The Fat Man smiled sinisterly, "Fortunately for you geniuses he did survive. Danger was sent a decoy." He grinned at Max. "Now, tell me Chinaman, my good Mr. Nip, where is The Peking Duck?"

Max immediately motioned toward the closet. One of the dwarfs attempted to reach the closet doorknob but couldn't. He was taller than a midget but shorter than a human. The Fat Man swatted him away and threw open the closet door to find Sheldon and Lana in a very compromising position that Gumby and Pokey would have trouble getting into.

"Well, well, well, if it isn't the great private detective Sheldon Danger caught with his pants down and his hand in the proverbial cookie jar...so to speak," The Fat Man gushed.

They all aimed their guns at Sheldon. Lana froze.

"No one told you to stop!" Sheldon snapped at Lana. Then he looked down at the second dwarf. "Do you think you could reach the call button for me, Big Guy?"

The second dwarf climbed up on the hospital bed and pressed the call button. "Thanks Goliath," Sheldon said, as he turned to The Fat Man. "The duck wasn't a decoy, Tiny. That was a ruse to get you here. My partner already returned the duck to the Ming Dynasty exhibit. You're too late and you could lose a few thousand pounds."

Suddenly the police burst in with weapons drawn, disarmed the bad guys, and cuffed them all.

"Glad you could make it Lieutenant," Sheldon said. "Max was getting nervous. Take them all away." He handed over Lana too. "This one's responsible for a trail of murder, larceny, and cases of the clap that could circle the Earth a million times over."

"I didn't want to come, Danger," the Lieutenant admitted. "I hate seeing you. But you did good. Washington will be pleased."

"Isn't he dead?" Sheldon asked.

Lana got all phony emotional all over Sheldon, "I did it all for you, my darling love!" she slobbered. Sheldon started unwrapping Max, and spoke to Lana with sensitivity and sincerity. "You wanna prove your love to me? Make some of those *Women Behind Bars* and *Women in Cages* movies. We love those movies, right guys?" Cops and crooks alike all agreed. Max, unwrapped, made a confession. "Boss, I didn't quite get The Peking Duck to the exhibit yet. I was on my way to meet the contact and there was this grand opening of a new deli and-".

"And you had to eat," Sheldon glared, cutting him off. "Where's the duck?"

Max slowly pulled his zipper down. As he did, a magnificent resounding choir sang accompanied by a brilliant blast of golden glittery Heavenly light from above. Everyone looked Heavenward for the source of all this hoopla and then everyone stared at Max's crotch. Sheldon was disgusted. Lana and the Lieutenant were thrilled as Max reached into his fly and pulled out The Peking Duck. He started to hand it to Sheldon who quickly shoved his hands into the pockets of his trench coat. "I'm not touching that thing. Give it to the Lieutenant." Max handed the priceless statuette to the Lieutenant who caressed it a little too affectionately and barked at his officers, "Alright, let's take these scamps downtown and book 'em."

Cops and crooks took their leave. Sheldon patted Max on the back. "I did it again, Max. I solved that case like the great Sheldon Danger that I am."

"You really were amazing, Boss."

"I just said that, Max, using different words. But it's nice to hear it again. And you were a good little helper, even if you didn't do anything but lie there doing nothing."

An orderly wearing thick black-framed 1950s faculty style eyeglasses, a medical mask, and a bow tie, came in carrying a tray of hospital food, set it down, and quickly exited.

"Yummy disgusting hospital food, Max! You earned it doing nothing. Enjoy it."

Max lifted up the cover of the plate, "One spaghetti noodle! And it's alive!"

"Spaghetti shouldn't be alive, Max. It should be dead. Let me see that." Sheldon leaned in close to the spaghetti noodle. "That's not a spaghetti noodle. That's a worm! And not just *any* worm. That's the calling card of-"

This time Max cut Sheldon off, "You don't mean-"

Sheldon was stunned and looked a bit frightened.

"He's back, Max. Does your new boom box, the cost of which is coming out of your salary, have a radio?"

Max turned on the radio, "Peter Gunn" was playing and the announcer broke in. "We interrupt the theme from Henry Mancini's "Peter Gunn" to bring you a special news bulletin. Notorious criminal mastermind Stanley Jerkins, known as 'Squirm' to the underworld, has escaped from California's Supermax Pelican Bay State Prison. Jerkins is considered armed and dangerous. If spotted, do not approach him. Contact the authorities immediately. Let's hope he can be captured before he strikes again." Max turned off the radio.

"He'll come looking for me, Max. I put him away," Sheldon said, somewhat fearfully.

"You put him away, Boss," Max said. "He'll come looking for you."

"I just said that, Max, only in a different order. I don't like this one bit."

Max, seeing that Sheldon was worried, changed the subject. "You know, Boss, when I saw The Fat Man dressed up like a doctor it reminded me of the story of 'The Drums of Mount Hingo', because The Fat Man looked like a mountain and he played a doctor, and there's a real doctor and a witch doctor in the story. It seems that there was a buried mountain in Africa. Very few people knew about it. The natives called it 'Mount Hingo' meaning 'Drums of Death'. The natives were very superstitious. Every night they would have a ceremony for the Great Mountain God who they called the Great Mountain God. They would make a sacrifice of one native girl and a white man, when one was available, because they thought that if they didn't, the mountain would blow up. It was really a volcano but none of them had gone past high school. One night the king of Shanolake was attacked by a king cobra. He had 30 minutes to live. He couldn't live longer because he did not have proper care. Three miles away a doctor who had come from the white country was exploring the land. Three natives captured him and brought him to the king. They told him to make the king well or they would kill him. He agreed to save the king. Twenty minutes had already gone by and the king was almost ready to cash in his chips. The doctor had no choice but to try to escape. He got away from the guards but the spearmen, who were men with spears, captured him. The king died and his son became king. The new king ordered the doctor to be thrown into a snake pit. There was a rock in the snake pit. A snake tried to bite the doctor and the doctor picked up the rock I mentioned and threw it at the snake. The snake bit into the rock, but the rock was a rock, and broke the snake's fangs. The doctor used the snake as a rope, lassoed a low-hanging tree branch which hung low over the snake pit and pulled himself out. He ran into the jungle, but the men with spears, known as the spearmen, surrounded him, captured him, and brought him before the new king. The new king had the doctor thrown into a large hole that the natives named after a white girl they had once sacrificed for the heck of it named Vivian Harper. The hole was called 'The Vivian Harper Hole'. That night, while the doctor was inside Vivian Harper's hole it got very cold. He noticed that there were some quartz and jasper rocks in the Vivian Harper Hole and rubbed them together to make a fire so he could keep warm. As he was making sparks with the rocks, one of the natives saw what he was doing and thought that the doctor had strange and mystical powers. Word spread and the doctor was looked upon as a new god. The local witch doctor who had not spent five minutes in medical school became jealous and claimed that he was a better god and doctor than the board certified doctor. A bridge was set on fire and they had to knock each other off the bridge. One was on one side of the bridge and one was on the other side. At the sound of the drum they would meet in the middle of the bridge and start fighting. The drum sounded. They both moved to the middle of the bridge. As the board certified doctor was about to take a swing at the witch doctor, the bridge collapsed, landing on all the natives and the king and everyone died."

Sheldon stared at Max. "Are you done?"

"Yes," Max said.

"What in Hell does that ridiculous absurd pointless stupid story have to do with anything?"

"Nothing," Max said. "I was just trying to distract you from being worried about Squirm."

"I appreciate it, Max. But it didn't work. It wasted everybody's time. It wasted Howard Camner's time. It wasted the reader's time. It wasted my time. But you tried to do a good thing and as usual you screwed up. Since you only had one piece of spaghetti that turned out to be a worm, I'm hungry. Let's get something to eat and figure out how to rescue Los Angeles and maybe the world, from Stanley Jerkins. He'll have this city hostage soon enough."

CHAPTER 9

With lunches packed and a full tank of fuel, The Outlaws of Asteroid #9 were soon on their way to rescue the kidnapped star maiden Zelda Borealis. They threaded their way between tremendous meteoroids and other cosmic debris to the outer rings of Shlump. They passed through the uppermost levels of Shlump's atmosphere and glided into stationary orbit. There was the usual red glow from re-entry friction, while outside the thick protective portals of the ZX-12 the Outlaws saw what at one time must have been a thriving industrious space colony. Now what was left of it smoldered in the bright light of the system's suns. Eternal fires here and there still licked at the remnants and ruins of structures. The only standing structures visible were a tremendously tall tower and a sphere. No life forms were in evidence anywhere. Slowly and cautiously they descended to the planet's surface landing the pod in a spherical sitara swamp. The Outlaws disembarked and began their perilous trek through the icky quagmire when suddenly the Digby orb streaked by just overhead followed by Marty and Bink in hot pursuit. Startled, the Outlaws dove faces-first into the swamp muck. When the orb and saucer passed, the Outlaws tried to stand up but couldn't move. At first they assumed they were simply stuck in the muck and it was preventing any movement. But then they realized, to their chagrin, that their wrists and ankles were clamped by gripping claws and projecting appendages. For the first time in ten minutes The Outlaws of Asteroid #9 were absolutely helpless and at the mercy of their captors. Quick as a cricket, Rollo Starguy, their lightning fast leader, started thinking up a plan of escape, but Rollo was not lightning fast enough; for a moment later the Outlaws were pulled down into the mire, completely submerged. *What a ghastly way to die*, they thought to themselves collectively as they felt themselves slowly and agonizingly suffocating. Just as Mr. Reaper was about to guide their spirits to the next level of the game, they were mysteriously and miraculously pulled through the muck to the shallow side of the spherical sitara swamp. They gasped frantically for air, shook the muck and yuck away from their eyes and blinked around trying to focus. They were in some sort of underground dwelling beneath Shlump's surface. Whatever or whoever had dragged them down was gone, or so it seemed. They began sliding downward; steadily, twisting and turning, on and on they went, down and down and more down. They slid for what seemed an eternity until they landed hard, tush-first, next to an underground canal. There was no sound. There was no movement. The silence was deafening. And then the still murky waters of the canal began to ripple and gurgle and sizzle, slowly at first, building to a fierce rolling boil; a time-to-put-in-the-pasta boil. Strange-looking bubbles rose to the surface and popped like a yellow sick toad giving off a smell of both Poet's Jasmine as summer turns to fall, and expired Dinty Moore beef stew that's been sitting on the shelf for nine years because the people who work at the grocery store aren't making a living and don't give enough of a crap to check expiration dates. The bubbles became larger and larger, the pops louder and louder. And then bursting out of the canal with ferocious horrifying screams popped the Moola Boola Agboos, a group of nasty looking trolls who inhabited the underground of Shlump. They were the absolutely grotesque result of several catastrophic collisions between The Evil One and anything that moved, or didn't move. It was under Shlump where they were conceived and it was under Shlump where they remained, unleashing the whomp on any trespassers. It was easy to see that abnormal levels of radiation, low barometric pressure, and heavy gamma rays had really screwed these guys up. One was a hulking blob of protoplasm; a writhing oozing amoeboid mass of pulsating protoplasmic putrescence with a large rotating bloodshot eyeball on top, a long lapping tongue, fuzzy tendrils, and dragon jaws. It carried its pea-sized brain in a stolen Buster Brown shoebox under one blobby appendage. Another was a giant cone-shaped, mobile, cucumber creature with a tadpole head and one huge bulging black bubble eye the size of a Buick Skylark, long groping arms with suckers on pencil-thin fingers, short little centipede legs, razor-sharp gnashing fangs, and frightful snapping pincers. And last, and certainly least, there were dozens of small shriveled amphibious ichthyoid-ish winged demons with pinched-in faces, long stringy hair, red eyes, flippers with crab-like claws, webbed hands and feet, antennae, spikes covering their rock-hard scaled bodies, long shaggy beards, and distorted points of view. They all came toward the Outlaws chomping on everything and anything in their path, including rocks, boulders (which are like rocks only bigger), old beer bottles, mobile home siding, you name it, they chomped on it, and The Outlaws of Asteroid #9 were next on the menu.

The canal was narrow enough, so the Outlaws took a few steps back to launch themselves and then jumped over to the other side. They all landed on their feet and ran like the devil, smashing into a wall and then quickly switching directions. The hulking blob of protoplasm moved so slowly that it was no threat at all. However, the cucumber creature and the demons were very fast and this was their turf, so they knew their way around. The Outlaws found themselves drifting deeper and deeper into Shlump's belly. The descending passages were tangled and crossed in all directions, so it became very confusing. The walls echoed with the horrifying howls of the Moola Boola Agboos giving chase. They knew the Outlaws could not possibly escape and took pleasure in taunting them. Through a maze of arteries and crevasses, pits and caves, the cucumber creature and the demons were also in pursuit of the intruders. When, for a moment, the Outlaws thought they had lost the Moola Boola Agboos they stopped to think of a plan of escape, but they were too scared to think. Then they forgot how to breathe. They went blank. They went stiff. They were desperate. They had to get away. Just the thought of being eaten alive by a cucumber beneath a swamp was enough to inspire them to leave any way they could. It was a ridiculous way to die for intergalactic legends.

Squinting through the subterranean darkness, they saw a passage, low and rough. With the slavering slobbering Moola Boola Agboos hot on their heels, they took their chances. Soon the passage that had been sloping down began to ascend again. After a while it climbed steeply, so steeply in fact, that several times they almost lost their footing and began to slide back down, which would have meant certain death. But they persisted, and at last the slope leveled off; the passage turned a corner, hit a sharp incline, and led into a cavern. At Rollo's signal the Outlaws scuttled as fast as they could and leaped into the cavern where they found themselves face to face with the cucumber creature and the demons. These particular Moola Boola Agboos were filled with rage and frothed and spluttered (yes, it's a real word, look it up) and hissed at the Outlaws. They were upset.

Drat the luck, gee whiz, and fiddlesticks, what a rotten break for our anti-heroes. But right when the demons grabbed the Outlaws for to chomp on, there was a blazing flash like lightning in the cavern, two loud bangs, the smell of sulfur, and several of the demons giggled like insane little girls suffering from Pseudobulbar Affect or PBA, which is a strange medical condition that can cause sudden uncontrollable laughing or crying, and fell dead. If you saw the *Joker* movie with Joaquin Phoenix, he had it. Also, demons always giggle just before they die. That's a fact. Look it up. No one knows why, but it's tradition. Where was I? Oh yeah, so the cucumber creature shed its skin (peeled itself without using a vegetable peeler) and out stepped none other than Mr. Green Jeans the old farmer who had given the Outlaws the ZX-12! With him was his good friend Daisy, his shotgun.

"I hate little demons," commented Mr. Green Jeans as he stroked Daisy adoringly. "Since Bowser's gone, the crops have been great! I got some special fertilizing sauce from a swamp witch near Percy that makes the vegetables grow really big and squeal like pigs. How 'bout that there cucumber, Boys?"

The Outlaws applauded and praised Mr. Green Jeans on the size of his cucumber.

"Follow me quick, Boys!" insisted Mr. Green Jeans as the remaining demons started attacking. The Outlaws and Mr. Green Jeans scrambled as fast as they could through dark corridors and tunnels with the Moola Boola Agboos swiping at their tushies. Eventually and accidentally they discovered a crack in a tunnel wall leading up to Shlump's surface. They pushed and pulled and squeezed each other (and there was some inappropriate touching) through the crack until they were all above ground. Mr. Green Jeans was the last one to start up toward the surface, but by then the demons had caught up and…well…this is grisly, but there's no other way to put it. The demons chewed off the old farmer's legs below the knees. It was a pity, and all that, but what can you do? As long as it's not me I don't really care. The good news is that at least most of him got through the crack to the surface of Shlump. To show their gratitude to Mr. Green Jeans for saving their lives, the Outlaws sent him to space mechanic Manny "The Wrench" Sanchez who was not only an ace mechanic, but a doctor as well. And I don't mean a "doctor" like these guys who lost their license and practice medicine with a wire hanger in the back seat of a broken down '71 Ford Pinto up on cinder blocks in Hampton, Florida, I mean a *real* doctor. In addition, the Outlaws insisted on paying Mr. Green Jeans' medical bills since Dr. Manny "The Wrench" Sanchez usually charges an arm and a leg and Mr. Green Jeans was…a little short. (I'm sorry for that one. I don't drink, but I feel drunk.) Let's continue. The Outlaws figured they had enough excitement for one- (I just looked up "What is a 24 hour period in space?" and I get articles on girls having their periods in space. Now I'm sick. I feel like the tail end of a misspent life. I'm taking a nap and I'll be back later.)

Alright, it's later and I'm still queasy. Where was I? Oh yeah, so the Outlaws decided to postpone the rescue mission for now. Remember they were on Shlump to rescue Zelda Borealis, the star maiden. When they got back to the ZX-12 and prepared for takeoff, the ship wouldn't move. Why wouldn't it move? It wouldn't move because it was surrounded by the hulking blob of protoplasm which was digesting the pod and the Outlaws within. They were tired and frustrated and they really didn't want to deal with this blob creature, so Alfie who had taken an electrical wiring course at Palm Beach State College but dropped out after only twenty minutes because the only girl in the class, butch dyke Peggy Foreman, was a butch dyke and didn't like him, rerouted the pod's electrical current to the *outside* of the craft, shocked the hell out of it, and the blob just slid off. It's an old trick for getting rid of unwanted things that cling to your spaceship, or ex-girlfriends who crawl out of the sewer because they found out that you wrote the greatest novel ever written. Rollo Starguy had second thoughts about leaving Shlump without attempting to rescue the star maiden, so they decided to give it a try. Slowly, carefully, cautiously, and circumspectly (whatever that means) they made their way toward what appeared to be the hub of Shlump. The only intact structures remaining on the entire planet, as previously mentioned, were a tower and a sphere, both fifty stories high. Because the giant sphere had two tremendous jackass ears sticking out of it, a 300-foot salamander's tail footbridge, and was sitting just beyond a Meridian Marsh in disgusting putrid ooze, the Outlaws took a wild guess and figured that it was The Evil One's headquarters. The moons were high and unusually luminous. The glow of the stars also beat back the night making the Outlaws easy targets. They crept through the Meridian Marsh and the disgusting putrid ooze toward the sphere. Surprisingly no one was outside of the sphere and all seemed quiet. Access was easy. There were no questions, no guards, no sweat, and no problems. The Outlaws took the shuttle stairway to the top level of the sphere and cautiously entered the control room. Immediately all possible exits slammed shut, and that awful cloud of putrid smoke billowed about the room signaling the arrival of The Evil One. He was not pleased to see the Outlaws alive.

"You're supposed to be dead!" snarled The Evil One.

"We don't always do what we're supposed to do, you slimy jackass!" snarled Rollo right back at him. "We know you kidnapped the star maiden Zelda Borealis. Where is she?"

"She's in the tower."

"Let her go."

"Never," proclaimed The Evil One. "She's my main squeeze, my hunny pants, my sugar muffin, my boo."

Rollo tossed the Golden Fleece at The Evil One and whipped out the Remus Opus.

"Here's your precious Golden Fleece, now let's have your seal on the Remus Opus."

"Nope," The Evil One grinned blackheartedly.

Rollo was beyond beginning to lose his patience.

"Look donkey shithead, you said that if we brought you back the Golden Fleece you'd put your seal on the document."

"I lied," admitted The Evil One. "They call me 'The Evil One' because I'm Evil. Hello? I'm one of the main bad guys in this book; remember? Bad guys lie. It's part of what makes us bad. As the Bard wrote, 'The evil that men do lives after them; the good is oft interred with their bones.' So what's the point in being good? Being evil is where it's at. And I'm a happening."

"We'll swap you the Golden Fleece for the star maiden," Rollo proposed.

"No deal, Starguy. I told you, she's my boopsy, my psycho hose beast, my sideline ho. Now you and your band of idiots get out of here before I vaporize you into vapor."

Rollo pretended to shudder (though not like Irma). "You vapid venomous vicious villain, you're attempting to tap into my fear mechanism which is that unpleasant strong emotion in each of us caused by a distinct awareness and anticipation of danger that often manifests itself in the individual retreating from that particular bad situation which caused the unpleasant emotion."

"What are you talking about, Starguy?"

"I don't know," Rollo admitted.

The exits opened up and the Outlaws stormed out of the sphere in lousy moods. The Evil One, also upset, wanted to be entertained, so he sent for his android comedian who entered wearing a cap and bells. He was a rotten comedian, but he was much better than that giant mouth comic in Percy. He stood before The Evil One, himself a frustrated comedian, and fired off a series of one-liners.

"I just flew in from Jupiter and boy are my android arms covered with artificial skin made up of hexagon-shaped silicone cells approximately one inch in diameter which can detect temperature, proximity, acceleration, and touch, tired."

There was no reaction from The Evil One, so he resorted to derogatory Martian jokes.

"Did you hear the one about the Martian who fired his laser pistol into the sky and missed?"

Again there was no reaction. The android comedian started to sweat, which means he was pretty nervous because androids don't sweat. He said, "This is a tough room. Did somebody die and I wasn't told?"

"Yeah, you," said The Evil One pointing his disgusting claw at the android comedian and blowing him to bits. The Evil One looked at the smoldering pieces of the android comedian scattered all around and broke out laughing a real laugh, a genuine laugh, a really real laugh, a soulful laugh. Exhausted from laughing, The Evil One fell asleep and had a dream about a cave worm defending its underground nest from an egg eater. A sudden rap on the control room door woke him with a start. The majestic bi-fold doors opened to a thunderous sound as some droids rolled in a gigantic wooden donkey on wheels. The Evil One read the attached card with a lump in his slimy jackass throat; for it touched him deeply.

"May this gift bring you joy and prosperity for all eternity, and may happiness be yours for just as long.

Affectionately,
A few extremely close friends"

The Evil One was at once delighted and suspicious of this peculiar gift. Delighted because it reminded him of his mother, and suspicious because it also reminded him of the story of the Trojan Horse when Greek warriors hid in the belly of a large wooden horse. The horse was brought inside the gates of Troy as a gift for the goddess Athena. It seems that that night while the Trojans slept, the Greeks came out of the horse's belly and captured the city of Troy. We'll get to all that later in this book. The Evil One quickly ordered the droids to turn their weapons on the gigantic wooden donkey.

"COME OUT FOOLS! YOU ARE SURROUNDED!" The Evil One yelled at the huge donkey. "YOUR CLEVER TRICK THAT WASN'T SO CLEVER DIDN'T WORK AGAINST THE LIKES OF ME WHO IS MORE CLEVER THAN YOU!"

There was no response.

"I SAY COME OUT OF THERE THIS INSTANT!" yelled The Evil One again.

Again, there was no response.

"OPEN THAT THING UP!" commanded The Evil One to his droids. They scurried around the gigantic wooden donkey on wheels searching for an opening and when at last they found the hatch they climbed inside and looked around. After a few moments they returned with the news that no one was inside the donkey. Incredulous, and needing to see for himself, The Evil One was lifted into the donkey (remember, he was only half an inch tall) and the droids, who were really The Outlaws of Asteroid #9 disguised as droids (which if you have any critical thinking skills at all, you already knew) closed the hatch behind him, trapping the bastard.

"Alright, let's get these asses outta here," Rollo ordered.

The Outlaws rolled the gigantic wooden donkey outside the sphere with The Evil One trapped in the belly of the beast and screaming to be set free, which wasn't on the menu. They hitched the donkey to the back of the space pod and towed it across three galaxies to Neutros, a neutral base for all factions. Think of it like a strange Camp David that is nothing at all like Camp David, in outer space. The journey to Neutros was not a joy. They spent most of the journey crash driving through hundreds of "invisible lightning" storms which in outer space is really luminescent plasma. There's also something called "sferics" which has something to do with it, but I'm getting a headache and tensing up just thinking about trying to explain what a sferic is, so I'll skip that. You go ahead and look it up if you want. The rest of us are moving on. So on their journey visibility was zero. They lost power twice, and when they did finally get to Neutros, Sluggo cut the jets too soon and the ZX-12 crash-landed in some really yucky unlovely substance which I won't get into. The hatch to the gigantic wooden donkey was thrown open and the jackass within was dragged out by his grotesque salamander tail. Again Rollo shoved the Remus Opus in The Evil One's repulsive face for his seal, and The Evil One shoved it back at Rollo. And then *they* started coming. "They" were thousands of disgruntled creatures from all over the universe, distinguished members of the Multi-galactic Congress, and even some salvaged parts of Mr. Green Jeans' upper torso in a bag mounted English style on the horrific Pig Boy from the Percy Zoo who had been launched into space just to get rid of him. Apparently Dr. Manny "The Wrench" Sanchez couldn't help Mr. Green Jeans, which was sad to see. They all surrounded The Evil One aiming their odd assortment of weapons at him which ranged from dark energy ray guns to hypersonic scimitars to Saturnian slingshots with ballistic trajectory loaded with meteoroids and pulled back to fire. Under the circumstances and having given the matter careful consideration, The Evil One put his seal on the Remus Opus.

The Evil One's seal upon the Remus Opus was definite cause for celebration and for The Outlaws of Asteroid #9 it was just another excuse to get absolutely crocked. Bidding The Evil One a stern bye-bye, they were able to latch on to the long tenuous tail of the Digby orb as it zigzagged around the universe with Marty and Bink doing their best to keep up. The Outlaws rode the tail to anywhere it would take them. The Digby orb was moving so fast (1,270,000 MPH) that the Outlaws' clothes actually disintegrated, leaving them wearing nothing at all. That's right; you read that correctly. The Outlaws were naked, nude, in the raw, el buffo, without a stitch, unveiled, stripped, peeled, starkers, and absolutely threadbare. So there they were, wild nasty naked illegal lads streaking through the universe in all their minuscule glory for all to see. However, at 1,270,000 MPH you really couldn't see them, but you could *hear* them hollering, screeching, yelling, yelping, shouting, screaming and carrying on like the bare-assed little weenies that they were. The Digby orb took a sudden drop and started veering toward Earth, which meant nothing, considering how erratic and unpredictable it was. Its tail momentarily fizzled out and the Outlaws were catapulted backwards toward Earth's moon. The hatch came unhinged from the phenomenal speed the ZX-12 had to stomach and the Outlaws were launched out of the space pod and landed bellies-down in Mare Humorum, the Sea of Moisture, where they composed themselves enough to sit around in the altogether, tell lewd jokes, and moon each other just so they could say that they mooned each other on the moon. Basically they were lightheaded from the trip and acted like total jerks. But I'll give them a break and let them blow off some steam. After all, they did manage to get The Evil One's seal, and that was no picnic, as you are well aware. When they got sick of mooning each other on the moon, they crawled out of the Sea of Moisture to drip-dry since they didn't have any towels. That reminds me of when I was in high school and the psychotic P.E. teachers, who if they were upset at something, would make us drip-dry with no towels right out of the showers. Thinking back on it, that was *really* weird to force a bunch of high school boys to stand there wet and naked while the P.E. teachers watched feverishly. While the Outlaws were drip-drying, they heard the annoying yet stimulating sound of girlish giggling. Then out from the Copernicus Crater sensually slinked half a dozen gorgeous moon maidens who giggled some more and joined the ogling outlaws in what will undoubtedly be known henceforth throughout time, space, and history as the greatest skinny-dipping session ever held. At the ding of a single bell tone the moon maidens quickly slipped out of the Sea of Moisture and scurried toward the source of the ding. The Outlaws, naturally curious and aggravated because their fun came to an abrupt end, followed the wild lunar ladies to the lunar domes which split wide open revealing a magnificent mansion within. Standing majestically on the balcony of his mansion having just dinged the bell, and stroking his telescope, was Chester Flemlock aka "Flem." To most inhabitants of the universe he was known as the classiest, most sophisticated, and suavist (If that wasn't a word before, it is now) gentleman in the Milky Way galaxy. He was known to those on the planet Kreplach as "The Milky Way Mensch." He was wearing his iconic Fendi windbreaker smoking jacket which sells for $23,000 on Earth (true) and puffing on his also iconic Smoking Dragon pipe which was created by the Russian company Bon-Cadeau and sells for $85,000 on Earth. Also true. Look it up if you don't believe me. And if you don't believe me, what in hell are you reading this book for? I don't make this stuff up. I research. Some of you probably think I do make stuff up, but there's not one thing in this book that isn't true except this sentence. Let's move on. Earthlings know Chester Flemlock as "The Man in the

Moon." That's right. You knew who he was and didn't even know that you knew who he was until I told you that you knew who he was. Flem dinged the bell again and the moon maidens giggled girlishly and skipped over to the crater Tycho which was filled with margarita Jell-O. The maidens jumped into the crater and then jumped on each other. This was moon mud wrestling using Jell-O instead of mud. Flem smiled toothlessly to himself, popped a PEZ having seen Private Detective Sheldon Danger do it on occasion through his telescope, puffed on his $85,000 Smoking Dragon pipe, sat back in his Zarifa Z Three Dimensional Full-Body Massage Chair, and enjoyed the spectacle of his little moon maidens rolling around giggling and tribbing in the Jell-O filled crater. Sluggo and Alfie decided to spice things up and jumped into the crater with the girls. Lucky for them they had both once moonlighted in drag as female mud wrestlers in the Tropicana star system to supplement their income, so they knew all the moves. While the wrestling was heating up, Rollo introduced himself to Flem and they joked about how the earthlings are so fascinated by the fact that Flem looks down on them and follows them everywhere they go. Flem aka "The Man in the Moon" commented that he is fascinated by Earth as well, because to him Earth looks like a big meadow muffin with a bunch of morons on it. He mentioned that in the 1800s murderers on Earth used the defense of "lunacy" if the moon was full when they committed their heinous acts, and it usually worked to set them free. He also explained how he controls the menstrual cycles of women on Earth because on average menstrual cycles are the same length as the 28-day cycle of the moon. That is a fact. The wrestling match ended with the moon maidens on top of Sluggo and Alfie who weren't complaining. After the match, everyone was tired and hungry, so Flem suggested a barbecue…

Hey, diddle, diddle, the cat and the fiddle
The cow jumped over the moon

Well, the cow *tried* to jump over the moon, but when she started her descent Flem grabbed her, butter-basted her, and threw her on the grill. It was gruesome.

Back on Shlump, The Evil One who had been banished back there by the Multi-galactic Congress, called a meeting of the minds with his commanders in the conference room of the sphere. He was extremely upset, claiming that he was kidnapped, beaten, mugged, raped repeatedly (sometimes without his consent) and forced to put his seal upon the Remus Opus against his will. Something caught his filthy disgusting bloodshot slimy jackass eye and he stopped talking mid-sentence. He pinched his first commander's nose shut and reached into the commander's mouth with his hideous teeny tiny arm and pulled out a wad of chewed Bazooka chewing gum. Now he was *really* mad! Chewing gum was absolutely forbidden in the conference room! The Evil One was always finding used chewed up chewing gum under the chairs and tables and it was very difficult to remove! As punishment he had the first commander flogged with ten pieces of Hot Wheels track stuck together with Hubba Bubba chewing gum and then returned to bitching about what he was bitching about. In effect he said that there would be no more Mr. Nice Guy. He wanted the Remus Opus and would stop at nothing to get it. He stated that he would gladly sacrifice all of their lives (except for his) to get that document. He added that he was still determined to take over the universe since it was his destiny according to Madam Brittney and Dionne Warwick on the Psychic hotline at $3.99 per minute and he needed the Remus Opus to do it. A devious and diabolical plan was in order. The plan would involve coaxing the Outlaws back to Shlump where The Evil One would have the upper hand without the threat of the Multi-galactic Congress. Several suggestions were suggested on how to coax the Outlaws back into the game: parties, women, booze, more booze, Mexican train, pizza, Mahjong, and booze, were put forth, but The Evil One rejected them all because none of them were overly challenging (I'll hear about that) and The Evil One was well aware that The Outlaws of Asteroid #9 loved a challenge. Just when he was about to throw up his tiny little disgusting hands out of frustration, an idea came to him. It was a deviously clever and cleverly devious idea, and a sinister smile crept across his ugly slimy donkey face.

The Outlaws of Asteroid #9 had repaired the hatch of the ZX-12 and were back on Asteroid #9 just sitting around staring at each other, not saying a word. They were still not a pretty bunch and they still knew it. In fact, they probably looked worse now than when they first set out to save the universe, which was understandable considering what they'd been through. I failed to mention that on the way back from Neutros the pod had passed through an anti-matter storm. The ship shuddered and the Outlaws were thrown about. The power went out several times.

Auxiliary lights flashed on and off. The lads turned green. They started evaporating. And then by sheer contrived luck the pod spiraled through a vacuum and was hit by a wave of electromagnetic energy which caused the anti-matter effects to subside and everything returned to normal, except for Alfie. Alfie got weird. Not P.E. teachers watching wet naked high school boys drip-dry weird, but weird nonetheless. He started imitating Pearl Bailey singing "Saturday Night Fish Fry" and then tried to stand on his own tongue. It was obvious to Rollo and Sluggo that an alien being had planted itself inside of Alfie and that he was in the grip of the alien's mind force, so they did what any good pals would do and they beat the alien crap out of him. Just as Sluggo gave Alfie one last kick in the teeth, a familiar brilliant beam of glittering Persian blue light pierced the musty haze surrounding Asteroid #9 sending the boys scurrying as always, and Dweezle Dwindle, the peculiar intergalactic messenger dwarf, appeared, took a bow, and handed Rollo Starguy a lovely scripted invitation. He then extended his hideous little hand and waited impatiently for his tip. Alfie snapped him to Sluggo who held him steady on his toe, laces out, and Rollo place-kicked him out into the starry universe, beating Broncos' place-kicker Matt Prater's 64 yard field goal against the Tennessee Titans on December 8th, 2013, by 55,946 miles. He then read the invitation and addressed his outlaws like the terrific leader he pretended to be.

"Boys, we have been cordially invited to the 'First Annual Shlump Blowout' hosted by The Evil One. There will be all kinds of galaxy games, supernova skill booths, vacuum volleyball, parallel universe puppet shows, cosmic carnival rides, open mic poetry readings, pancake and egg races, dancing competitions, and a musical lineup featuring The Bonzo Dog Doo-Dah Band, Michael Bolton, Fitz and the Tantrums, and a special appearance by outer space's own William Shatner performing his hit covers of "Rocket Man", "Space Oddity" and "Lucy in the Sky with Diamonds". There will also be intergalactic food prepared and catered by Chef Dewey who will come out now and then and play guitar. It says it will be fun for the whole universe. It all begins at the next rising of Venus on Shlump. It says it's half-price for infamous outlaws, but it also says that if we bring the Remus Opus that we can get in free! Plus, there's a contest to win back Zartov from The Evil One. If you ask me, something seems a bit peculiar about all this."

"I didn't know we had volleyball in the 29th century," Alfie pointed out.

"Yeah, that's it," Rollo nodded. "It's a definite trap, but so what? We've been in traps before. What are we gonna do, sit around on this stupid floating rock staring at each other while the rest of the universe is having a great time? Michael Bolton will be there! Besides, it says we can win back control of Zartov from The Evil One. I say we go for it."

So the Outlaws decided to chance it and attend the "First Annual Shlump Blowout" with the hopes of winning back Zartov, saving the universe, and maybe eating some corn dogs, fried pickles, and banana split funnel cake. However, they would need disguises since The Evil One and his droids would undoubtedly be looking for them. Their disguises needed to be subtle, yet elegant and elegant, yet subtle. I couldn't think of anything and neither could the Outlaws. They did consider using the droid disguises again, but that was nixed because they could get mixed up with the real droids, and considering they could be in dire danger, it was important that they knew where each other was at all times. And just for the heck of it, Rollo decided to visit the star maiden being held captive in the Shlump tower. Maybe she could help him come up with something. So he gritted his teeth, crossed his fingers, and dematerialized. With Rollo gone, Alfie and Sluggo grew very tired of staring at each other, so they decided to strike up a conversation which went precisely like this. In fact, this was the conversation verbatim:

"What do you wanna do?"

"I dunno. What do *you* wanna do?"

"I dunno. Wanna keep staring at each other?"

"Okay."

You get the picture. They kept repeating those same exact four lines for just under four hours. Finally they decided that since Rollo left them the ZX-12 that they would take a little outer space road trip to pass the time until he got back. So they put their bikinis on under their outlaw uniforms and headed the pod toward the Tropicana star system where, as I previously mentioned, they had moonlighted as female mud wrestlers. Rollo never knew that they had done this professionally and they never told him, fearing he would be ashamed of them. He did comment on their skill with the moon maidens in the Jell-O filled crater when they left Earth's moon, but that was the extent of it. Unfortunately the pod never made it to the Tropicana star system as they were accidentally sideswiped by Marty and Bink's saucer as Digby's best scouts continued chasing the extremely erratic and uncooperative Digby orb. The ZX-12 spun into Earth's perimeter, somersaulted 18 times, and skidded to a stop on New

York's George Washington Bridge causing a major traffic jam. Within seconds angry commuters were yelling and cursing at Sluggo and Alfie for holding up traffic. Earthlings are like that. Even the guy who Nick Nero introduced to the limo door in Los Angeles was in New York on vacation and jumped on the ZX-12. Alfie zapped him with his ray gun and blew off his nut sack. He was in a lot of pain and I'm glad. Minutes later, several of New York's Finest (who I myself had a few run-ins with) drew their weapons on the Outlaws. Alfie threw Sluggo in front of him and they both raised their hands in surrender.

"What seems to be the problem, officers? Do we have a taillight out?" asked Alfie with a grin.

"License, registration, and proof of insurance," the officer demanded.

Alfie could produce none of the necessary documents to prove he was eligible to drive, so the ZX-12 was towed to an impound lot where it whimpered like a lost puppy behind the barbed wire security fence, and Alfie and Sluggo were taken to jail and booked. They were thrown in a cell which was already occupied by a huge terrifying deranged killer who had slaughtered his family, his elementary school teachers, and the Good Humor Man who only had strawberry shortcake ice cream bars when this psycho wanted a chocolate éclair bar. That killing was justified and understandable. The killer glowered hatefully at Alfie and Sluggo, like he wanted to kill them. The guard reassured them that if by chance the deranged killer did kill them, that they shouldn't worry because he was already in jail. As the guard walked away, Alfie and Sluggo frantically called after him, "DON'T LEAVE US HERE WITH THIS MADMAN! ARE YOU OUT OF YOUR MIND?! YOU CAN'T LEAVE US ALONE WITH THIS PSYCHOPATH! HE'S A HOMICIDAL MANIAC! HE'S A COLD-BLOODED INSANE KILLER!" When they realized that the guard was gone, they turned around and politely introduced themselves to the deranged killer who then tried every trick in the book (and then some) to get them to bend over. He used lines ranging from "Your space boots are untied" to "You dropped the soap" to "Would you mind bending over so I can take your temperature with my hands on your shoulders?" But the Outlaws' mommies didn't raise no chimps, so they didn't fall or bend over for it. When that didn't work the killer revealed his elaborate plans to break out of the joint (that's jail talk) when it occurred to our anti-heroes that there was really no need for them to stay in jail since they hadn't dematerialized in a while and their molecular structure should be strong enough to do so. So they bid the deranged killer farewell and dematerialized their butts outta there. Naturally they *re*materialized in the West End Bar on the Upper West Side because where else would outlaws from outer space go when in Manhattan? They ordered a dozen Harvey Wallbangers and got totally blitzed out of their noggins. There was a lousy local jazz band called "The Seven Member Quartet" playing a lousy jazz rendition of ZZ Top's "Tush" and a tremendously disgusting fat broad that looked like The Fat Man in drag, but wasn't, dancing with a midget that looked like a midget, but was really a dwarf disguised as a midget. I was there too, sitting in the corner disguised as someone who cared, nursing a mudslide, and writing a poem about a poem that couldn't be written. In their stupid drunken stupor, Alfie and Sluggo decided that the fat broad was The Evil One in another form (a really big form) and the midget who was really a dwarf disguised as a midget was one of his droid commanders. So they created a strategic diversion by picking a fight with a teacup Chihuahua that was in some woman's purse. They allowed the teacup Chihuahua to tear them apart on purpose when they could have just blown him to bits with their ray guns. Come to think of it, they could have blown the deranged killer in the jail cell to bits too, although the ray guns probably would have been confiscated by the cops. I'm not going back there to that scene to add all that in, so let's just move on. When everyone (including yours truly) was congratulating the teacup Chihuahua on a job well done, Alfie and Sluggo forced the fat broad and the dwarf midget thing outside at the point of their aforementioned ray guns. Once outside on Broadway not far from Barnard College where lots of hungry girls are (and by "hungry," I don't mean "hungry") they hailed a cab, shoved the fat broad and the dwarf midget thing in the back seat, and then vaporized the cab driver into another dimension. No, it wasn't very nice, but an intergalactic outlaw's gotta do what an intergalactic outlaw's gotta do (to quote John Wayne…sort of). Alfie took the wheel and Sluggo rode shotgun, an expression which was thought to originate from the old west where on stagecoaches in the late 1800s a man with a shotgun would sit next to the driver just in case the stagecoach was attacked by Indians or robbers. That said, the phrase was first used in the 1939 movie *Stagecoach* which starred, you guessed it, John Wayne as the Ringo Kid. Ringo Starr was only one year old when that movie came out. I really got off track. Where was I? Oh, so, Alfie was driving the taxi through the Upper West Side. He's zigzagging all over the place because he's used to piloting a space pod and not a cab. Soon there were flashing lights and sirens on his tail. He hit the gas and the taxi sped up, but not by much. The buffet slayer in the back seat was slowing them down.

"THIS IS THE POLICE! PULL OVER IMMEDIATELY!" commanded the police. But outlaws are outlaws, so Alfie veered off to Riverside Drive and a ferocious chase ensued with the cops in hot pursuit. Ironically, at the same time, the Digby orb flew by overhead with Marty and Bink in hot pursuit. Talk about irony. The two cars wound through the main streets and side streets of Manhattan smashing through obstacles like pedestrians, hot dog carts, hot pretzel carts, and the always dependable "two guys carrying a big sheet of glass" across the street. Eventually the taxi turned onto the road leading to Hell Gate Bridge, which if you don't know, is a railroad bridge. The fat broad and the midget dwarf thing tried to cry out when they saw they were headed for Hell Gate, but they were gagged (which I forgot to mention) and couldn't cry out. But Sluggo wasn't gagged, so he cried out, "ALFIE, IT'S A TRAIN BRIDGE!" Alfie was cool as a cucumber.

"Don't worry about it, Slug; remember that Spielberg flick where the big lizard makes those Earthling kids fly on their bicycles? If a lizard could do that, then I can make this thing soar, no sweat. Hang on to your gonads. Here we go."

The patrol car stopped at the foot of Hell Gate Bridge and the officers watched in disbelief as the taxi flew into the air and immediately dropped 135 feet down toward the Hell Gate. It seems that Alfie forgot to take into account that he had Earth's largest salad dodger in the back seat. Ironically, Long Island's infamous Mobro 4000 garbage barge that hauled the same load of garbage from New York to Belize in 1987 appeared because I wanted it to, and the taxi crash-landed on it. Alfie looked around in disgust.

"I think we're in Kearny, New Jersey," he cringed. "Man, it stinks. Get those two whatever-they-ares out of the taxi while I try not to heave."

After much pushing and pulling, Sluggo found an old ratchet hoist someone had tossed in the garbage on the barge and used it to remove the fat broad from the taxi. She rolled down the mountain of trash and landed face-up. She wasn't smiling. Sluggo threw the dwarf midget thing over his shoulder and gave chase. "THE EVIL ONE IS ESCAPING!" he yelled. Alfie grabbed him by the midget as he ran by.

"Let her go. She's not The Evil One. If she was she would have tried to vaporize us or eat us by now. And I think this midget is just a midget. In a way I always wanted to be a midget. I think it would be great to be so small that you can see under a girl's skirt just by looking up. And you could walk out of restaurants without paying and no one would know. But I was dealt a bad hand and I'm not a midget, so I resent them."

With that, Alfie rifled through the dwarf midget thing's pockets, took his money (being an outlaw and all), and then rolled him down the same mountain of trash that the pork party rolled down. The dwarf midget thing landed between her enormous legs and was sucked into her gargantuan coochie never to be seen or heard from again. Alfie and Sluggo jumped off the barge, made it to the opposite side of Hell Gate away from the cops, and set out to retrieve the ZX-12. They walked the six miles to Times Square where they took in a few girlie shows, got conned in a few con games, vaporized a few con men, and wandered into the Funtastic Family Fun Center just off of Mott Street. They were mesmerized by the colorful lights, clanging bells, buzzing buzzers, hookers, and pings and pangs of the games. They wandered through the arcade in wide-eyed amazement watching hordes of teenaged Earthlings, who should have been in school, playing the various video games and pinball machines. They stopped at one particular video game called "Space Attack" and watched some juvenile delinquents badgering the machine and beating it up.

"This game is too hard. It's for wimps! Let's go rob a blind man and beat up old ladies!" one of them said, and the hooligan Earthlings left. Alfie and Sluggo sat down at the console to play the game.

Speeding missiles and plasma balls zipped down the screen and fired on Alfie and Sluggo. Faster and faster they came! Closer and closer they came! Having never played a video game before, the Outlaws thought they were really being attacked, especially when several Punk, Emo and Goth kids with wild peacock Mohawks and mullets, outrageous attire, frightening makeup, and not a GED or a job in sight, surrounded them to watch them play. Immediately they shrunk down and projected themselves inside the video screen and materialized as characters in the game, not avatars, their actual selves in miniature. They took control of the weapons inside the game, raised them out of the screen, and turned them on the Punks, Emos and Goths. Alfie drew his ray gun and blasted the Funtastic Family Fun Center just off of Mott Street's breaker box which didn't destroy it, but rather caused a bizarre short-circuit, causing all the games in the arcade to spring to life, shooting their weapons at each other and at the Punks, Emos and Goths. It was a madhouse. There were explosions, screams, flashes of things flashing, rockets and missiles flying everywhere. Plasma cutters, fire flowers, gravity guns, energy swords, crowbars, shrink rays, and Koopa shells were all activated and all hell broke loose. (These are all video game weapons. I had to look them up. I know nothing about video games.) It was total pandemonium. It looked like the Fourth of July gone haywire, a dazzling display of lights, colors, sounds, and screaming. There was lots of screaming. The arcade had become a war zone. It was a battle royale never seen before or since in the history of video games. As police cars and fire engines approached from all directions with sirens wailing, Alfie and Sluggo popped out of the game, returned to normal size, and staggered out of the arcade. They turned around for a moment and watched this spectacular display of a war won, feeling cocky and victorious. They swiped some Nathan's hot dogs for the road and agreed that New York was a nice place to visit, but it was time to head home. They blasted through the impound fence, hotwired the ZX-12, and lit up and out. Meanwhile in a galaxy far far away, their phenomenal leader Rollo Starguy was materializing in the Shlump tower where Zelda Borealis, the star maiden, was in bondage, held captive by that half-inch tall disgusting slimy nasty part donkey part jellyfish part salamander…The Evil One. Zelda looked great in bondage, as many women do. Rollo noticed the guards heading for the tower. He spoke quickly to the star maiden. "I came to tell you that I'm crazy in love with you. I love the way you exhale. I especially love the way you inhale. I'd love to stay and rattle your chains but I really must be going." Rollo tried to dematerialize but it was too soon after materializing and his molecular structure was too weak and he couldn't, so he started taking off his clothes.

"What are you doing?!" asked the startled shackled star maiden.

"What does it look like I'm doing? I'm getting naked."

This was a stunt Rollo always pulled whenever he was about to get caught with a woman he was not supposed to be with, which in his mind was quite often. Because he was very dignified and proud, he refused to hide under a bed, or in a closet, or in a tub, or anything like that. Rollo Starguy would not be intimidated. He would remove his garments and simply stroll out of the sticky situation stark bare-assed naked. Rollo's theory was that psychologically most people have paranoia about handling a live naked body in public, so they would avoid him instead of doing him harm. Candid Camera's Allen Funt sort of addressed this with his 1970 feature film *What Do You Say to a Naked Lady?* So Rollo had a point. He opened the tower door and excused himself walking through the guards. One of them did pat him on the hiney as he passed. Once he made it outside the tower, Rollo skipped through the frosted fields of Fodder where he was being tailed by the Seething Aardsnarks, carnivorous creatures who inhabited the fringe of Shlump and were ashamed of nothing. Since they were meat-eaters, Rollo covered his Jimmy Dean and skipped as fast as he could toward the thick tangled vegetation of the perilous peaks of Pettiness where forgetting to empty the dishwasher or putting a pen back was a big deal. Unfortunately Rollo was not fast enough. However, he was lucky enough. For just as the Seething Aardsnarks were about to clamp down on his one-eyed wonder weasel, the dematerialization kicked in and he was transported back to Asteroid #9. En route he did make one quick stop to pick up disguises for himself and his boys to wear to the First Annual Shlump Blowout. Anybody who was anybody would be there, including Nelly Bly the investigative reporter who posed as a patient in a nuthouse to expose abuse, Wally Cox, Audrey Munson the first actress to appear nude in a movie, Agent 355 a spy for George Washington during the American Revolution, Lee Van Cleef, Ching Shih a Chinese hooker who became a pirate, Arnold Stang, and of course, the cast of *Petticoat Junction*. It promised to be the social event of the season, and that it was indeed. Excited life forms from all over the universe, as far away as Mizar Alcor, gathered on Shlump for the festivities. They were some of the most peculiar and disgusting creatures imaginable: clusters of blobs, thin wiry creatures with oval heads, six elbows, and three tongues, and several certified public accountants. If it was beyond comprehension, it was there. Many of the attendees were natural enemies, but they put their differences aside to enjoy the fun and thrills of the First Annual Shlump Blowout.

The Evil One was sitting on his throne on a raised platform overlooking the festivities and scanning the crowd. He mumbled to himself, "'Uneasy lies the head that wears a crown', to quote the Bard. But I don't wear a crown. I tried it once, but they're too uncomfortable, and it's annoying to have a heavy 20-carat gold hat with assorted gemstones sitting on your head. I don't need a crown. Everyone knows who I am. I'm the evil handsome one who runs the show." Yes, well, the evil handsome one knew the Outlaws would show up and instructed his droids to keep alert. He wanted the Remus Opus and would stop at nothing to get it back. Unnoticed by The Evil One or his droids, the space pod once again took the back door in and The Outlaws of Asteroid #9 made the scene. The hatch to the ZX-12 popped open and out came Alfie disguised as a little girl, Sluggo as Santa Claus, and Rollo as a grandfather clock.

"Remember," Rollo Starguy reminded his lads, "Blend in. Mingle. And don't forget why we're here. We have to win back Zartov, rescue the star maiden, overthrow The Evil One, and save the universe. And we have to do it all without anyone recognizing us."

It sounded simple enough, so the Outlaws entered the festival grounds and split up. They had their missions, but they were also very excited to be there with all the different games, contests, carnival rides, and freak shows. It was just a heck of a lot of fun. On his way to the Shlump tower, Rollo (as the grandfather clock) passed by the throne. The Evil One saw him passing by and asked him for the time. Like the courteous guy he was, Rollo gave The Evil One the time with a smile, explained that he was a little slow, and continued on his way. The Evil One scanned the crowd again but still saw nothing suspicious. Alfie (as the little girl) entered a Granny Smith Earth apple-bobbing contest against two one-legged knock-kneed Krakulas from the Ginga Star Sector. They were kneeling over a tub of Jupiter juice with the Granny Smith Earth apples floating in it. Just as the referee blew the whistle to start the contest, a Globbo from the planet Rimbam seven galaxies away and a Mabmir from Obbolg, who were sworn enemies, got into a squabble about whose plonker was longer. The ref was distracted by the squabble. Alfie seized both the opportunity and the heads of the Krakulas and held them under the Jupiter juice while he alone bobbed for the apples. The ref blew the whistle, spun back around, and declared Alfie the winner. The angry one-legged knock-kneed Krakulas hopped over to The Evil One and accused Alfie of cheating. The Evil One called Alfie over to him.

"Oh little girl, come here to your Uncle Francis!"

Yes, you read that right; "Francis" was The Evil One's name. I couldn't believe it either. Alfie reluctantly approached the platform. The Evil One beckoned her (him) to the throne.

"You're a pretty little thing. What's your name?"

Alfie's response to The Evil One is not fit to print. Let us surmise to say he strongly suggested an intimate activity The Evil One might do with himself in only two words, slapped him, and took off. Meanwhile Rollo was under the tower trying to get the star maiden's attention with ice giant impersonations, planetoid poetry, and a not half-bad rendition of Buddy

Holly's "Look at Me". When finally she looked down and saw him, she immediately assumed that Rollo had been eaten alive and swallowed whole by a cannibalistic (in a clockish way) grandfather clock. She was heartbroken and horrified, but she did ask him for the time. Rollo explained as best he could, and in terms she could comprehend, that he had not been eaten alive by the clock but was actually wearing the grandfather clock as a disguise so he could come and go as he pleased and no one would notice him. Rollo vowed to free the star maiden from captivity at a later time and waddled off to join in the contest to win back his beloved hometown planet, Zartov. The contest to win Zartov was a good old-fashioned archery tournament.

Alfie (as the little girl) approached Sluggo (as Santa Claus) and asked Santa for a new Muttnik plush toy which was based on Laika the Soviet space dog who was the first animal to orbit Earth. He was a stray mongrel off the streets of Moscow who made space flight history. Alfie had forgotten that Santa Claus was really Sluggo and Sluggo had forgotten that the little girl was really Alfie. Sluggo had gotten into the spirit of the festivities and had been getting soused on Big Bang beer.

"That dog was a dog," he slurred. "I'm not a dog; I'm an outer space outlaw who's not a dog. Now beat it kid before I do something that has nothing to do with anything."

Alfie walked away feeling dejected and hurt. The Evil One took a puff on his cigar and beckoned Alfie the little girl back to him. "That wasn't very nice what you said to me before," said The Evil One. "But I'll forgive you if you give your Uncle Francis a nice big kiss."

Alfie took the cigar from The Evil One, gave it a puff, and cooed, "A nice hot one," as he stubbed out the cigar in The Evil One's jackass face. The Evil One brayed in agony drawing his droids' attention. Alfie started to run but tripped on the platform causing his little girl wig to fall off. When The Evil One saw that the little girl was really one of The Outlaws of Asteroid #9 he immediately ordered all exits and entrances shut and sealed so there was no possibility of escape. "HELL IS EMPTY AND ALL THE DEVILS ARE HERE!" announced The Evil One, quoting the Bard. He then ordered a search to commence for the others. The droids and commanders searched everyone, everything, and everywhere. With no other option at hand the Outlaws tore off their costumes and grabbed the bows and arrows from the archery tournament. Fortunately they had some archery experience from when they were kids at Camp Comet where the counselors who later became sadistic P.E. teachers at my high school used to watch them shower. The Evil One commanded his droids to capture them, but The Outlaws of Asteroid #9 had no intention of being captured. They formed a defensive semicircle facing the droids with weapons poised. They assumed the proper stance. They nocked (an archery term meaning some archery thing having to do with the bow or something). They set their draw hands (another archery term meaning to grip the pinkie finger with the thumb while keeping the other three fingers together). They set the bow hand (whatever that means). They pre-drew, they drew, they anchored, they aimed, they set up their shots, and they were ready to release the arrows.

** (I need to stop a minute. If I had known archery was such a pain in the ass to describe I would have chosen water balloons or some other weapon. I always thought you put an arrow in a bow, you pulled back the string, and you shot the arrow. But no, it's incredibly complicated and there are all kinds of crazy archery terminologies and complex procedures and I'm getting really annoyed. That said; let's continue.)

"Stand together Outlaws!" Rollo ordered with the confidence of a man who had absolutely nothing to be confident about. "These creeps don't scare me. There are three of us and only thousands of them."

The Evil One ordered the Outlaws to drop their bows and arrows and hand over the Remus Opus, which they refused to do. They were holding fast. Surrounded by an army of thousands of droids armed with vaporizing lasers, Rollo took advantage of his predicament and demanded that the army of droids drop *their* bows and arrows and surrender. The droids didn't know what to do because they didn't have bows and arrows, and several started to self-combust out of sheer confusion. Rollo also demanded that the star maiden be released from the tower. The Evil One was so amused that Rollo had the gall to give orders when the odds were so overwhelmingly against him, that he seemed to go along with it. He unlocked the ground entrance to the Shlump tower so that the star maiden might be easily rescued, but at the same time he activated the emergency tower vaporizer and the tower started disintegrating from the bottom up. The star maiden started screaming hysterically like star maidens tend to do when they're hysterical and the crowd hissed in horror. The Evil One blurted out some beaten-to-death dumb cliché like "If I can't have her, no one will!" It was a lousy break for most everyone concerned except the bad guys. The Evil One would be victorious, the star maiden would perish, and worst of all the Outlaws never got to try the banana split funnel cake or ride the Tilt-A-Whirl. Just as all looked hopeless, Rollo Starguy made an offhanded comment to one of the droids about irony in literature. Irony in this case because the Remus Opus that The Evil One wanted so desperately was stuffed in the push-up brassiere of Zelda Borealis aka the star maiden. The Evil One overheard this (which was intended) and rushed into the disintegrating tower. As the tower was about to completely vanish The Evil One poked his hideous head out of the top window and called down to Rollo, "I THOUGHT YOU SAID THE STAR MAIDEN HAD THE REMUS OPUS!"

"I lied," smiled Rollo Starguy as he watched the tower disappear with The Evil One and the star maiden inside and thought to himself *this book has some great special effects.*

The Evil One screamed, "I'M DISINTEGRATING! I'M DISINTEGRATING! WHO WOULD HAVE THOUGHT AN IDIOT LIKE YOU COULD DESTROY MY EVIL EVILNESS!" and The Evil One disintegrated. The droids threw down their weapons and cheered. The Wicked Witch was dead! I mean, The Evil One was dead! The universe was saved by The Outlaws of Asteroid #9! Rollo was a little broken up about Zelda being a goner too because she was the only girl he never had to pay. But what can you do? The head droid approached Rollo and handed him a broom. He said, "Take this with you!"

"Gee thanks," Rollo said. "I'll give it to my mother-in-law as a new car."

The Cosmos Command appeared before the Outlaws with a bottle of Mogen David Blackberry wine and an opened bag of Herr's Salt & Vinegar potato chips. They were very proud of the Outlaws for saving the universe and officially decreed that Rollo, Alfie, and Sluggo were now the official ministers of the Remus Opus and it would be their duty to protect and defend the provisions of the document. This would have been quite an honor except for the fact that the Remus Opus did actually disintegrate along with the star maiden since it was stuffed in her panties, not her push-up brassiere. The Cosmos Command was not thrilled to hear this, and as punishment continued their banishment of the Outlaws. Rollo Starguy, the unamused leader of the Outlaws, looked up at their home planet Zartov and sneered. "Someday," he said. And The Outlaws of Asteroid #9 nodded in agreement, knowing exactly what he meant.

CHAPTER 10

From his mansion on the moon some 240,000 miles from Earth, Chester Flemlock aka "Flem" aka "The Man in the Moon" looked through his telescope at the Blue Planet. He could see oceans, continents, the Great Wall of China, the Staten Island Fresh Kills garbage dump, the Great Pyramid of Giza, and the Percy sign. He adjusted the extremely expensive custom-made Orion lens of his telescope and focused in on the Percy sign, reading aloud to himself. It had been changed to read:

"WELCOME TO PERCY!
PIG SEMEN CAPITAL OF THE WORLD!
Population 26
HOME OF THE PERCY MONSTER!"

Tourists wearing colorful shorts with rubber Percy monster tails, caps with Percy monster ears, and shirts with renderings of the Percy monster were milling around the Percy sign. Many were posing for pictures next to it giving the thumbs up like a bunch of assholes with nothing to live for. Mr. Percy himself was directing buses full of the curious to park in a separate section away from the shanties. He held up a handwritten sign that read:

"FREE PARKING 5 BUCKS"

The "Hollywood Exposed" story about the Percy monster had turned the once quietly insane desert town of weirdos and crackpots into a major tourist attraction, so the people of Percy (the Percy People) decided to take advantage of their new notoriety and milk it for all they could and a lot more. They had set up booths and businesses exploiting "The Percy Monster." A group of about twenty tourists gathered in front of "The Historic Percy Monster Museum," a small spray-painted building dedicated to perpetuating the monstrosity that in reality was a very unlucky mob underboss turned bad actor who at the moment was frantically heading into the odd wooded area of Percy. The tourists were paying close attention to their tour guide Ivan Kash, the resident Percy historian. Ivan only wore his left shoe and limped when he moved about.

He cleared his throat, counted to three softly, and addressed the crowd.

"Folks, to me, this here Percy Monster Museum is the feast de la resistance of Percy other than The House of the Choking Chicken. Watch your step as you enter."

The tourists stepped inside and the door slammed shut behind them. It was totally dark inside the museum other than a green glowing object on a table. Some of the tourists were getting nervous and said so.

"Don't be afraid yet. Here we go!" Ivan said as he pulled a cord and a 40-watt light bulb went on overhead.

He pulled the cord several times and the light bulb went on and off. For the moment he kept it off.

"Ain't that the damndest thing?!" he said. "You're in the dark now, but I'm going to enlighten you. This here cord that I've been yankin' on is like that French Napoleon fella, very powerful. Napoleon, who was named after chocolate, vanilla, and strawberry ice cream all in one box, was only three feet tall and he kept his hand in his coat to keep his legs on. If he took his hand out of his coat his legs would've fallen off. But like this here light cord, he was a powerful son of a bitch. Folks, there has always been much debate about whether or not man should play God. I must confess that sometimes after I leave The House of the Choking Chicken, speakin' of yankin', I come in here late at night when no one's around and I play God Almighty like this here…" In a booming voice he bellowed, "**LET THERE BE LIGHT!**"

With that he yanked the cord and the 40-watt light bulb dangling overhead went on. Ivan bowed to the crowd. Two people from Tennessee clapped. No one else cared. "Thank you," Ivan said bowing again as the same two people from Tennessee clapped. "Now step right this way," he instructed the crowd as he limped forward. Red faux velvet ropes on faux silver barrier poles like those used in theaters (or "theatres" if you want to feel special) surrounded a small stolen plastic table with chewing gum stuck to the bottom of the top, to deter people from touching what was on the table. What was on the table were two clear plastic display boxes. Inside one box was Ivan Kash's right shoe. Inside the other box was a pile of caca. It was monster caca to be precise. It was green and glowing and was in fact the green glowing object that was seen when the museum was dark. It looked as though it had been sprayed with some cheap 1960s neon green model paint. It looked *exactly* like that. And that's all there was inside The Historic Percy Monster Museum: Ivan's right shoe, a pile of poop, and a 40-watt bulb. Mr. Percy dressed as a security guard stood silent and vigilant next to the glowing caca. We should assume that this was in case someone might try to steal it. Ivan Kash let himself inside the roped off area and pointed to the box containing the caca.

"Folks, what you are seein' with your own two eyes, unless you're from another planet and you have more than two eyes, is genuine authentic Percy Monster leavins'. You may have heard the legend around town about how I myself, Ivan Kash, resident Percy historian, almost stepped in this damned stuff. That ain't just no legend, it's true."

Ivan bowed to the crowd. The two yahoos from Tennessee clapped. No one else did. To sweeten the reaction to his tale of almost stepping in the monster whoopsy, he pulled out a small tape recorder and pressed "play". Several "OOHS" and "AAHS" came from the recorder. He turned it off and pointed to the shoe in the display box.

"Folks, to your amazement, this here is the actual shoe I was wearin' when I almost stepped in the official Percy Monster leavins'. Come on and feel free to get a closer look. Don't be shy, but don't come past the ropes neither. This is a once in a lifetime experience to be near this shoe; somethin' to tell your grandkids about."

The tourists moved in a circle around the display of the Percy Monster doody and the very fortunate shoe that just missed it. One of the tourists from Tennessee pulled out a camera and snapped a picture of the pile of shite. Mr. Percy, the security guard, immediately slapped the camera out of her hands. Mr. Percy pulled out his gun and shot the camera 28 times, killing it. Ivan was extremely upset and let the crowd know it.

"NO PHOTOS!!! This is a delicate archeological find!! The microwaves and radioactive fumes that come out of a camera could destroy this priceless artifact of discovery!"

The tourist from Tennessee apologized. Ivan started sobbing and the tourist held him until he composed himself. When he calmed down he held up an 8 x 10 glossy photograph of himself with a big toothless smile and his right foot (with shoe on) precariously dangling over the Percy Monster caca, about to step in it.

"Folks, although we discourage picture takin' here, you can purchase this here official photograph of a reenactment of me about to almost step in the monster's leavins'. The cost is only ten dollars. For an additional forty dollars I will personally autograph the photo. For another thirty dollars on top of the forty and the base cost of ten, I will personally personalize it. For example, if your name is Joe, then I will write "To Joe" on the photograph along with my autograph. I am feeling especially generous today since it's the anniversary of the mysterious disappearance of my brother-in-law, so to celebrate I will allow you to touch the shoe that almost stepped in the monster mess. Would that make you folks happy?"

The two geniuses from Tennessee clapped. No one else did. Ivan pulled out his recorder and pressed "play". The sound of many people cheering came from the recorder. He carefully removed the clear cover to the display box and a few tourists reached in and touched the shoe. Mr. Percy reacted like it was an attack, and shoved them away from the shoe. Ivan quickly dropped the clear cover back over the shoe and snapped at the tourists: "BACK OFF! YOU'LL DESTROY IT! ONE AT A TIME! YOU'LL GET YOUR DAMNED TURN!"

Back outside, tourists were lined up "around the block" to get into The House of the Choking Chicken. As usual, those coming out the exit door looked disheveled, spent, and exhausted. Right next door to The House of the Choking Chicken was a booth with a sign that read:

"PERCY MONSTER LEMONADE
So good it's scary!
Always freshly squeezed right next door!"

Tourists were making sour faces as they sipped from their lemonade cups, locals were guzzling it down. A father and son rushed over to the booth. The boy was holding his crotch and frantically dancing in place. Both were wearing souvenir T-shirts that read, "I was killed by the Percy Monster."

"That boy's got rhythm," the lemonade clerk, who was actually the giant mouth Percy comic, remarked. The boy's frantic father asked, "Where's the restroom?!" and the comic handed the boy a lemonade cup. Meanwhile back in the museum, Ivan Kash was busy signing his 8 x 10 glossy photos for the tourists. Mr. Percy glanced at his watch that didn't work and quickly exited. Ivan didn't notice as he was making chitchat with the tourist whose camera Mr. Percy shot to death. "Where ya from, Darlin'?"

"Nashville."

"Y'all got caca there in Nashville?"

"Not like here. Ours don't glow in the dark."

"That don't shock me," Ivan said proudly. "Percy is an amazing place." He noticed a teenager staring at him. "What is it you kids say, 'Percy's groovy, Daddy-O! Percy blows my mind!' Right? Ain't that what you kids say?"

72 yards away Mr. Percy was on a sand dune about to push down on a detonator box plunger. He spoke aloud to himself sinisterly…"My attempts to plunge this book *The Greatest Novel Ever Written* into the depths of readers' despair have been futile. Therefore I'll do this instead. Enjoy this here blow job, you phallic bastards!" With that, Mr. Percy pushed down on the plunger and the tour buses were blown to smithereens. As pieces of buses rained down all over Percy, killing several people, Mr. Percy looked Heavenward and exclaimed, "The Good Lord's takin' a major dump!" A bus driver's seat fell out of the sky and knocked Mr. Percy out like a 40-watt light bulb hit with a brick. The bus driver's seat then flipped over and crushed a tourist from Harrison, Arkansas, the most racist town in America, killing him instantly, which was fine with me. Black buzzards swooped down for lunch.

Back at the museum Ivan Kash was still collecting cash and signing photos. He was approached by the same teenager who was staring at him before. The teen brought along another teen to help him stare at Ivan. This teen had green spiked hair, skull tattoos, and a ring in his nose. Ivan looked at him and said, "And where are *you* from son, Pluto?"

"I am from the abode of the eternally tormented damned," said the teen.

"I'm married too," Ivan said. "Next picture-purchaser step right up!"

"Hey! When are we gonna see the Percy Monster for real?! This place is a scam!" the first teenager asked loudly to attract attention. And attention it attracted. The crowd followed the teenager's lead and started getting riled up. Several people started chiming in with "We wanna see the monster! We wanna see the monster!" And then a chant started swelling, as the crowd grew progressively angrier. "SHOW US THE MONSTER! SHOW US THE MONSTER! RIP OFF! RIP OFF! SHOW US THE MONSTER!" Ivan raised his hands in an attempt to pacify them.

"Now y'all calm down and listen! Just this mornin' we sent the Percy Posse to escort the monster here for your very eyes to behold. He'll be arrivin' shortly. So stop your moanin', groanin', twitchin' and bitchin'. He'll be along. Now who's next for an autographed photo of yours truly about to step in his poop?"

Nero was frantically running through the woods. His breathing was heavy and fast. His monster claws were ripping, tearing, slashing, and knocking away brush and tree limbs as he fled from the Percy Posse who was about 50 feet behind him carrying torches in broad daylight. Nero spotted a cabin up ahead and ran behind it. The back door opened and Nero ducked down between a garbage can and a large red wheelbarrow. Someone tossed a stack of newspapers next to the garbage can and the door closed. Nero grabbed his rear, mumbled "Oh crap!" and ran behind a brittlebush where he frantically began to dig a squat hole with his claws.

While Nero is digging this would be a good time to tell you that in spite of all the hell he was going through, that he was in fact honored by the very prestigious International Cryptid Society for being the world's newest and most mysterious cryptid. If you don't know, a cryptid is a strange creature whose existence has been claimed but never proven. Nero/The Percy Monster/formerly The Creature from Gruesome Gulch now belonged to an elite group of luminaries which included the Loch Ness Monster, Sasquatch (Bigfoot), the Abominable Snowman (Yeti), Chupacabra (the goat-sucker), the Ozark Howler, the Skunk Ape, Mothman, the Honey Island Swamp Monster, and Junior, the unseen vicious lake monster of Junior Lake in Interlachen, Florida. To be recognized and honored by the International Cryptid Society was something special he could always be proud of. It wasn't the Academy Award he had hoped for, but it was close enough. As an actor, Nero's biggest fear about not being able to ever get out of the monster costume is that it would probably typecast him for life.

As Nero continued to dig, a 14-year-old boy knocked hard on the front door of the cabin. Perpetually pissed-off Old Man Perkins answered the door.

"What do you want?"

"Hello Old Man Perkins, is Molly here?"

"Why?"

"We have a date."

"I wouldn't let you date my dog because you'd knock her up like you knocked on that door."

"Can I see Molly?"

"You can see the wrong end of my shotgun," snapped Old Man Perkins aiming his shotgun at the boy.

"I don't want to knock up your dog, I wanna see Molly."

"Are you callin' my virginal daughter a dog, boy?"

"No sir, Old Man Perkins, sir. Is she here?"

Mrs. Old Lady Perkins called to her husband, "Who is it, Sherman?"

Old Man Perkins called back, "Some kid who wants to date the dog and have his way with her."

"Land sakes! Ain't that against the law?!"

"She's right, boy," Old Man Perkins pointed out. "You are under arrest!" He then called to his wife, "Read him his rights, Miranda!"

As Miranda Perkins came in from the back room with the law book that she had written, Nick Nero darted out from behind the brittlebush while holding his tail. He grabbed a newspaper from the stack by the garbage can and darted back behind the brittlebush. As Nero was frowning at the headlines, Miranda was reading the boy his rights from her book.

"You have the right to remain silent and refuse to answer questions. Anything you do say may be used against you in a court of law-"

The boy interrupted her. "I'll just say that there's a monster taking a dump behind your house. He's probably going to kill you and eat your guts for supper. And your daughter's no virgin; she's a whore. There's not a human or an animal or a kitchen utensil within a hundred miles of here that she hasn't screwed. Have a nice day."

The boy turned and walked away. Old Man Perkins called after him, "That ain't no excuse for wanting to date a dog! Here in Percy we do things white and right!"

The boy spun around, shot Old Man Perkins dirty birds with both hands, and yelled, "HAVE FUN GETTING RIPPED APART BY

THE MONSTER! YOUR DAUGHTER PROBABLY SCREWED HIM TOO!"

The Percy Posse arrived at the cabin with torches blazing in the sunlight, and scoured the area. The lead tracker of the posse, Seymour Most who once found the keys to his first car, a 1976 AMC Pacer, when they fell out of a woman in Walmart, discovered the monster's clawed footprints in the ground and followed them around back to the garbage can, red wheelbarrow, and newspapers. The garbage can had been overturned and the newspapers were in disarray. The wheelbarrow was okay, so you can relax.

"He's been here," the tracker said.

"How do you know?" asked the Percy Posse simultaneously like the one mindless entity that they were.

"These are his footprints with claws," the tracker said measuring with a tape measure, "unless you know someone else with 16 inch feet and claws." He pressed the release button on the tape measure and the tape quickly slithered back into its casing. "But the defining piece of evidence is that he has been through the garbage. Monsters love garbage. That's a fact."

The rest of the posse watched carefully as the tracker continued following the footprints which led directly to the brittlebush Nero went behind. Slowly, cautiously, tracker Seymour Most, former owner of an AMC Pacer, pulled out his machete and with one fell swoop cut down the brittlebush. There he saw an opened newspaper, the Percy Gazette with the headlines: **"PERCY MONSTER LOOSE! WATCH YOUR ASS!"** The entire Percy Posse simultaneously backed up in fright like the one mindless entity that they were. One monster claw was holding up the newspaper from the top. The newspaper seemed to be moving a bit like it was being bumped. The other monster claw was out of view. Nero, who was taking a dump in the squat hole he had dug (yes, there was that poopy flap that Madam Mancowitz installed in the rear of the costume for him to do so) slowly lowered the Percy Gazette and glared at the posse. With his other claw he was holding a turkey leg that had been discarded in the garbage. The posse members were terrified but they had a job to do. Nero chewed on the turkey leg like he meant it. One posse member, Earle Higgins, who really didn't want to be in a posse chasing a bloodthirsty monster, but wanted an excuse to get away from his crazy bitch wife, bent over like he was ready to heave, and choked, "Oh God! He's eating Old Man Perkins' leg!"

Nero snarled, "It's a turkey leg, you moron."

The posse was startled (all at the same time). They were at once terrified and fascinated. Together they all said, **"IT TALKS! IT TALKS! THE MONSTER TALKS!"**

Seymour said, "Some monsters talk and some don't. It's a fact. This one here talks. And he speaks English, so he's not a foreigner." Seymour reached into his fanny pack, pulled out some baby wipes, and handed them to the monster.

"Clean yourself up and let's go."

The posse all said to Seymour at the same time as Nero wiped, "Baby wipes? You carry baby wipes?"

"They keep me clean as a whistle and minty fresh," the tracker said. The entire posse simultaneously snickered at Seymour who added, "I'm cleaner than all of you. And now this damned monster's cleaner than all of you."

The posse stopped snickering and subtly stepped away from each other. Nero stood up and they all moved back nervously as anyone would. He was intimidating enough out of the costume, but with it on he was terrifying. He addressed them. "Listen to me, you nutjobs. I'm not a monster. I'm an actor."

"Was you in *Gunsmoke*?" the posse asked.

"No," Nero answered, "that was before my time."

"Then you ain't no actor," the posse said as they all jumped on him... simultaneously.

The people of Percy (the Percy People) and tourists alike lined the main stretch through Percy in anticipation of the Percy Monster's arrival. Charred tour bus parts were scattered here and there. Some still on top of bodies as buzzards snacked away. A tourist was examining a charred tour bus door that was on top of the bottom half of Percy's resident romantic Edmond Stout, who was being fought over by two female buzzards as they tore him apart. One of the boys who led Nero and Izzy into town purposely bumped into the tourist, snatched his wallet, and spoke to him. "That ain't no bus door, Mister, that there is the door of the flying saucer that the Percy Monster came out of. Me and my friend who don't like girls saw him come out of it with my own eyes and my daddy blowed it up to protect the United States of America."

The anticipation was like nothing the town had ever known before.

The whole place was tingling with excitement. Izzy was sitting in the shade of a Joshua tree out of sight, watching nervously for a different reason. She looked over at the Percy sign which now read "population 426." Mr. Percy, now in his capacity as the mayor wearing a top hat and tails, stood at a microphone on a pig semen shipping crate ready to address the crowd. Milo Mabbitt was perched on the roof of The House of the Choking Chicken watching for the monster's arrival as some tourists who were only interested in themselves waited to get inside. The Percy High School and Flower Shop Marching Band wearing stolen uniforms that didn't match from high schools throughout Los Angeles stood silently, poised to play at their drum major's signal. Suddenly came the news that the tiny twisted town had been waiting for. Milo Mabbitt jumped up and down on the roof of Percy's self-love shack, and pointed down the center of town. **"THEY GOT HIM! THEY GOT HIM! HERE HE COME!"** With that Milo crashed through the roof landing on a female Congresswoman from Georgia's 14th district in the bologna room and they both died. Milo's death was tragic. Hers wasn't. The crowd cheered wildly as the Percy Posse came swaggering down the main drag pushing the red wheelbarrow that they stole from Old Man Perkins. The drum major raised his mace (his baton, not tear gas) and struck up the marching band which played a not-so-fabulous (sucked) rendition of Richard Wagner's "Here Comes the Bride." Nero, of course, was in the wheelbarrow bound with rope and covered with a tarp. He was hidden from public view. Every once in a while he would thrash around attempting to break free, but he really couldn't move much because the posse had tied him with constrictor knots which are extremely difficult to escape from. As my arrest record shows, I know from experience. The Percy Posse parked (say that five times fast) the stolen wheelbarrow and its incensed contents right in front of the mayor who was adjusting the microphone stand. The drum major cued the Percy High School and Flower Shop Marching Band to stop playing, and thankfully they did. But it was a train wreck as none of them stopped at the same time. Mayor Percy tapped on the microphone to test if it was working and then addressed the crowd.

"People of Percy, Percy People, foreigners, tourists, and honored guests...Percy is wonderful. And so is this town." He and the tourists from Tennessee laughed, but no one else did. He swept his arm across the landscape of his beloved Percy and continued. "The trees we have outside are just like the trees we have on our train sets only bigger. Every Saturday night we have our annual snail fights." He got suddenly stern and wagged his finger at the crowd with a warning. "Now y'all know them snail fights is the only gamblin' we allow here. If you can't follow the law in Percy, then start walkin'."

Someone in the crowd yelled, "Sure as heck can't drive!"

"Who said that?!" asked the mayor angrily.

"Stop stallin'!" Someone else yelled. "LET'S SEE THE MONSTER! WE WANT TO SEE HIM!" Others joined in demanding to see the monster too and chanting, "SHOW US THE MONSTER! SHOW US THE MONSTER! SHOW US THE MONSTER!" Mayor Percy raised his hands to quiet them down.

"You'll see the monster soon enough, but I have one more thing I need to address. Folks, education is important, especially if you want to be successful in life. We have too many sheep and hogs runnin' around here pregnant. You boys gotta get back to school! I'd like to congratulate our fine Percy Posse for capturin' the hideous and very dangerous Percy Monster!" The Percy Posse applauded themselves. No one else did. Even the Tennessee tourists didn't. Alright they did. I'm just sick of them clapping at everything. The mayor continued.

"This here Percy Monster who's in this here wheelbarrow under this here tarp has turned this here lovely law-abiding God-fearing community into Hell North!" He turned to the posse. "Y'all boys bring that son of a bitch over to the tent. They're waitin' for him."

Nero thrashed some more under the tarp as the posse wheeled him toward a newly erected large circular tent a short distance away. The crowd followed eagerly. Everyone was excited and scared at the same time. The drum major cued the marching band and they played a lousy rendition of "(Na Na Hey Hey) Kiss Him Goodbye." The mayor headed for the tent and was tripped by Izzy. She let him hit the ground and then grabbed him by the collar, pulling him up to face her. She was seething.

"That poor creature didn't do a damned thing to you, or this town, and you turned all these half-wits against him just so you can make money! You're a very bad man!"

"Oh, no my dear," said the mayor, "I'm a very *good* man. I'm just a very bad mayor."

"And a lousy car mechanic!" someone yelled.

The mayor brushed off his top hat and said, "Now if you'll excuse me, the good people of this glorious town want to meet the monster who is responsible for destroying their lives."

The mayor headed into the tent where the posse had taken Nero. Izzy thought for a moment, realized that the whole town would soon be under the tent, and then took off toward Percy's mechanic shop.

Talk show host Barry Slinger was acting as a barker outside the entrance where everyone was gathered. Ivan Kash was seated at the same small stolen plastic display table with the chewing gum under it that was in the Historic Percy Monster Museum. The same red faux velvet ropes on faux silver barrier poles that surrounded the table were now set up to deter people from entering the tent just yet. The Percy boys were selling cups of "monster food" (which we refer to as peanuts) for a buck a cup. Just in front of the entrance to the tent a large sign read:

"IT'S HIDEOUS! IT'S HORRIBLE! FROM HELL TO HERE!

The World Famous PERCY MONSTER!

$20 gets you in…Pray that you come out
*(no refunds if he kills you)"

Slinger wore a loud parakeet green striped jacket, a skimmer hat, a fake handlebar mustache, and spoke through a pink plastic toy megaphone: "Ladies and Gentlemen! Boys and Girls! Locals and foreigners! In the tent behind me is the most hideous, horrifying, and rudest monster in the history of mankind! Buy your ticket, step right up, and see it with your own two eyes! It's live in person! The Evil of all Horrors! The Horror of all Evils! The one and only *PERCY MONSTER*!"

Nero (as the monster, of course) was sitting on a round wooden rotating pillory in the same exact position as Rodan's "The Thinker", with one exception. He was shooting a bird at the crowd who gawked at him in amazement. His ankle was shackled to the pillory so he couldn't escape or lunge too far. Several of the gawkers held cups of "monster food" and tossed the peanuts at Nero. He growled menacingly at the crowd as Mayor Percy addressed them.

"Folks, we promised you the monster and we delivered!"

The crowd clapped and cheered wildly. The mayor continued. "And now, here's our resident historian and Percy Monster expert, Ivan Kash!" No one clapped other than Ivan. Not even the tourists from Tennessee. Really, they didn't. Alright, they did. Ivan was holding a cattle prod. Nero snarled when he saw it.

"Thank you, Mayor Percy," Ivan said. "Is my car ready yet?"

"Nope," Percy said.

"It's been eight years."

"I'm still waitin' on those plugs," said the mayor.

Ivan addressed the crowd passionately. He pointed at Nero with the cattle prod. "Folks, as most of you know, this son of a bitch almost ruined a good shoe for me!" The crowd booed Nero. Ivan lashed out. "It ain't easy gettin' from here to there and there to here in the condition he put me in!" Again the crowd booed Nero. Several threw monster food at him which he swatted away. Some he ate. Ivan was really getting steamed. "Look at him! Sittin' there all high n' mighty demonstratin' the secret monster hand signal! Notice the word *demon* in '*demon*stratin'. The secret monster hand signal means–"

Mayor Percy interrupted Ivan, "Percy is a great place, folks. We really wish you was here."

Nero noticed swamp witch Madam Mancowitz in the crowd, munching on monster food. The mayor pointed at Nero.

"This here monstrosity of a monster has soiled the good name of Percy, California!"

"California?!" Madam Mancowitz mumbled. "How the hell did I get to California? I hope I don't have to hear those damned Beach Boys and that nutjob Mike Love."

A tourist from American Fork, Utah, aimed a camera at Nero, and Ivan immediately knocked the camera to the ground, smashing it and warning, "NO PHOTOS! YOU'LL ONLY GET HIM MAD!"

Nero snarled, "Too late."

He grabbed the cattle prod and slammed it into Ivan's crotch. Ivan hit the ground in agony. The teenagers applauded. The crowd gasped and ran for their lives, which was kind of dumb because Nero was still shackled to the pillory and they really didn't have any lives to run for. As the crowd fled, a classic silver whiskey flask flew out of someone's pocket and landed at Nero's feet like 94 proof manna from Heaven. He decided to get very religious.

That night Nero was alone in the tent. Now both ankles were shackled to the pillory which was no longer rotating. He was holding the whiskey flask just as Hamlet held Yorick's skull, and just as he held the smoked ham on the billboard. Only this time no cigar and he wasn't smiling. He was extremely drunk, teary, depressed, and very dramatic as he gazed at his monstrous reflection in the flask, and slurred and slaughtered Shakespeare.

"Toby, or not toby, that be the question: whether jizz nogler in the mind you surf the zings and sparrows of outstanding futures, or to take harm against she who caused trouble, and, by opposing, send them." Nero took a long hard swig from the flask, squinted at it, and said, "What the fuck does that mean?" As he pondered, Izzy snuck into the tent carrying a satchel. Nero looked up from the flask in his drunken stupor.

"Oh, look who's here, Little Miss Shortcut. Great little town."

"I see you've been bar-hopping," Izzy said.

She was distraught, but tried not to show it.

"I'm not a froggy or Mr. Nowicki, I'm a monster. We don't hop, we just sort of roam around doing the terrible things that monsters do."

Izzy looked at the shackles on Nero's ankles and started going through the satchel.

"I figured they wouldn't want *you* roaming around, so I borrowed a few things from your car mechanic who likes to blow things up."

Out of the satchel she removed some C4 explosive putty, a spool of wire, a fuse, and a friction igniter.

"Please explain what you're going to do," Nero said. "My curiosity is aroused."

Izzy explained. "I'm putting exploding putty on your shackles. Terrorists use it to blow up ships and buildings. Percy uses it to blow up buses."

She attached the C4 putty and wire to the two shackles, and trailed the wire to behind some stacked crates about twenty feet away. She then fastened the other end of the wire to the friction igniter. Nero was getting concerned.

"Ships and buildings and buses are bigger than my ankles."

"You want to get out of here or not?" Izzy asked.

"Yeah," Nero said. "While you're at it, blast off that stun jewelry my dear old daddy gave me."

Izzy quickly attached some of the explosive putty to the stun bracelet too, and ran a joining wire to the main wire.

"Cover your monster ears if you have any. This could be a loud Boom Boom."

She ducked behind the crates and struck the friction igniter. There were three rapid sudden sharp **BANGS** as the shackles and stun bracelet cracked off in shattered pieces. Nero flew off the pillory and crashed to the ground grasping his charred ankles and shrieking and writhing in agony.

"What a baby!" Izzy said, "I only used a little. Stop the floor show and let's blow this Popsicle stand before the yahoos get here!"

She helped him up, and with Nero limping in obvious pain, they exited the tent as quickly as they could. 37 minutes later back in the clearing in the woods, Izzy was sitting on the ground watching Nero who was limping around the clearing cursing his head off, and pausing now and then to grab his ankles and scream in pain. The booze was wearing off and he was becoming more "sensitive."

"You are so dramatic," she said. "You chose the right career."

"SHUT UP! You almost killed me!" He spied something on the ground. It was a hand mirror. "What the hell is a hand mirror doing in the woods?"

As he reached down and picked it up, the movement of the mirror released a cocked tree branch which sprang upward. Attached to the top of the branch was a rope which lassoed Nero's monster foot and flung him straight up and back, suspending him swaying upside down. The hand mirror was still in his "hand." He looked in the mirror and saw the upside down reflection of Nigel Daw. Daw looked at Nero hanging there helpless and almost felt pity, but not quite.

"There is one thing monsters and actors cannot seem to resist… mirrors. Both creatures are fascinated by what they see. You were trapped by your own vanity, Mr. Nero, how poetic."

"Bring him down!" Izzy demanded.

"Oh, I will. I promise. You like the trap, luv? Very primitive, yet very effective. I learned how to make them when I did my Oscar-nominated documentary on the Sentinelese tribe."

"I learned how to make them watching *Gilligan's Island*," Izzy said. "Now get him down!"

"A branch, a rope, and someone or some*thing* in the wrong place at the right time; and Nick Nero's time has come," Daw mused. Nero took a swipe at Daw's head and just missed him.

"Now, now, don't be a naughty monster," Daw scolded. "You don't want to give monsters a bad name, do you? You'll be happy to know that I've decided that you're my ticket to some big money. The merchandising on you alone will make me millions. These buffoons in Percy have no idea what they have or what they're doing. But I do. Let's get you down from there." He called sweetly toward the woods, "Come out, come out, wherever you are..."

Nigel Daw's giggling film crew entered the clearing from the surrounding woods wheeling out a large wooden crate marked "HANDLE WITH CARE" and "HAZARDOUS." They positioned the crate directly under Nero, removed the lid, and lowered him down into it.

"Let him go you scumbag," Izzy demanded again.

"I'm sorry luv," Daw said. "I didn't go to all this trouble just to let him go. By the way, one of my more graceful crew members accidentally stepped on this when we were interviewing the old witch." He tossed her a busted radiophone. "I don't think it works anymore. I don't know who it belongs to, but I thought *you* might know since this place is far from the madding crowd."

She looked just past him. "Not as far as you think."

Suddenly the Percy Posse, torches in hand, burst on the scene.

"We figured on trouble," lead tracker Seymour Most stated. "That's *our* monster. Get your own," he told Daw. Izzy came up from behind Daw and cold-cocked him with the busted radiophone.

"It works," she grinned.

Seymour turned to the film crew. "Unless y'all wanna join him in La La Land, I suggest you beat it."

The film crew scattered. Seymour then turned to Izzy.

"Now, Mam, I ain't just a tracker. When I ain't trackin' I spend my free time thinkin'. And I thought of somethin' while I was thinkin'. I figured out how to get rid of these here Hollywood weirdos who have invaded the peace and tranquility of Percy the town, not the man. I don't give two hoots about the man. He blew off my penis 'cause it looked phallic."

After a few moments of letting that sink in, Izzy asked, "And what about all the money this town is making because of the monster?"

"We don't need the money," Seymour said. "We have Percy. And when a man has Percy, that's all he needs."

Izzy (and you) thought about that statement for a few moments. Izzy looked over at Nero who was just sitting in the crate with his monster head in his monster claws, sulking. Then she said to Seymour, "Alright. What's your brilliant idea?"

Two days later at high noon the Percy High School and Flower Shop Marching Band (in blackface) was on the main drag playing a slow mournful funeral dirge as six members of the Percy Posse acted as pallbearers for a large casket with the words "This End Up" stenciled on the lid, moving slowly behind the band. The casket was put down in front of the raised platform the mayor used to address the people of Percy (the Percy People). The drum major cued the band to stop playing, and they did, like the train wreck that they were. Mayor Percy tapped on the microphone a few times to see if it was working and then addressed the crowd. Behind him, unnoticed except by you, Izzy, Seymour, and yours truly, Nick Nero (the Percy Monster) slipped into The House of the Choking Chicken. The mayor spoke.

"People of Percy, foreigners, and honored guests…This is a very sad day for our little town. Today we say farewell, adios, sayonara, toodle-oo, and don't take any wooden nickels to a good friend of us all. Folks, just because somethin's different from you, don't mean it's evil. Except for that damned Pig Boy and that Wilkins boy. That Wilkins boy was straight from Hell. That son of a bitch got three nipples and seven toes on each foot! Food poisoning couldn't get you sicker than that little freak! Now y'all know that I got a lot of respect for the man upstairs, but he really dropped the ball with that boy. Folks, we have gathered here today to say bon voyage and good riddance to the Percy Monster."

A few mourners sobbed. One asked, "Mayor is my car repaired yet?"

"Nope," the mayor said. "And now's not the time to ask me."

"My gun's repaired," the mourner shot back.

"Should be ready any day now," the mayor said. He continued the eulogy. "The demise of the Percy Monster came sudden-like in a freak accident. Here now is our resident historian and monster expert Ivan Kash to explain what happened to our dearly departed compadre."

The mayor and Ivan and maybe the Tennessee tourists were the only ones who clapped as Ivan stepped up to the microphone. He was clearly affected by the monster's death. His voice quivered as he spoke and he blotted tears.

"Thank you Mayor Percy. Friends and foreigners, I'm told that the monster was in the clearin' in the woods that we call 'God's Bald Spot' when the flyin' saucer that first brought him here came back to pick him up. The saucer was tryin' to land on God's Bald Spot and…and…"

Ivan lost his composure and broke down sobbing like a little baby girl who had her rattle stepped on and crushed by a guy who her mommy was screwing while her daddy was at work. The mayor moved Ivan aside, patted him on the shoulder, and resumed speaking to the mourners.

"Bein' a monster expert and historian, Mr. Kash, not Johnny Cash, Ivan Kash, although I'd rather have Johnny Cash here instead of Ivan Kash, gets attached to his work in an emotional way. So we can certainly understand his sorrow and grief at this sad and sorrowful time of grieving sadly. What Ivan was tryin' to explain is that when the flyin' saucer was comin' down…well…when you're goin' down on somethin', you can't really see where you're goin'. That saucer squashed that poor monster bastard like a pancake."

Ivan, still choking on tears, grabbed the microphone. He was livid. "Them aliens in flyin' saucers got them big eyes, but they can't see shit!"

Again, the mayor moved Ivan aside, patted him on the shoulder, and took back the microphone. "Folks, we'll all miss the Percy Monster terribly." The mayor saluted the casket and nodded to the pallbearers while swatting a fly. "Now go plant him before he stinks up the whole goddamned town. I don't want no smelly Percy."

The pallbearers picked up the casket and headed down the main drag toward the Percy graveyard. The drum major cued the Percy High School and Flower Shop Marching Band and they broke into a rousing (and actually not half bad) New Orleans style Dixieland jazz rendition of "When the Saints Go Marching In." The mourners started dancing wildly en route to the graveyard. Nigel Daw, with his head wound in bandages, was watching the proceedings from a tour bus driver's seat that was on top of the skeletal remains of that tourist from Harrison, Arkansas, that had been picked clean by black buzzards. *Hollywood Exposed* reporter Jerry Juxson was back on the scene and approached Daw.

"Percy just lost its superstar."

"Bloody rude of him to leave now," Daw said.

"Messed up some plans, Mr. Daw?"

"C'est la vie. At least he got out of this residential rectum."

"We can take you and your crew in the van," Juxson offered. "You may have to leave some of your equipment if there's no room."

"I'd rather leave my crew," Daw said seriously. "The equipment's worth something."

Daw and Juxson gathered a few things and prepared to leave. Daw paused for one last look and said, "Farewell sweet Percy. I would have accomplished more spanking my monkey."

When Daw and Juxson were gone from sight and everyone else was at the graveyard, Nero came out of The House of the Choking Chicken looking as exhausted and disheveled as a monster could look. He glanced around seeing no one and said, "People come and go so quickly here." Meanwhile at the graveyard the pallbearers started lowering the casket into the ground as the bugle player for the Percy High School and Flower Shop Marching Band played a really crappy rendition of "TAPS." Mayor Percy stopped him as an act of mercy and presided over the burial, reading from the Percy Bible:

"Ashes to ashes, dust to dust. Why do they call it 'love' when it's lust?"

The mourners all responded with "Amen."

"Alright boys, flip it," the mayor ordered.

The pallbearers flipped the casket upside down and dropped it into the grave. Mayor Percy explained what just happened. "Folks and foreigners, if this is your first Percy burial, and we hope it ain't your last-"

"Keep 'em comin'. Is my car ready yet?" a mourner asked.

The mayor ignored the outburst and continued. "Let me explain that we always bury our dead upside down so they can see where they're goin'. Not like aliens with big eyes that can't see what they're landin' their saucer on. It's just our way of sayin' 'thank you for dyin' in Percy'. Alright, let's head back. No need to hang around here."

Late that night outside the Caribou Inn, Nero tossed a hangman's noose over one of the huge antlers protruding from the roof. He climbed up and stood on the same large wooden crate marked "HANDLE WITH CARE" and "HAZARDOUS" that Nigel Daw and his film crew tried to hold him in when he was captured. With the noose around his neck, Nero was gathering the "courage" to step off the crate. He was distraught and in turmoil. Izzy stepped out of the darkness and looked at the monster about to hang himself from the giant antlers. She was shaken, but tried not to show it.

"Now there's something you don't see every day," she said. "One funeral for you today wasn't enough?"

Nero was flustered. "How'd you know I was here?"

"I did all sorts of scientific and mathematical calculations to figure out where you were. And when that didn't work I followed the giant monster footprints. They give you away Nero. So are you rehearsing for a tragedy here?"

"I don't need any rehearsal for that. I've had enough. I lived as a monster; I'll die as a monster."

Izzy teared up and got very serious.

"Listen…Nick…Everything changes. You were bad news, but you had the balls to leave a terrible situation and chase your dream and change what you could. That takes courage. I respect that. Look at me. I have a lousy personality, so making a friend isn't easy for me. I'm hard to take. People don't hang around; pardon the pun. But now I have a friend who's a famous actor. That's pretty special."

Nero looked at her and then at the four foot drop under his feet. "Maybe this is what I am inside. Maybe I got turned inside-out. Go to my old man. I'm sure he'll see you. Tell him I'm sorry I was a fuck-up…No; don't say 'fuck-up', say 'loser'. He'll like that better. Tell him to give you my inheritance if he hasn't written me out of his will. I don't have anyone else."

Nero stepped off the crate. For a moment it looked like he had made himself taller. And then, from his weight pulling down on the antlers, the already-tilted Caribou Inn toppled over. Nero hit the ground on his tail with a jolt, as though the Earth had stood up to greet him. The noose was still around his neck. He wasn't hurt at all. Izzy, who had just stifled a scream, stared in absolute amazement as Mr. Percy in his capacity as the Caribou Inn desk clerk, crawled out of the back door of the "hotel" which was now facing the Percy sky. The Caribou Inn toppling over had also caused Mr. Percy's bad blond toupee to topple over, and it hung off his head. He saw the Percy Monster staring at him and threw a fit for all to hear,

"IT'S THE PERCY MONSTER ZOMBIE! IT COME OUT OF THE GRAVE! BRING BASEBALL BATS! KILL THE ZOMBIE BASTARD! BASH THE BRAIN! BUST HIS BEAN! KNOCK HIS NOODLE!"

Completely frazzled, Nero dropped his monster head between his monster knees. Izzy sat down beside him and put her arms around him as Mr. Percy continued to rant and rave and the people of Percy (the Percy People) emerged.

"This place is like the asshole of Oz," Nero sighed.

Mr. Percy glared at him. "Well, if you hate it so much zombie monster, why don't you click your heels together three times and scoot!"

Nero lunged. Mr. Percy screamed like a little Girl Scout girl who had her Do-si-dos cookies crumbled. Then he started yelling at the moon, "YOU'RE MY WITNESS, BILLY! THE ZOMBIE MONSTER TRIED TO KILL ME! WE'LL TAKE HIS ZOMBIE MONSTER TAIL TO COURT! YOU'LL HAVE TO TESTIFY!"

On the moon, Chester Flemlock watching all this with his telescope shook his head, puffed his pipe, and mumbled, "Schmuck Nirvana."

Back in Percy Mr. Percy turned to Nero and said, "I am judge and jury in Percy."

"I'm sure I'll get a fair trial," Nero mumbled.

"Billy saw it all," Percy said. "I *will* put him on the stand. Celestial orbs do not lie in court."

Again Nero started after Mr. Percy. Izzy jumped in front of Nero and stopped him. She pointed back toward the entrance to Percy as a bright light headed toward them.

"Look! Here's someone who can help you!"

The approaching bright light separated into two headlights and a black limousine pulled up, headlights shining directly on Nero who squinted to see who it was. The driver's side door and the passenger door opened simultaneously. Angelo and Toto got out. Nero fell back and just sat on the ground. Angelo opened the rear door and helped Don Neroni exit the limo, walking stick in hand. He walked slowly over to Nero and stood over him, taking in the sight of his only son in the guise of a monster with a noose around his neck. With the headlights behind him and Nero at his feet, Don Neroni appeared absolutely menacing. Angelo looked down at Nero, shook his head, and smirked. "Did you think we wouldn't find you, Superstar?" He looked around. "You ran away and joined the circus, or whatever the fuck this place is?"

Don Neroni addressed Angelo with his eyes fixed on his son. "Shut your face and turn those lights off. They bother me."

Angelo did as he was told. Toto removed the noose from around

Nero's neck with a comment, "Superstar got a little dick so he's trying to get hung."

He laughed alone at his remark. Don Neroni wasn't amused. "That's enough sampling of your lack of mentality for one night. I want to talk to my son alone."

Angelo and Toto offered to get the don something to sit on, but he refused it, so they helped him sit down on the ground next to Nero and walked away to give them their privacy. Toto pulled out his little note pad and started writing. Father and son sat together in silence for several very tense moments. Finally the don spoke. His voice trembled.

"I don't like seeing my son with a noose around his neck…Especially if I put it there."

"And I don't like what you do," Nero said sadly. "I don't like who I've become."

"Cosa ci consiglia?" the don asked.

"My Italian doesn't work right now," Nero said.

"I asked what you would recommend."

"I don't know," Nero said. "All I know is I don't like that I was part of it. It kept me stupid. And you treat me like the dirt you're sitting in."

"I think you do stupid things and you play games, but you're not stupid, Nicolo." He pointed his walking stick toward Angelo and Toto. "*That's* stupid."

They both watched Angelo and Toto as they wandered around and stopped to read the Percy sign aloud, "Pig Semen Capital of the World." They both laughed. Angelo said, "Even a pig can join the fuckin' navy."

The don shook his head. "I didn't hire them for their brains. They're babbos with muscle. That's all they'll ever be. I'm hard on you because you're my son…and I love you."

"Love me less," Nero said.

After a few awkward moments the don said, "You know on that *Hollywood Exposed* show, they showed the Percy Monster going after that lousy Nigel Daw, that son of a bitch that did that documentary on Cosa Nostra. I knew that monster was you when I saw it on television. This get-up is from your first movie *The Thing from Gopher Gulch*."

Nero corrected him, "*The Creature from Gruesome Gulch*."

"The Thing, Creature, whatever. I thought you were terrific in that. The monster didn't talk, but you did good."

Nero was surprised. "You saw that movie?"

"I've seen all your movies. I don't like the language in most of them, but you don't write them, you just say the lines. I know I give you a hard time with the acting thing, but no one's ever left the family unless they were leaving life at the same time. And my mother was defiled and deflowered by that troupe of actors in Palermo. The truth is I'm proud of you. Your mother would be proud of you too. You took a big risk. Speaking of which, I want my book back, Nicolo. You used it to blackmail half of Hollywood to get where you are. Don't deny it." He looked around. "I don't mean *here* where you are."

"It's sewn into my crotch," Nero said. "And (he got loud and angry) I CAN'T GET THE GODDAMNED COSTUME OFF!!!"

Angelo called over to him, "You wearin' a costume, Superstar?" Nero had enough. He jumped up, ran over to Angelo, and swiped him with a claw, drawing blood. Angelo pushed the button on the remote for the stun bracelet repeatedly but nothing happened. Nero knocked it away and clobbered Angelo with a solid backhand. Toto pulled his gun on Nero, but Don Neroni motioned him to stop, which he did. Nero returned to his father and sat back down next to him.

"He had that coming," Don Neroni said. "So what are you going to do now, Nicolo?"

"I don't know. You're right. I blackmailed my way through my career."

"You think you're the first to do that? You didn't invent it, my boy. That doesn't mean you're a bad actor. You just took a different road."

"I think it's time I got off this road and took a new one," Nero said. "I could ask Izzy to marry me. She hates me and loves me at the same time. Isn't that what marriage is? I could start over; a white picket fence and a station wagon."

"Isabella? Your driver? You can't marry her, Nicolo," the don said.

"Why not?"

"Because she's your sister, that's why not."

There was a heavy silence as that bit of information sank in like the Titanic.

"My *WHAT*?!"

"Let's get back to the house. It's been a long night," the don said. "I'll explain the birds and bees to you tomorrow. You have my word. In the mean time, you try to figure it out."

Don Neroni waved Angelo and Toto over to him. As they started walking over, Nero motioned for them to stop and they did. He helped his father up and walked him slowly toward the goons. Don Neroni stopped walking for a moment and looked at his son. "There is a Jewish proverb that says when a father helps a son to walk, they both laugh. But when a son must help his father to walk, they both cry."

"You should think of things like that before you do what you do to me," Nero whispered. He passed his father to Angelo and Toto who helped him over to the limo.

"Isabella drives," the don ordered.

"Terrific," Nero said. "No shortcuts."

Izzy sneered at him and got behind the wheel. Nero got in the passenger seat. He closed the door on his own tail, pulled it in, and closed the door again. The limo peeled away, leaving Percy (both the man and the town) in the rearview mirror. As they drove away Angelo said to Toto, "Hey Shakespeare Junior, let's hear another poem." Toto pulled out his little note pad.

"Alright, I just wrote this one. It's called "Fuhgeddaboudit.""

""Fuhgeddaboudit'. Good title. Lots of mystery in it," Angelo said.

"Pure genius," Don Neroni remarked.

"Yeah…It's like a love poem, only different," Toto revealed. "It goes like this…" He cleared his throat and got dramatic.

"You think you mean shit to me?
Fuhgeddaboudit, my love
When I look in your eyes
you know what I see?
A tramp what screwed half the fuckin' country
under the stars above
So don't come knockin' on my front door
you stupid ugly fuckin' whore"

Angelo clapped. "Who knew you was so sensitive under all that–"

"Stupidity," the don interjected. "If the literary world has a toilet, it's sitting next to me. If you write another word I'll kill you myself." The don turned his attention from Toto to Nero. "Nicolo, that Percy place is not a bad spot for a casino. Would they gamble there?"

As the limo was heading out, the Percy comic (the giant mouth with one eye, one leg, one arm, and a bowler hat) was prowling the stage of the Percy Comedy Club.

"So a guy says to a girl, 'Will you go out with me?' She says 'No, because you'll fall in love with me and you'll propose and I'll say 'yes' because I want your money and we'll go skydiving on our honeymoon and our chutes won't open and we'll fall to the ground and die and you'll come back reincarnated as an electric chainsaw and I'll come back as a fish. An electric chainsaw and a fish wouldn't work because if you put the electric chainsaw in water to be with the fish it will electrocute the fish who will die and the chainsaw will get all ruined and rusty. You're asking me to die twice for you, which I will not do. So no, I won't go out with you.'"

Some women in the audience laughed. The comic stared with his one eye at the large chest of one of the laughing women. The woman said, "My eyes are up here." The comic said, "I know, I was staring at your tits." A few men laughed. The comic continued. "I accidentally pushed my grandmother off the roof of a ten story building. Why do people scream when they're falling off a building or a high place? What the hell does that accomplish other than 'Hey look at me, I'm falling!'? People are dumb, aren't they? Here's a true story for you history buffs. A guy named Benjamin Boyd was a counterfeiter who had been caught and was in the slammer. His buddy wanted to spring him from jail, so he planned to steal Abraham Lincoln's body, and quote, 'return it unharmed' if Boyd was set free. 'Unharmed'?! The guy's dead! 'Oh please don't hurt dead Abe. We'll release Boyd and give you whatever you want. Just don't hurt the dead guy.' So last night I was mugged, true story. I was coming out of the Laundromat where I hang out between shows because there's lots of poor broads there who would do anything for detergent, when a guy pulled a gun on me. I said, 'How much do you want for the gun? I'll give you fifty bucks.' He said, 'How 'bout I shoot you?' I said, 'Then it becomes a used gun and depreciates in value. Now I'll give you five bucks for it.' He agreed. I gave him five bucks and he gave me the gun which I immediately pointed at him and demanded my five bucks, plus a thousand bucks for my time and trouble. He didn't have the thousand. He said, 'I won't lay down and die.' I said, 'Then you can do it standing up,' and I killed him. I'm hiding out here with all you fine people. Anyone here watch porn? I watch it now and then but only because I wait for *the question*; the famous porn question." The comic pointed to a guy in the audience. "He knows what I'm taking about; Right?"

The guy in the audience smiled and nodded.

"Here's how the question works. A couple is screwing like crazy.

They're moaning, howling, really going at it. The camera pulls back so we can see the door to the room. Moments later the door opens and another woman, typically an older mother figure, enters the room, watches them banging like mad with this look of total confusion on her face, and inquires… *'What are you doing?'* That's the famous porn question. People are screwing like mad six feet in front of you and you have absolutely no idea at all what they're doing. 'I'm doing my taxes, Mom. Wanna join in and help me do my taxes with my girlfriend? We're filing a joint return.'"

Speaking of returns, late that night the Neroni limo had returned to the compound and the following day the don was keeping his word in his office. Angelo and Toto were standing by the door, their hands folded respectfully in front of them. Izzy was seated. Nero was standing, still in his monster costume, of course. Don Neroni was seated at his desk.

"Sit down, Nicolo," he said.

"No thanks," Nero said, expecting to hear things he didn't want to hear.

"Suit yourself. I promised you both I would explain some things. Isabella's mother and I were…friends, *good* friends. She was my-"

"Comare," Nero interjected.

"Yes. Elvis set me up with her in Vegas." He gestured to Izzy. "As you can see, that was a long time ago."

Izzy cringed. "Gee thanks…*Daddy.*"

Don Neroni came around his desk, grabbed her face, and kissed her on the forehead. He laughed. "I didn't mean it like that, my dear. You look… like you. Your mama was a hell of a dancer."

"That's good to hear," she said. "I'm so proud."

Then father looked at son. "So Nicolo, as I told you, you can't marry Isabella because she's your sister."

Izzy spun and stared at Nero. "And I'd rather die anyway, so that's two strikes. Who wants a bunch of baby lizards running all over the house?"

Angelo turned to Toto. "Superstar can't get a broad so he wants to marry his sister."

Toto shook his head, "In Night School they told us that in Greek mythology Zeus married his sister Hera. But these days, that's disgusting. Superstar has no moral compass. It's like in Florida they had to make sex with dead bodies illegal. It doesn't occur to the people in Florida that maybe you shouldn't bang a corpse. It has to be written law. You screw a corpse in Florida and it's a second-degree felony and maybe two years in the joint. Superstar inspires a poem in me that goes like this: No other broad let him kiss her, so he had to marry his very own sister."

Angelo looked at Toto in total awe. "You are some kinda genius. You're like a poetry Eisenstein. When are you going to New York to do your poetry? They love that crap there."

"Maybe soon," Toto said. "Since I'm like the voice of my generation."

A shot was fired at Toto. The bullet hit the wall inches from his head. Don Neroni was holding the gun.

"That's your second warning," he said. "There is no third. Write one more word and see what happens."

Toto was shaken; "What?! I didn't *write* it. I *said* it!"

"That's true, Godfather," Angelo said. "I watched him the whole time. He didn't write nuthin'. It just came out of his head like...like somethin' that comes out of people's heads. Like a water fountain."

The don, Nero, and Izzy all stared at Angelo. After several moments, Don Neroni pointed his walking stick at Toto. "Your poetry career is hereby over. Don't write it. Don't say it. Don't even think it in that tiny brain of yours. Capisce, Toto?"

"Can I do my poetry in New York?" Toto asked nervously. "I'm the voice of my generation, Godfather."

"You're the voice of a sewer system," the don said, "But you'll be almost 3000 miles away in Castellano's turf, so go ahead, with my blessing." Don Neroni addressed Nero. "The truth is I recently found out that Isabella was my daughter. So a big part of this, Nicolo, was to test her loyalty to me, the family, *and* to you."

Nero was seething, "So all this was a setup."

"No. Only Isabella being your driver was set up, nothing else. You should know she kept me informed of your whereabouts when she could."

"Informed? How?"

Izzy broke in. "I had a radiophone, but it broke. And then I broke it again on Daw's head when he wouldn't set you free."

"So you conned me and then you ratted on me."

"She's your sister. She was looking after you," the don said.

"You mean she was looking after your precious book!"

"Both. She was looking after my precious son *and* my precious book. In light of recent events I've decided there will be some changes around here with our... Cosa Nostra." He addressed them all, "My son has opened my eyes to some things, whether he knows it or not. Therefore, since my health is not going to win any awards, and as the Americans say, I'm no spring chicken long in the tooth, my daughter Isabella will run the show until I say otherwise. If I like what she does she might stay in that position. Maybe she can…modernize. I believe that it's time for a woman's influence. Maybe there won't be so much violence and trouble among the families. That idea was your mother's many years ago, Nicolo. Maybe I should have listened."

"Maybe Izzy can muscle in and take over the fashion industry. I know a good seamstress in the woods," Nero commented.

Don Neroni ignored him and continued, "Nicolo will be in charge of security for the time being." He looked at his son. "I'm not breaking your position, Nicolo. This is temporary while you're here. I don't like that you took the book. It was dangerous and disrespectful. You put a lot of very important people at risk by doing that. This will give you time to reflect on your mistake. Don't fight it." He turned to Angelo and Toto. "Tie him up to the back fence. Give him a long leash so he has room to run around. And make sure he has plenty of water."

Angelo and Toto escorted Nero out the door. He was so beaten down that he didn't struggle.

"That's a good boy, Superstar. Don't hump my leg," Angelo winked.

"That's Toto's territory," Nero said, "He's the expert."

Izzy and her father remained in the office.

"Nicky doesn't like to be tied down," Izzy said.

The don took her face in his trembling hands and kissed her forehead again. "Don't worry about your brother. He'll be okay. Come with me, I'll show you the ropes."

That night from the back of the compound under a knowing moon, there was a strange howling. Minutes later Angelo and Toto were back there putting the new "top dog of security," wise. Angelo warned, "Close your head before we close it for you, Fido! Humans are trying to sleep!"

"Give him a bone to chew on so he'll shut up," Toto said.

"Screw you, Toto," Angelo snapped, "you give him *your* bone."

Izzy came out of the main house and motioned Angelo and Toto to leave, which they did, acknowledging her newfound authority. Nero was sitting on the ground with his monster head in his monster claws "chained," not tied on a long leash per the don's instructions, to the high barbed wire security fence at the back of the compound. A bowl of water was next to him. Izzy approached cautiously, not quite sure what to say, but saying it anyway, "so…how ya doin' brother dear?" Nero just looked at her, like the answer should be pretty obvious. Izzy looked up at the moon. "Billy's lookin' good tonight." Again, Nero just looked at her. "I got good news," she said.

"Let me guess," he said. "The old man arranged for me to perform *Hamlet* with Pig Boy in the role of Claudius, the King of Denmark."

"Not *that* good," Izzy said. "But I know how to remove the costume." Nero stared at her. "Don't stop now, talk!"

"Datu Puti vinegar, a solvent-based degreaser, and refined pomace olive oil mixed. We use 33 1/3 percent of each one. We inject the solution through the seams and it slides right off. Madam Mancowitz's maid told me how to do it."

Nero was thrilled. But after a few moments of being thrilled he had a question, "And how long ago did Madam Mancowitz's maid tell you this?"

"It doesn't matter," Izzy said. "We couldn't get what we needed in Percy anyway. I tried. We'll get you out of that thing tomorrow. And if we can't do it we'll just go back to Percy with the stuff and Madam Mancowitz's maid will do it. We'll get there quick, I know a shortcut."

Nero delivered the nastiest glare in cinematic history, even though this is a book, and Izzy backed away just as the Digby orb zoomed by overhead followed by Marty and Bink in their flying saucer closing in fast. In the saucer's tailwind was the ZX-12 which seemed to be flying erratically. That was because the windshield and the porthole windows were dirty because the pod had passed through space dust from exploding stars, and they couldn't really see where they were going. You see, even though they were still stuck and banished on Asteroid #9 as their home, the Outlaws still had the ZX-12 and did take it for a joyride now and then to cruise for star maidens and Big Bang bimbos that they wouldn't have to pay. Rollo, being the leader, volunteered Alfie to tether up and go out and clean the portholes and windshield. Alfie volunteered Sluggo to do it, but Sluggo said that his hair hurt and he needed his rest, so Alfie ended up doing it.

CHAPTER 11

Alfie got into his space suit, grabbed some Dollar Store glass cleaner spray, a 2-ply paper towel, and floated out of the ZX-12 to do the windows. *Here I am an expert in Greek mythology cleaning windows in outer space,* he thought to himself. Suddenly, and without any warning (which is pretty much what "suddenly" means) the perfect space storm happened. Alfie was wiping down the porthole. Sluggo was at the controls. Rollo was visiting the crapper, which was a slang term first used by soldiers in 1932 inspired by Thomas Crapper who (despite what you think) did *not* invent the toilet, but *manufactured* them in England. He did however invent the nastily named "ballcock," the tank-filling mechanism still in use as of the writing of this magnificent book. Where was I? Oh yeah, so while at the controls, Sluggo glanced out the still-dirty windshield which Alfie should have cleaned first, but that would make sense, and there's no place for that here. Anyway, while glancing, Sluggo thought he saw a Deep Space Zaus, which is a lot like a flying scorpion with wheels only completely different, fly across the path of the pod and to avoid hitting it he slammed on the brakes. There was a loud THUD and a scream and lots of bad nasty words that I won't repeat here, coming from the crapper. Alfie was flung forward so fast that he was faster than light. For the more skilled and competent amongst you, go outside at night and turn on a flashlight. He was faster than the light that comes out of that cheap thing. As Alfie was flinging forward, an energy density field lower than a negative mass appeared and he hit Alcubierre warp drive named after Mexican theoretical physicist Miguel Alcubierre who based his findings on Albert Einstein's field equations of relativity. Alfie landed on the traversable wormhole and the

Einstein-Rosen Bridge which links contrasting points in the spacetime continuum. And then, if all that wasn't enough to blow up your skirt, Alfie sensed some gravitational-wave radiation and two infinite loops of parallel cosmic strings approaching. You know what the result of all this scientific lunacy was? Alfie was sent back in time to the year 2999 BCE, the time and place of Greek mythology, something he knew a lot about. But just because you might know a lot about rattlesnakes doesn't mean you should cuddle with them. That said, if you're still reading this it means you have nothing better to do, so let's go for the ride. Alfie landed ass-first in the beginning…the *very* beginning. I'm talkin' the *very very* beginning when there was nothing but Atlas holding the planet Earth (and the heavens) on his shoulders as punishment for leading the Titans against Zeus and the other gods in a battle for control of the heavens. It was a bad move and it pissed Zeus off, so you get what you get. What Atlas got was a hernia the size of Texas, Alaska, and California combined.

So how did it all begin? It all began with Heaven and Earth screwing one night because they got a little tipsy, lost their heads, and got some stankie on the hang down. Out of that fateful drunken night came three children who were Cyclopes. They were big strong guys about 15 feet tall and weighing in at about 2500 pounds. They each had only one eye in the middle of their forehead as round and as big as a wagon wheel like you would see in the television series *Wagon Train* which ran from 1957 to 1965. *Star Trek* creator Gene Roddenberry based *Star Trek* on *Wagon Train* which is an interesting fact that you never knew until this very moment. He saw it as *Wagon Train* in space. The Cyclopes were not the best-looking boys, but they sure could wink at broads. The next three kids each had a hundred hands and fifty heads. They were a favorite of theater performers because they made great audiences and always applauded loudly. However, they seldom dated. Father Heaven refused to believe that he was their father claiming no resemblance, and accused Mother Earth of cheating on him. He was embarrassed by these offspring and had them imprisoned in a secret place within the Earth's core. The last group of kiddies was the Titans. You've heard of them. No, I don't mean the football team; I mean the mythological entities. They were the children of Heaven and Earth, and I already explained how booze and broads are trouble. The most important Titan was Cronus who became ruler of the universe, sort of like what The Evil One aspired to be, but a hell of a lot taller than half an inch, and handsomer. When Cronus was about to become a father he heard a rumor that one of his children would attempt to overthrow him as ruler of the universe. So Cronus did what any decent father would do under the circumstances and swallowed his children whole as they were born. When the last child Zeus was born, his mother had him secretly carried off to Crete while she wrapped a great stone in swaddling clothes which Cronus thought was the baby and swallowed down accordingly, which must've really been a bitch passing. And that was long before Thomas Crapper made the scene. Years later when Zeus was grown, he returned from Crete and with the help of his Grandma Earth, forced Cronus to upchuck his brothers and sister who were now full-grown. I'm glad I didn't have to see that. I get sick watching final expenses commercials on television. So there followed a terrible war that almost destroyed the universe, though not at the level that The Evil One had his microscopic heart set on, as Zeus and his brothers battled Cronus and the other Titans. Well, to make a very long story short, Zeus and his siblings took over the universe and made their home on the tippy-top of Mount Olympus in Greece. Although it wasn't actually the tippy-top, it was just under it. I want to inform you at this point, dear reader, that any establishing scenes involving Mount Olympus will be matte paintings rendered by my friend Louisa in France and not the real thing as I simply could not afford any real location work and not one single hotel, motel, or flophouse would accept these actors. Let's move on. So Zeus punished the Titans terribly, like Atlas there who must bear the cruel weight of the crushing world and apparently has something to say. What? I'm busy writing, what do you want?

"I gotta go to the crapper. Will you hold Earth a sec?"

No. I'm not that gullible. I survived New York, mister! You'll take off and I'll get stuck holding that nightmare, which is probably too heavy for me anyway. Forget it.

We pick it up centuries later in ancient Greece around 400 BCE at the foot of Mount Olympus, home of the gods (and our first look at Louisa's matte painting) where Alfie, now wearing a toga which he probably stole, being an outlaw and all, was sitting against a boulder counting his toes when suddenly there was a flash of a figure running toward him at blinding speed. Alfie was startled by a loud BANG as fleet-footed Mercury, messenger of the gods, wearing winged sneakers, a full-bodied electric orange spandex suit, and a low-crowned hat with wings on it, tripped, stumbled, and landed smack on his tush right in front of Alfie.

"Shit...That's the third pair of sneakers I blew out this week." He looked at a piece of paper, then at Alfie. "Are you Alfie the Outlaw from Asteroid #9?"

"Could be," Alfie said. "Who wants to know, even though I know who wants to know because I'm an expert on Greek mythology, you know."

Mercury stood up and brushed himself off.

"Well, my Greek name is Hermes which sounds like an STD so I go by my Roman name Mercury. It has more zing to it. You can call me Merc, everyone does." He extended his hand and then quickly pulled it back as Alfie reached to shake it. "Ha! Too slow. I've been sent to bring you to meet the Big Guy."

Alfie panicked. "Is it my time already?! I haven't lived! I never sang karaoke and I never had a lap dance!"

"No, you don't understand," Merc said. "As far as I know you still got plenty of time. Zeus knows that you know a lot about mythology, so he wants you to write the story of his life. He thinks it'll sell. Personally I think it's a waste of paper. The guy's boring as hell. Me, I'm electrifying."

A bolt of lightning flashed through the air and electrified Mercury right in the rear. He screamed in pain and changed his tune. "Or it could be the greatest book ever written. Not as great as *this* one, but close enough."

Alfie said, "I'm flattered, but I'll pass. Tell him thanks but no thanks."

The sky grew suddenly dark and rumbled with thunder. Merc looked up at the sudden change nervously and warned Alfie, "I wouldn't refuse him. He doesn't handle rejection very well."

"I'd like to really, but I'm more of an intergalactic outlaw than a writer," Alfie said.

Another thunderbolt flashed across the sky, took a sharp turn, and hit Mercury right in the sack. In a very high-pitched voice, and holding his roasted nuts, Merc pleaded, "*Please* change your mind!"

Thunderbolts started carpet-bombing Mercury and Alfie and they ran around dodging them. Alfie dove under a low stone overhang and Mercury was moving so fast he was a sparking blur. Angry, he stopped, looked up to the top of Mount Olympus and yelled, "GIVE ME A BREAK WILL YA?! I'M TRYING!" Then he turned to Alfie in desperation. "Look, this guy's crazy. Temper-wise he goes from zero to sixty almost as fast as me. If you don't come with me right now, he's liable to destroy the world, and you wouldn't want that on your conscience, would you?"

"No, I guess not," Alfie said. "But in the future The Evil One went for the whole universe, so threatening to destroy one little planet doesn't do it for me."

Mercury thought for a minute, and a minute to him was a zeptosecond for you and me. A zeptosecond is the smallest measurement of time. It's a trillionth of a billionth of a second, which you didn't know until this very zeptosecond.

"Look at it this way," Mercury said to Alfie, "you'll be the first mortal, and probably the *only* mortal ever allowed in to the home of the gods. That looks pretty good on a resume. You'll like it. It's a cool place: palaces made out of gold and marble just under the peak of Olympus. Some folks call it the tippy-top, but it's really not, it's just under the peak. They recently put in a tennis court, an acoustic recording studio, and a home theater with Surround Sound and a concession stand that sells Raisinets."

"Really, I'll be the first and they have Raisinets?"

"Yep," Merc said.

"Okay, I'll go," Alfie agreed. "But just to have it on my resume. How do we get there? I'm not climbing 9,570 feet."

"That's a good question. Let me talk to my supervisor." Merc yelled up to the top of Olympus, "HEY! HOW DO I GET HIM UP THERE?!"

Suddenly the dark sky was parted by the sun which gave way to Zeus's son Apollo in his golden chariot. It was Apollo's job to pull the sun across the sky every day because he really didn't have any other talent besides playing the lyre, and it was hard to get gigs on top of a mountain. Of course it was the four horses pulling the chariot who did all the work, but they weren't about to get the credit they deserved. The sky turned a blazing golden yellow as Ra known as Apollo here, descended.

"Oh just swell. Put these on," Merc said handing Alfie a pair of UV 400 sunglasses. Merc slipped a pair on himself.

"Do you always carry two pairs of sunglasses?" Alfie asked.

"No, I just bought these five seconds ago. Don't forget, I'm Mercury, the fastest cat around. You could think I'm right here listening to you but I'm really a million miles away. You're not married are you?"

Apollo's chariot giving off intense rays of golden light pulled up alongside Merc and Alfie. Apollo pulled back on the reins and pulled on the hand brake. He said, "Hey Speedy, 'sup dawg?"

"Not much, bright boy. I blew out another sneaker."

"Damn bro. That's like the third pair this week!" Apollo pointed out.

"True dat," Mercury said. "Zeus wants to see this guy. Alfie, this is Apollo, Apollo this is Alfie."

Alfie extended his hand. Merc shook his head. Apollo shook Alfie's hand and burned him badly. Alfie jerked his hand back, shook it vigorously, and blew on it as hard as he could to cool the pain. "That's like touching the sun!"

"Bingo," Merc said.

"Sorry," Apollo said looking at Merc questioningly.

"He's not a god. He's a mortal."

"A *mortal*?! Zeus is letting in a *mortal*?" Apollo asked in amazement.

"Remember those stories we used to hear about Thales and the cosmos? He would talk about a small group of outlaws who in the future were gonna save the universe. This guy is one of them. But he won't be born for thousands of years. He got caught in some weird time warp where there was gravitational-wave radiation and two infinite loops of parallel cosmic strings and he was thrown back to this time. If I had to guess I would say that Big Daddy was behind that to get him here. Zeus wants him to write a book about him."

Apollo pondered. "What's it gonna be called, *A God's Guide to Picking Up Mortal Women* or *How I Single-handedly Screwed Up the Universe?*"

Apollo was struck in the rear with a thunderbolt. He told me later that it *really really* didn't feel good. Then he reached into his toga and pulled out his golden lyre. "Wanna hear a tune?"

"Nah, we gotta get goin'," Merc said. Apollo played the opening to "Purple Haze." Merc cut him off by clapping. "Great tune, brother. What a guy. What a musician. Let's go or there's gonna be trouble."

"You two are brothers?" Alfie asked, not really caring.

"You're the mythology expert," Merc said. "You know Zeus is everyone's father, but we all have different mothers. All he does is scream and screw. And sometimes he screams while he's screwing and screws while he's screaming."

There was booming Earth-shaking thunder. Mercury flashed out of the way of a huge thunderbolt and jumped into the chariot pulling Alfie in with him. *"FLOOR IT!"* he commanded, and Apollo snapped the reins of his horses, Pyrois, Eous, Aethon, and Phlegon who took off like a shot toward the peak of Olympus passing through a breathtaking maze of clouds, rainbows, brilliant colors, and joyous sounds. The winged steed Pegasus flew by and Alfie watched in amazement as the horsey did flips as he flew and was showing off like an ass. The winged one's daddy was Poseidon and his mommy was that hideous Gorgon bitch Medusa, the crazy broad with snakes for hair who would turn men to stone if they looked at her. As you might recall, she's been mentioned in this book as the maternal grandmother of the purple sisters. I guess Poseidon was really hard up and put a bag over her head when he took *that* tapping trip. The chariot pulled up to the majestic golden gates of the home of the gods which was surrounded by a blanket of gold-flecked cyan blue clouds and guarded by two huge muscle-bound Minotaurs. A Minotaur has a bull's head, human torso, a bull's bottom half, and ironically most of what he says is bull. I'm not sure about the weenie and I don't care. I have enough problems. The gatekeeper looked at Alfie suspiciously. "Who is the stranger, Apollo?"

"He is called 'Alfie', one of The Outlaws of Asteroid #9. Remember Thales used to talk about them saving the universe in the future. He hasn't been born yet, but here he is."

"Yeah, I remember Thales used to talk about them saving the universe in the future. This Alfie hasn't been born yet, but here he is."

"I just said that," Apollo said. "You didn't have to repeat the whole thing."

"I'm part bull. It affects the brain. I have great respect for The Outlaws of Asteroid #9, but no mortal shall pass through these gates."

Merc piped up. "Zeus summoned him."

"I wasn't informed," the gatekeeper said.

"Frank, I blew out another sneaker. This is my third one this week. I had a bad day. Just open the gate."

"Look Speedy," the gatekeeper said, "I'm just trying to do my job. You know the rules. No mortals are allowed in, period."

Merc thought for…a zeptosecond and said, "He's not really a mortal, Frank. He's also the god of male sex organs, and if you don't open that gate and let us in right now, he'll make yours, whatever it is, fall off."

Frank called to the other gatekeeper, "Let 'em through, Charley!" The gatekeepers opened the gates and the chariot entered the home of the gods. Spectacular palaces of glittering gold and gleaming marble dazzled with a dreamlike ambiance. It was a sight no mortal could ever imagine. Several gods were lying around the grounds being fanned and fed ambrosia and nectar by beautiful women. The nine Muses and the three Graces were also hanging around with a few Sileni (part man, part horse) and a couple of Satyrs (goat-men). They all put on UV 400 sunglasses when the chariot arrived. Apollo, Alfie, and Mercury stepped off the chariot. Apollo pulled his lyre out of his toga and commanded Pyrois, Eous, Aethon, and Phlegon to pull the chariot back into the sky and wait for his whistle when he needed the chariot again. Everyone removed their sunglasses and Apollo asked them if they wanted him to play a tune on his lyre. No one did, so he started playing "Smoke on the Water." The nine Muses got up and danced the monkey, which would become a popular novelty dance over 5000 years later in 1963, in choreographed unison. The three Graces provided background vocals and Pan (part man, part goat, all a-hole because he wanted me to pay him for his little cameo appearance here, which I won't do) played his flute. He was no Ian Anderson. As Apollo "sang" the beautiful mesmerizing Aphrodite, Goddess of Beauty and Love, slinked by. As she passed, flowers bloomed behind her but not in front of her. Most things happened behind her. Alfie stared at the vision of loveliness that was Aphrodite and asked Mercury, "Who is that?"

"*That* chick?" Merc replied. "That's Aphrodite, the Goddess of Beauty and Love. In 1969 Shocking Blue will put out a song called "Venus" that's really about her. She's got it. And you can get it too if you bonk her. When she's not selling it, she's the greatest prick-tease in history. Her legacy isn't beauty and love, it's blue balls. She's a Pillow Princess. She just lies there and makes you do all the work. In the 1970s she'll be a porn star called "Mona Lott." She'll be famous because all she'll do is nothing, and moan. Does that answer your question?"

Aphrodite saw Mercury, waved, and said, "Hi Speedy!" Merc frowned. Just behind Aphrodite stomped Athena, the Battle-Goddess. She was a fierce ruthless woman in battle armor, carrying thunderbolts over her shoulder. As she stomped along, the flowers that bloomed behind Aphrodite wilted and died. She knocked down anyone and anything in her path including Merc and Alfie.

"And that delicate little flower is Athena, the Goddess of War. She's the daughter of Zeus, of course. She didn't have a mother. She just popped out of his head one night, full-grown and in full armor. She created the very first migraine, the strap-on, and femdom. She's the Queen of Bitchdom; the dyke of all dykes."

Athena spun around and stared at Mercury.

"*Oh shit*," Merc mumbled under his breath.

"What did you say?" Athena growled.

"*Like*...I said that you I *like*."

"Good," Athena said, "then you can carry these thunderbolts to my daddy for me."

She unloaded them on Merc and slapped him hard on the back, knocking him down. "Thanks Twinkle-Toes. You're okay. I don't care what they say about ya."

Athena stomped away. Alfie took some of the thunderbolts from Merc to carry.

"Let's go see the big guy," Merc said.

Lamia who was a nymphomaniac shape-shifter who hunted children as a hobby and was one of Zeus's mistresses happened to be passing by Mercury and Alfie. Mercury conned her into changing into a Radio Flyer classic red wagon which he and Alfie loaded the thunderbolts on and pulled toward the living quarters of Zeus and Hera. After a few feet of travel, Merc stopped and looked at Alfie. "No one here understands the plot of this book. Do you?"

"I think it has something to do with the Digby orb," Alfie said, "because it zooms by now and then with Marty and Bink chasing it in their flying saucer. That's what I think."

Suddenly the sky above rumbled and the Digby orb flew by overhead with the flying saucer closing in fast.

"There it is and there they are!" Merc said. "I think you nailed it."

The orb just missed slamming into Atlas's crotch, and continued on. Had it hit Atlas's crotch, he would have dropped this rock and you wouldn't be here. Inside the living quarters of the aforementioned Zeus and Hera, things were not going well. Hera, who was a huge woman with an equally huge temper, was hurling things at the almighty Zeus, god of the sky, god of thunder, ruler of all gods and humans. Zeus came up to Hera's knees in stature, but what he lacked in height he made up for in gruffness. He always wore gold satin boxers, a majestic robe with "The Big Guy" printed on the back, and always chomped on a robusto cigar. Hera hurled a Winter Palace table lamp which retails for $2,438 at Zeus's head. Zeus ducked and the lamp shattered against the wall behind him. Cupid, the god of desire, affection, attraction, and erotic love, was cowering in the corner trying to escape Hera's fury. A duck in a dress was running around. Merc and Alfie arrived and dumped the thunderbolts.

"YOU SCUM!" Hera screamed. "DO YOU HAVE TO PORK EVERY GIRL YOU SEE?!"

The Radio Flyer classic red wagon slowly moved backwards and rolled away quickly on its own. Merc and Alfie exchanged glances.

"She fainted!" Zeus lied, like a god who was just caught screwing around. "I was giving her mouth-to-mouth resuscitation!"

"Naked?!" inquired Hera while picking up a 3 door mahogany wardrobe to throw at his head.

"I thought she might be allergic to clothing! Later I insisted that she put on a dress! Did you have to change her into a duck?!" asked Zeus as he ducked the 3 door mahogany wardrobe.

"I'm fed up with you and that horny dwarf!" Hera screamed while hurling a foot and calf massager she bought at Bed Bath & Beyond at her husband.

"Cupid is not a horny dwarf!" snapped Zeus. "Technically he's a cherub. He's also the God of Love. He makes his home in all men's hearts. All men serve him of their own free will. And he whom Cupid touches walks not in darkness."

Cupid chimed in, "Hera, I get girls for Zeus because he tells me to, not because I want to."

"Shut up you horny dwarf!" Zeus snapped.

Mercury knocked on the doorframe. Zeus was happy for the distraction. "Speedy! Great to see you! Come in! Hera look, Mercury's here!"

"I'm thrilled," Hera sneered, hurling a discontinued Signature 6-piece Bath Towel set at Mercury who easily dodged the incoming projectile, but kept it, because it will be alluded to in an upcoming scene. While they both continued ducking, diving, and dodging Hera's air-to-floor attack, Mercury asked Zeus, "Where do you want these thunderbolts?"

"Put them by the throne," Zeus answered while ducking a discontinued Ellen DeGeneres Romero 6-drawer Double Dresser in Barnwood Grey. Merc and Alfie piled the thunderbolts by the throne as instructed. I don't know if "throne" meant the toilet or Zeus's majestic chair. It doesn't specify in my notes. My feeling is that it meant his majestic chair. Mercury introduced Alfie to Zeus.

"This is Alfie, the Outlaw of Asteroid #9 who you sent for to write your biography."

This only added to Hera's...displeasure. "What is a *mortal* doing here?! It's forbidden!"

"You heard what Mercury said. I sent for him to write the story of my life."

Hera broke up laughing. "What's it gonna be called, *The Life and Times of a Complete Asshole Who Screws Anything That Moves or Doesn't Move As Long As There's a Hole to Fill?*"

"It's an honor to meet you, Your Majesty," Alfie said nervously in the midst of this domestic quarrel.

"Did you hear that, Hera? He called me 'Your Majesty'. You should take a lesson from the mortal and show me as much respect as he does."

Hera snickered, not like the candy bar, like a bitch, "I'll show you respect when donkeys fly."

Zeus shrugged, gestured with his middle finger, and changed his wife into a donkey with wings. She brayed in an infuriated sorta way and flew out the window. He turned to Alfie. "Are you married, Mortal?"

"No, Your Majesty," Alfie said.

"Never get married," Zeus advised. "You could be the ruler of all gods and humans and your wife will still treat you like something she stepped in. Merc, go tell Hera I'm sorry and promise her that I'll never screw around again, at least not until the next time."

Mercury stood there.

"Merc, I told you to apologize to Hera for me," Zeus glared, getting annoyed.

"I already did," Merc said. "I just got back right now."

"I didn't see you move," Zeus said. He then looked at Alfie. "Did you see him move?"

"Nope," Alfie replied, like someone who didn't see Merc move.

"I'm a fast guy," Merc shrugged.

Zeus changed the subject because there was nowhere to go. "Let me tell you boys a little story about women." He looked at Alfie again. "Mortal, take notes for the book."

Alfie pulled a pad and pencil out of thin air, literally. If you believe what's gone on in this book so far, you'll believe that too.

"Is this the Pandora's Box story?" Mercury asked, bored to death already.

"Have I told you this story before?" Zeus asked.

Mercury nodded. "Every single time I see you, which is at least 25 times a day. It gets really really old."

"Well, I'll make it brief for the mortal because I want it in the book."

"I know the story," Alfie said. Zeus ignored him and proceeded with the tale. "Pandora was a beautiful girl. I could look at her for hours playing pocket pool she was so beautiful. One day all the gods got together and filled a jar with bad evil nasty things: plagues, sorrow, misery, I threw in a picture of Hera, lots of disgusting things. Pandora's Box was really a 5 gallon pickle jar, but over time they started calling it a box because a guy named Erasmus who will be a 'Renaissance humanist' (whatever that is) in the 16th century which hasn't happened yet, will screw up the story and call it a box. That's probably where you'll get the word 'erase' because 'Erasmus' will erase the truth and call things whatever he damn well wants to call them. So we'll call it a box in that idiot's honor. Anyway, the gods gave the box to Pandora and warned her not to open it. Then we pulled out our bankrolls and placed bets. Being a female, she couldn't stand it. Her curiosity was killing her. So she opened the box and out flew troubles galore, all over the world. From that moment on, women became evil to men, with a nature to do evil. It's in their blood. If they're not doing something evil, they're lost. I won $127 bucks that day, because *I KNOW WOMEN!*"

Merc whispered to Alfie, "Ask him how he became king of the gods. You won't believe this one."

Alfie cleared his throat and said, "Your Majesty-"

"Yes, common ordinary mortal?" Zeus answered like a god who thought he was really something special.

"Your Majesty, I know that your brother Poseidon is Lord of the Sea, and your other brother Hades is King of the Underworld. How did you and your brothers determine who would be in charge of what?"

Zeus looked at Mercury. "Did you tell him to ask that question?"

Merc shook his head. "I don't remember doing that. But now that you brought it up, it is one of the most asinine stories I've ever heard in my life. Why don't you enlighten this common ordinary mortal? And add some of your phenomenal wit."

"Alright, but this is off the record, Mortal. This doesn't go in the book. We drew straws. I drew the longest straw so I chose to be the god of the gods. Who wouldn't? Poseidon drew the second longest straw so he chose to rule the sea because he always liked going to the beach, surfing, and looking at broads in bikinis. And poor Hades got stuck with the Underworld. He accused me of cheating so I told him to go to Hell. (He laughed alone). Put that in the book. I have a great sense of humor and I'm very witty. I don't have to have a great sense of humor, you know. I could be any way I want because I'm top dog around here." The phone rang and Zeus answered it. "Harry's Pizza, we deliver." He winked at Merc and

Alfie, then covered the mouthpiece with his mythological right hand and whispered to Alfie. "That's an example of my incredible sense of humor and wit. Put that in the book." He listened for three zeptoseconds and said "Speak of the devil, it's Hades." Then he spoke into the phone, "I was just complaining about you, little brother...*YOU DID WHAT?!* ARE YOU OUT OF YOUR MIND?!...No, I'm not coming down there. That place stinks and it's too damned hot. The humidity is like being in Fort Meyers, Florida, in July...No, you're not coming up here either...Because I don't want you here...Stop crying...I'll tell you what, I'll send Speedy and one of the Outlaws from Asteroid #9 who's visiting to write a book about me and how great I am. Do you still have that damned dog? I hate that dog. If I see him again I'm going to kill him...because all three of his heads bit me on the ass the last time I was down there. In fact, I'm also sending Hercules to slap him around a little as a reminder not to screw with me. They'll be there soon. Talk to you later." Zeus hung up and turned to Mercury. "Go tell Hercules I want him to come here and then go to Hell with you." Merc stood there. Zeus looked at him. "Did you hear what I just told you to do?"

"I already did it," Merc said. "I'm so fast I can enter a room before I get there."

Zeus squinted at Merc. "I don't believe you. You didn't move an inch. I've been looking at you the whole time."

Zeus turned to Alfie. "Did you see him move?"

Alfie shook his head, "Nope."

Hercules entered, busting through drywall, plywood, and plaster like an asshole, when he could have just come through the door which was wide open. He was incredibly strong and powerful, extremely muscle-bound, and not one to win a Mensa High IQ award any time soon. Zeus glared at Mercury who grinned. He then explained what was happening down below. "It seems that my dear brother Hades got a little lonely down in the Underworld and kidnapped Demeter's daughter Persephone to be his wife. If you've read your mythology you know that Demeter is the goddess of the harvest; fruit, veggies, things like that. I have two kids with her. One of them is a horse. I have no idea what that's about. So, if Demeter doesn't get Persephone back from my dipshit brother, it's really gonna hit the fan. I don't know what she'll do, but I guarantee you it won't be fun. She's a woman." He turned to Hercules, "Hold Speedy tight. Don't let him move."

Hercules grabbed Mercury around the waist from behind and locked his muscle-bound arms in front of him. Merc grinned, "Not too tight big fella. You musclehead boys stretch my spandex."

Zeus stepped up on a piece of the mahogany wardrobe that Hera threw at him so that he was nose-to-nose with Mercury.

"Now Mister 'So-fast-I-can-enter-a-room-before-I-get-there', I want you to go get Pegasus so that you and Hercules and the mortal can ride him down to the Underworld."

"I'm back," Merc smirked.

Hot magenta steam erupted out of Zeus's ears which happened when he became confused and upset at the same exact time. "No, you're not back, because you never left," he snarled. He looked at Alfie. "Did you see him move, mere mortal?"

Alfie shook his head again, "Nope."

He then asked Hercules. "Did you see him move? Did he leave your strapping muscle-bound arms at all?"

Hercules thought for a few moments and said, "Well, I felt him vibrate a little, but that's all."

Pegasus, the magnificent winged steed, flew to the doorway. Mercury grinned at Zeus. Zeus, fuming, commanded Hercules to release his hold on Mercury who mounted Pegasus. (No, not that way, you are so disgusting.) Hercules lifted Alfie up on the steed's back and then climbed on himself. Let me be clear because there are certain people who will read this book, like the Pulitzer Prize Board, who will take that literally. Hercules didn't "climb on himself." You can't climb on yourself. He climbed on the back of the winged steed Pegasus. Crap. Now some of you have stopped reading so you can try to climb on yourself. Have fun. The rest of us will continue on. Pegasus made an odd groaning sound that told me he wasn't overly thrilled with all that weight on his back.

Zeus commanded, "I want the three of you to go straight to Hell, no detours. Hercules, slap that three-headed mutt for me." He pointed his right pointer finger that he had once got stuck in a stripper, at Mercury. "When you're done dealing with Hades, take the mere mortal around with you and show him my kingdom to impress him with my greatness even more than he's already impressed."

Merc smirked. "We're back! *Now* what do you want us to do?"

Zeus lunged at Mercury who swatted Pegasus who bolted into the sky and made a U-turn toward the Underworld. Seventeen minutes later, Pegasus touched down at the entrance to the Underworld. On guard before the gate sat Cerberus, the giant hideous seething slobbering three-headed red-eyed serpent-tailed dog. Pegasus was hesitant to enter through the gate, and I don't blame him. I would've turned around right then and there, and so would you whether you think so or not. It's easy to sit there reading this and think that you could just swagger through those gates and Cerberus wouldn't mind, but I could write you into this thing and let Cerberus have you for a snack. You know what? I will. Cerberus saw _your name here_ and ate _your name here_. Never screw with a writer. So Mercury tried to encourage Pegasus to go through the gate in an assuring encouraging kind of way, sort of.

"Go on horsie…That doggie might not kill you."

The winged steed took a few cautious steps toward the gate and the vicious three-headed mongrel attacked him. Pegasus bolted. Merc, Alfie, and Hercules were thrown on their tushies. Hercules jumped on Cerberus and they battled fiercely. While he kept the mean vicious puppy busy, Mercury and Alfie entered through the gate to the Underworld. They both glanced back and saw that Hercules had two of Cerberus's heads in a full nelson, a wrestling move which is not permitted in high school wrestling matches because it can be very dangerous even though it does impress the cheerleaders.

Hades was a dark shadowy place of torment as in a horrific nightmare, like marriage. I kid! I'm kidding! But seriously, that's what it was like (and probably still is). The eternal flames of Hell burned eternally, sinners were flogged mercilessly without mercy, and their screams could be heard all the way to Last Chance, Iowa. Charred bodies were in piles having been ripped of their souls. It was an atmosphere of utter gloom, torment, and horror. Yet in the midst of all this misery, the big cheese of it all, Hades, dressed to the nines in a red tuxedo, and Persephone, the lovely young innocent girl, kidnapped daughter of Demeter, were seated at a lovely table set for a quiet intimate romantic dinner with candles burning pointlessly and hot red wine because there's no refrigerator in Hell. However there are many refrigerator repairmen with eternal flames being blasted into the cracks of their asses. Sadly, Persephone was sobbing, and Hades, who was a lot more sensitive than you might think, was trying to console her.

"What's the matter Honey? Is your Chateaubriand overcooked? I'll send it back and put the chef on a rotisserie."

Merc and Alfie crept in and looked around, feeling plenty queasy.

Merc approached the table, looked at Persephone sobbing, and said to Hades, "What in Hell is going on here?"

"He kidnapped me!" Persephone sobbed.

"Yeah, I know that," Merc said. "No chick would be here because she wants to be." He looked at Hades. "Do you have something to add, Last of the Red Hot Lovers?"

Hades was emotional. "It's lonely here, Speedy. I'm tired of the bachelor life and being a swinging single."

"'A swinging single'? You never had a date in your life other than with your hand. What are you doing to this poor girl?"

"I want to settle down and start a family. Is that too much to ask?" Hades asked in a way that was too much.

Mercury looked around. "Well, it is a good environment to raise kids. I'll give you that. And I'm sure you have lots of school teachers around here to educate them. And high school coaches who like to watch boys drip-dry out of the shower." He looked at Persephone who was still sobbing. "Don't you like it here? It's so warm and cozy."

A bloodcurdling scream pierced the romantic atmosphere inspiring Alfie to crawl into a corner and lose his lunch. Persephone was shaking and hysterical. She cried, "This is the most *horrible* place!"

"You've never been to Trenton have you?" Merc asked, not wanting an answer. "Look, you hang a few curtains…some wallpaper maybe with flowers or hearts on it. I know where there's some smashed bedroom furniture that could maybe be repaired. I can get you a few autographed headshots of Zeus to hang around. You lay down some shag carpet, install an AC unit, and you're all set. I bet you could turn this place of torture and pure horror into a nice little home."

Hades took Persephone's hand. "That's right my love. After we redecorate, your family will love me!"

Merc pulled Hades aside. "Don't bet on it, Hot Stuff. You're not exactly a mother-in-law's dream. And when her father asks what you do for a living what are you gonna say?"

Hades shrugged, "Her father's dead. I got him here somewhere."

Merc rolled his eyes like loaded dice in a crap game (literary genius or what?). "You're missing the point," he pointed out. "Can you imagine this girl's mommy playing mah-jongg with the broads? 'My son-in-law's a doctor, my son-in-law's a lawyer, my son-in-law's the king of Hell…' That'll go over real big. Let me tell you something, Sparky. Her mother's very upset. She covered the earth with snow and stopped everything from growing and will keep it that way until she gets her kid back. Everyone will starve. Do you understand what you've done? Do the right thing and let the girl go."

Hades started tearing up. "But I love her."

Mercury put his arm around Hades consolingly. "You'll find another one whose mother can't kill us all. That hoo-haw between her legs ain't a gold mine. It's a four inch deep petri dish of bacteria and two rounds of penicillin." He pulled Persephone out of her seat. "C'mon kid, let's scram before he breaks into a medley of Broadway torch ballads."

As Persephone was leaving she paused and turned back to Hades who was dejected, distraught, and really sad. She said, "Thanks for dinner, Hades. I had a really nice time."

Heartbroken and staring at his hand, Hades mumbled, "Sure."

Persephone continued spewing her patronizing poppycock like Francine Horwich did when we were in kindergarten. She was the love of my 5-year-old life. She broke my heart even after I buried myself in the sandbox to impress her except for my nose sticking up so I could breathe. I almost died, but I learned a valuable lesson. Never try to impress a girl by burying yourself in a sandbox. It's just not worth it.

I need a minute to compose myself.

Okay. I'll be alright...outwardly anyway.

So Persephone said to Hades, "I really think you're a swell guy who got stuck with a lousy job."

"Thanks," Hades said, looking up from his hand. "Please think about marrying me. If you play your cards right, someday this could all be yours."

More screams of torment and torture pierced the foul air. Persephone looked around, shuddered (not like Irma), and said, "I'll think about it."

"Before you go, I'd like you to taste something," Hades said reaching into his trousers. Merc and Alfie cringed like few have ever cringed before. Persephone screamed and covered her eyes with her hands. Hades grunted and whipped out a pomegranate seed. Persephone peeked through her separated fingers and observed, "It's so tiny!"

Hades said, "No, Snookums, this isn't my one-eyed trouser snake, it's a pomegranate seed. It tastes like popcorn. Try it."

He tossed it up into the foul air and Persephone caught it in her mouth like a performing seal catching a sardine tossed by her trainer. Persephone swallowed the seed. Mercury shook his head. "Swallowing that seed wasn't a great idea, my dear. I'll explain why when we're heading back." Merc turned to Alfie who was still queasy in the corner. "Let's go, Life of the Party. You're a real dynamo at social gatherings."

Mercury, Persephone, and Alfie took their leave. They came to the gate and looked around for Hercules. Merc called out, "HERC, WHERE ARE YA?"

Cerberus emerged from the dark with a bloated stomach, picking his teeth, and belching. Mercury swatted him on the tuchus and scolded him: "*Bad Doggie! Bad Bad Doggie!*" Then they mounted Pegasus and flew up from the Underworld. Persephone was relieved to be leaving. She said, "Thanks for getting me out of there. I'll never go back!" Mercury corrected her, "I got news for you, my dear. When you swallowed that pomegranate seed, that was your contract with Hades. Now you gotta stay with him three months a year. And Alfie, if I know my mythology, and I think I do, that's why you mortals have winter, because when Little Miss Swallow Anything here is in Hades, her pissed-off mommy covers the earth with snow and stops everything from growing and causes skiing accidents and other problems until she gets her kid back. And when Persephone comes back, the seasons change."

Speaking of change (How's that for a segue?) Toto made it to New York to read his poetry. So let's pop in to the Jazz Room of the West End Bar also known as "The West End Gate" at Broadway and 114th Street in Morningside Heights on the outskirts of Harlem where the Beat Poets used to hang out. The Not Quite Right Quintet finished their final number of the set with the Miles Davis composition "So What" to enthusiastic applause. The emcee, Herb Gilbert, an odd little fellow with absolutely no magnetism, charisma, or stage presence, hopped on stage and the applause stopped immediately. Most of the audience lost interest and talked amongst themselves, totally oblivious to Herb who spoke into the microphone.

"We're glad you liked the band," he said, to no response. "They'll be back later if they can't pick up any women at the bar. Now it's time for the poetry readings!"

A few people got up and left. Some booed. Herb's mother who was in the front row yelled, "TAKE A HIKE CLOWN!" Herb ignored her and pressed on.

"These self-proclaimed poets are amazing. They have the phenomenal ability to recite their poetry without revealing an ounce of talent. Our first reader tonight is Roberta Castle-Smith. She is the author of this chapbook (which he holds up) *Poems to Kill a Bastard By* which is about an old lover who screwed her and split, leaving her with a rotten kid and a deep-rooted hatred toward men. And now here's Roberta Castle-Smith!"

A few women clapped. Herb stepped down off the stage as Roberta Castle-Smith stepped up on it and sat on a stool in front of the microphone. She read her poetry viciously.

"This first poem is called "Woodpecker."
You bastard!
You left me alone
with your tadpole in my belly!
If your pecker was made of wood
I would pour gasoline on it
and set it ablaze
and then I would feed the ashes to termites!"

The same women clapped. She continued.

"Thank you. This next poem is called "Rooster."
You bastard!
You left me alone
with your tadpole in my belly!
If I could I would take your rooster,
that squawking cock,
and run it through a meat grinder.
I would make it into a cock burger
and make you eat it…with fries!
Thank you."

The same women clapped again that clapped the first and second time. In fact, those same women that were in the audience came to all of Roberta Castle-Smith's poetry readings and they were always the only people who clapped for Roberta Castle-Smith. All of them (there were four) had been in bad relationships with men, hated them, and considered Roberta Castle-Smith their voice of retribution. Roberta Castle-Smith stepped down off the stage as Herb Gilbert stepped up on it and got behind the microphone.

"Thank you Roberta Castle-Smith. The date's off." He laughed alone and then pulled a sheet of paper out of his coat pocket and read from it. "As you know, Roberta Castle-Smith is a regular reader here at the West End, but our next poet came all the way here from Los Angeles just to read for us tonight. His name is Toto, but he wasn't the dog in *The Wizard of Oz* and he's not that 1970s rock band. He's a professional enforcer who works for Mafia boss Don Neroni, and he's the voice of his generation. And now here's Toto."

A few people clapped. Herb stepped down off the stage as Toto stepped up on it and sat on the stool in front of the microphone. He was nervous, but excited to be there. He cleared his throat…for several minutes, and it wasn't pleasant.

"This first poem is called "The Problem."
What's *your* problem?
We all got problems.
Your problem ain't too far.
Your problem is very near
'cause I got your problem *right here*!"

A few people clapped. Toto nodded and continued.

"This next poem is called "Where Can I Hide the Body?"
This hit was a pain in the rear
I can't hide the body here!
Too many people come and go.
If it was winter I could hide the body in the snow-"

Suddenly an awful cloud of putrid smoke billowed about the Jazz Room, as a strange entity materialized. And there right at the foot of the stage in front of Toto, appeared that half inch tall, part donkey, part jellyfish, part salamander, wicked evil nasty sadistic monstrosity…The Evil One! He bowed and addressed the audience.

"HELLO NEW YORK! ROLLO STARGUY AND HIS RIDICULOUS OUTLAWS THOUGHT THEY COULD DISINTEGRATE ME! BUT IT DIDN'T WORK! FOR I AM THE EVIL-"

Toto picked up the microphone stand and slammed the heavy cast iron base down on The Evil One squashing him to death.

CHAPTER 12

Zeus and Cupid were looking down on Earth using Zeus's special "T & A Telescope" which came highly recommended to him by Chester Flemlock. They were searching for easy Trixies to tutor. Cupid pointed one out. "There's one!"

Zeus focused in on her.

"Are you kidding? Look at those thighs. She'd kill me!"

Cupid looked again, "How 'bout the one next to her?"

Zeus looked through the scope and adjusted the focus knob. "With the flowers in her hair? She's no Aphrodite, but she's not bad. Shoot her."

Zeus and Cupid took a quick detour into their old vaudeville routine when they were billed as "Snooky Rabinowitz and Wally Wings." Cupid said, "Hey Snooky, what do you look for in a woman?"

"Me!" Zeus quickly replied like the ham-on-high that he was. Cupid placed a golden arrow in his golden bow, pulled back, and let it fly. It wasn't his best shot. The arrow ricocheted off of two satellites, hit the ZX-12 space pod, soared to Earth, and struck the young maiden in the head, killing her instantly.

"You killed her!" Zeus snapped.

"Sorry. I did my best!" Cupid said.

"That's the problem, you did your best. Alright, just go ahead and shoot every bimbo you see. Get as many as you can. I prefer them alive so they can move, unlike Hera who thinks she's a throw rug. I'll take them all on at once."

"All of them?"

"Cupid, I am a sexual animal, and a god to boot. I can handle them."

Cupid took out many more arrows and fired away one after the other. When he was done, Zeus looked through the T & A scope and saw a slew of women slayed and scattered everywhere with golden arrows sticking out of them. It was a bloodbath. "Good job, you little shit!" Zeus snarled. "You wiped them out!"

Cupid examined one of his few remaining arrows and said, "I think I know what happened. I think those were old arrows and the love potion I dip them in that I got from Madam Mancowitz expired. So because of her, they became just regular golden arrows and killed everyone. Not my fault. Blame the witch." He pulled out a brand new glistening arrow and showed Zeus. "This Carbon Express Maxima was dipped in fresh love potion this morning. It'll do the trick."

Zeus looked through his T & A scope and saw a beautiful young maiden skipping through Whorehouse Meadow on the western slope of Steens Mountain southeast of Frenchglen, Oregon, so named because in the days of the Old West (watch *Gunsmoke, The Virginian, Bonanza, Wagon Train*) women would set up tents there and offer services to sheepherders and cattlemen. And I don't mean they would wash their cars. The beautiful young maiden was skipping through the meadow picking daisies around the rotting fly-swarmed corpses of lots of women with arrows sticking out of them. She was totally oblivious and laughing that annoying Disney princess laugh that infuriates me.

Zeus said, "This one's not real bright, but she's a piece of ass. Shoot her."

Hera's delicate voice interrupted them, "ZEUS! GET YOUR SCRAWNY USELESS ASS INTO THIS BEDROOM AND PICK UP YOUR SOCKS! RIGHT NOW!"

Cupid fired the arrow and Zeus changed into a field mouse. He scurried away just as Hera stormed into the room. She glared at Cupid. *"Where is that rat, you little creep?"*

"You mean the boss?" Cupid asked.

Hera grabbed Cupid by the ear. *"I'm* the boss, you little pervert. Where is he?"

In Whorehouse Meadow, the fair maiden, with Cupid's Carbon Express Maxima arrow sticking out of her patootie and totally oblivious to it, bent down to pick another daisy when she came upon the field mouse who was leering at her aforementioned patootie. "Oh, what a cute little mouse!" exclaimed the fair maiden, and then followed her exclaimation with that damned Disney princess laugh that pisses me off. The fair maiden lied down in the meadow driving the arrow further into her ass, and the cute little field mouse crawled on top of her. She giggled a really annoying giggle that wasn't as irritating as that Disney princess laugh, but was damned near close. Lightning flashed through the meadow and the mouse changed back into Zeus lying on top of her. "SURPRISE!" exclaimed Zeus like a mythological god who had just transformed from a field mouse and was on top of a fair maiden. Suddenly an arrow with a message attached struck Zeus in his mythological ass. Zeus said some bad words that I won't repeat here, pulled out the arrow, and read the message aloud, "Hera's coming. Love, Cupid". *Oh shit!* Zeus thought to himself and said out loud simultaneously, which isn't easy to do. To quote Gordon Livingston, M.D., "Only bad things happen quickly." Thunder blasted the meadow and Hera appeared in front of Zeus who was still atop the fair maiden. He was eye-level with his wife's huge not-so-pleasant-smelling tootsies. He slowly looked up past the tapping foot, the knock-knees, the growling stomach, and the defiantly folded arms, to the extremely livid mug of his beloved bride.

"Hello dear," Zeus grinned. "I was picking flowers for you in this lovely meadow when I tripped and fell. Fortunately this young lady was lying here and she broke my fall, as you can clearly see. I think we can both be very grateful to her that I wasn't severely injured. Don't you agree?"

Hera reached down, picked Zeus up with one very annoyed hand, and tossed him aside. She then changed the fair maiden into a heifer, which wasn't very nice. Zeus got mad.

"Did you have to change her into a cow?! She broke my fall and saved my life!"

Hera grabbed Zeus by the ear. "You left your socks on the bedroom floor, *Sweetheart!* Now let's go home so you can pick them up. You don't want to eat dirty socks, do you? Remember, what you leave on the floor, you eat. Now let's go."

Thunder roared, lightning flashed, and they were gone. The Digby orb zigzagged overhead with Marty and Bink hanging back to see which way it would go as Pegasus and his riders busted through a cloud from the opposite direction.

"We'll let you off here Persephone, bye," Merc said, shoving her off the winged horsie and watching her fall through the clouds screaming. "Nice girl," Merc said. "Not exactly a spark plug, but sweet."

"Yeah," Alfie agreed as he spotted something and pointed to it up ahead. "Look at that!"

Mercury looked where Alfie was pointing and saw the Titan Prometheus bound with chains on the rocky peak of Mount Caucasus. Mercury explained the situation, though Alfie already knew some of the story after taking a correspondence course in Greek and Roman Mythology from the University of Pennsylvania.

"That's Prometheus. You'd probably like him. He's done a lot for mankind. Some say he created man, then he stole fire from the sun and gave it to man. He even arranged for man to keep the meat of the sacrificed animals and gave the bones to the gods. Zeus didn't like that at all."

"Is that why he's chained up?" Alfie asked.

Merc shook his head. "No. He's chained up because he's an asshole, which reminds me, I gotta give him a message from Zeus. Head that way, Horsie." Pagasus flew forward, veered left, and touched down beside Prometheus on the rocky peak of Caucasus. Merc waved. "How's it goin' there, Sport?"

Prometheus stated, "My body is bound, but my spirit is free."

"Good for you!" Merc said like a mommy whose kid just told her he won Honorable Mention in a "Match the City to the State" contest. "Zeus wants to make a deal with you, Einstein. He heard you said he's gonna be dethroned by a son and that you know who the kid's mother is. I would've asked who the son is, but he doesn't think like that. If you tell him who the mother of the son is, he'll set you free."

"Go and persuade the sea wave not to break.
You will persuade me no more easily," Prometheus said.

Merc grimaced. "Oh, I see we're gonna talk classical. Okay.
Hath not thou any brains, Peckerhead?
An eagle red with blood shall come
A guest unbidden to your banquet.
All day long he will tear to rags your body
Feasting in fury on the blackened liver."

Merc turned to Alfie who was taking notes and whispered, "I don't think Olivier could've done better than that. I was so great I gave myself chills."

"There is no force which can compel my speech
So let Zeus hurl his blazing bolts
And with the white wings of the snow
With thunder and with earthquake
Confound the reeling world

None of all this will bend my will," Prometheus stated with about as much emotion as my portable bidet.

"His mind is fried," Merc whispered to Alfie. He then addressed Prometheus more directly than my portable bidet tends to go. "Been up here a long time have you, Big Guy?"

Prometheus repeated, "My body is bound, but my spirit is free."

"That answers my question," Merc grinned. Suddenly a monstrous two-headed eagle the size of a Cessna Skyhawk swooped down and swiped at Prometheus, drawing blood. Merc cringed. "Don't be a jerk. Tell Zeus what he wants to know or that bird is gonna make you the mythological version of Golden Corral."

"None of this shall bend my will," Prometheus stated with about as much pizzazz as raw tofu.

"I'm not worried about your will bending," Mercury stated like someone who knew how to state things, "I just don't want your guts spilling on my new sneakers."

Again the giant two-headed eagle swooped down on the chained Titan, this time ripping through his stomach, spilling some guts on Merc's new sneakers. Merc said some bad words and Alfie ran behind a boulder to barf. Merc shook his head. "There he goes again, the Life of the Party. You're paying for these sneakers, Promie."

Again the big bad bird took another swipe spilling more guts. Merc zoomed behind the boulder with Alfie and did some heaving of his own. Just as the eagle circled back around and dove down for another swipe, Hercules appeared and a tremendous battle ensued. I can't describe the battle because I didn't see it. I was busy with my bidet. But I can report that eventually Hercules did in fact kick the big bad birdie's tail and broke the chains that bound Prometheus who was in tremendous agony but didn't let on because he was a Titan god and you know how they are. He thanked Hercules for freeing him but said that it really wasn't necessary since his spirit was free and that was the important thing. Merc and Alfie staggered out from behind the boulder and in unison said, "Hi Hercules! We thought you were dead. What happened?" Hercules showed off his new shoes and beamed, "Hercules made doggie boots!"

Hera, Aphrodite, and Athena were standing before Zeus striking different poses. Hera squinted at her husband, "So, Big Shot, who is the fairest?"

Zeus was sweating from terror. "I don't want anything to do with this because if I don't choose Hera, Hell would be Heaven and I'd never hear the end of it."

Hera snarled, "*CHOOSE*, SCUMBAG! AND YOU BETTER BE RIGHT!"

"I can't choose between you. You're all so (he swallowed hard)... different." All three goddesses slugged Zeus hard. Hera threw him across the room. "And charming!" Zeus added in agony. "It's too bad this isn't a personality contest. Look, Ladies, go to Mount Ida near Troy and find Paris. He's really good at this stuff. He's a great judge of beauty, much better than me. You know me; a hole's a hole. I got enough problems. I don't need to be in Loonville with three powerful crazy broads." Hera, Aphrodite, and Athena all slapped the hell out of Zeus and dematerialized to find Paris.

At the foot of Mount Ida the young prince Paris was sitting under a fig tree smoking a joint when the three goddesses materialized in front of him. He looked at them and then at the joint.

"Are you Paris?" Hera asked in her delicately abrasive way.

"No, I'm Czechoslovakia," Paris answered like an asshole, breaking up laughing hysterically and then stopping abruptly.

"And you are?"

"I am Hera, wife of Zeus, goddess of women, the first bitch."

"And you?" Paris asked Athena.

"I am Athena, the Battle-Goddess, creator of femdom," answered Athena the Battle-Goddess, creator of femdom (and the strap-on).

Paris took a toke. "And you, you gorgeous thing you?" Paris asked Aphrodite as Hera and Athena frowned.

"I am Aphrodite, the Goddess of Love. Shocking Blue's 1969 hit "Venus" will be about me."

Paris took another toke. "What can I do for you gals?"

"My husband said that you are a good judge of beauty," Hera said. "Is that true?"

"I know a dog when I see one," Paris replied, taking another toke.

Hera flipped her Bitch Switch and commanded, "You are to judge between us who is the fairest. If you choose me, I will make you the Lord of Europe and you shall have beer, pizza, and chocolate anytime you want it."

"That sounds fair," Paris nodded.

Then Athena said, "If you choose me, I will make you a great warrior." Paris grunted.

Then Aphrodite said, "If you choose me, I will do things to you that haven't even been invented yet. I'm talkin' non-stop raw wild wet sex day and night. My naked body will be yours to do whatever you want with, and we will quiver together in orgasmic ecstasy."

Paris looked at Hera. "What *kind* of pizza?"

"Any toppings you want," Hera said.

Paris pondered. "Can I get it delivered or do I have to pick it up?"

"There's no delivery here. You'll have to pick it up," Hera answered with a frown, knowing that she was now out of the running.

Paris said, "Well Ladies, you're all wonderful, but I'm going to have to go with the slutty chick even though it probably means several visits to the clinic."

Aphrodite took his hand in hers. "Come with me, Paris. I want you to meet my friend Helen of Troy. She's picking a husband today and I really should be there."

Puzzled Prince Paris paused. "She's *picking* a husband?"

"You have to get to know Helen to understand Helen," Aphrodite said. "She can be very Jappy."

Helen Rothenstein of Troy was slouched in her "throne" which was really a beach chair covered in aluminum foil that had been spray-painted metallic gold with a fast drying high gloss decorative finish primarily used for arts and crafts. She was wearing a hideous tangerine orange strapless tiered ruffle gown, gaudy acrylic jewelry with bugs trapped inside, and full makeup that would make Barnum and Bailey check their inventory. Behind her on the wall was the framed credo "More is Not Enough". She was snapping gum between here teeth, blowing bubbles, and painting her fingernails with Beverly Hills Burgundy nail polish. Her father, King Tyndareus, sat on a real throne nearby. An extremely long line of suitors awaited their turn to propose to Helen. They were primarily princes from very wealthy families. In line were also a few Amazon women, Mercury, Zeus, a Satyr (part man, part goat or horse, depending where you are), a Seleni (part man, part horse), and a Hippocampus (part horse, part fish). Helen never looked up at her suitors when they proposed, as she was more concerned with doing her nails. She spoke with an obnoxious whine. The kind of whine that would make me stand over her with a meat cleaver while she was sleeping at night, asking myself which would be better, prison or putting up with this shit. Helen's daddy, King Tyndareus, addressed her suitors.

"Gentlemen, strange creatures, and Amazon dykes, you have each come here today to propose marriage to my lovely daughter, Helen. She will select, of course, only one amongst you to be her husband. Because Helen is such a prize, I am fearful that those who are not chosen may unite against the man, strange creature, or Amazon dyke who is chosen. Therefore, I ask all of you to promise that you will champion the cause of Helen's chosen husband should any wrong befall him…or it…or dyke. It is, after all, to each of your advantage to take the solemn oath, since each of you is hoping to be selected. Do you take the oath?"

"WHAT?" They all asked in harmony having not understood a thing the king said.

"GOOD!" said the king. "Let's have the first suitor please."

Prince #1 approached and knelt before Helen who didn't acknowledge him at all, focusing only on her nails.

"Lovely Helen, if you consent to marry me, I will cover you with furs and fine jewelry. You will have servants at your command, and anything you desire shall be yours for the asking. What say you, my love? Will you be mine?"

"Daddy, I wanna go to Saks!" she whined to the king.

"Helen, dear, you've just been proposed to. Show the young man some courtesy."

Helen sighed, "We'll do lunch…NEXT!"

Prince #1 exited and Prince #2 knelt before her.

"My sweet Helen, my dearest Helen, Helen of my dreams-"

"NEXT!" Helen yelled.

Prince #2 exited and Mercury zoomed up, knelt before her, and took her hand.

"Watch the Beverly Hills Burgundy nail polish. I'm wet," Helen said.

"I do that to broads," Merc smirked. "Darling Helen, I am but a lowly incredibly handsome messenger. I have nothing to offer you but love. The emotion of love is all-powerful. Love is what all who seek, truly seek. Say you'll be mine and you shall have all the love that someone who seeks love shall have. We will know nothing but bliss born of love. Life will have new meaning, and together we shall be as one, in love."

"NEXT!" Helen yelled.

"You are a filthy whore!" Merc sneered. "I wouldn't touch you with a Lake Rake!"

A part man, part horse Sileni next in line charged at Mercury who left in a blinding blur. The Sileni knelt before Helen who yelled "NEXT!" The Sileni exited and Menelaus, King of Sparta, son of Atreus, brother of Agamemnon, approached and stood over Helen. He knocked away the nail polish and grabbed Helen's face with his hand, lifting it up. King Tyndareus took notice.

Menelaus snarled, "You look at me when I speak to you, Bitch! You're nothing but a spoiled little brat. If you're lucky I'll let you marry me. But if you give me any crap about 'I want this and I want that' I'm gonna knock your teeth out. Now what'll it be, are you gonna marry me or what? You have three seconds to answer."

King Tyndareus jumped to his feet. "She'll marry you! In fact, as king of this kingdom, I pronounce you man and wife. There, it's done. Welcome to the family. What's your name?"

"I am Menelaus, King of Sparta, son of Atreus, brother of Agamemnon!" said Menelaus, King of Sparta, son of Atreus, brother of Agamemnon.

King Tyndareus addressed the remaining suitors. "Thank you all for coming gentlemen, creatures, and dykes. The position has been filled. You will each receive an autographed 8 x 10 glossy of Helen, a bag of roasted peanuts, and a year's supply of Turtle Wax. Thank you for coming."

All the rejected dejected suitors exited grumbling. King Tyndareus exited to another room just as Aphrodite and Paris entered the parlor. Paris was stoned and staring at his pinky trying to figure out what it was. Aphrodite and Helen screamed for joy like two dopey schoolgirls when they saw each other. They ran to each other in slow motion and kissed the air by each other's cheeks, which always seemed like a futile act to me.

"How are you, darling?!" Aphrodite asked excitedly.

"Just fine, darling!" Helen answered, also excitedly. "This is my new husband. I forgot his name."

Her new husband introduced himself to the point where I'm so annoyed that I'm already thinking up ways to kill him off. He said, "I am Menelaus…" And you know the rest.

Aphrodite said, "And this is *my* new guy, Paris. He's a prince but he doesn't know what his pinky is. Paris, this is my BFF Helen of Troy and her hubby, whatever his name is."

Paris looked up from his pinky. "Mind if I call you 'Hell'? Helen of Troy is too much to remember."

Menelaus snarled, "She is Helen of Troy. I am Menelaus, King of Sparta, son of Atreus, brother of Agamemnon."

"You look like an Esther to me," Paris said. "I'll just call you Esther. Actually I'm probably not going to call you at all." He looked at Helen. "Did you get your nose fixed? Someone really botched that job! I can spot 'em a mile away. Fake boobs too."

Aphrodite swatted Paris on the bottom. "Paris, that's rude!"

"I'm originally from New York," Paris explained.

In actuality Paris was right about the botched nose job. The only plastic surgeon at the time was Dr. Leopold Klopper who was a Monopod, which was a dwarfish creature who had only one leg coming out of the middle of its body with a giant foot attached to the leg. Dr. Klopper, although board certified, had terrible balance and kept falling when he would perform surgeries, so many of his patients looked god-awful.

"Well I'm famished," Aphrodite said, changing the subject. "Anyone for The Bistro Garden?"

"What do you think; I'm made of money, honey? All I do is sit under a fig tree, judge beauty contests, and get high," Paris pointed out. Aphrodite thought for a moment. "Then let's just get tacos and bring them back here," she strongly suggested in a demanding kind of way.

"Sounds good to Menelaus," said Menelaus.

"Come on Paris, let's go," Aphrodite demanded in a demanding (now bordering on bitchy) kinda way again.

"No, I'll stay here," Paris said. "I can't be all things to all people. And where are you going to find tacos in ancient Greece?"

"He's right," Helen said. "You and Mene…whatever his name is, go hunt for tacos in ancient Greece. We'll wait here."

"Alright, suit yourselves. Let's go…whatever-your-name-is," Aphrodite commanded like she'd been taking wife lessons from Hera. She and the guy I'm ready to drop a boulder on left to find tacos. Helen started painting her toenails with yellow pineapple polish as Paris wandered around the parlor. He spied a gold box and opened it. He reached in and took out some rocks and broken glass. He was ecstatic.

"OH WOW! ROCKS AND BROKEN GLASS!"

Helen spun around and said, "Oh my Gods! What are you doing?! That's my secret collection! I leave it out in the open to remind me to hide it."

"I can't believe it!" Paris said in total amazement. "You collect rocks and broken glass too?! I thought I was the only one!"

"You collect rocks and broken glass too?!" Helen asked, getting all tingly and a little bit wet.

Paris proudly proclaimed, "I've been collecting rocks and broken glass for ten years. That's almost a century. I'm somewhat of an authority. The best places to find them are vacant lots, chariot parking lots, and…" Together they exclaimed simultaneously at the same time in unison **"AROUND THE DELPHIC ORACLE!"** They laughed and laughed at their mutual insight and interest and then paused for a moment in all seriousness gazing at each other lovingly.

"This is blowing my mind," Paris whispered. "I'm sorry what I said about your nose job." He gazed into Helen's Jack Elam-esque eyes. If you've ever seen a western, Jack Elam was in it. And he had weird eyes. When he was a kid he got into a fight with another boy who stabbed him in the eye with a pencil, which was a horrible thing, but it most likely gave Elam his acting career.

"I can't deal with this!" Helen squealed practically whinelessly. "We have so much in common!"

"I know another cool place to find really awesome rocks and broken glass and old Cracker Jack prizes from the 1930s which hasn't happened yet," Paris said affectionately. "Wanna go?"

"Sure!" Helen said back affectionately also. "Let me get my Gucci rock and broken glass collector's bag. You leave a note for Aphrodite and… whatever."

Helen handed Paris pink construction paper and a blizzard blue crayon and he scribbled a note. Helen returned with her Gucci collector's bag and Paris gazed at her even more lovingly than before.

"Is something wrong?" Helen asked.

Paris answered thusly, "You know, a long time ago I fell in love, and now I have someone to share it with. It's a good feeling."

Paris and Helen exited just as Aphrodite and...Menelaus entered. I mean they literally walked right past each other in the hall and didn't notice. That's how dumb they are.

"We're back!" Aphrodite announced to the empty room. "We found the very first tacos in ancient Greece! It was the weirdest thing. We ran into Hestia, goddess of the hearth. She told us that Apollo and Poseidon both wanted to marry her and she was so repulsed that she became a baker. She put some cornmeal on a stool and had me, Aphrodite, sit on it because she knows I never wear panties. So the cornmeal took the shape of my coochie. She shoved some meat in it and sour cream and invented the taco! So every time someone eats a taco, it's like they're eating me! Next week she's moving to Mexico." There was no response. Aphrodite looked around the room. "I don't think they're here," she said. Menelaus saw the note that Paris wrote and handed it to her. Aphrodite read it aloud:

"Dear Aprodite and Esther,
We aren't here because we left. We went to Troy, but don't try to figure out where we went.

P.S. I painted the walls the same color they were before we left. They should be dry by the time you get back."

The Greek Army was assembled on the Greek shoreline. Many of the soldiers were Helen's rejected suitors. King Tyndareus and Menelaus stood before them. A thousand ships awaited departure...

I want to break in here and explain an interesting historical fact to you. I'm sure you have heard that Helen's face was so beautiful that it was "The face that launched a thousand ships" which is this story where we are now. But that expression has been misinterpreted through the centuries, just like, as you learned earlier, Pandora's "Box" was never a box. You see, between the botched nose job and the Jack Elam-esque eyes, Helen was no Medusa, but she was no picnic up close either. Everyone who looked at her went immediately to a bar and had to have a drink. So in reality, the expression was that her face launched a thousand *sips*. Not ships, *sips*.

King Tyndareus addressed the Greek army. "Gentlemen, creatures, dykes...as you recall, you took an oath to champion the cause of Helen's husband should any wrong befall him through his marriage. As you know, a great injustice has been done to Helen's husband, Menelaus.

"*WHO?*" They all asked in unison.

"You know...Menelaus...King of something...son of someone... someone's brother...This guy here," King Tyndareus tried to explain.

"OH!" They all said in unison.

The king continued. "Helen has been kidnapped by Paris who has taken her to Troy. To get her back, we must destroy Troy."

"OY!" replied Corporal Allen Lipschitz who really doesn't belong in this particular story, but the casting director for this book blackmailed me. 565 nautical miles later, the Greek ships pulled up on the Trojan shore. The soldiers disembarked and headed for the city which was surrounded and protected by gigantic walls. From a watchtower a sentinel saw the entire Greek Army advancing. "TO ARMS! TO ARMS!" he yelled. "I THINK WE GOT A LITTLE PROBLEM HERE!"

As the Greek Army advanced further or farther, whichever one it is, the Trojan Army quickly assembled, advanced (but not quickly enough to impress me) and a tremendous clash ensued. Battles and wars are very complex and hard to write about because there's too much going on, so let's just zoom in on a Greek warrior and a Trojan warrior involved in hand-to-hand combat.

"Hey Trojan," the Greek warrior said ducking a spear jab, "If you guys win this war maybe they'll name a prophylactic after you."

"Good," the Trojan replied ducking a sword swipe, "Then you and your buddies won't have to worry about getting each other pregnant."

Meanwhile on the tippy-top (the real tippy-top) of Mount Olympus, Apollo, Zeus, Hera, and Athena were watching the warfare.

"I got five obols on the Trojans," Zeus said confidently.

"I'll take that bet and I'll raise it to three drachmas," Hera said. "I want Paris to suffer for not choosing me the most beautiful woman alive."

"Three obols on the Trojans," Apollo piped in.

"I'm with Hera," Athena added.

"So it's the boys against the girls," Zeus grinned. "Then let's add a little zing to this thing. If we win, you're not allowed to speak for the rest of your lives."

Hera sneered. "And if *we* win, I get to cut off your slut slayer and feed it to you."

Down on the battlefield the armies drew back on both sides, and in the space between, Menelaus and Paris faced each other. Menelaus held a sword and shield. Paris held Helen's Gucci bag.

"Give Helen back!"

"Oh, is that what this is all about? Why didn't you just say so, Esther? You didn't have to make a big stink," Paris pointed out.

"She is mine. You will return her!" Menelaus mentioned.

"But she loves my rocks," Paris professed.

Menelaus drew his sword to strike. Paris reached into Helen's Gucci bag, pulled out a rock, and nailed him in the nuts. In a voice reminiscent of Little Anthony of "Little Anthony and the Imperials" Menelaus said, "You have guts, Paris, to strike Menelaus, King of Sparta, son of-"

Paris cut him off, "Yeah, I know who you are, Esther. I want that rock back. That was a classic Colosseum piece, circa 76 CE in mint condition, which doesn't make sense because this is circa 1194 BCE. Don't ask me how I got it. It's a long story and not a very pretty one, involving time travel, a farmer's daughter, monkey gland sauce, and three tubes of silicone-based lubricant. The point is, you got me mad, and I still am."

Paris pelted Menelaus mercilessly with more rocks and both armies charged each other and clashed again until ultimately the Greek Army was pushed back to their ships. That night on the Trojan shore, the General of the Greek Army, Odysseus, was speaking to his soldiers who were sitting on the beach before him. As the tide swept in, they got soaked or knocked down, but they didn't move away from the very wet waves. That takes thinking ability, reasoning, and logic, and there was none of that around.

"We need a plan to get inside those walls," General Odysseus announced, "Any ideas?"

A soldier raised his hand. Odysseus pointed to him.

"Sir, we could get a really big electric drill and drill our way through the wall."

The General shook his head. "Young man, this is 1194 BCE. We don't have electric drills."

"Sorry," the soldier said, embarrassed. The others razzed and taunted him. Another soldier raised his hand. The General pointed to him.

"Sir, I happen to know that the sentinel goes on his break every two hours. We can wait till he goes on his break and just walk in."

"Too easy," the General said. "I don't do easy."

Corporal Allen Lipschitz chimed in, "We could build a giant soldier and hide horses in his belly, and they could come out of his belly and capture Troy."

General Odysseus looked at the soldier sternly. "Did you raise your hand?"

"Yep," said the soldier. The others all shook their heads and shouted out, "He's lying!" "He didn't raise his hand!" "He's a liar!"

"What is your name?" the General asked sternly.

"Corporal Allen Lipschitz, Sir. I have a master's degree in drama from Yale. This is just a part I'm playing."

"Oh yes. Camner was blackmailed by the casting director for this book. I know the story."

Alfie raised his hand and explained to General Odysseus in detail how in the faraway future The Outlaws of Asteroid #9 will capture The Evil One by wheeling a giant wooden donkey into The Evil One's headquarters and tricking him, which they will be inspired to do by the Greeks wheeling a giant wooden horse with warriors in its belly, through the gates of Troy and capturing the city. Odysseus was impressed with Alfie's story and had some of the ships dismantled to build the giant horse. You know the tale. I told you before. Here it is again real quick with a few more historic details. The giant wooden horse was wheeled in as an offering to Athena so Troy would be protected from enemies. When everyone was asleep the belly of the giant wooden horse opened and Greek soldiers slipped out. They opened the Scaean gates, and let the rest of the Greek Army in. Within minutes Troy was captured. And that's exactly what they done did. Menelaus found Helen and Paris in a room together examining rocks and broken glass. Menelaus grabbed Helen and yanked her out the door. Paris was preoccupied looking at a rock formed of chryselephantine which was a combination of gold, ivory, and iron, and didn't hear Helen's screams. Or if he did hear them, the chryselephantine rock was more important at the moment. Paris moved on to a piece of broken glass from an A & W Root Beer bottle and was studying it intensely. It was a different kind of glass. He was transfixed. It was a glass that intrigued him, and rightly so, as the brown glass of the A & W Root Beer bottle is to prevent UV rays from altering the flavor. You didn't know that until right now, did you? Apollo knew it, and spent his free time trying to screw up root beer. Helen was whining to Menelaus as he carried her over his shoulder toward the Scaean gates that she needed to go to Saks to buy a new wardrobe. Moments later she was tossed back into the room where Paris was studying the piece of broken glass and Menelaus left her there. Without looking up from the piece of glass from the A & W Root Beer bottle and not realizing that she was ever even gone, Paris, who was full of emotion gazing at the piece of broken glass, spoke to Helen in a way that expressed his deepest thoughts as he thought deeply. "To think deeply" comes from the Latin word "ruminatus" which also means, "to chew the cud."

"Helen, when I look at this piece of broken glass I wonder what its life was like before it got broken. Was it married? Did it have any kids? Did it have any pets? If it could talk, what story of despair would it tell?" Paris started to cry. "*Why* did it have to die?! *Why*?!" He inquired rhetorically as he broke down sobbing.

Meanwhile back in the living quarters of Zeus and Hera, Alfie was in a corner staring at his hand pretending it was Sluggo. Merc was sitting at a table playing a game with himself. He placed two coins on the opposite side of the table two feet apart. He then sat back in his chair, arms folded across his chest, fists clenched. He didn't appear to move. A moment later both coins were gone. Merc opened his fists and the coins were there, one in each hand. He grinned, impressed with himself. Hera was pacing in front of Zeus, lecturing him.

"You call yourself a god?! Not just a god, but the god of all gods and all mortals! You're supposed to set an example, but you're a bum! All you think about is sex, sex, and sex. It's the same way down there with the mortals. All they care about is themselves, just like you. Have you seen what goes on down there? Sex, drinking, sex, gambling, sex, cheating, lying, sex, and more sex. It's disgusting, just like you!"

Hera stormed out. Zeus and Mercury looked at each other. Zeus said, "Let's see what's shakin' on the Blue Planet circa 1980s CE. I have an idea."

Moments later there was a loud clap of thunder and blue lightning filled the sky over Wilshire Boulevard in Los Angeles as Zeus and Mercury disguised as life-worn filthy derelicts materialized before a row of luxurious houses.

"Why are we dressed like this?" Mercury asked in disgust. "I feel like my brother-in-law."

"This way the mortals won't recognize us," Zeus explained. "And I can prove to my darling wife that they do care about each other and are very generous. Just like me, their god. I love it when she's wrong. She doesn't speak to me for weeks."

"You're generous with your weenie," Merc said respectfully.

They approached the first house and knocked on the door. An older distinguished-looking man answered.

"Yes?"

"Good day sir," Zeus said. "We are two hungry mortals–"

The man cut Zeus off, "Get off my property and get a job."

The door slammed in their faces. They looked at each other and cut over to the next house. Zeus examined the bottom of his shoe like he stepped in something. Mercury knocked on the door and a woman answered. As Zeus was looking at the bottom of his other shoe in disgust, Mercury did the talking.

"Good day Mam."

"It was until now," the woman said slamming the door. Merc knocked again and the woman answered, irritated.

"We are two mortals who haven't eaten anything in many centuries–"

"Then you should have dropped dead a long time ago," the woman said. "Why don't you do it now?"

Again the door slammed. Zeus scraped the bottom of his shoe on her step and they continued on to every house on the street and were refused each time. Finally they came to the last house on Wilshire and were greeted by two older men. One was dressed in a Zeus Halloween costume and the other as Mercury. The real Zeus and Mercury exchanged glances. Merc whispered to Zeus, "Faygelehs." He then addressed the two men.

"Good day. We were wondering if you could spare something to eat... bad choice of words...I'll start over. Good day. We are two mortals who are hungry for food as we have not eaten any food in many centuries."

"Oh, you poor dears, you must be famished!" Mercury #2 said. "Come in, come, come, come."

Mercury stepped aside and allowed Zeus to enter first. As Zeus entered, Merc patted him on the tushy. Behind his back, Zeus gestured with his middle finger and knocked Mercury halfway down the block. Merc was back in a flash, literally. They entered the house and looked around with their jaws dropped. The interior was an exact replica of the living quarters of Zeus and Hera. The guy dressed as Mercury grinned when he saw their reaction.

"Do you like it? We did the interior ourselves because, as you can tell, we're both big Greek geeks. Zeus here is a mythology maven. How rude of us. We haven't introduced ourselves. I'm Mercury, messenger of the gods, and this honey here is Zeus. I call him 'The Big Guy', if you know what

I mean." He winked and giggled, like no man should wink and giggle. If Jack Nicholson's laugh in *The Shining* was a giggle by a little girl instead of a laugh by Nicholson, that's exactly what it would sound like. The real Zeus looked at the fake Zeus and cringed like he just bit into an umeboshi plum.

"This fake Zeus looks nothing like the real Zeus," said the real Zeus. "I mean, the real Zeus might not be Paul Newman, but he's a lot better-looking than this guy." He turned to Merc. "Do you agree?"

"Not particularly," Merc said. Zeus gestured again, sending Merc crashing through the door and knocking him six blocks away. Merc was back before the next breath. The fake Zeus said, "I have a thunderbolt. Wanna see it?"

"No," the real Zeus said. "Don't you know that it's fatal for mortals to emulate the gods? What do you think Zeus would do if he saw you like this?"

"I don't know, but he's a crazy guy. He married his own sister. He turned into a swan and forced himself on a girl. He became a golden shower and got another girl pregnant. He turned another girl into a cow. He disguised himself as a goddess, led another girl into the woods, took off his disguise, forced himself on her, and knocked her up. She was turned into a bear and her own child shot her while he was hunting. Before he married Hera, Zeus was married to the Titan Metis. He turned her into a fly and ate her. He's done a lot of crazy things because he's crazy," the fake Zeus said. "So I really don't care what he thinks."

Mercury felt that things were about to get extremely bad on Wilshire Boulevard and suggested that it was time for them to go. He guided Zeus, who was about to explode, out of the house and down the street.

"I need a drink," Zeus said. "Hera was right. These mortals are heartless, they have no compassion, and they suck."

As they got to the end of Wilshire, Zeus gestured with his middle finger, and blew up every house on the block. Thirsty and aggravated, Zeus and Merc wandered into Madame Wong's, the same rough dive where Sheldon Danger had his ass handed to him by Toto in drag. Merc looked around at the dregs of society that frequented the place. Even bit part actor Allen Lipschitz was there. In fact, those dregs hadn't left since our last visit. Smoke hung thick and heavy in the noisy air from the explosion in the stripper's dressing room, as well as from cigarettes, cigars, and other things. Card games and pool games were accompanied by flaring tempers. Men slugged it out with women who were really men, people were shot and stabbed, real women were grabbed, drinks were guzzled; the place was as chaotic as usual.

"This is what I like," Merc announced to himself, "a nice quiet charming little lounge where one can relax, sip a cocktail, and forget his woes." A hooker was thrown into Mercury who nonchalantly dropped her (or him) on the floor and swaggered up to the bar.

"What'll it be, Mac?" Big Mama asked.

"Two Shirley Temples straight-up," Merc said.

All the action in the bar stopped as everyone looked hatefully at Merc. "Make mine a double," Merc said. The action resumed. The club DJ addressed the crowd through the PA system and announced, "Ladies and Gentlemen, for your listening pleasure, here are The Beatles!"

Apollo and his band took the stage wearing funky costumes that looked like a really bad attempt to recreate the Sgt. Pepper's look and Beatle wigs. Pan's goat horns were protruding out of his Beatle wig, but no one at Madam Wong's seemed to notice or care. The Three Graces were set to sing background vocals. Apollo counted down and they performed a trainwreck rendition of "You Know My Name, Look up the Number."

"That band looks familiar," Zeus remarked.

"All these rock bands look the same to me," Merc remarked back.

Two mortal girls, Flora and Hilde, approached Zeus and Merc who were nursing their Shirley Temples. The girls were giggling that stupid giggle that girls giggle sometimes.

"Hi. I'm Flora and this is Hilde," said Hilde, which is a great indicator of just how drunk and dumb they were. "Would you guys like to dance?"

"Thank you, that was nice," Merc said.

"What was nice?" Flora or Hilde or both asked.

"The dance," Merc said.

"What dance?" Hilde asked.

"You just asked me to dance and we danced," Merc said.

"I don't remember dancing with you," Hilde said.

"I can't help what you remember or don't remember," Merc said.

The girls giggled, which is already annoying me to no end.

"You're cute!" Hilde said. "What's your name?"

"I don't think I should tell you my name, because if you know my name, you'll look up the number," Merc said. "Then you'll want to go to bed with me just because of who I am, and I'm tired of being treated like a piece of meat. You see, I'm wearing a disguise right now so no one will recognize me."

"Please tell me who you are," Hilde or the other one said. "I won't tell anyone. I swear."

"Oh sure, you won't tell anyone, you'll tell *everyone!* Then you'll force me to sleep with you just so you can brag to all your friends! You'll tell Biff and Scooter and Brittany."

"No, I won't tell," she promised.

"Alright, I'll tell you who I am, but it's our little secret. I'm probably Annette Funicello's stand-in on those *Beach Blanket Bingo* movies. And don't ask me what Frankie Avalon's really like. I only knew his stand-in, and she was a jerk."

"Let's dance again, even though I don't remember the first time," Hilde said, pulling Merc up. She started dancing and Merc stood there.

"Why aren't you dancing?" she asked.

"I already did, but I'll slow it down if you want."

A strange shimmering translucent veil surrounded Mercury as his speed, even slowed down considerably, was difficult for the mortal mind to comprehend, and visually nearly impossible to perceive. He was basically a blur doing flips, splits, spins, twirls, reverse turns, Michael Jackson's Moonwalk, spinning headstands, the Twist, the Mashed Potato, the Swim, the Hitch-Hike, the Shimmy, the Time Warp dance from *The Rocky Horror Picture Show* and finishing with the Frug. A few of Madame Wong's putrid patrons clapped and Merc and Hilde returned to the table to sit with Zeus and Flora. Zeus raised his Shirley Temple, "Very nice, Bojangles." Mercury called over to Big Mama, "SOME MORE SHIRLEYS OVER HERE, BIG MAMA. AND KEEP 'EM COMIN'!" There was some awkward silence at the table until Zeus decided to break the ice.

"I like it when a girl talks dirty to me. *That* keeps me interested. When a girl talks just to talk and isn't talking dirty to me, I immediately lose interest. And when we're doing the nasty I want her to call me 'Master of the Mattress'."

Merc stared at Zeus for several moments and then leaned over to him. "Why don't we start with some small talk about the weather? Get to know them a little before you destroy any chance we may have of getting laid. Although at this point the effort may be futile, think of something clever to say."

Zeus thought for a while and then said, "So...do you mortals like cheese?"

Merc dropped his head on the table.

"'Mortals'?" Flora asked.

"Sometimes he thinks he's God," Merc said attempting damage control. The girls laughed. Zeus gestured and Merc flew across the room and crashed into the bar. When he got up Big Mama handed him the Shirley Temples and warned him not to drink too much. Merc brought the drinks back to the table and raised his glass for a toast. "To love, romance, and tenderness; may we keep those passions alive tonight."

They all clinked glasses and drank up.

"So what do you girls do?" Merc asked, not really caring.

"We're hookers," Flora who was a hooker said like a hooker admitting she was a hooker. Toto, who had just returned from New York after his poetry reading and killing The Evil One, and Angelo, approached the table in a very intimidating manner. "What are you bums doing with our chicks?" Angelo snarled.

Mercury (who was now drunk from too many Shirley Temples) warned Angelo, "Skedaddle Cyclops. You have no idea who you're messing with. I just flattened your tires, trashed your place, screwed your mother, and now I'm back."

Hilde said, "You tell 'em, Annette Funicello's stand-in!"

Zeus, who was also drunk, also warned, "You heard him Lady, you and your dog better beat it or I'll make you live with my wife."

"Is that a threat, Big Man?" Angelo asked pulling one of those little paper cocktail umbrellas out of Zeus's Shirley Temple and crushing it with his bare hands. Angelo and Toto picked up Zeus and tossed him. He landed on stage with the band. Apollo looked down at him.

"Zeus?! What are you doing here?"

"I came to hear shitty music," Zeus said.

Pan took his Beatle wig off and butted Zeus in the caboose with his horns. Zeus flew into Angelo and Toto and knocked them down. The hooker girls screamed, Mercury sipped another Shirley Temple, and a barroom brawl broke out. Thunder clapped, hot pink lightning flashed, and Hera and Athena materialized in the doorway. They looked at Zeus and Mercury in the midst of all this mayhem.

"What'd I tell you?" Hera said to Athena, "You can't leave them alone for two seconds."

Hera and Athena entered the bar and took femdom charge. They beat up Angelo and Toto and clobbered everyone in sight. During the destruction and chaos Zeus was knocked down and landed on top of Flora. Lightning flashed again and Hera appeared in front of Zeus. Again, he was eye-level with his wife's huge not-so-pleasant-smelling tootsies. He slowly looked up past the tapping foot, the knock-knees, the growling stomach, and the defiantly folded arms, to the extremely livid mug of his beloved bride.

"Hello dear," Zeus grinned. "You were right about this place and these mortals. It's nothing but sex, drinking, gambling, lying, cheating, and more sex. It's disgusting here!"

"And you're setting a bad example again, *Darling*," Hera growled. She reached down and picked him up by his ear. "It's time to go home now, *Sweetheart*. So we can mop the floors...with your face." Thunder clapped, lightning flashed, and they were gone.

CHAPTER 13

At the foot of Mount Cithaeron, Alfie was leaning against a statue of Zeus staring at his right foot (his, not the statue's) pretending it was Sluggo. Suddenly Merc came running toward him at blinding speed. There was a loud BANG, Merc tripped, stumbled, and landed smack on his tush in front of Alfie.

"Damn!" Merc exclaimed, "Another sneaker blowout!"

"You should try sandals," Alfie suggested. "They're very popular Greek mythology footwear."

"Too gauche," Merc said in disgust, "and I can't run in them. How's the book coming?"

"I finished the part about Zeus. There wasn't much to tell. He just screws everyone, everybody, and everything. So now I'm writing about my experience here. Let me finish what I was just writing." Alfie said the words out loud as he wrote them down. "Damn...Merc...exclaimed... Another...sneaker...blowout

...How...is...the...book...coming?"

Alfie heard soft footsteps, looked around, and saw a lovely young bare-assed naked girl come out of a nearby cave. When she saw Alfie she was startled and ran back inside the cave. Her name was Echo and she was an Oread, which is a nymph. An Oread wasn't a goddess, but actually a mortal who could live for thousands of years and usually ran around naked. Zeus fooled around with them all the time. The word "nymphomaniac" which is a girl who constantly needs that jiffy stiffy, was derived from the word "nymph". You're learning a lot from this book, aren't you? Alfie was intrigued.

"Merc, who was that girl?"

"What girl?"

"Some naked girl just stepped out of that cave and when she saw me she ran back in."

"It's probably Echo the Oread." Merc hobbled over to the cave and called into it, "ECHO!"

From inside the cave, Merc's voice came back at him: "ECHO! ECHO! ECHO!"

"Yeah, it's her," Merc said. "She's beautiful, but she's a pain in the ass. Everything you say to her she repeats back to you."

He called back into the cave: "ECHO COME OUT!" His voice came back at him: "ECHO COME OUT! ECHO COME OUT! ECHO COME OUT!"

Echo timidly came out of the cave. Cupid popped up from behind the statue of Zeus and fired new arrows freshly dipped in Madam Mancowitz's love potion at Alfie and Echo. Alfie gazed at Echo lovingly.

"I love you. Marry me," he said.

"I love you. Marry me," Echo echoed.

Merc was stunned. "How could you love each other? You just met! You don't know each other's favorite color. You don't know each other's pet peeves. You don't know each other's favorite ice cream topping. You don't know-" (Merc noticed the arrows sticking out of their keisters) "what I know."

Merc pulled Alfie aside and said, "Excuse us Echo."

"Excuse us Echo," Echo echoed.

"You're under the influence," Merc told Alfie. "Can you understand me?" Alfie nodded.

"Cupid shot you and her. There's an arrow sticking in your ass."

"I'm just in love, I'm not stupid," Alfie said.

"Same thing," Merc smirked. "Maybe she is the girl for you, I don't know. But I should tell you the lowdown on your intended. There's a reason she repeats everything you say to her. A while back she had a fling with Zeus and Hera found out about it. So Hera punished Echo. Hera told Echo she'd always have the last word, but never the power to speak first. Now, I don't know about you, but being with a woman who always has to have the last word would drive me up a wall. Every guy she's been with, which is a lot, has tried to kill her, but Zeus stopped them because she's good in the sack."

"It's not her fault that she has to have the last word," Alfie said.

"I didn't say it was," Merc replied. "If you can live your life with someone who repeats every single word you say every time you say something, fine. Millions of men do it. I can't. It's up to you."

Alfie pulled the arrow out of his butt and thought a minute.

"She can't speak unless I speak to her first. That's great."

"You're right," Merc said. "It's terrific. Just don't talk to her."

"You wanna be my best man?"

"Me?" Merc asked, emotionally touched. "I'd be honored."

He shook Alfie's hand and said, "Mazel tov!"

Perseus flew down on Pegasus. He carried a shiny bronze shield, a sword, and a satchel. Mercury was upset.

"How did *you* get Pegasus?"

"It's possible that Zeus let me borrow him," Perseus proclaimed.

"The last time you 'borrowed' him, you sideswiped Apollo, knocked the sun into the sea, and nearly boiled Poseidon. And you brought him back with one mile due till empty and an orange warning sticker for a parking violation stuck on his tail that took two weeks to remove. You're irresponsible and a lousy driver," Merc mentioned.

Perseus got off the flying horsie and pulled Merc aside. Behind them, Alfie and Echo were gazing lovingly at each other without saying a word.

"I heard the kid's getting married," Perseus said.

"News and me travel fast," Merc marveled.

"Cupid told me."

"He should know."

"I want to get them a wedding gift and I want you to come with me to get it," Perseus proposed.

"I'm giving them a used Signature 6-piece bath towel set, what are you getting them?"

"Medusa's head."

Mercury pondered. "Why don't you get them a magazine subscription to *Deity Digest* instead?"

"You know me, Speedy. I like to do things different."

"Yeah, I'm aware."

"I'm not sure where to find Medusa."

"Either am I," Mercury mulled. "But I know who would know."

Mercury looked back at Alfie and Echo who were still gazing silently at each other.

"We're going off for a little while. You kids just keep gazing at each other like a couple of comatose zombies."

"We're going off for a little while. You kids just keep gazing at each other like a couple of comatose zombies," Echo echoed.

Under his breath Merc mumbled, "If he doesn't kill her, I will."

Mercury and Perseus climbed up on Pegasus. Mercury sat up front and took the reins. "I'll drive," he insisted. Pegasus spread his magnificent wings, reared up, and bolted into the sky. A short time later he touched down just outside the entrance to The Gray Place, home of The Gray Gilfs. Merc and Perseus dismounted and entered. It was a cavern, dim and shrouded in twilight, where no ray of sun or moonlight ever entered. Everything within was entirely gray. And if it wasn't naturally gray, it was *painted* gray. The shades of gray in The Gray Place were slate, ash, charcoal, graphite, flint, pebble, and pewter. It was really gray in there. Merc and Perseus waded through treacherous gray muck to get where they were going. They saw skulls, spleens, orthodontic night retainers, three public defenders, and expired car warranties stuck in the muck.

"Where are we?" Perseus asked nervously. "What is this place?"

"This is called 'The Bright Red Place'," Mercury said.

"Actually this is the home of The Gray Gilfs, second cousins to the purple sisters who shared one eye. The Gray Gilfs share a vertical smile, if you know what I mean."

"What's a vertical smile?"

Mercury shook his head: "A banana basket, a sausage wallet, a va-jay-jay, a coochie."

"Oh," Perseus pondered. "Yuck."

Mercury explained. "Three old bags with only one penis fly trap between them. They can tell us where to find Medusa. This is the kind of crap we have to go through because you have to do things different. There's nothing wrong with a magazine subscription for a wedding gift. I don't give that marriage a week anyway. He'll cut off her echoing head and go bowling with it."

Suddenly a shrill chilling voice shook the gray cavern walls:

"WHO DARES TO ENTER THE GRAY PLACE?!"

That caused the muck to mingle and Merc to mention, "It is I, Mercury, extraordinarily handsome and fleet-footed messenger of the gods, and Perseus, the bad driver."

Merc and Perseus turned the corner and came face-to-face with The

Gray Gilfs. They were three gray sisters joined at the hip and withered from extreme old age. But they were hotties in their prime and won several swimsuit competitions back in the day, as the kids say. Their trophies and photographs of them modeling swimsuits were proudly displayed on a gray shelf in The Gray Place. And yes, they shared but one…honey pot… between them, which they took turns with, each removing it from her forehead (you read that right) when she had it for a time and handing it to another.

"Eech!" Perseus eeched when he saw what he saw.

"That's right," Merc whispered to Perseus, "make a good impression so they'll tell us what we want to know." Merc looked at the Gilfs. "You ladies should get out more. Go to the beach and get a tan. I know it's 400 years too late, but it is bikini season. I love what you've done with the place. The colors just burst."

"What message do you bring from the gods, Mercury?" the Gilfs asked.

"I bring no message from the gods. We seek the Gorgon Medusa but have no recent address for her. I need to update my address book. Can you tell us where to find her?"

"Yes, we can tell you," said the Gilfs, "but we won't."

"Why not?" asked Mercury, getting annoyed.

"Because we don't wanna," replied the Gray Gilfs like three stuck-together crazy dames. Perseus snatched their snatch off the forehead of the middle Gilf.

"Maybe you *wanna* tell us now or I'll keep this to put my jockstrap in, since every statue and painting of me in the future has me with my nuts hanging out. Tell us where to find Medusa and you can have your panty hamster back."

The Gray Gilfs agreed and explained how to get to the Gorgon: "On the back of the North Wind fly over the sea to the Terrible Sisters' Island. There you will find the Gorgons. But beware, do not look at Medusa directly, or you will turn to stone."

Perseus slapped the snatch back on the middle Gilf. (Now there's a sentence I never thought I'd write.) They thanked the Gilfs and left The Gray Place. The Gilfs cranked up their phonograph while looking at their photographs, played "Glory Days" by Bruce Springsteen, and pined for the past, as a tear fell from their vagina.

In a New York minute Pegasus was hovering over Terrible Sisters' Island. The three Gorgons were on top of mounds sitting on portable camping chairs with built-in cooler bags containing Nehi grape sodas, those orange salted crackers with the thin schmear of cheap peanut butter between the halves, and green olives without pimentos. What the hell is the point of eating green olives if they don't have pimentos? The Gorgons were dreadful creatures with large wings, bodies covered with dragon-ish scales, fangs, claws, and hair a mass of twisting venomous pit viper Bothriopsis snakes. Mercury slipped on a pair of 1993 ACE Polarized mirrored sunglasses ironically called "Pit Vipers" (true, look it up) that sell for $99.00 or four payments of $24.75. I would just pay the $99 and be done with it. You don't need that $24.75 hanging over your head for three more payments, do you? And what if the glasses get lost or break before you're done paying for them? Now you have to keep paying for something that you don't even have! Just pay the whole thing up front. So Merc slipped on the sunglasses, looked down at the Gorgons from above, and said, "There they are, three wild sexy chicks for the taking. I don't know about you, but I'm in heat. You sure you wanna go through with this asinine venture?"

"I am an adventurer," Perseus reminded Mercury. "I do things like this."

"You're also a horse's ass," Merc added as Pegasus reared up. Mercury patted Pegasus, "Just an expression, you handsome horsie you." Pegasus calmed down. "Okay, it's your show, Perseus. Remember, don't look them in the face or you'll be standing in Athens Square with pigeons dumping on your head. In my latest book *How to Decapitate a Gorgon* I explain that the Gorgon's reflection is harmless. It's looking at them directly that causes problems. So if I may suggest, use your shield as a reflector. I would let you borrow my shades, but I'm a major character in this book and Camner can't afford to lose me now. It's in my contract." He patted Pegasus. "Take us down, handsome boy."

Pegasus reared back and dumped Perseus and Mercury on the island, like two large pigeon droppings.

"BAD HORSIE! BAD BAD HORSIE!" Merc yelled. The Gorgons were seething.

"WHO DARES INVADE MY ISLAND?!" Medusa howled.

Perseus and Mercury looked every which way but at the Gorgons. They looked at their hands, feet, crotch, everywhere but at them.

"It is Mercury, messenger of the gods, and Perseus the putz who doesn't seem to think that a magazine subscription is a good enough wedding gift."

"What do you want, Scum? Look at me when I speak to you!" Medusa demanded like a snake-haired crazy bitch.

"I'd rather not," Merc said. "You're not exactly a sight for sore eyes. No offense."

Perseus held up his shield and saw Medusa's reflection.

"Lovely hair Medusa, ever find any spiders in it?"

"Thank you Groucho Marx," Merc winced. "If you don't mind, I'll do the funny stuff. It's in my contract." He looked at his new sneakers but addressed the Gorgons. "We were just talking about you gals and we got so hot and bothered that we just had to stop by and get some head."

It was the perfect cue. Perseus glanced at Medusa's reflection in his shield, reached back, grabbed his sword, spun it, and cut Medusa's head off with a single sweep. He picked up the head and dropped it in his satchel jerking his hand back quickly. "Her hair bit me!" Horrified at the sight of their slain sister, the other two Gorgons started after Perseus and Mercury who urgently called to Pegasus: "HORSIE! COME DOWN QUICK! CRAZY BROADS ARE ATTACKING!" Pegasus swooped down to the island to rescue Mercury and Perseus when his horsie eyes met those of Medusa's youngest sister Euryale. Sadly he turned to stone and fell into the sea sinking like a stone pony, which is not to be confused with the folk rock trio Stone Poneys that Linda Ronstadt was in. Moments after Pegasus fell, the sea rose up in fury, the waters parted, and Poseidon appeared, rubbing his head in agony.

"Who the hell dropped a statue of Pegasus on my head?" He noticed Perseus. "I should have known. Have you boiled anyone lately?"

"That was a long time ago, Earthshaker."

"Gods are like elephants," Poseidon pointed out, "we never forget."

"I don't want to interrupt all this delightful reminiscing," Mercury interrupted, "but the Gorgons will be here any second and I'm not supposed to die. It's in my contract."

"Why are they after you?" Poseidon asked, still rubbing his noggin.

"The Outlaw Alfie is getting hooked, I mean *hitched* with the Oread Echo (say that ten times fast) and Professor Einstein here wanted to give them Medusa's head as a wedding present."

Poseidon looked at Perseus like he was nuts. "Why don't you just give them a magazine subscription?"

"You see!" Merc said, "Even Poseidon thought of that."

Poseidon glared at Mercury. "What do you mean *even* Poseidon thought of that?"

Mercury swallowed hard, "What I meant...was that..." (There was a long awkward and extremely uncomfortable silence as Mercury tried to think his way out of this one as the Gorgons were about to strike.) I can't think of an excuse and I respect you too much to lie to you, Earthshaker. What I meant was that the wires in your head don't touch and I'm amazed that an intelligent thought came out of your mouth, something other than fish breath. No disrespect intended."

The Gorgons charged. Poseidon shook his trident and the whole island shook, causing the Gorgons to retreat. Mercury was stunned.

"Why'd you do that after what I just said to you?"

"I figured you must be telling the truth. You're stranded on a very dangerous island in the middle of the sea which I lord over. And on that island are the Gorgons who want you dead. Believe me, there are lots of nasty creatures under these waters and on these isles that would devour you if I let them. That was a very ballsy thing you did, Herpes."

"Um...It's not 'Herpes'...It's '*Hermes*' which is my Greek name. But I go by my Roman name 'Mercury' because it has more pizzazz and the chicks dig it." Herpes said...I mean *Hermes* said.

"Whatever. Do I really have fish breath?"

"Why do you thnk they call you 'Earthshaker', Earthshaker?"

"I thought it was because when I shake my trident I can shake and shatter whatever I want to shake and shatter."

To prove his point Poseidon shook his trident and Mercury and Perseus went flying. When they recovered, Mercury said, "No. It's because your breath is so bad that every time you exhale, some portion of the Earth is annihilated."

"Alright, I get it," Poseidon said. "When you get back home get me some mouthwash."

"You got it. I'm back. Here you go," Merc smirked like a jerk tossing Poseidon a bottle of Listerine.

"Thanks Herpes. You need a ride?"

"We'd appreciate it."

Poseidon called down into the sea between his legs, "TRITON!" Triton, the Trumpeter of the Sea, rose up from between Poseidon's legs with his trumpet which was a great queen conch shell.

"You called, Earthshaker?"

"These guys need a lift."

Triton blew a long sour note on the queen conch and Poseidon flinched. The surface of the sea stirred madly and two giant pot-bellied seahorses rose up as Triton went down from whence he came. Poseidon addressed Mercury and Perseus. "They'll take you as far as the lagoon under the Orlias Waterfall, but they can't stay long, so dismount quickly and let them go. Give Zeus a message for me. Tell him to go to Hell and say 'Howdy' to Hades for me. Even above sea level I'm amusing."

"You're all wet," Merc quipped, as he thought to himself, *I can't believe I said that. My wry sense of humor and natural knack for understatement and sarcasm are slipping like giggling moon maidens with lesbian tendencies jumping all over each other in a crater filled with margarita Jell-O.* Poseidon sank back into the sea. Mercury and Perseus mounted the giant sea horses and headed back to Olympus. And the two surviving Gorgons looked on, with tears falling from their snake hair.

Love and industrial carbon dioxide was in the air as the wedding day for Alfie and Echo had finally arrived ("finally" in this case means three days.) The ceremony was held at the foot of Mount Cithaeron where the lovebirds had met. Zeus was officiating. Alfie stood nervously in a charred tux borrowed from a billionaire televangelist that Hades had burning in Hell. Mercury stood next to Alfie as his best man. Merc was wearing a dazzling neon yellow tux with tails and a top hat with wings on it to match his new gold-sequined high top sneakers that also had wings. The guests sat on wooden folding chairs that were never picked up by the company that set up my Bar Mitzvah reception in 1970. The chairs were divided up the middle to form an aisle from Echo's cave for the bride to walk down. Echo's family and friends sat on one side appearing rather normal, while Alfie's guests sat on the other side. These included Poseidon, who was dripping wet with seaweed hanging off of him and head bandaged, Hercules, who was flexing in his doggie boots, Athena the Battle-Goddess in full armour, several Sileni (part man, part horse), Cupid who was beaming and telling everyone that he was responsible for the couple getting together, Hera who was being Hera, Helen of Troy, who was wearing the latest Halston designer gown, chewing gum, and painting her nails, the Outlaws of Asteroid #9, the remains of Mr. Green Jeans in a Jetsons lunchbox, Alfie's parents, Al and Frances Koppelman,

Paris, who was examining a rock under his chair, Aphrodite, who was gazing lovingly at herself in a hand mirror, a few Amazons, Perseus, who was holding a wrapped gift that was hissing in his lap, several Satyrs (part man, part goat), and Jason and the Argonauts. Echo's father studied the group, leaned over to Echo's mother and said, "I'm not losing a daughter, I'm gaining a carnival freak show." Zeus took his place in front of all the guests and motioned for silence. Poseidon yelled, "CLAM UP!" and they did. Echo's mother said to Echo's father, "They're ready to start. Go to your daughter's side and try to look the proud father."

"I'm very proud," he said. "It's not every day my daughter marries into Ripley's wet dream."

Echo's father walked into her cave. Zeus cued Apollo's band and they played a snappy rendition of Felix Mendelssohn's traditional "Wedding March" even though Mendelssohn wouldn't be born for many many centuries yet. Echo, wearing a lovely...well, she never wore anything and wasn't about to start now. Echo came out of the cave on the arm of her father, who didn't appear overly happy, and they walked in step, down the aisle toward Zeus who had screwed the bride many times. Behind them trailed a small cow, formally a beautiful but shallow maiden, who was now a maid of honor (yet, still a cow) carrying a basket of daisies in her cow mouth, and wearing a lovely gown that sort of matched Mercury's tux, but not really, at all.

Apollo and the Graces sang:

"Here comes the bride, not wearing white
And she won't be wearing white, after tonight..."

Everyone turned and looked at Apollo who shrugged. Echo took her place beside Alfie. Zeus was ready to begin when Apollo started playing "All You Need Is Love" by the (real) Beatles. Zeus hurled a thunderbolt which missed Apollo and killed the drummer.

"Can anyone here play drums?" Apollo asked.

Echo's Uncle Jake (who used to sell sardine sandwiches and phony driver's licenses from a pushcart just outside of Dead Horse Bay in Brooklyn) volunteered.

"I'll sit in, but not now."

Zeus began. "Gods, friends, monsters and mortals, we are gathered here today in the sight of the Almighty, which is me, to bond or bind, whatever it is, this couple together in matrimony. I hear that marriage is a wonderful thing, but I'm married so I wouldn't know." He laughed. Hera glared. He stopped laughing. "But seriously folks, let's get this over with. Do you Alfie the Outlaw of Asteroid #9 take this nymphomaniac Oread Echo to be your lawful wedded wife, to have and to hold, for richer and for poorer, in sickness and in health, until death do you part? Don't do it kid. Run!"

"I do," Alfie did.

"Big mistake," Zeus mumbled. "And do you, Echo the Oread nymph, take Alfie-"

Alfie clamped his hand over her mouth. "She does."

"The ring please," Zeus said.

Mercury froze, "The ring! I forgot it!"

"Where is it, genius?" Zeus asked; a bit perturbed.

"I left it on Crete. I'll go get it. I'll be back in a few seconds."

"That's impossible," Zeus decided. "Crete is an island 286 miles away from here. I know because I made it. You're telling me that you can get to shore, swim 286 miles to Crete, get the ring, swim back another 286 miles which totals 572 miles, and get back here in a few seconds."

Merc frowned. "I could be faster but I'm wearing a tux. It doesn't crank the motor like spandex."

"Fifty drachma says you can't do it."

"Can we please get on with the wedding?" Alfie asked, getting annoyed, but not wanting to upset Zeus.

"We need the ring. Speedy's going to get it." Zeus spoke to the guests. "Excuse us folks. We'll be with you soon. Talk about how great I am for a few minutes. Hercules come up here and hold Speedy as tight as you can without killing him."

Hercules did as he was told.

"You got him?" Zeus asked.

"Yep," Hercules grunted.

Zeus grinned and leered at the same time. "Alright smartass... ready...*GO!*"

Mercury was suddenly soaking wet. Hercules released him. Mercury reached into his pocket and pulled out a flathead mullet, a damselfish, a black goby, and the ring.

"Where's my fifty drachma?"

"Sue me," Zeus scowled. He then continued with the wedding. "Outlaw

Alfie, place the ring on her finger and repeat after me, "With this ring, I thee wed."

Alfie slid the ring on Echo's finger and repeated, "With this ring, I thee wed."

Zeus looked at Echo. "I know I don't have to say this, but repeat after me, "With this ring, I thee wed.""

"I know I don't have to say this, but repeat after me, "With this ring, I thee wed."" Echo echoed while putting a ring on Alfie's finger.

"I now pronounce you husband and wife. Do whatever you want to her. I give it a week before she mysteriously goes missing." Zeus turned his attention to the guests. "Gods, friends, monsters and mortals, we'll have cheap food and bad music in a moment, but before the festivities begin I'd like to take this opportunity to plug this new book about my life, written by our very own bridegroom, Alfie!" There was some light clapping. Zeus held up a hardback copy of the book with his smiling face on the cover. "It's called *Zeus, How'd You Get So Great?* The title was my idea because I'm constantly asked that question. Gods and mortals and even some monsters come up to me all the time and say, 'Your Majesty-' (He glanced at Hera who shot him a bird.) "They say (he glared at her) *'YOUR MAJESTY*, how do you do it? How do you manage to do what you do so well and stay in such great shape?'" Hera burst out laughing. Zeus turned to Alfie. "This is what you have to look forward to Kid." He continued. "The answer to that question and many more are probably all right here in this magnificent book. I haven't read it yet, but I think it's great."

The guests started to get up, but Zeus started talking again and they reluctantly sat back down.

"Sure there's steamy sex and violence and all that good stuff, but it isn't all fun and games being King of the Gods. There were tough times too, like when I had to make major decisions that affected all of you. This book explores how I came to those decisions, and what I thought about and considered and reconsidered during those trying times when I realized that the fate of history was in my hands. It's not easy being Number One. The trials and tribulations, the joys and the sorrows, are all here between the covers. I think."

The guests started to get up again, but Zeus started talking again and they reluctantly sat back down.

"I inspired the creation of many things that the world will use in the future: alarm clocks, marathons, umbrellas, maps, theater, the Olympics, central heating, bridges, and chewing gum, which Helen of Troy is never without. There's another side to me too–"

Hera yelled to him, "THIS BETTER BE THE LAST SIDE TO YOU OR I'LL SHOVE THAT BOOK WHERE IT *REALLY* BELONGS!"

Zeus turned to Alfie again, "You see? This is the train you just jumped on." He continued. "This book probably also reveals to the reader my tender, merciful, and sensitive side. But again, I haven't read it, so I don't know."

Echo's Uncle Jake sneezed. Zeus hurled a thunderbolt at him and killed him. Zeus was livid. "That's what happens when you interrupt me! Now where was I?"

Mercury answered, "You were mentioning your tender, merciful, and sensitive side. And while I have the floor, I think The Beatles need a new drummer."

Zeus continued, "So if you want to know what makes me tick, buy this book. I haven't read it, but I think it will answer all those questions about me that keep you awake at night twisting and turning."

Mercury grinned at Zeus. "You're telling me that if I read that book that I'll fall asleep. No more long agonizing nights pacing the floor wondering what makes you tick. Is that right?"

Zeus gestured and sent Mercury flying into the taco bar as the other guests moved into the reception area. Some went directly to the buffet and waited in line to be served by such Olympian luminaries as Poseidon, wearing an apron and dishing up seafood quiche, poached salmon, and lobster bisque; Artemis, serving roasted lamb and both chocolate and banana Moon Pies, and Dionysus, serving a variety of wines ranging in price and quality from J Roget Brut at $2.49 a bottle all the way to Barefoot Fruit Moscato at $5.99 a bottle. Others stood in line to buy Zeus's book and get his autograph. Table seating had been arranged according to name cards so that Echo's guests and Alfie's guests were mixed and seated together at the same tables. I was sitting alone in the corner watching and taking notes. Aphrodite kept winking at me, but I have enough problems without getting caught in that nether region. Apollo's band The Beatles was on the makeshift stage and there was room for dancing. The Titan Hyperion was seated at a table with an older couple, Sam and Midge Benowitz. They were both looking him up and down.

"He's a big one!" Midge commented, pointing out the obvious, as she tended to do.

"How tall are you son?" Sam asked, "Ten feet?"

"25 feet," Hyperion answered. "And I weigh 14,000 pounds, since that's your next question."

"You must eat a lot," Midge commented.

"What do you do for a living?" Sam asked, really wanting to know.

"I am Hyperion, the God of Heavenly Light."

"You don't say! I sell light fixtures! That's probably why they put us at the same table! I can get you a deal on flush mounts, pendant lights, and track and rail lighting."

Echo's second cousin on her mother's side, Norman Cousins (yes, ironically, that was his last name) sat across from Aphrodite. He was history's first nerd, complete with bow tie, plaid jacket, and horn-rimmed glasses. He smiled at Aphrodite who was still winking at me.

"What's your major?" Norman asked as The Beatles started playing "Bitch" by the Rolling Stones, with Pan on flute, Cupid sitting in on drums, and the three Graces doing background vocals. Apollo pranced around the stage as he sang, imitating Mick Jagger who imitated Tina Turner. He cued the band to bring it down and the music mellowed. He took the microphone off the stand and wandered around to different tables to converse with the guests. I should tell you that this was the same microphone stand that Toto used to squash The Evil One in New York. I can't afford to bring in all new equipment for each scene in this book, so I cut corners where I can. I got the idea from producer Irwin Allen (*Lost in Space, Voyage to the Bottom of the Sea, Land of the Giants, Time Tunnel*) who would use the same props on each of his shows and would just have them repainted or redecorated to save money. My point is that the remains of The Evil One were still on the bottom of the cast iron base of the mic stand, and they were rotting and smelled bad. But some of the creatures at that reception smelled a lot worse, so it wasn't a big deal. Apollo paused at Sam, Midge, and Hyperion's table.

"You folks here for the wedding reception?" he asked.

Midge pulled the mic to her mouth. "Yes. It's a lovely reception, Mazel tov to the lovely couple."

"And where are you from?"

Sam pulled the mic away from Midge to his mouth. "The Big Apple, New York City. I'm Sam Benowitz and this is my wife Midge, and our big friend here is Hy and he's in the lighting business like me. I sell fixtures wholesale if anyone's interested. I can make you a great deal."

"We'll keep that in mind," Apollo said as he cued the band and sang the first verse of Sinatra's "(Theme from) New York, New York." Across the way Alfie was next in line to have his book autographed by Zeus.

"Make it out to Alfie and Echo."

Zeus signed the book and then hit some buttons on a calculator. "That's $19.95 for the book plus $1.50 for the personalized autograph. Your total comes to $21.45."

"You're gonna make me pay for a book that I wrote?"

Zeus thought for a moment. "I'll tell you what. Because it's your wedding day, and I know what you just did to your life, I'll let you have it for half price. That'll be my gift to you."

Alfie frowned while paying Zeus. "Your generosity overwhelms me, Your Highness."

"If you forgot to mention my generosity in *this* book, you can write all about it in the sequel. I already got the title for it, *ZEUS, HOW'D YOU GET SO TERRIFIC? THE SAGA CONTINUES.*"

"I'm not writing the sequel," Alfie announced. "I'm giving up writing and becoming a god instead. It's less work." He grabbed the book and stalked away.

"Ungrateful outlaw," Zeus mumbled.

The band played another verse of "Bitch" and Apollo paused at another couple at a table. He cued the band and the music mellowed as he interviewed them. The husband purposely dropped his fork and went under the table to pick it up so he wouldn't have to speak.

"Are you enjoying yourselves?" Apollo asked the wife.

"Yes, we are," the woman said into the mic.

"Here for the wedding reception, are you?"

"We are. They're a terrific couple. I wish she would put on some clothes. I hear she repeats everything you say to her, but there are worse things, like not wearing clothes at your own wedding."

"Point taken, and where are you folks from?"

"San Francisco."

Apollo cued the band and the husband sat back up as Apollo sang the first verse of the Tony Bennett hit "I Left My Heart in San Francisco" to some scattered applause. "Guys, grab a gal, or ladies be bold, and I don't mean Athena, and ask a gentleman to dance. This isn't the old days. This is 400 BCE, the night is young, and we're swingin', as we celebrate the marriage of Alfie and Echo!"

There was some light applause. The music picked up and several gods, monsters, and mortals got up to dance. Norman was still smiling dumbly at Aphrodite who was smiling dumbly at me.

"Would you care to cut a rug and boogie down?" Norman asked Aphrodite.

"I wish there were two of me to help you but there's not so I can't," she said.

Just then Athena grabbed Norman by the seat of his pants and carried him with one hand to the dance floor where they both started doing a fascinating Rumba. As they were dancing, Norman asked Athena, "What's *your* major?" Paris and Helen were sitting with Alfie's parents, Al and Frances Koppelman. Helen was painting her toenails opaque pastel peach and popping chewing gum between her teeth. Paris was holding forth philosophizing.

"Most people take rocks and broken glass for granted, but if you really think about it, when mankind destroys itself, which it will, only rocks and broken glass will survive. So I think we should teach rocks and broken glass how to read and write and use their minds, so they can carry on for us and make a whole new race of rock-like-glass people who will live in peace and harmony and not just throw themselves at each other."

Al and Frances Koppelman looked at each other.

"Ain't he smart?" Helen asked popping her gum.

"Brilliant," Al responded.

Echo's mother and father were sitting at a table with a Satyr (a goat-man), a Sileni (part man, part horse), and a midget. I don't really know where the midget came from. He just wandered in. Echo's father was staring at them. Echo's mother stood up.

"I'm going to the buffet," she looked at her husband, "do you want me to fix you a plate?"

Echo's father didn't answer. He just stared at his table companions. The Satyr got up and headed to the buffet too. The band started playing "All of Me". The dance floor was getting crowded with mortals dancing with monsters and gods dancing with monsters and mortals. It was quite a sight. Alfie's cousin Allison was dancing with Poseidon and was pulling seaweed off of him.

"You've been swimming? What's with the pitchfork?"

"It's not a pitchfork, it's a trident," Poseidon corrected her.

"LIKE THE GUM!" Helen yelled across the room.

The Sileni looked around and said to Echo's father, "Hey Father of the Bride, looks like your old lady's a bedswerver. Check it."

He pointed to the dance floor with his hoof. Echo's Father stood up and looked on in disbelief to see his wife on the dance floor kicking it with the goat guy. Cupid was sitting with a group of children from both the bride's side and the groom's side. They were all staring at him. A boy asked, "Are you going to be in *The Wizard of Oz?*"

Cupid snarled, "Screw you Kid! I'll make you fall in love with Norman Cousins."

He placed an arrow in his bow and fired at the boy, but the boy ducked and the arrow struck Echo's mother who immediately fell in love with the Satyr.

"I love you!" she professed.

"It's probably just a physical sexual attraction," the Satyr said. "Lust is a very powerful thing. Mortals often mistake it for love."

The music ended, the dancers clapped, and Apollo brought his mic over to Echo's Aunt Goldie.

"You must be Echo's Aunt Goldie. I heard a lot about you. All the way from Flatbush, you came. Are you here for the wedding reception too, Goldie?"

"No, I came here to pole vault in the Olympics. What kind of schmucky question is that? Of course I'm here for the wedding reception. I want to say mazel tov to the children. May they have many happy years together. Not like me and Bernie. I hate to say it but I'm glad he's dead. Every day with him started and ended with Rod Serling making a speech."

"And we all want to say mazel tov with you, Goldie. And we'll do it like this..." He cued the band, closed his eyes, let the feeling overtake him, and sang passionately. As was tradition, he started slowly at first and kicked it to a rousing finish, the song of course, "Ha-va na-gi-la, ha-va na-gi-la, ha-va na-gi-la ve-nismeha ..." Everyone formed a circle and danced the hora, lifting Alfie and Echo in chairs and dancing them around, and then parents were lifted in the chairs, then some mythological creatures. The Titans were too big to be lifted in chairs. 25 feet tall and 14,000 pounds is begging for a hernia. Apollo spoke while The Beatles continued to play the music to Hava Nagila. "Let's have a round of applause for the Earthshaker who supplied the fresh seafood. Was it great or what?"

People clapped, Poseidon bowed. Mercury flashed in and handed Apollo a telegram. Apollo glanced at it and addressed the guests. "Alfie, Echo, Gods, Monsters, Mortals, and Honored Guests, I have just received a telegram from Hades, God of the Underworld, who says he's sorry he couldn't make it to the wedding but his mother-in-law's visiting him for an extended stay. He says he doesn't see her leaving any time soon. He wishes the bride and groom the very best and says that if they ever need a warm place to stay, they can go to Hell. Camner's running that joke into the ground, isn't he? Let's have a hand for Hades."

There was some light clapping and Apollo cued the band for the final verse of "Bitch." When "Bitch" ended, the band segued right into a mellower "Hava Nagila" reprise and Apollo addressed the guests over the music. "We thank you all for coming. We are The Beatles. We're available for weddings, Bar Mitzvahs, Bat Mitzvahs, funerals, divorce parties, birthday parties, bachelorette parties, or any time you get something notorized. We wish the lovely couple much happiness and a joyous life together. L'Chaim! I believe the bride and groom are going to open their wedding gifts now, so let's all gather 'round!"

Just as the guests gathered around Alfie and Echo to watch them open their gifts, Echo's father saw his wife kissing the Satyr. He ran up, forcefully pulled her away, and angrily confronted the Satyr.

"Go find yourself a sheep!"

"But I love him! I want to be with him!" Echo's mother cried.

"You're leaving me for a goat?! I won't have it! People will talk!"

"Let them talk. I don't care!"

"Then either do I!" Echo's father cried. Distressed and distraught he took the stage and spoke into the microphone.

"Ladies and Gentlemen and whatever the hell the rest of you are, I have an announcement to make. My wife of 25 years is leaving me for a goat!"

He broke down sobbing. There was a low murmur of reaction expressing shock and disappointment among the guests. Aunt Goldie mumbled, "I'm surprised it took her this long." Mercury glared at Cupid who shrugged. Some time later, Alfie and Echo were surrounded by empty boxes, bows, ribbons, and gift wrapping paper. Alfie looked at the gifts piled all around.

"My love, we've gotten some swell gifts so far: giant eagle wings, dragon parts, horse manure (two Sileni high-fived each other with their hooves), assorted rocks and broken glass in a Gucci bag, goat cheese from the Satyrs, a lifetime supply of sardines from the Earthshaker, and Mercury gave me an assortment of mouth gags and duct tape. That red one looks great on you." He addressed the guests. "I think I can speak for both my wife and myself when I say we appreciate all these fine and functional gifts." Aphrodite handed him an envelope. He opened it and read the card out loud. "'This card entitles you to one free fabulous blow-' me down, what's next?" Alfie shoved the card in his pocket, opened a rather large box, and pulled out the Golden Fleece. The guests all gasped. "This is from Jason and the Argonauts."

** (Let me step in here. I honestly don't remember who had the Golden Fleece last or what happened to it, and I don't have the time or the patience to go back and look. So let's just say that Jason and the Argonauts had it last, although I seem to remember Rollo Starguy tossing it to The Evil One so he would put his seal on the Remus Opus, which he refused to do at that time. I don't know and I don't care. Now back to Alfie.)

"It's a beautiful bath mat. Thanks guys. I'll enjoy stepping on this when I get out of the shower. Thank you all for the great gifts and thanks for coming. Bye."

"There's one more gift," Perseus said, stepping forward with his gift for the newlyweds. "I wanted to save mine for last because I like to do things different."

"I have to take a whiz," Alfie said. "You open it and show everyone. I'll be back in a minute, unless I'm having prostate problems and then it will be longer."

Alfie walked away and Perseus unwrapped the box.

"Why is that box hissing?" Echo's father asked. "Why is everything here so insane?"

Perseus excitedly said, "I think you're all going to like this. It makes a good conversation piece and would go well on any coffee table." Perseus put on gloves, took the lid off the box, reached in, and pulled out Medusa's head. It was hideous. A horrific scream came out of its mouth as the snake hair hissed and snapped at the guests. Perseus held up the head for all to see. Everyone looked at it and turned to stone. As Mercury was turning to stone he thought to himself *I can't believe I forgot what that schmuck was giving them. This is embarrassing.*

Realizing what he did, Perseus said, "I could return it and get them a magazine subscription instead."

Perseus looked at the head and also turned to stone. A few moments later, Alfie returned (from the head) and wandered through the statues. He paused at Mercury and sadly tapped his knuckles against the hard stone that was once his friend.

"See what happens when the Life of the Party leaves, Merc? Everything just stops."

He sat down with his back against his friend and looked up into the sky which rumbled loudly as the Digby orb flew by overhead with Marty and Bink closing in again. If this were a movie the camera would remain fixed on the shot, which would dissolve slowly into present day, with a tour guide leading her group of picture-snapping tourists through the statues which have deteriorated somewhat through the centuries, as she explained.

"These statues were constructed around 400 BC in tribute to the mythological characters of Olympus. For the most part, mythology served to explain nature, the origins of mankind, religious rites, customs, institutions, and so on. The myths usually involved the exploits and adventures of gods and heroes like those we see represented here." Several tourists posed by the statues for photos as the tour guide continued. "As you can see, the statues have deteriorated somewhat through the centuries, but it is still possible to tell some of your favorite characters from mythology." She pointed some out. "Here is Hermes, the fleet-footed messenger of the gods. He's more widely known by his Roman name, Mercury. Over there in front of the other statues is the great hero Perseus holding Medusa's head that he famously removed from the rest of her. According to legend, anyone who looked at Medusa's head would turn to stone, so don't look at her!"

The tourists laughed. One tourist said, "Maybe that's what happened here. They all looked at her and turned to stone." The tourists all laughed again. The tour guide continued.

"Here's Aphrodite, the Goddess of Love. Some of you who were around in the 1960s might remember Shocking Blue's song "Venus" which was about her. Venus was her Roman name, just like Mercury was Hermes' Roman name. And over here is the one and only Hercules. In 1970 a movie came out called *Hercules in New York* about Hercules being sent from Mount Olympus to New York where he becomes a professional wrestler and gets involved with some mobsters. Who do you think played Hercules in that movie?"

"Arnold Schwarzenegger," a tourist said.

"That's right. It was the first movie that he acted in and he's billed as

'Arnold Strong, Mr. Universe'. The ancient Greeks believed that Zeus, who I believe is represented by that statue over there holding the book, and several of the other gods, lived in a palace on top of Mount Olympus."

The tourists looked up.

"This isn't Mount Olympus. This is Mount Cithaeron," the tour guide said, slightly annoyed. "You just wasted your time and mine looking up."

"Did these characters ever really live?" asked one of the tourists who was from Tennessee.

"No, not really, but people needed something to believe in and a way to explain things, like I explained before, so they created the gods."

Meanwhile, down in the Underworld, as the flames of Hell burned, and sinners were flogged without mercy in this dark shadowy place of torment, eternal suffering, gloom, and misery, Hades' mother-in-law Demeter was giving him her own special kind of Hell.

"You call this a home for my daughter, you bum?! Get a *real* job! Be a mensch!"

A tortured soul screamed behind her and she spun around.

"Don't interrupt me when I'm talking! Have some manners!"

She turned back to Hades and continued blasting him, "I'm the laughingstock of my mahjong club because of you! When I told them what my son-in-law does for a living I almost got blackballed. It's hot as Hell in here! There's a new thing called *AIR CONDITIONING*! Ever hear of it?! Don't be cheap where my precious daughter is concerned! Thank the gods my Irving isn't alive to see this. It would kill him!" Another tortured soul screamed. Demeter continued, "Shut up Irving, I'm talking!"

If this was a movie the picture of Demeter nagging Hades in Hades would freeze and become a photograph in a very bizarre family album. A hand would move into frame and close the album. We would pull back until we were at the very very beginning where the Titan Atlas was holding the world on his shoulders. There he is and it looks like he has something to say. What is it now, Atlas? I'm very busy.

"Could you hold Earth for one quick second? I really got to tinkle bad."

I don't have time to waste on you, Atlas. Right now, in the future, as we speak, Private Detective Sheldon Danger's archenemy, Squirm, has escaped from prison and I have to run along to tell that tale. Try not to drop that rock. I have enough problems.

257

CHAPTER 14

Back in the City of Angels, private detectives Sheldon Danger and Maximus Moore were walking toward their office, trench coats and fedoras making them look like total twits in the hot L.A. heat. The theme from "Peter Gunn" was playing on Max's boom box which he carried on his shoulder. Sheldon stopped to look at himself in a storefront mirror. Max stopped with him and paused the music.

"Do you know who I see when I look in this mirror, Max?"

"Yourself?"

"No. I see someone who's not you. And that makes me very happy."

"I'm happy you're happy, Boss."

"And I'm happy that you're happy that I'm happy. Squirm's on the loose, Max. And we both know he's got big plans. There's only one man who can stop him. Do you know who that man is, Max?"

"Spider-Man?"

Sheldon glared at his partner. "I've said it many times. Quick Draw McGraw had a jackass for a sidekick and so do I."

"Baskin-Robbins just opened a new place and I need to see if they have Caramel Macchiato," Max said.

"Alright Max, but don't be too long. We need to stop Squirm before he gets started."

But it was too late for that. "Squirm" was already well under way under the Hollywood National Savings and Trust drilling into the strong room where a small portion of the floor appeared to be "moving." Within minutes that portion broke away neatly and up popped the head of notorious criminal mastermind Stanley Jerkins, known to authorities and the underworld as "Squirm." He was wearing a yellow hard hat embossed with his personal "logo", a sinister-looking worm in the shape of the letter *S* wearing Stanley's iconic coke-bottle- thick black-framed 1950s "Faculty style" eyeglasses, and his ever-present bow tie. Stanley's own spectacles were covered with dust and particles from drilling. He blew the tip of the drill like it was a Colt-Frontier Six-Shooter Revolver belonging to Dale Robertson on *Tales of Wells Fargo*, put it down, and removed a small spray can and a lens wipe from his shirt pocket. He removed his glasses, sprayed the lenses, and wiped them clean. He put his glasses back on and calmly surveyed his surroundings. There were hundreds of safety deposit boxes of various sizes and a massive safe. Squirm grinned to himself and then turned his full attention to a security camera. Knowing he was on camera something snapped and he became very dramatic and frantic in his delivery, because in his mangled mind this was a major production for the world to witness.

"Greetings Ladies and Gentleman, and welcome to *the Stanley Jerkins Show!* Are you ready for some fun?! I'm your host, Stanley Jerkins, and I'm buzzed to be here. I just tunneled through 200 yards of dirt and 12 feet of cement and boy are my arms tired! Yesterday I came here incognito, rented a safety deposit box, and got to work. The alarm was almost as dopey as your employees. I melted the insulation off the wires, and then connected the NC switch wires with crocodile clips leaving the tamper wires untampered. Piece of cake! Then I put delicious maple syrup all over the diffusion lenses of your costly microwave/Passive Infra-Red motion detectors, and repositioned eight of your nine security cameras. They're all taking exquisite shots of your cheesy flea market artwork that hung themselves in this dump! Now we have this one remaining camera, which I'm happy to say is no longer a live feed. Live audiences give me stage fright. Therefore, this broadcast is being taped for the enjoyment of future generations. We have a great show for you tonight, Ladies and Gentlemen. When I was in the cage I became something of a domestic diva. I'm a bad cook, so I won't give you a cooking demonstration, but I will show you how to clean out your house, or in this case, your bank."

Squirm smiled big at the camera just as Sheldon Danger slammed down a newspaper with the headlines: "ESCAPED CONVICT 'SQUIRM' STRIKES AGAIN!" He stomped out of his private office and stormed over to his secretary Irma Finkelstein who was at her desk, chewing Trident gum, and on the phone. "No darling, only use tartar sauce for fishermen...

He's a lawyer? Tabasco. But that might burn you too. Let me think about it." She noticed Sheldon glaring at her. "I gotta go Sweetheart, the live version of *Fantasia* just walked up." She hung up and glared back.

"Where's Max?" Sheldon growled.

Irma read off a phone message pad while chewing her Trident. "Mr. Moore called to say he'll be late because he was leading a safari through the Amazon and they were attacked by cannibals. There was a fierce battle and he was hit on the head with a heavy club. His pith helmet was dented and he was knocked unconscious. He narrowly escaped with his life."

"He doesn't have a pith helmet," Sheldon snarled. "He tried all 31 flavors. Today's my interview with *Detective Magazine*."

"To quote the Greek gods, 'mazel tov'. Marty Doyle from *Detective Magazine* is in your office. He's been there for over an hour."

"No one's in my office but me and I'm not even there, I'm here."

"You may be here, but Marty Doyle is in there."

Sheldon, totally confused, turned around and stormed into his office to find Marty Doyle sitting at his desk, feet propped up, newspaper opened with the headlines facing Sheldon to purposely taunt him.

"So your old nemesis is back in action, Danger. Not good. Stanley's been a busy little beaver since he busted out. There's been five major heists so far with his signature all over them, and he's been out ten minutes."

"He's just warming up," Sheldon said. "You got some interview questions for me?"

"I know you 20 years, Danger. I have all I need. We're doing a special issue on strange cases and you've had a few gems, so we'll put you in. It's a rush job. The issue prints tonight and comes out tomorrow. Camner needs it for the next scene, so we're speeding things up. You think Stanley's gonna come after you? You did put him away. You nervous?"

"I don't get nervous, Marty. I get overly concerned. But if I nail Stanley first, there won't be a problem."

"Try to do it soon 'cause he's gonna gut this city good. I need a recent photo for the article. The only ones we have of you on file make you look young, handsome, and energetic, and we don't like to deceive our readers."

"My girl up front has pictures. We usually charge, but I'll make an exception."

Irma yelled, "YOU WANT THE GLOSSY 8 x 10 OR THE POSTER? THEY'RE BOTH STAMPED AUTOGRAPHED."

"Her medication is wearing off. You know Marty, I learned in this business long ago that even a criminal mastermind like Stanley Jerkins has an equal, or in this case a *more equal un*criminal mastermind to stop him, and I'm that guy."

Doyle stared at Sheldon and wrote down what he just said.

"You can use that quote in tomorrow's issue."

"You can bet on it, Danger. Where's your partner? I'd like to interview him."

Sheldon put his arm around Doyle and steered him toward the door. "Sadly, tragically, there was a terrible accident and Max didn't make it."

Doyle was shaken. "I'm sorry. I didn't hear a word about it."

Sheldon appeared to get misty-eyed and emotional. "When a man loses a partner–" He paused getting choked up. "I'm sensitive, Marty, not just tough. You might want to mention that in tomorrow's issue. Broads read it too, and broads like sensitive guys like me."

"You like sensitive guys, Danger?"

"No, I like *real* men. Put that in the article, so your readers get to know the man inside the trench coat."

"I'll make sure of it. If it's not too painful, tell me what happened to Max."

Sheldon blotted his eyes and gazed out the window. "Max was skiing and he fell off a mountain and into a river. He survived that, but when he climbed up the riverbank, he was eaten alive by 31 wild pigs of all different colors. They tore him to pieces, Marty. He never had a chance!" Sheldon broke down sobbing.

"That's horrible!" Doyle said, patting Sheldon on the back consolingly.

"What a way to go," Sheldon said wiping his eyes. "Ripped to shreds and eaten alive. What could be worse?"

Max walked in.

"Damn," Sheldon mumbled.

"Sorry I'm late, Boss."

Doyle was confused. "I thought he was dead!"

"Well, he is in a way," Sheldon said, "look at him."

Doyle wanted to interview Max, but Sheldon ushered him out. "We don't have time for that, Marty. You have to write up your story on me and get that issue out. Squirm's loose and I've got some fishing to do."

Irma handed Doyle an 8 x 10 of Sheldon and Sheldon gave Doyle the bum's rush.

Late that night inside Fishman's Jewelers in the Diamond District on Hill Street, Sheldon's nemesis was ready to strike again. If this was a movie the camera would rocket inside and from its point of view we would snake around Fishman's Jewelers admiring all the dazzling diamonds and precious gems. We'd hear a slight noise above our heads and the camera would rocket up just as Stanley "Squirm" Jenkins popped his head through a ceiling panel and smiled big. Stanley loved his work. Hanging upside-down, he extended a collapsible fishing rod, opened the bail, and slowly lowered the line. He paused and put on some strange-looking steampunk goggles, along with an earpiece which he adjusted for sound sensitivity. With the goggles on, Squirm could see infrared beams crisscrossing at many different levels, and very heavily around the display cases. Fishman's was known for never putting their jewelry in safes after they closed because it would make this scene too tedious to write and I have things to do. Squirm proceeded to carefully lower the fluorocarbon fishing line through the infrared beams until it reached the lock on the first display case. Attached to the end of the fishing line was an odd-looking magnet that attached itself to the lock, opened up, and made clicking sounds. Squirm adjusted his earpiece again and pushed some numbered buttons on the reel. He heard pins and tumblers fall and the lock snapped open. Still hanging upside-down he addressed a security camera directly, as his "show" continued from this new location. "Like my new hangout?" He let go a sinister laugh which was okay, but not great compared to the previous sinister laughs you've heard in this book, even though they weren't great either.

The next day the theme from "Peter Gunn" blasted from Max's boom box as he and Sheldon walked down Hill Street passing a man on a bench with an opened copy of *Detective Magazine* hiding his face (you're way ahead of me aren't you?).

On the cover was a picture of Sheldon Danger and in large bold print the cover lines: *DANGER LIKES REAL MEN!* A sexy woman walked past Sheldon and commented, "You look really hot in that trench coat." Sheldon turned around to look at her and slammed right into a light pole. Max quickly pushed pause and caught Sheldon just before he hit the cement.

"You okay, Boss?!"

Sheldon said woozily (yes, it's a real word): "Women are dangerous, Max. Did you see how that girl looked at me like she was falling in love?"

"I looked at her, Boss. She didn't look at you; she just looked at your trench coat."

"Max, it looked like she didn't look at me to you because I'm wearing dark glasses. When are you going to start using your brains? You're a private detective. It's time you started acting like one." Sheldon looked across the street at Fishman's Jewelers. "Stanley hit that place hard last night. The cops were here earlier. I know that because there are 128 doughnut boxes in that expanded metal outdoor park trash receptacle over there. The Lieutenant called me because he knows Stanley and I go way back. I have a feeling Squirm's in the neighborhood, Max. He likes to watch the flies swarm. But he's tricky. We can't assume he'll be where we think he'll be. So first we'll check out places he would never go, and then work our way up to places he might be but won't be. Don't forget, Max, the garden may look good, but there's lots of worms in the Big Apple."

"We're in Los Angeles."

"Don't contradict me, Max. It makes you look worse than you already do. Are you with me or not?"

"Four inches away."

"That's too close. Back up and let's go."

As Danger and Moore walked toward Fishman's, the man on the bench slowly lowered the *Detective Magazine* hiding his face, and yes, you were right...it's Squirm, who said to himself out loud and with anger in his voice..."Sheldon Danger!"

A few buildings away was an adult movie theater called "The Wormhole". On the marquee was *SEX KITTENS FROM OUTER SPACE*. Sheldon pointed it out. "Now there's a place Squirm might be but won't be. Let's check that out first since we're right here, and then work backwards to places he would never go, and then forward again to places he might possibly be but most likely won't be, again," Sheldon said.

"Whatever you say, Boss," Max said.

Inside the dark dingy Wormhole Theater, Danger and Moore sat next to each other, mesmerized by the movie. On screen was some of the greatest acting ever to appear on celluloid. Here now is a scene from *Sex Kittens from Outer Space*.

Mistress Athena

"Welcome to Planet Pussy. I am Athena, your mistress. You will now be exhibited in our Human Zoo. We will take advantage of you to fulfill our desires."

Astronaut

"We have traveled zillions of miles to be here and are hungry. Do you have anything to eat?"

Sex Kitten #1

"Will I do?"

A loud rumble filled the theater through the speakers. The "actors" looked up.

Astronaut

"What was that loud noise, Mistress Athena?"

Mistress Athena

"That was the Digby orb passing by overhead. Now let me see your orbs that I will twist until you scream."

(End scene)

Max had a box of popcorn on his lap. Without looking away from the screen, Sheldon reached into the popcorn box, froze as if he grabbed something he wasn't expecting to grab, and quickly glared at Max. While the theatrics in the theater were going on, Squirm was plotting his next hit.

Late that night inside the Los Angeles Museum of Art, the crotch on a life-size portrait of frilly monarch Louis X1V, the Sun King, began to bulge and then burst open as Squirm's head popped through the aforementioned crotch, grinning madly. "I LOVE ART!" he announced to a security camera he had previously rigged for a twenty-minute time delay. He pulled his head back in through the crotch and moved the portrait out of the way as he stepped through a huge gaping hole the size of the entire painting. He carefully took select paintings off the walls and deposited them through the hole behind the Sun King while addressing his "audience." "It's a burglar's buffet in here! Vibration sensors, environmental sensors, motion detectors, closed-circuit TV cameras, surveillance scanners, and behind every painting, eye hooks attached to L hooks with metal boilerplates screwed into both the frame and the wall! But not to worry, Ladies and Gentlemen, I've taken the liberty of disconnecting all of the above...except for one...the piece de resistance by the exit door. Ta-Daaa! I give you the Reverse Man-Trap! A series of sets of doors designed so that one set of doors cannot be opened until the other set is closed. They both lock quickly to trap an intruder. But I'm not an intruder, I'm an uninvited guest!" He let go his sinister laugh, but we've all heard better.

Outside the Wormhole Theater, Sheldon was letting Max have it, "That was disgusting, Max. I can't believe I let you bring me down to your level of sleaze!"

"Sorry, Boss. It'll never happen again."

"Why not?"

"I don't think you want it to."

"Don't think for me, Max. You're not qualified, and my thoughts are too powerful. Your head would explode and that would be disgusting. Did you see the way the girls in that movie were looking at me? They wanted me bad, Max."

"I saw that," Max lied.

Sheldon looked down at his shoes and frowned. "What I can't see is my reflection in my new opera pumps, which is very upsetting."

Max immediately pulled out a shoe polishing cloth and squatted down to shine Sheldon's shoes.

"They say you can tell a lot about a man by looking at his shoes," Max said. "I can tell you're a dirty guy, Boss."

Sheldon looked down at Max and scowled just as Don Neroni's limo sped around the corner, hit a mud puddle, and drenched Sheldon like a box of popcorn on someone's lap drenched in disgusting glow-in-the-dark butter-flavored oil...or something like that.

A few hours later Sheldon was sitting at his desk in his Betty Boop boxer shorts and wife beater undershirt rapping his fingers on the desktop and scowling at Max who was reading *Detective Magazine* with Sheldon's face on the cover. The face on the cover was no picnic, but much better to look at than the one in that office. Irma walked in carrying Sheldon's clothes from the dry cleaner.

"The dry cleaner wanted to know if you were hit by a truck; from his mouth to God's ear."

Irma exited to the outer office and Sheldon talked to Max while getting dressed.

"Stanley's making mincemeat out of this town. He's hit banks, art museums, jewelry stores, one after another. I need to trap him. I need something big and important that he'll go for."

"Like the Peking Duck," Max said.

"Sort of, but something he could fence faster. The Peking Duck will always have trouble behind it. We need something different, something easier to sell."

"You think of something, Boss. I need to twinkle...I mean, tinkle."

"Say that again, Max."

"I need to tinkle."

"No, not 'tinkle', what you said before that."

"Twinkle?"

"*That's it!* What twinkles, Max?"

"Davy Jones's eyes when he falls for a girl."

"And *diamonds!*" Sheldon said.

"But he already hit Fishman's. He has lots of diamonds."

"But he doesn't have the most valuable diamond in the world...the Priceless Sacred Blue Diamond from the Vivian Harper Hole of Mount Hingo."

"From my story!"

"Yes, Max. Your ridiculous absurd pointless stupid story may have just saved the day. Let's make the mountain come to Muhammad. Go out on the street and spread the word to all your disgusting street rat pals that I have the Priceless Sacred Blue Diamond from the Vivian Harper Hole of Mount Hingo stashed here in the office. Slip them a few bucks and tell them to make sure Squirm gets wind of it. When he comes here to grab it, we grab him."

"Can I see it?" Max asked excitedly.

266

"It doesn't exist, Max. I made it up. Now go and do what I told you to do."

"Okay, I'm back," Max grinned.

"Really? You need to do the Mercury scene? You're not Mercury, Max; you're Max. But we can do the scene if you want. This is coming out of your paycheck and I charge a lot for my acting skills. Here we go… So… you're back already…you really are fast…I didn't see you move."

"I was on the track team in high school," Max grinned.

"I only remember you at the concession stand. End scene. Now go talk to your street rats."

"Okay. I'm back."

Sheldon, getting aggravated, pushed the button on his desk intercom and told Irma to come in. She walked in annoyed.

"I'm watching my soap. What do you want?"

"I don't want to get you sick, but if you can, put your arms around Max and hold on tight."

"That's not in my job description."

"Either is anything you do. We're acting out a scene from earlier in this book and you're playing Hercules without the looks. I'll give you ten bucks, which is coming out of Max's paycheck."

Irma wrapped her arms tightly around Max the best she could and wasn't happy about it.

"Alright Max, go talk to your rats," Sheldon ordered.

"I'm back!" Max cracked.

"Irma?"

"He vibrated a little."

"Well that's something you should know a lot about. End scene. And I mean it."

Moments later on the street below, one of Max's informants herein known as Street Rat #1, limped along suspiciously, bumped into a businessman, and lifted his F.P. Journe wristwatch valued at $30,000. He slapped it on his own wrist, admired it with a glance, and turned down an alley where Street Rat #2 was relieving a young couple of their belongings. He had the couple facing the alley wall with their hands and feet spread apart as he searched them. The knuckle of his left pointer finger was pressing into the upper center of the young man's back as though it was a gun barrel. He removed a wallet from the man's back pocket and stuffed it into his own back pocket. #2 acknowledged #1 approaching. #1 whispered in #2's ear as he lifted the wallet from #2 and shoved it in his own back pocket. #2 took off running. #1 emptied the wallet of all cash and credit cards and graciously handed it back to the young man who thanked him profusely, grabbed the young woman by the arm, and ran. Street Rat #2 creeped into the next alley where he saw Street Rat #3 trying to pick the lock of the back door of a reptile pet shop that opened into the alley. #2 whispered to #3, pulled a Bronx pry bar out of his pants, and popped open the door which set off an alarm. #2 quickly dashed inside and ran back out screaming with a bag full of cash and a large boa constrictor around his neck strangling him. He got a block away and fell down dead. #3 grabbed the bag of cash and watched the snake slither into the sewer. Police sirens were approaching swiftly in response to the alarm and #3 ran into a nearby park. Street Rat #4 had his ill-gotten overcoat open and was exposing himself to a senior citizens exercise class who were all pointing to his winky and laughing. #3 saw what was happening, rushed over, and whispered to #4 who closed his coat to wild applause and ambled over to a man sitting on a park bench reading the Los Angeles Times with the headline *SQUIRM L.A., SQUIRM!* #4 whispered to the man behind the newspaper, which lowered slowly, and Stanley "Squirm" Jenkins grinned wickedly.

The next day Danger and Moore were down on the street meandering about. They appeared not to know what to do next, but that appearance was only what it appeared to be. It wasn't what it really was. Max wasn't quite sure himself what they were doing.

"Boss, if we're waiting for Squirm to show up at the office to steal the Priceless Sacred Blue Diamond from the Vivian Harper Hole of Mount Hingo, shouldn't we be in the office waiting for him to show up?"

"Don't second-guess me, Max. It upsets the balance of nature. We'll look for him here while we're waiting for him there. That way he has nowhere to turn."

Sheldon scanned the street, looked down at his feet, and saw a manhole.

"Go down that manhole, Max. You're no stranger to that. Sniff around. See if you can come up with something. Maybe Stanley's down there. If you run into him tell him I'd like to see him."

"Do I have to go down there?"

"Is there anyone better qualified?"

Max struggled to remove the manhole cover. The Congresswoman from Georgia walked up and handed Max a Bronx pry bar she had found in an alley where she was spending the week turning tricks to see how ordinary people live. Max thanked her, pried up the manhole cover, squeezed inside, and disappeared. Sheldon was getting worried but refused to admit it to himself. 23 minutes later, Max came out of the manhole with what seemed to be a push from below. He was now wearing the coveralls and protective gear of a sewer worker, not what he went in with.

"Well, Max?"

"No, it's a sewer."

Sheldon grit his teeth and turned Torch Red. Max realized that he was wearing the wrong clothes, ducked back into the manhole, and returned in his trench coat and detective garb. Horrible screams were coming from inside the manhole.

"I didn't see Stanley down there, but there is a really big snake killing everyone."

The same sexy woman that walked by Sheldon before, when he slammed into the light pole, walked by again. Sheldon said to her, "You look really hot in my trench coat." She ignored him and kept walking.

"I love when broads pretend to ignore me," Sheldon said.

"They do that a lot, Boss."

"It's all a game, Max. It's all a game."

Sheldon went silent and just stared into space, grinning.

"You alright, Boss?"

Sheldon snapped out of it.

"I'm okay, Max. Thanks for asking. I was just thinking about how great I am. Let's get some hot dogs."

They approached a hot dog cart in Skid Row's San Julian Park. Inside the park two young boys were digging into the ground with shovels. Sheldon took two hot dogs from the vender and handed one to Max. They sat on a bench to eat and watched the boys dig.

"Let me explain the concept of women to you, Max. Look at those boys digging. Even as young boys, we have a fascination with holes, which is why when we get older, we're attracted to women. Here's another way of looking at it. You can eat a hot dog without a bun, but the bun holds the hot dog steady. The bun keeps the hot dog warm, unless you get a cheap bun that falls apart and makes a mess and leaves you naked with mustard and relish all over you. So a good quality bun is what every man needs."

Max thought a minute. "So women are hot dog buns?"

"Pretty much, but they talk. They're like talking hot dog buns."

They finished their hot dogs and approached the boys digging. Sheldon showed them a photo of Squirm and they paused briefly to glance at it.

"Have you seen this guy around?"

They looked at the photo and got excited.

"SQUIRM! He's our hero!"

"He's no hero, boys. He's a bad guy. He's a criminal."

"We just like how he digs to places he wants to get to. That's cool," one of the boys said.

"Have you seen him around here?"

"Nope."

"Where are you digging to, China?"

"Yep."

"Max, enlighten these boys."

"Boys, to dig to China you gotta go through the Earth's crust," Max expained. "Then the lithosphere, the asthenosphere, the mantle, the mesosphere, the outer core, the core, the inner core…and that just gets you halfway."

Max stopped and looked at Sheldon to see if he should continue.

"Go on, Max, tell them. They need to know what they're up against."

Max continued, "When you guys reach the inner core-"

He stopped, getting choked up.

"Tell them," Sheldon said.

"When you reach the inner core, it's really hot. It's 10,000 degrees. You could get burned."

"Wear light clothes and bring one of those portable fans and Gatorade," Sheldon recommended.

"You won't end up in China anyway," Max said. "If you dig straight down you'll end up in the Indian Ocean."

"Bring a bathing suit," Sheldon recommended again. "Let's head back to the office, Max."

Danger and Moore walked away; the boys shrugged and continued digging. A short time later the detectives were standing in front of a construction site watching a hydraulic excavator digging into the ground. The noise from the equipment and the workers yelling to each other was pretty prominent. Sheldon yelled to Max over the noise.

"THESE GUYS DIG HOLES. I WANT TO SEE IF THEY'VE RUN INTO STANLEY!"

Max nodded. Sheldon walked through the site and approached the foreman with the photo of Squirm. They talked for several minutes and then Sheldon returned to Max who posed the question: "WHAT DID HE SAY? HAVE THEY SEEN SQUIRM?"

Sheldon said sharply, "I DON'T KNOW. I COULDN'T HEAR HIM. YOU KEEP LOOKING AROUND. I'M GOING BACK TO THE OFFICE. DON'T BE LONG."

Max nodded and Sheldon headed back. A short time later he entered his office to find Irma tied to her chair and gagged. Stanley "Squirm" Jenkins was sitting in Sheldon's chair with his feet propped up on Sheldon's desk. He grinned at Sheldon.

"We meet again, Mr. Danger. There's no big deal priceless diamond here. You lied."

"Hello Stanley." He motioned toward Irma. "How much do I owe you for that?"

"You can pay me the years of my life that you took away."

"You're cutting up paper dolls, Stanley. I didn't put you in prison, you put yourself there."

"Great line, Danger, may I quote you?"

"It's not original. I heard your old man say it when we were kids and he was the cop on the beat."

Squirm looked dejected and affected by what Sheldon said.

"He liked you and Max better than he liked me."

"That's 'cause we weren't his kid. He didn't expect anything from us, so we couldn't let him down. You were the smartest guy I ever knew and you turned out rotten. What happened Stanley?"

Squirm pulled a pistol. "Shut up Danger!"

Squirm kicked Sheldon's chair next to Irma and tied them up together. "Get cozy with your girl."

"Shoot me. How *is* your old man?"

"The truth? Right after you left the neighborhood he bailed to Mexico and became my second mother. They kicked him off the force and he became 'Bubbles Bongo' the star attraction at the Blue Flamingo Strip Club and Cabaret, that's how he is."

Sheldon was stunned. "Mexico?!"

"It's been a pleasure reminiscing. I'll be back to deal with you later. Right now I'm going to college."

"College! That's great! I'm glad I convinced you to turn your life around. Your mothers will be proud."

"Actually, Danger, I'm tunneling into the UCLA Film and Television Archive to relieve them of their holdings which I plan to ransom back to them. I sent them a compilation tape of my security camera shows that I host when I rob a place. I wanted them to put it in their archive so generation after generation could study the genius of my work, *BUT THEY REFUSED MY SHOW!*" he yelled angrily. "They just turned it over to the cops. So now they'll pay for their mistake!" He let go a long sinister laugh which wasn't too long and wasn't so sinister. No one was impressed. He wheezed and left. Sheldon struggled to untie his ropes and Irma made muffled sounds through the gag.

"Be quiet!" Sheldon snapped. "I need to concentrate to untie these knots the exact reverse of the way they were tied!"

A moment later Max walked in.

"Sorry I'm late, Boss. I was discussing the Rise and Fall of the Roman Empire with a guy who sells organic honey and calls himself Attila the Huney. Time just got away."

"Max, do you see that Irma and I are tied up?" Sheldon inquired.

Max quickly covered his eyes. "Oh! Sorry! I guess rough love is better than no love."

"Untie me you idiot!"

Max untied Sheldon. Irma was frantically trying to talk.

Sheldon explained what was going on to Max.

"Stanley was here, as you can see. He's going to tunnel into the UCLA Film and Television Archive to clean them out. We gotta stop him."

"That's 350,000 motion pictures, 170,000 television shows, and 27 million feet of newsreel footage. Can he carry all that?"

Irma was going berserk, frantically rocking back and forth in her chair making loud muffled sounds. Max removed her gag and she started bitching up a storm. Behind her back, Sheldon shook his head *NO* and Max put the gag back on. Leaving Irma bound and gagged; they left to stop Squirm in his slimy tracks.

Late that night outside The Film Archive and Preservation Center in Santa Clarita which houses the UCLA Film and Television Archive, Maximus Moore was more than ready. He had his ear to the ground a short distance from the surrounding wall of the building. Sheldon watched him.

"Hear anything, Tonto?"

Max gave Sheldon the thumbs up, removed a can of orange glow-in-the-dark spray paint from his trench coat, and sprayed a line on the ground from where he was listening, to the entrance. He then blew a doggie whistle, silent to human ears, but it did cause dogs to bark and three muscular UCLA frat boys appeared from behind bushes, each carrying a keg of domestic beer. They set the kegs down directly on the orange glow-in-the-dark line at designated points that Max had marked. Next, Max blew a predator call whistle and a trained hawk swooped down and dropped three powerful magnets, one on each keg. At that same precise moment in a tunnel-in-progress leading toward the archive, the sharp tip of Squirm's pickaxe flew up to the "ceiling" of the tunnel three times, each about 12 inches (a foot) apart. Suddenly Squirm's tunnel started filling with beer from the kegs. You see, the magnets caused the sharp tip of the pickaxe to fly up and puncture the three kegs, thus releasing the flowing beer into the tunnel. Squirm was totally confused (as we all are) and panicked. Not wanting to drown, he started frantically picking toward the surface. The ground over the tunnel started to move and Squirm's head popped up. He was gasping for air and tipsy. Max nodded to the frat boys who pulled Squirm out of the tunnel and held him so he couldn't get away. Sheldon told a passing student to call the police to tell them he captured Squirm. The student ran off to call as Sheldon patted Max on the back.

"Max, I always thought you were the dumbest thing I ever saw until I saw the way you helped me capture Squirm. It was absolutely the most ridiculous plan ever, but it worked! I'm very proud of you. I'm going to give you an autographed picture of myself for free."

Sheldon reached into his trench coat and pulled out a glossy 8 x 10 photo of himself and a pen.

"Let's do this quick before I change my mind. Who do I make it out to?"

"Me, Maximus Moore."

Sheldon said what he was writing as he wrote it: "Meee. Maximusss Moorrrrr...Beeesst Wissshhhes, Shellldonn Daangerrr, Priiivate Detecccctivvvv."

Sheldon handed the signed photo to Max, and then turned to Squirm who was being held by the frat boys and wasn't going anywhere except back to the prison. Sheldon lost his temper.

"And *you*! You killed my partner and you're going over for it!"

"I'm right here, Boss," Max said as police sirens blasted their way.

"I know that, Max. I just love that line so much. I can't wait to use it."

Another frat boy ran up to the others. He was breathless, but got out what he had to say.

"Somebody stole our pledge paddle! For some reason that no one understands, if we don't get it back, we'll lose our charter and our fraternity will cease to exist! They say that Beta Alpha Delphi, the Witch Sorority, stole it! Those evil scantily clad, usually always naked, easy girls took our paddle. Who can help us?! Who?!"

Danger and Moore looked at each other. Max pressed play on his boom box as the theme from "Peter Gunn" filled the air. A dozen cop cars arrived, as well as the Lieutenant and Marty Doyle. Stanley Jerkins was cuffed and put in the prisoner cage of a police interceptor. He and Sheldon made eye contact and just looked at each other wondering if their paths would ever cross again. An earsplitting BOOM pierced the night sky and they all looked up as the Digby orb zoomed by overhead and appeared to be falling, straight into Beverly Hills.

CHAPTER 15

The night sky over Beverly Hills looked like a night sky over any other place you could name except that it was over Beverly Hills. It was a night sky. Parked up on scenic Mulholland Drive was a sky blue 1963 Cadillac Series 62 Convertible Coupe, and inside of that automobile was Marvin "Moose" Morgan and Sandra Morgan. They were not related. They were on a first date. Marvin pretended to yawn and stretch. During the stretch he attempted to put his outstretched right arm around Sandra. Sandra didn't like that, reached into her purse, pulled out a SIG P365 handgun which was named the 2019 "Handgun of the Year" by *Shooting Illustrated* as well as being named the 2018 "Handgun of the Year" by *Guns & Ammo*, and blew Marvin's miserable member clean off. As Marvin was screaming in agony and regretting having asked Sandra out, he pointed toward the sky as the Digby orb fell straight down, smashed into the hood of the car, flipped the car over, and sent it soaring down the overlook some 1,342 feet killing both Marvin and Sandra. Marvin was having a lousy night anyway. Sandra got what she gave. The Digby orb rolled down Mulholland and wound its way through the streets of Beverly Hills as erratically as it moved through outer space. It rolled across Doheny Drive causing lots of car honking, swerving, cursing, and near misses and eventually came to rest behind the West Hollywood home of famed B movie schlockmeister director Leo Sachs who was inside his home office standing on a footstool in a cold sweat with a noose around his neck. This was no tiny tilted Caribou Inn with antlers; these were strong ceiling beams that would do the job. Ironically, Leo's first directing job was *The Creature from Gruesome Gulch*. Maybe you've heard of it. It would become a cult favorite because both star and director tried to hang themselves. Leo looked around at the accolades awarded to him throughout his esteemed schlock movie career which were displayed around the room: the Sci-Fi Saturn Award for Best Director, an induction plaque for inclusion in the Science Fiction Hall of Fame, the George Pal Award for Best Director and The Independent Horror Movie Award, among many others. On the walls were posters/one sheets of some of his films including *Nanny Nightmare, Passage to Purgatory, Attack of the No-See-Ums, The Creature from Gruesome Gulch,* and *The Stepmummy.* There were also many framed photographs of Leo Sachs with actors he had directed in his heyday including John Agar, Gloria Talbott, Allison Hayes, Jeff Morrow, and the previously mentioned and ill-fated Yvette Vickers. Leo was gathering the nerve to take that final fatal step just as the Digby orb started behaving badly, which is usually the result of lousy parenting. It sprung up into the air about 50 feet and then came crashing down causing Leo's house to shake violently. All those awards, photos, and posters also came crashing down. Leo lost his balance and slipped off the footstool. Just as the noose was about to do what nooses do his ex-wife Doris burst in and caught him.

"Before you hang yourself pay me the alimony you owe me."

"Can't I at least *die* in peace? The insurance from my death will pay your precious alimony."

"I forgot about the insurance," Doris remembered. "Sorry I interrupted. Please continue."

"Do you know why I'm ready to be on the wrong side of the grass, Doris? I'm washed-up. I'm finished. I haven't made a decent picture in decades. I'm through, Doris."

"Good, I was getting tired of hearing you," she said sensitively. "When you're done, put yourself in a bag out by the curb. I'm not cleaning up after you."

Suddenly a blinding blast of dazzling green light coursed through the office window. Leo and Doris turned their eyes from the light's searing brilliance. After several moments it faded to a softer incandescent green glow. Leo stared out the window in wide-eyed amazement at the Digby orb. Doris came up next to him and they both stared at it.

"DORIS!" Leo yelled.

"I'm right here Leo and I'm busy. What do you want?"

"There's a giant...thing...in the yard, and it's glowing."

"I see that," Doris said staring at it.

Leo fumbled with the phone, dialed nervously, and spoke into it. "Leo, it's Elliott, I mean Elliott, it's Leo, get over here now!" He dropped the phone and just kept looking at the glowing orb.

"I thought you were going to have brunch with the Grim Reaper," Doris declared.

"I changed my mind. I want my agent to see this."

"You're so cheap the Reaper would have to pay for brunch anyway. Maybe that's why he made you change your mind."

22 minutes later, Hollywood Super Agent Elliott Fineberg was with Leo in the backyard mesmerized by the glowing Digby orb.

"Are you sure it's not a prop?" Elliott asked, staring.

"It's not a prop. Whatever it is, it's the real thing. It's also my next picture, Elliott. This will be the greatest sci-fi flick ever to hit the screen! I'll be king of Hollywood again! When people hear the name 'Leo Sachs' they won't say they thought I died long ago. They'll know I'm ruling this town with an iron fist! I'm back, Elliott!"

"I WANT MY ALIMONY MONEY, LEO!" Doris yelled from inside the house.

Leo cringed. "That witch will get her alimony and I'll be the Toast of Tinseltown! Audiences will flock to see...*It Came from Outer Space!*"

"You're too late," Elliott the super agent who wasn't so super when it came to finding work for Leo, pointed out. "1953. Universal. Jack Arnold directed. Based on a Ray Bradbury story. Starred Barbara Rush, Charles Drake, and Russell Johnson before he got to Gilligan's Island. The plot has been passed around like an old whore. The special effects were okay for the time. Shoestring budget, no big deal."

"But this is *real*, Elliott. Look at it! No special effects. No tricks. This is the real deal!"

"Maybe it's an egg. Why don't you sit on it and see if it hatches?"

Leo grabbed his crotch. "Sit on this."

Just as Leo released the hold on his crotch (his, not Elliott's) a hoodlum named Mad Dog Leibowitz tore through the backyard on his motorcycle, stopped at the Digby orb, and Leo and Doris's teenaged daughter Fran let go of his waist and got off the bike. She was slightly drunk and dressed like she didn't own any opaque clothes. She tottered over to Leo and looked at the Digby orb.

"Who's that, Daddy?"

"That's not a *who*, it's a *what*. And *where* the hell have you been with this parental nightmare?"

"She was licking my stamp collection," Mad Dog replied like you would expect from a guy named Mad Dog.

"Don't you have a murder to go to?" Leo asked. "I wouldn't want you to be late."

"Made any lousy movies lately, Mr. Sachs?" Mad Dog replied again like you have come to expect him to. Leo started after Mad Dog and chased the motorcycle around the yard, cursing and throwing things at the hoodlum who was having a good laugh and taunting Leo. Just as Leo was about to collapse from exhaustion, several government vehicles including black sedans with tinted windows and a very large armored van surrounded the house.

"This looks official. I'm gone," Mad Dog mumbled as he ripped through the yard and sped away.

Several government officials including a few operatives in ebony attire (See how I got around that?) and an Aerospace Research Team in protective hazmat radiation suits surrounded the Digby orb and ran scan wands over every inch of it. There were some hand signals among those in the hazmat gear and they proceeded to move the Digby orb into the van for transport. Leo, who was extremely upset, went up to the man who appeared to be running the show.

"This is private property! You can't take that!"

"Sir, that object is officially government property now."

"Do you know who I am?" Leo asked, trying to play the Hollywood card.

"Yeah, I thought you looked familiar. You're that movie director who was a big deal years ago. I thought you died. What's your name again?"

"Leo Sachs. I'm not dead, and that thing is a movie prop."

"I'm glad you're still with us, Mr. Sachs, but this is no movie prop. We've been tracking this sucker for a long time. It's no ordinary meteorite. There's something strange about this one. But that's all I can say. Just pretend you never saw it. Forget about it." One of the operatives in ebony attire reached into an inside pocket and the man talking to Leo motioned him to stop, which he did. "Mr. Sachs, as far as you're concerned, this is top secret government property now, and there's no one in this world who can get near it."

The next morning it was rush hour on the Hollywood Freeway. Traffic was horrendous. Cars were honking and tempers were flaring. Suddenly the flying saucer with Marty and Bink, our two little green bug-eyed extraterrestrial Digby scouts at the controls, dropped out of the sky and crash-landed right there on the 101 causing major pandemonium.

Marty smacked Bink's antenna.

"Who taught you how to drive?"

Bink caressed his throbbing appendage. "I never drove a stick shift before, Marty."

There was pounding on the outside of the saucer as the same commuters who attacked Nick Nero's limo attempted to break in with crowbars and other implements of destruction. Even the guy who Nero introduced head first to the limo door was back in L.A. swinging at the saucer with a nine iron. Sirens could be heard approaching. People were screaming and going wild. All hell was breaking loose. Inside the saucer, Marty and Bink were covering their earholes attempting to block out the unrelenting noise.

"I'm getting a migraine already, and I've been on this planet for three minutes," Marty mumbled.

They heard a flutey ringtone and their leader Emperor Zee appeared on the screen above the control panel and addressed his scouts.

"REPORT!"

"Greetings from planet Earth, Emperor Zee," Marty said, rubbing his migraine. "The weather's great. Perfect day for the beach. If I had my board I could catch a wave and a tall blonde babe. I'd throw her in the back of this orange crate and make her see stars."

"Cut the crap, Marty. Did you find it?"

"A funny thing happened on the way to Earth, Sir. We ran into a little problem called 'a freeway'. It seems that Bink here drives like someone who doesn't know how to drive."

Emperor Zee frowned, "Is that true, Bink?"

"I never drove manual before, Sir. And I couldn't really see where I was going, so we crashed."

"You got eyes the size of New Jersey, Bink. Use 'em!"

The pounding and screaming got louder and the hatch to the saucer was being pried open with crowbars. Marty interrupted the conversation.

"Sorry to break in, but the crazy Earthlings are about to break in to this sardine can. Would you mind beaming us up Scotty...Emperor Zee, Sir, because I have a headache and I'm not really in the mood for this. You know what Earthlings do to things they don't understand. They'll probe us and put things in our tushies and then tear us apart. You've seen those movies."

"Quit whining and find the orb. Have a nice day." Emperor Zee signed off and the screen went dark.

"If I looked like that I wouldn't appear in person either," Marty snarled.

Bink looked at Marty. "You do look a little like that."

Marty swatted Bink's antenna which hurt. "You're no George Jetson, Binky Boy."

Government and military helicopters hovered menacingly over the flying saucer. Police lights were flashing. There were television crews, news cameras, reporters, photographers, UFO fanatics, curious onlookers, and a growing mass of humanity becoming an absolute raving mob, along with the angry crazed commuters. It was total chaos. The National Guard tried to keep people at bay while Military Special Forces surrounded the saucer with their weapons trained on the hatch. Inside the saucer Marty and Bink heard this warning announcement spoken by the tactical operations leader through a bullhorn: "WELCOME TO EARTH! YOU ARE SURROUNDED BY ARMED FORCES! COME OUT OF YOUR VEHICLE IMMEDIATELY AND PEACEFULLY! YOU HAVE THIRTY SECONDS TO COMPLY OR WE WILL COMMENCE FIRING!"

Marty scowled, "I hate this planet, and I just got here."

"We gotta get lost Marty. My tushy's an exit door and that's it. You said that humans will put things in it."

"My thoughts exactly, Bink. This calls for drastic measures. Activate the emergency boosters. Let's make like a baby and head out."

"YOU HAVE 20 SECONDS!" came the second warning.

"The emergency boosters won't carry us very far, Marty," Bink warned.

Marty nodded. "I know. But if we stay here they'll turn us over to some scientists who will conduct all kinds of awful experiments on us. You yourself said that I said so myself; these humans go right for the ass. And then they'll exploit us like they did with E.T. Our faces will be on T-shirts, blacklight posters, lunch boxes. There will be action figures of us, board games, and Marty and Bink Ice Cream which will probably be mint green with little chocolate flying saucers in it! I never understood the whole E.T. thing. He's got the brains of a turnip, he looks like hell, he only says a few words, and now he's got houses on eight planets and he's a major shareholder in AT&T. It's all public relations and who you know."

"I wouldn't mind my face on a lunch box and that ice cream sounds good," Bink said.

"YOU HAVE THREE SECONDS TO COMPLY OR WE OPEN FIRE!" came the final warning.

"Where's your Digby dignity, Bink? E.T. sold out like Dylan did when he went electric. Let's boogie!"

Bink threw the switch to actvate the emergency boosters. The saucer popped straight up about 20 feet off the Hollywood Freeway and spun off to most everyone's amazement and excitement. Several shots were fired by those who weren't impressed or amused. The military fired also, not just the commuters. The choppers attempted to chase the saucer, but couldn't keep up with its speed. Inside the saucer Marty glanced in the rear-view mirror at the distant helicopters and Bink checked the power gauges.

"We're out of reserve power, Marty. We have to land."

Marty cringed. "Alright, let's ditch this jalopy. We'll find the Digby orb and figure out how to Garfunkel this greasy globe."

Famed finished forgotten movie director Leo Sachs and his agent Elliott Fineberg were in Leo's 1967 Rolls Royce Silver Shadow shadowing the large armored van transporting the Digby orb to the Aerospace Research Facility in Simi Valley. The strange green glow from the Digby orb could be seen through the small rear security window of the van. Leo followed the van like he had stalked Maila Nurmi (Vampira) from 1952 to 1965 when she finally got a restraining order to stop him. He was close enough, but not close enough.

"Elliott, when I get that thing back, you're going to see the greatest comeback in the history of modern cinema when my new picture comes out...*IT CONQUERED THE WORLD!*"

Elliott shook his head. "You're too late. 1956. A Corman quickie. Starred Peter Graves, Dick Miller, and Jonathan Haze. A real bomb."

"I need a new agent," Leo mumbled as he followed the van onto the private road toward the lab. The van was waved through the security gates, but the Rolls was stopped by a barricade and an armed security guard approached.

"This area is off limits, sir. Turn your vehicle around please."

"I'm with the van," Leo said.

"And *I'm* with the band," Elliott added with a laugh. "You get it?"

"Yes, very humorous... Your name?" he asked Leo.

"Leo Sachs."

The guard checked his list. "Sorry. You're not on the clearance list. I can't let you in."

"Do you know who I am?" Leo asked, trying to play the Hollywood card again.

The guard looked at him. "I give up. Who are you?"

"I'm Leo Sachs, the movie director."

"Oh! Leo Sachs, the movie director! I'm Sergeant Dalton, the armed guard at the gate. Turn your vehicle around....*Now*!"

Leo was impatient and getting angry. "What if I drive through the barricade, would you shoot me?"

"That's a very strong possibility."

"If you gave me a screenplay to read I would pretend to read it and throw it in the trash," Leo threatened.

"I'll keep that in mind. Go home Mr. Sachs, and get some rest."

Leo turned the Rolls around and headed back to his house. When he got back, Elliott left, and the frustrated director turned on the television and sat down in his easy chair. Just as he did, several large repo men walked into the house without knocking or ringing the bell. The oldest repo man handed Leo some papers. He didn't do any lifting, just the formalities.

"Bank repossession; they want the furniture. Tough break. Hey, ain't you that guy that did all those crazy monster flicks back in the day?"

Leo watched sadly as his furniture was being taken out of the house and loaded into a truck. "I was."

"I always liked your movies. I used to take my wife to 'em when we were dating. I even proposed to her at one of your flicks. I wasn't paying too much attention to the screen, if you know what I mean."

"I know what you mean...Look, could you do me a favor and leave the TV and my chair. They're showing one of my pictures tonight and I want to see it so I can remember back when I had furniture."

"Oh yeah? Which flick?"

"*Day of the Night Creature*."

"I remember that one. That's the one where the gravedigger who works the graveyard shift at the graveyard turns into a six-foot owl and makes sleepwalkers walk into graves he dug. I remember the poster, a giant owl in overalls holding a shovel and the poster said, *This is Dave. He doesn't give a hoot about you!*" He sees that Leo is hurting. "I'll tell you what Mr. Sachs, since it's you, I'll cut you some slack. But I'll have to come back for the chair and the TV in a few days."

"I appreciate it," Leo said, shaking his hand. The repo men left. Leo sat back in the chair and watched the television like a man who had nothing left but to watch television. When *Day of the Night Creature* came on and he saw the opening credits with his name as the director he changed the channel and saw a *special news bulletin*.

"What the Pentagon is claiming to be an actual flying saucer from another planet crash-landed on the northbound lanes of the Hollywood Freeway during rush hour this morning causing major pandemonium, as you might imagine."

Leo was spellbound, literally sitting on the edge of his seat as video of the crashed saucer and the mayhem that ensued filled the screen. As the video continued, the news anchor spoke in a voice-over: "After several very tense and historical minutes on the freeway, witnesses say the saucer appeared to regain power and took off. The whereabouts of the saucer at this time are unknown. Authorities stated that they are even more bewildered by the fact that the saucer which some witnesses claim had a license plate that said, 'DIGBY 1', did not register on any space or ground surveillance radar."

The video ended and back in the studio the anchor, Michelle Roberts, who had been a masseuse who rubbed the right guy right, had two guests to talk about the saucer landing. The first was J.T. MacCah a 16-year-old high school dropout and punk rock enthusiast who collects graphic novels and hopes to create his own one day. He can't write or draw so that should be a neat trick.

"J.T. MacCah witnessed the saucer crashing on the freeway," Michelle said by way of introduction. "J.T., what did you see?"

"When?"

"When you saw the flying saucer crash. What was that like?"

"It was like when your mom is holding a good china plate that your grandma gave her and you trip her because she stopped your allowance because you don't do anything but get high and the plate falls on the floor and breaks. Except the flying saucer didn't really break, it just fell. But it's not a plate. A flying saucer isn't a plate. And I don't think it's from China. Am I getting paid for this?"

Michelle stared at him briefly and then moved on.

"My next guest is Dr. Arnold Kazazian from the Aerospace Research Facility. Dr. Kazazian, could this flying saucer have been some sort of hoax or perhaps a Hollywood publicity stunt to promote an upcoming film? We're right in the thick of where all that happens. Was this some kind of staged media event?"

"Absolutely not. This is indeed an actual flying saucer, probably from within this galaxy although we can't be certain. We speculate because of the greenish-blue hue of the saucer that it must be from one of the three outer planets of the solar system: Uranus, Neptune, or Pluto which may or may not be a planet. The jury's still out. We don't know too much about these three planets because they are so far away. It's difficult to see them even with the most powerful telescopes. To give you some idea of our limited knowledge, the two sets of rings around Uranus were only discovered in 1977. We assume those planets are dark frozen worlds made up primarily of gases, which might explain the coloring of the saucer. It's also possible that the saucer can change colors. We just don't know anything at this point. That said, I don't see how any life form can possibly exist there. What is extremely fascinating to me personally is that, as you mentioned, some witnesses claimed that it had a 'license plate', for lack of a better term, that said, 'DIGBY 1'. We're trying to figure out what that means."

"Which brings me to the question most likely foremost on everyone's mind, who was piloting this flying saucer?" Michelle asked. "Who or what was inside?"

Dr. Kazazian thought for a moment before answering. "Obviously some life form was in control of this vehicle, but considering that it crash-landed, we have some doubts as to its intelligence."

"And do you think this was a friendly visit?"

"I have to answer 'no' to that question because it was asked on several occasions to exit the craft and refused, so therefore I have to deduce that this is indeed a hostile life form. Possibly scouts for an upcoming invasion, but you didn't hear that from me. Let's not put the cart before the horse."

"One final question Dr. Kazazian, where do you think the saucer went to when it took off from the freeway? I heard that it was very fast but didn't fly very high."

"There's no telling. It could be heading back to where it originated from, to the far reaches of space, or it could still be within Earth's perimeter. We simply don't know at this time. But you can believe we're making a concerted effort to locate this saucer, which will be difficult because as I explained, it did not register on any surveillance radar when it arrived. Therefore we were unable to determine its position, velocity, or size, by analysis of radio waves reflected from its surface. This is all quite astounding. The saucer and its occupants could be right under our noses and we wouldn't know it."

Leo Sachs was ecstatic. He rummaged through his hall closet and pulled out a telescope. He rushed out to the backyard, set up the telescope on its tripod, and gazed up at the sky. Suddenly the optical tube slammed down to a much lower position and Leo saw Marty's bug-eyed eye gazing back at him. They were both startled, fell back, screamed in horror, and scurried away. After a few moments they both cautiously came out of hiding and slowly approached each other. Leo was terrified but thrilled at the same time. Bink came from behind a bush and stood by Marty. Leo couldn't take his eyes off of them. "You were in that flying saucer, weren't you?"

Marty turned to Bink. "I told you, these Earthlings are brilliant."

"YOU CAN TALK!"

"And you can yell. Keep it down, will ya? You're two for two. Keep goin'."

"Do you have names?"

Marty glanced at Bink. "No, we just call each other 'Hey You'. I'm Marty Mooncricket and this is Bink Le' Dink. And you are?"

"Leo. Leo Sachs. Where are you from?"

"Yonkers."

"No, you're not, you're from outer space."

"Why do you assume that we're from outer space?"

"Because you're little green guys with big bug eyes, antennae on your heads, and propellers on your rears. What would you think?"

"Have you ever been to Gibsonton, Florida? We blend."

Bink interjected, "We're from the planet Digby which is the only square planet in the entire universe. Digby has four lines of reflectional symmetry and is a polygon with four sides of equal length and four right angle 90 degree corners and we're on a recovery mission."

Marty got mad. "Bink, you dink, Earthlings like to torture people to get information out of them. You don't just volunteer information."

Leo reached down and yanked on Marty's antenna.

"OW!" Marty yelped.

"YOU *ARE* REAL!" Leo exclaimed.

Marty slugged Leo in the nuts. Leo hit the ground yelping too.

"SO ARE YOU!" Marty exclaimed back. Suddenly came the sound of cutting wind as a Bell OH-58 Kiowa Warrior military chopper hovered ominously above, searching for the saucer or its contents. Marty and Bink dove into a very large hole in the ground hoping not to be seen. Apparently missing sight of them, the chopper moved on to search elsewhere. Leo helped them up. Marty examined the hole in the ground. He knew what he was looking at.

"Nice crater, Leo. How'd it get here?"

"I don't know. It's a hole."

"Bull doody," Marty remarked. "The Digby orb landed here. Where is it?"

They heard the chopper returning for another pass.

"Quick, get inside before they see you!"

Leo rushed Marty and Bink inside the house. Marty looked around. "Nice place, Leo. You don't believe in furniture? Just tell us where the Digby orb is so we can get off of this rotten rock."

Bink piped up, "But Marty, the saucer-"

Marty cut him off, "You piped up, now pipe down, Binky Boy."

Leo sat them down...on the floor. "You don't understand. The government is looking for you. The Men in Black are looking for you, and that's not just a comic book and a movie, that's a real organization. Look it up. The military's looking for you. You're all over the news. If they find you, you know what they'll do."

"They'll stick things up our butts," Bink said.

"Yes, they will, and a lot more," Leo warned.

"I'm hip," Marty said. "Humans suck. I still can't believe what they did to King Kong and the Creature from the Black Lagoon. This planet is ridiculous. And I might add, Earth is the laughingstock of the entire universe. Do you know we have joke books on Digby that are only about Earth and Earthings? Bink, how did the Earthlings die?"

"They used toilet paper and wiped themselves out," Bink grinned.

"We can help each other," Leo said. "I'm a movie director. I used to be very famous and respected even though my pictures were what they call B movies. I made schlock science fiction and monster movies. To be honest, things haven't gone so well for me the last thirty years or so. I'll help you get the Digby orb if you'll star in my next picture...*Marty and Bink and the Search for the Digby Orb.*"

"No deals," Marty said.

"I wanna be in the movies, Marty. Please!" Bink begged.

"No, Bink. We get the orb and we go home. That's it!"

Outside and overhead, the helicopter descended and hovered over Leo's house as several Marines slid down a Fast Rope to explore the grounds. Leo, Marty, and Bink panicked. Leo quickly ushered them into a bathroom and locked them inside. He then watched out the window as after a careful combing of the area, the Marines were pulled back into the chopper and it flew away. Leo went to free Marty and Bink from the bathroom, but stopped himself and dialed the phone which he whispered into. "Elliott, get over here. I have something here that will make my next picture the greatest in the history of the business. Hollywood is gonna love me again."

He hung up and sat in his chair, well, the bank's chair. From the bathroom the toilet flushed twice. Leo turned on the television. The picture on the screen became wavy. When the picture refocused, Marty and Bink were on the television screen, smiling big, and soaking wet. Leo ran to the bathroom, unlocked it, and threw open the door to find them gone. He returned to the television and watched in amazement as they addressed him directly.

"HI LEO!" Marty and Bink called out while waving.

"It sure is a tight squeeze down that toilet! Cool ride though. It was like one of those rapid water parks with free admission," Marty pointed out. "We were gonna leave you a note but the toilet paper was only one ply and too flimsy and we didn't have any lipstick to write on the mirror with. So here's the deal. Since you won't tell us where the Digby orb is without blackmailing us into being in one of your unOscar-winning movies, we're gonna find it ourselves."

"And we borrowed your car," Bink blurted.

"BYE LEO!" Marty and Bink called out while waving. The screen went black.

"MY CAR?!" Leo said in a panic out loud to himself.

Leo's 1967 Rolls Royce Silver Shadow was weaving down Sunset Boulevard. They had wanted to weave down Wilshire Boulevard but there was nothing left of it. Apparently someone had blown it up. Bink was on the floorboard working the gas and brake pedals. Marty was sitting on three phone books steering. They swerved all over the place hitting things here and there and causing a good bit of trouble. Eventually Marty turned down Larrabee Street and crashed the Rolls into the front porch of an old house. Marty looked down at Bink.

"You can get up now. We stopped. We'll just go door-to-door and ask the Earthlings if they've seen it. It's a simple 'yes' or 'no' question, it shouldn't be that difficult for them."

They got out of the car and approached a kindly old woman who had been rocking in a rocking chair on the front porch but had been thrown into her flower garden upon impact.

"Howdy Earthling! By any chance did you happen to see the Digby orb around here?" Marty inquired politely.

"No, Sweetheart. Oh, how adorable you are! Help me up, Cutie."

Marty and Bink each grabbed an arm and helped the old woman to her feet and out of her flower garden.

"I'll be right back!" she said as she stepped through the rubble that was once her porch and entered her house.

"All that 'sweetheart', 'adorable', and 'cutie' stuff, she was referring to me," Marty mentioned.

"Bull ca-ca!" Bink blurted. "She was looking right at me when she said it."

The old woman returned with bags of candy corn which was originally called "Chicken Feed" invented by George Renninger and first produced in 1888 by the Wunderle Candy Company in Philadelphia, which you didn't know until just now. She had these particular bags of candy corn in her house since 1942. They were expired.

"HAPPY HALLOWEEN, KIDS!" she said as she handed the bags of expired candy corn to Marty and Bink and went back inside. Marty and Bink looked at the candy corn and then at each other.

"Earthlings are such weenies," Marty said.

They approached the next house. Marty gave Bink's propeller (on his rear) a starting spin and Bink flew up tush-first to ring the doorbell. A fat cigar-chewing shlub in his stained boxers and stained wife beater shirt answered the stained door. He looked Marty and Bink up and down unfazed, took a swallow of cheap beer, and called to his wife.

"Blanche! It's your mother and her sister!"

Blanche came to the door looking like every husband's nightmare with curlers in her hair and cold cream on her face; you know the story – just lovely. Marty, Bink, and Blanche all screamed in fright when they saw each other. Blanche slammed the door and Marty and Bink got the hell out of there leaving smoldering tracks through the yard. They dove behind a hedge and tried to catch their breath. They were in shock.

"Have you ever seen anything like that before?! Scared the willies out of me!" Marty whispered to Bink who was petrified and trembling. "Calm down Binky Boy, it's not chasing us." From behind the hedge Marty spied two Girl Scouts selling cookies door-to-door. He saw how they were warmly received and said to himself and to Bink at the same time, which isn't easy, "I got an idea."

** (*Reader discretion is advised for this next scene*)

The Girl Scouts left a house and walked by the hedge. Marty and Bink grabbed them and pulled them behind it. There was a bit of a tussle. Cookies flew everywhere.

** (*End reader discretion advisory*)

A short time later a door opened and our little green bug-eyed Digby scouts were standing on the doorstep in torn Girl Scout uniforms holding broken boxes of cookies. They both looked very high up at the person who answered the door and they both swallowed hard. They were terrified. Marty spoke nervously.

"Greetings Earthling. I'm Ilene and this is my friend Trudy. We are Earthling Girl Scouts selling Earthling Girl Scout cookies. We are also trying to earn our Outer Space Merit Badges. If we see the Digby orb we can get our badges. Do you know where we might find it?"

A tremendous menacing man six foot, seven inches and 354 pounds took a step out of the house and looked down at the "Girl Scouts" in disgust. At his side was a ferocious Pit Bull on a short leash, growling, seething, and snapping at Marty and Bink who were quivering in fear.

"You ain't no Girl Scouts," the menacing man said using atrocious grammar. "You're some kinda weird lizards."

"LIZARDS?!" Marty and Bink exclaimed as though they were insulted, which was indeed the case.

"My pup Executioner here loves to kill lizards. Don't you boy?"

The dog growled and snapped.

"That's a 'yes'. I think I'll let him go."

Bink babbled, "It would be impossible for Earthlings to visit Venus which is 480 degrees centigrade because they'd be pushed over by the wind and crushed and suffocated by the carbon dioxide air which is sixty times thicker than the air on Earth and they'd be poisoned by the acid clouds."

Marty looked at Bink. "What the hell does that have to do with anything?"

"Nothing, I just thought the nice big mean Earthling man would like to know in case he was thinking of going there."

"I don't like you ugly lizards," the nice big mean Earthling man snarled.

Marty pulled Bink away.

"C'mon Trudy, Let's sell our cookies somewhere else."

As they turned to leave, Marty stopped, turned around, and addressed the dog.

"Executioner, would you like a doggie biscuit? It's like a Girl Scout cookie only completely different."

Executioner barked. "That's a 'yes'," Marty said. He gestured and turned the nice big mean Earthling man into a six foot, seven inch 354-pound doggie biscuit which toppled over and fell on Executioner killing him. Oh well. Shortly thereafter Marty and Bink were driving along residential backstreets in Leo's extremely battered and bent Rolls Royce.

Again, Marty was sitting on phone books steering and Bink was working the pedals.

"What do you think Emperor Zee will do to us if we don't find it?" Bink asked from the floor of the car.

"I don't know, Binky Boy," Marty shrugged, "but I don't want to be around when he does something to us."

CHAPTER 16

That night, which was exactly 36 minutes later, four teenaged girls: Cindy Sai, Janet Whitlock, Laura Lawson, and Fran Sachs (Leo's daughter, the prize we met earlier) were having a slumber party at Cindy's house. They were wearing scanty nighties, eating Domino's pizza that was supposed to have extra sauce but came with none, passing a joint around, and talking about boys. Laura Lawson was a huge rotund well-fed girl who collected old copies of *Tiger Beat* and pictures of Bobby Sherman and was seated in front of an open window that was facing the street.

"I think Mark Harris is totally gross. I saw him eating a hamburger once and he wasn't holding the burger tight enough and the insides fell out on the floor of the restaurant and an old lady slid on them and hit her head on the counter and died and he just got up and left like nothing happened and didn't even leave a tip, but I would still do it with him," Cindy revealed.

"Eeeeewwww..." the others responded like ridiculous teenaged girls tend to respond.

"The guy for me is Mad Dog," Fran Sachs said like a girl with the brains of a turnip. "He's tough and strong and he can hotwire a car in 19 seconds flat. He says that if he gets to 12 seconds he's going to try out for the Olympics."

Cindy had her annual idea... "Let's go around and tell what kind of guy we're looking for. Fran already went telling us about Mad Dog Leibowitz, so there's nowhere to go but up. I'll go next. I want a guy who's strong and sexy with big shoulders so he can carry sandbags on his shoulders just in case we're on the beach in Japan and Godzilla causes a tsunami and we need sandbags. Also he should be able to bake chocolate chip cookies and he needs to have a nice car with cup holders for my latte. Janet, it's your turn."

Janet thought for a moment and then let her feelings be known. "I want a guy with no legs and no arms so he could never leave me. I would buy him lots of hats and he would dream about playing guitar for me and serenading me under my window which he wouldn't be able to do because he doesn't have any arms to play the guitar with. He could play the guitar with his tongue like Jimi Hendrix, but I want him to use his tongue for other things, if you know what I mean."

"Eeeeewwww…" the others responded like dopey teenaged girls often respond. Then they all looked at Laura Lawson, the marvelously massive full-buttocked girl who (as you may recall) collected old copies of *Tiger Beat* and pictures of Bobby Sherman and was sitting in front of an open window that was facing the street. Laura's description of the man she wanted was full of sensitivity and passion.

"I want him to be the kind of guy who knows what he wants in life; the kind of guy who can see beyond the physical, to the person beneath who is crying out to be loved and held. I want a man who isn't afraid to reach out when he finds what he's looking for, and hopefully, someday, what he's looking for will be me."

Cindy, Janet, and Fran looked at each other and then at Laura. They were extremely moved by her emotional outpour. Cindy pondered, "I wonder if there are guys like that left in this world."

Leo's battered Silver Shadow turned down the street where Cindy's house was. Marty and Bink were singing the theme to The Jetsons, alternating lyric lines, while Marty looked around for their elusive holy grail. Suddenly he yelled, "*HIT THE BRAKES, BINK!*" Bink pushed down on the brake pedal as hard as he could and the car came to a screeching stop right in front of Cindy's house. Bink popped up from the floorboard and Marty pointed at Fat Sensitive Laura sitting in the window.

"THERE IT IS BINK! THE DIGBY ORB!"

Marty turned Bink's head in the direction of Large Laura in the window and Bink's antenna twirled with excitement.

"Wow Marty! Look how big it is!"

Marty looked at Large Laura longingly. "Let's get it!"

They crept slowly into the front yard, snuck up to the open window, and jumped on unlean Laura from behind. Laura screamed and ran around the living room with Marty and Bink clinging to her. The other girls joined in screaming and chased Laura, moments later pulling Marty and Bink off of her and throwing them on the sofa. When Bink saw the girls in their scanty nighties, his antenna which was normally limp, became rock hard and stood straight up on his head.

"You're disgusting!" Marty snapped. "Hide that thing!"

Bink, embarrassed, found a shower cap on the floor, and covered his head with it. The girls couldn't believe their eyes looking at our little green bug-eyed boys.

"What are you?" Janet asked. And quite frankly, it was a good question.

"Are you from outer space?" Cindy inquired just like someone named "Cindy" would inquire while looking at two little green guys with bug-eyes, antennae sticking out of their heads and propellers on their rears.

"No, we're two fraternity pledges who like to dress like aliens and this is a panty raid. If we bring back your panties we're in like Flynn. If we bring back the Digby orb's panties we're starting a circus," Marty answered sensitively.

Bink added, "We're on a recovery mission for our planet and Marty thinks the chunky chick here is the Digby orb which is what we're here to recover."

Then Marty added, "Not to be indelicate, but at first glance I thought she was the whole planet."

"We had a big thing land in our yard a few nights ago," Fran Sachs said.

Marty looked at her. "You're Leo's slutty kid, aren't you? I knew the Digby orb landed there, but daddy played dumb at first. With you it's not an act." Marty put his arm on Laura's gigantic shoulder. "*This* is the Digby orb pretending to be a jigglepotamus."

Fran reached out cautiously and touched Marty's antenna which sprang up.

"Don't get me going unless you want to take that trip, Sister," Marty warned.

The other girls joined in touching Marty and his antenna got stiff and started throbbing.

"Some things about this planet aren't so bad," he said.

The joint was passed to Bink who tried to eat it. Janet stopped him. "No, you don't eat it; you smoke it, like this." She demonstrated and passed it back. Bink took a hit, his propeller twirled, and he hit the ceiling.

"You two really *are* from outer space!" Fran finally realized. "That's so cool!"

"Does my coolness get you hot?" Marty inquired inquisitively.

"Do you girls have any Benny Goodman albums?" Bink wanted to know.

"I think my father does, why?" Cindy Sai said.

"Because we're hungry and Benny Goodman albums taste like kugel to us…and we want to dance."

Cindy found a Benny Goodman album (*Live at Carnegie Hall 1938*) and put it on her father's phonograph. Marty and Bink danced wildly together. They were swinging each other around, doing flips, splits, just going crazy. And then Cindy turned the phonograph on and they stopped. Marty grabbed Fran to dance and she pulled away.

"What's a matter, am I too good for you?" Marty asked.

"You're too short to dance with," she said.

"No sweat, sugar. You girls and the Digby orb close your eyes and count to three, if you can count that high."

As the girls (and Laura) closed their eyes and counted to three together in harmony, Marty and Bink locked antennae and spun around in midair gaining speed and moving from 33 + 1/3 rpm to 45 rpm to 78 rpm. Shimmering green sparks flew from their antennae followed by a whizzing whirling sound which was then followed by Lalo Schifrin's *Mission Impossible* theme. When the *Mission Impossible* theme stopped, Marty and Bink hit the floor. When they stood up, they were in human form, although they did still have antennae coming out of their heads and propellers on their rears. Marty would probably be considered fairly attractive to female Earthlings, sort of a combination of Tony Dow, James Dean, Tyrone Power, Ava Gardner, and Jonny Quest. Bink was on the cute side of short and dumpy. They looked at each other in utter disgust.

"YUCK!" they both said in unison while wincing.

"Gag me with a spoon!" Marty grimaced, looking at Bink. "You're so ugly you have to sneak up on air to breathe!"

Bink retorted, "And you're so ugly you look really bad!"

The girls squealed with delight and made comments like "I'm freaking out!", "They're so cute!", and the like. You know those ridiculous comments that girls like that make. The girls started dancing too and everyone was having a swell time until Janet left the room and returned with a life-size plush E.T. doll. When Marty saw the E.T. doll he stopped the Benny

Goodman record by dragging the needle across the tracks. He frowned at the E.T. doll, totally revolted, and glared at Janet.

"Why did you have to ruin everything with that monstrosity? Have any of you chicks ever met E.T.? First of all his name is Evan Teitelbaum. Where we come from he's a patio lizard who made it through the screen door to the big screen. It was pure luck. He's the only one on the entire planet that can't speak in complete sentences, and he's the one who makes it. If you're a dope, you get to the top. That's how life works."

Cindy Sai said, "We never met him. You're our first Martians that we ever met."

Bink, bitterly insulted, lunged at Cindy Sai who shouldn't have said what she said but said it. Marty grabbed him by the propeller and kept him back. Still, he blasted Cindy Sai for saying what she said.

"We are *NOT* Martians! We are from Digby, the only square planet in the entire universe, where recognizing that an energy density field lower than a negative mass would appear and an Alcubierre warp drive would be hit and as a result someone caught in the middle would land on the traversable wormhole and then on the Einstein-Rosen bridge linking contrasting points in the spacetime continuum while sensing gravitational-wave radiation and infinite loops with parallel cosmic strings approaching, isn't a major production! Bink Le' Dink and Marty Mooncricket, who are us, are touchy about being called 'Martians'. It demonstrates a profound ignorance on your part. It's like calling a worm, 'spaghetti'."

"I'm very sorry," Cindy Sai said sensitively. "So do you really know E.T.?"

"We met him before his breakdown and again when he was returning to rehab for the 53rd time. Talking to him is like having a conversation with a doorstop. You and Evan would get along real good."

Bink interrupted. "Say, Cindy Sai, is there a bathroom here?"

"Down the hall on the right," Cindy Sai said.

Bink headed for the bathroom as Marty eyed him suspiciously.

"Bink, why are you going to the bathroom?"

"I have to do my business," Bink blushed.

"Bink, we don't do our business like Earthlings do it. You have no need of an Earthling bathroom."

"I don't need your permission to go to the bathroom!" Bink blasted back.

"Yes, you do, and the answer is no."

Bink ignored Marty, entered the bathroom, and closed the door.

"Excuse me ladies," Marty mumbled.

He walked over to the bathroom, opened the door, and found Bink playing with his antenna.

"What are you *doing?!*" Marty asked harshly.

Bink was startled and nervous.

"Umm...I was...adjusting...the frequency."

"Sure you were. I know exactly what you were doing. In 1716 the Earthling Dr. Balthazar Bekker published a pamphlet all about what you were doing and another doctor named Samuel-Auguste Tissot also wrote about it. They said that you'll get pimples, you'll go blind, you'll go deaf, you'll turn into even more of an idiot than you already are, you'll get a hunchback, you'll get old before your time, you'll get a fever, fire will roast you from the inside, you won't be able to walk, you'll have nightmares, your teeth will rot and fall out, your propeller won't spin, you'll get hair on your palms, and you'll go mad and kill yourself. And one of The Outlaws of Asteroid #9 had a cousin who died from it. He had a stroke mid-stroke. Is all that worth it for a zeptosecond of glory?"

"I already got hair on my palms," Bink said.

Marty grabbed Bink and dragged him back to the living room where the music was playing again and the girls were dancing. Fran grabbed Marty and they danced together closely. Their eyes locked and there was a definite attraction between them.

"Don't you aliens from outer space take over human bodies?" Fran Sachs asked Marty Mooncricket causing his antenna to pop up. Marty glanced over at Bink who was sitting on the sofa staring at his palms. At that very inconvenient moment they heard the loud rumble of a Harley-Davidson Big Twin Shovelhead and the next thing they knew Mad Dog Leibowitz came plowing through the front door on his motorcycle and caught Fran dancing with Marty. Mad Dog was angry. He was always angry, but now he was a very special angry.

"What's going on here?" he asked like an older woman, typically a mother figure, who just entered a room to find a young couple banging like crazy six feet in front of her.

Marty explained. "We're playing water polo without a pool or water or a net or a water polo ball or caps or mouthguards or goals, and we don't have enough people for two teams, but we could use a good center forward if you're available. Say Cindy Sai, would you happen to have a D-1flying saucer viewing screen around here? We have one in our saucer but I don't even know where the saucer is. It's probably in a chop shop by now."

"No, I'm sorry Marty. I don't have a flying saucer viewing screen," Cindy Sai said.

"Oh! There's one!" Marty announced, looking directly at Mad Dog. Mad Dog turned around and looked behind him, seeing nothing.

"I don't see no kinda screen," Mad Dog mumbled moronically.

"That's the amazing thing about Earthlings," Marty grinned, "you can't see yourselves. You can only see reflections. Bink, go to your favorite hangout, the Earthling bathroom, and bring me a hand mirror."

Bink did just that. Marty held the hand mirror up in front of Mad Dog, gestured, and turned him into a 1953 Motorola television set. Fran screamed.

"Oh relax," Marty said. "Now he has a purpose. We need to contact Emperor Zee and tell him we found the Digby orb. Bink, wrap your antenna around the left rabbit ear television antenna and stand on your right foot."

Bink did what Marty said to do while Marty fiddled with the dials.

"Alright, now lift your left leg six inches, touch your tongue to your left knee, and hold still. Do not move."

"Snow" came on the screen and a very long thirteen minutes later some shows appeared as Marty flipped through the four available channels: *Rocky Jones Space Ranger, Lost in Space, Space Patrol,* and one that made Marty pause and simulate sticking his finger down his throat, *My Favorite Martian.* Marty set the dial between the third and fourth channels and instructed Bink to take his right pointer finger and point to Uranus. Bink pointed to his tushy and grinned.

"Very funny," Marty remarked. "Now with your propeller point to Digby and spin it counter-clockwise."

Bink pointed toward the sky. The picture got snowy, then wavy, and when it came into focus Emperor Zee was on screen looking at the centerfold of *Moon Maiden Magazine* and playing with his antenna. Marty cleared his throat, "AHEM!" Emperor Zee was startled, tossed down the magazine, and pulled out a pamphlet published in 1716 by an Earthling named Dr. Balthazar Bekker.

"Who's there?" Emperor Zee demanded.

"It is I, Marty Mooncricket," replied him, Marty Mooncricket.

"I can barely see you, Marty."

"Hang on a sec, Emperor Casanova…Bink, stand on your middle eight toes, maybe that'll help."

Bink was gazing lovingly at the 1953 Motorola and didn't hear.

"BINK!" Marty snapped.

"What?!" Bink replied, snapping out of it.

"I told you to stand on your middle eight toes. This isn't the time for your perverse electronics and appliance fetish."

Bink stood on his middle eight toes and it did the trick.

"Now I can see you better, Marty. I hope you can finally see me," Emperor Zee said on screen.

"I saw you fine before," Marty muttered, "and I'm devastatingly disgusted."

"REPORT!" Emperor Zee demanded, changing the subject.

"Good news, Emperor Zee! We found the Digby orb! We'll come home now."

Emperor Zee put his face (which wasn't overly attractive) up to the screen.

"Not so fast, Marty. Let me see it."

Marty left Emperor Zee's view and returned a few minutes later grunting, groaning, and straining, while rolling Laura in front of the television. Emperor Zee put on his tortoise frame glasses and looked at her through the screen.

"That's not it, Marty. That's a fat broad."

"What difference does it make?" Marty asked annoyed. "It's the thought that counts."

"Find the Digby orb, Marty, or you can't come home."

"Are you telling me that if we don't find that stupid thing we have to stay on Earth?! We can't live on this planet. Earthlings are crazy. They eat tofu and shoot each other. What kind of life is that?"

Emperor Zee warned, "It may be *your* life if you and Bink don't find the Digby orb. Have a nice day."

He reached down for his *Moon Maiden Magazine*, frowned, grabbed his antenna, and signed off. The screen went black.

"I hope your antenna breaks," Marty mumbled under his breath.

The screen flashed on again and Emperor Zee was scowling.

"*What* was that, Mooncricket?"

"Uh…I said that I hope we have what it *takes*…to find the Digby orb."

Emperor Zee offered a hand gesture that I won't demonstrate here, and the screen went black.

"Come on Bink, we gotta find that thing. Laura here has misled us, which I find particularly disturbing and unforgivable."

Bink didn't respond and was just gazing lovingly at the television set.

"*BINK!*" Marty snapped.

"I think I'm in love, Marty," Bink sighed.

Marty shook his head. "Not again, Bink. You fall for every electronic device and appliance you see. Last week it was Sally the satellite dish and you dated her just so you could tell everyone you were dating a real dish, the week before that it was Carol the can opener, and last month it was that psycho bitch Rosie the radio who wouldn't shut up. What a piece of work she was." He draped his arm consolingly over Bink's shoulder. "Don't fret Binky Boy, you'll find another broad. This one's too old for you and she's not under warranty. I'll find you a nice girl; don't worry. Have I ever let you down before?"

"Yes, many times."

"Oh…well…let's find our ticket home."

Fran Sachs approached Marty and tweeked his antenna.

"I never made it with a guy from another planet in the back seat of a Rolls Royce before," she said slutishly.

"It's good that you can narrow it down that way," Marty mumbled.

Fran grabbed him by the propeller and dragged him outside to the car. Exactly seven seconds later Marty came back into the house pulling up his trousers. A minute later Fran staggered into the house looking like she'd been hit by a train.

"That wasn't making love, Marty. It was too quick. There was no feeling. There was no affection. Earthling girls like to be held and caressed and told how beautiful we are. We like to feel like we're special."

"On Digby we use the Big Bang method. Let's go Bink."

Half an hour later Marty and Bink entered an electronics and appliance store wearing plastic novelty Groucho glasses with attached nose, bushy eyebrows, and mustache to disguise themselves.

"Why do we have to wear these, Marty?" Bink asked, and it was a good question.

"Because we're wanted aliens, Bink. This way the Earthlings won't recognize us," Marty answered, and it was a good answer. "Now look around for a nice sweet girl, and don't fall for the first thing you see."

If this was a movie Todd Rundgren's "We Gotta Get You a Woman" would play over this sequence if I could get the rights. But I don't have to get the rights, because this isn't a movie, not yet anyway. Bink moved through the store examining various electronics and appliances such as telephone answering machines, refrigerators, radios, toasters, blenders, vacuum cleaners, microwave ovens, etc. to see who struck his fancy. Eventually he came upon an adorable little portable TV who caused his antenna to immediately stiffen and his propeller to twirl, lifting him off the floor. Marty ran over and quickly pulled him back down.

"Are you crazy, flying up like that? They'll notice us!" Marty whispered.

"Sorry, Marty. I love this little TV. This is who I want to marry."

"How can you say you love her? You just met her! You're like Alfie the Outlaw of Asteroid #9 when he met Echo the Oread nymphomaniac. Learn from mythology, Bink. Those doomed to repeat the past should learn to read about it. You don't even know what this TV's favorite show is. You don't know if she wants the Archies to get back together as much as you do or if she likes paprika. Slow down. If it's meant to be, it will happen. If it isn't meant to be, it's because you screwed it up."

"I don't care about any of that. I just feel it."

Marty realized how happy Bink was. "Alright Binky Boy, I'll leave you two crazy kids alone so you can get better acquainted. I'll be over by the blenders." He pulled Bink aside. "Don't say anything stupid. First impressions are important."

Marty walked away and Bink turned to the TV. "So...do you come here often?"

A salesman, Rodney Hoover who had a forged autographed picture of Herbert Hoover vacuuming hanging over his bed, approached Bink and the TV set. Marty didn't notice. He was too busy pretending to look at blenders while he was actually looking at electric milk frothers.

"You like this little honey?" Hoover pushed. "We have an 85 inch wide-screen you might want to look at too, if you want to feel like you're in a theater. We have easy financing with no credit check."

"No, she'd be too big for me. She'd kill me in bed. I like 'em just like this, short and built."

"I hear ya," Hoover pushed again. "And built she is. She's got a fine body, solid state, and gets excellent reception. She's been sitting here just waiting for some lucky guy like you to take her home. Go ahead...turn her on."

Bink stared at Hoover. "Right here, in public, in front of everybody?"

"Sure. I'll bet this little lady gets turned on a hundred times a day… by men, women, kids…I even saw a guide dog do it once. Go ahead, turn her on."

"Okey-dokey," Bink blurted. He unbuttoned his shirt, started to gyrate, and sensuously rubbed his antenna against the antenna on the TV. Then he started fondling the power button and French kissing the screen as his propeller started to twirl. A crowd started to gather which drew Marty's attention.

"Oh shit," Marty mumbled to himself.

The salesman Rodney Hoover was flustered. "Not like that, pal, use the power button you've been molesting."

Hoover reached for the power button; Bink knocked his hand away and exploded, "HANDS OFF MY WOMAN, BUSTER!" Bink jumped on Hoover. Marty took a flying leap at Hoover too. Several of the other sales associates joined in defending Hoover and a tremendous brawl broke out. Ironically the little portable TV that was entirely to blame for all the trouble was killed during the chaos. As Marty was getting clobbered he turned to Bink who was also getting his tail handed to him.

"Are we having fun on Earth, Bink?"

"We're having a swell time, Marty," Bink responded politely.

Truth be told, they weren't having such a swell time at all. They were beaten up pretty badly. Marty did manage to eventually turn all the sales associates into an assortment of D, C, AA, AAA and 9 volt batteries, most of which didn't work. After the melee, Marty and Bink managed to hitchhike back to Cindy's house getting a ride with Charles Edward Malinchak, one of those three-name guys who was a former hand model turned trucker when his hands were injured in a horrific emory board accident. Charles Edward Malinchak always wanted to be a serial killer as most three-name guys aspire to be, but he got sick watching tampon commercials and didn't have the stomach for it.

Back at Cindy's house the girls bandaged Marty and Bink up and tended to them. Bink was holding a toaster sort of lovingly, but not completely lovingly.

Cindy, bandaging Bink's butt said, "Bink, I think what you did was very gallant. Not many guys fight for their women like you did."

Bink smiled sadly, "But I still didn't get the girl of my dreams."

"The toaster's cute, Bink," Marty interjected. "And she has a crumb tray and a bagel setting! You can't beat that."

"Why a toaster? Why not a real girl?" Fran asked, showing her ignorance.

"It's a long sad boring coma-inducing story," Marty said, "and it goes like this: On our planet Digby when it comes time for a young male to lose his virginity he goes to the Star-Riser Devirginizer which is sort of like a big vacuum cleaner that talks dirty to the young male while it does nasty things to him. It can also show movies to help in the process. When it was my turn I insisted on watching the double feature pornographic cult classics *Debbie Does Digby* and *Deep Inside Uranus* because the Star-Riser Devirginizer alone didn't do it for me. But when it was Bink's turn he fell head over heels madly in love with the Star-Riser Devirginizer and refused to leave it. We had to pry him out of it with extra extra extra virgin olive oil, crowbars, and a winch. It was terrible. Finally we had to destroy the Star-Riser Devirginizer because Bink kept proposing to it and serenading it with Bread songs when we were trying to sleep. Ever since then he's been crazy about electronics, household appliances, and anything that doesn't have a pulse and can't say 'no' and reject him, similar to many of your morticians here on Earth, and the reason for that law in Florida making sex with corpses a crime.

"But if the Star-Riser Devirginizer was destroyed, how do the other males on Digby lose their virginity?" Fran inquired. And to her credit, it was a good question.

"They don't," Marty said. "I told you it was a sad story."

"Why don't you guys come to my house for dinner tonight? I want Marty to meet my parents," Fran pushed.

"I already met your father," Marty said. "I shouldn't have to meet him again. It was bad enough the first time."

"Because when an Earthling girl likes a guy a lot she takes him home to meet her parents. Bink can come too. Even though you already met my father, you should still meet him again."

Marty cringed. "That's a strange ritual. When a Digby guy likes an Earthling girl he bangs her in the back of a Rolls Royce. But what the hey, let's eat."

Leo Sachs, his ex-wife Doris, Fran, Marty, and Bink were sitting on the floor of Leo's house since there was no furniture. Marty and Bink were in their human form and wearing Abe Lincoln-esque stovepipe hats to hide their antennae. Bink was clinging to his toaster. There were several moments of uneasy silence as Leo and Doris (especially Doris) stared at their guests who had finished their meal and were now eating the plates. Doris glared at Marty.

"Even though Leo and I are divorced, thank God, Franny is still my daughter. I wanted to meet you Martin because I don't want Franny to make the same mistake I made."

"And what mistake was that, Doris?" Leo asked, knowing the answer.

"Marrying a bum!"

"Great way to talk in front of company, Doris; you never did have any class."

Doris looked at Marty and Bink. "Some company; they're eating the plates."

"Mother!" Fran frowned.

"Alright, I'll change the subject," Doris decided. "Martin, where are you and your friend Linc, from?"

Marty was getting perturbed. "It's not 'Linc', it's Bink. This isn't *The Mod Squad*. We're from Cleveland."

"Do people in Cleveland wear hats at the dinner table or is it considered rude?"

"This isn't a dinner table, it's a floor. And nothing is considered rude in Cleveland."

"I have relatives in Cleveland. What part are you from?"

"The other part."

Bink interrupted to try to relieve the friction between Marty and Doris. "Did you folks know that the Earth's sun is 15 million degrees centigrade in the center? A pinhead as hot as that could kill someone standing 90 miles away. That's a fun fact."

Marty looked at Bink.

"How interesting," Doris commented. "Do you study outer space?"

"I love outer space, but I dropped out."

Marty dropped his head on the floor. Fran changed the subject.

"Marty protected me from Mad Dog."

Leo patted Marty on the back. "Thank you, Martin. I never liked that creep. A father wants his daughter to find a good man, not someone like him. How did you protect Franny from that monster, he's three times your size?"

"I know a few tricks. I turned him into a 1953 Motorola television set."

Leo and Doris both started laughing. No one else did.

"How many channels does he get?" Doris asked, as she and Leo continued laughing.

"Four, I think," Marty answered as Leo and Doris laughed hysterically. For a moment they held on to each other heaving with laughter, realized that they were getting too cozy, and turned away from each other. Doris looked at Bink clinging to his toaster.

"Why are you holding that toaster, Linc?"

"I'm not 'Linc'. Your brain cells stink. You need a shrink, that's what I think, you Earthling fink. I'm Bink Le' Dink, and this is my girlfriend, Proctor Silex. She's a cook."

Doris and Leo screamed with laughter. Bink, Marty, and Fran just looked at each other.

"Where's the bathroom?" Bink asked.

Marty eyed him suspiciously...again. Doris wiped away tears of laughter.

"It's the last door on the left down the hall, but you can cut through the kitchen, it's faster."

Bink picked up his toaster chick and went into the kitchen. Doris was drying tears.

"He's a riot! Where'd you find him?"

"Outside of the Digby Home for Strays," Marty said seriously. "He was trying to escape a very bad situation where he was being abused and I helped him. He's like a little brother to me."

Doris cracked up laughing, but she laughed alone. Leo and Marty looked at each other sadly. As Bink passed through the kitchen he looked at all the appliances and started quivering in ecstasy. His girlfriend Proctor Silex got jealous and without being plugged in heated up in Bink's hands. Bink screamed in pain and dropped her on his own foot. He screamed again. All the appliances started up full blast and the kitchen was suddenly alive and going wild. In pain and without realizing it, Bink changed back to his original little green bug-eyed alien form. The incredible racket could be heard in the room where the others were. Marty figured out what happened and quickly got up off the floor. "I'll go see what's wrong," he said, but Doris beat him to it. She ran into the kitchen and found Bink the alien in the middle of total havoc. At the sight of Bink as Bink, Doris was frightened out of her wits. She flew into the other room babbling nonsense. Leo slapped her, liked it, and slapped her again.

"CALM DOWN!" he demanded.

She pointed to the kitchen. Leo poked his head into the kitchen and saw Bink back in his human form cleaning up a few things. He went back to the other room shaking his head. Bink followed without the toaster and politely tipped his hat (but not too much) to Doris.

"Thanks for dinner. It was swell. Bye."

Marty followed Bink out the door. Once outside Marty stopped him. "What happened to your chick?"

"I dropped her," Bink said. "She was too hot-tempered and too possessive. I don't like that."

Marty and Bink walked a bit and accidentally found a twenty-dollar bill in the pocket of an old man who was passed out drunk under a tree. They came to a revival house showing the original *Star Wars* and went inside. 121 minutes later the movie let out and several people left the theater discussing and pseudo-intellectualizing what they had seen. And then Marty and Bink came out breaking up and howling with laughter.

"WHAT A BUNCH OF CRAP!" Marty yelled.

They continued walking while laughing hysterically.

"But I still wouldn't mind taking a tumble with Princess *LAY...Ahhh*," Marty commented.

"Or you could use your...*HAN...SOLO*," Bink shot back, and they both howled again with laughter.

"Make sure no one tries to...*JABBA YOUR BUTT!*" Marty warned, and they rolled around on the ground holding their bellies and cracking up as people stepped around and over them.

"Did you have the hots for the lightsabers, Bink?"

Bink ignored the question and calmed down.

"That R2-D2 was very believable," Bink commented. "The Academy really screwed him over for Best Supporting Actor."

Marty got irritated. "I couldn't see him much because Godzilla sat right in front of me and the Earthlings behind me had to narrate the whole damned thing. Earthlings never stop talking."

They walked a little more and came to a park bench. They sat down and looked up at the night sky which was breathtakingly beautiful, still, and peaceful. Marty wanted to say something and was nervous about it.

"Bink...I don't think I'm going back to Neptune."

"We're from Digby, Marty."

"I mean…I don't think I'm going back to Digby."

Bink sat silently for several moments.

"What do you mean?"

"I mean I'm staying on Earth."

"You just said Earthlings never stop talking," Bink said, trying to understand and getting scared.

"I can wear earplugs."

Bink thought silently. He was getting distraught.

"You mean even if we find the Digby orb you're still not going home?"

"Right."

Bink started to cry. "Did I do something wrong, Marty?"

Marty started tearing up too. "Oh no Binky Boy…" He put his arm around him.

"It's because of that Earthling girl, isn't it?"

"She does something to me, Bink. I can't explain it."

Bink got brave. "I can explain it. She makes you into a weenie! If you stay on Earth you'll have to get a job and wear pajamas and listen to Lawrence Welk."

"I made up my mind. I'm staying."

"You're thinking with your antenna, Marty. What about our mission? What about Emperor Zee?" And then sadly…"What about me?"

Marty lost it: "The hell with finding that stupid rock! The hell with Emperor Zee! And the hell with *you!*"

Bink was crushed. He rolled up into a pitiful little ball and didn't move. Marty felt terrible.

"I'm sorry, Bink. I didn't mean that."

Bink didn't move.

"Come on Binky Boy, I'm sorry."

Bink didn't respond. Marty got mad.

"Alright Bink, you wanna be a ball? You're a ball."

Marty kicked Bink hard and he rolled through the streets, down alleys, bounced down stairways, accidentally became the ball in a pick-up basketball game scoring 68 points and was taken to a bowling alley where he was acknowledged for the most gutter balls since the place opened. He was tossed out of the bowling alley, rolled through a park where he was tossed around, kicked around, punched around, passed around, escaped from there, and eventually rolled to the "Sweet Dreams Ice Cream

Factory." A worker was carrying in a heavy crate because he couldn't find a hand truck and also because he wanted to get a hernia so he could avoid screwing around with his wife for a while. The worker couldn't really see much that was in front of him and accidentally booted Bink up in the air. Bink landed inside a 3,000-gallon mixing vat along with the milk, cream, and sugar that acts as the base for the ice cream, including the milk fat, stabilizers, nonfat solids, and emulsifiers.

** (I need to stop a minute… again. This is about to get very complicated. If I had known that manufacturing ice cream was such a pain in the ass to describe I would have chosen something easier like…something easier. I always thought that ice cream came out of cold cows. But no, it's incredibly complicated and there are all kinds of machines and complex procedures and I'm getting more annoyed than I was describing archery. That said, bear with me, and let's continue.)

So then Bink was pasteurized at 175 degrees for 25 seconds. Then he was homogenized to become smoother and creamier which insured a better blend of all the ingredients. After that he was "aged" (as they call it in the ice cream biz) for four hours at 40 degrees which made the milk fat crystallize. That crystallization allowed his proteins time to hydrate. I hope you're following this, because I'm lost. The hydration time "improved his whipping properties." I don't know what that means, but I like it. He then had some liquid flavors added. They had to be liquid so that he could flow through the freezing machines, which are probably called "freezing machines." He was then frozen and mixed with air during that process. Then he was thrown into a rotating Continuous Ice Cream Freezer Barrel which was half filled with ice cream mix. As the barrel rotated, Bink, in the mix, was mixed with more air which creates the lightness or density of the ice cream being produced, which in this case was Bink, so it was dense. Inside the barrel rotating blades kept scraping ice off the surface of the freezer equipment. Suddenly Emperor Zee appeared on the rotating blades inside the barrel. Bink could only catch glimpses of him on each blade as it passed. His voice came through like hiccups like when you were a kid imitating an Indian (indigenous American) and repeatedly popped your palm over your mouth while making your version of the Indian warpath sound: "O-o-o-o-ohhh." You know what I'm talking about. In fact, you probably just tried it. Don't lie; I know you did. Or…or…think of the end of "Crimson and Clover" by Tommy James and the Shondells where Tommy used that tremolo effect with the vocals. The voice mic was plugged into a guitar amp with the tremolo turned on and the amp output was recorded while Tommy sang "Crimson and clover, over and over" resulting in the hiccup voice effect that symbolized the 1960s. That's how Emperor Zee's voice sounded in the barrel. Bink was semi-frozen but could still carry on a conversation through chattering teeth which were more like the wind-up novelty kind than the real kind.

"Greetings from inside a f-f-freezing rotating barrel in an ice cream factory on Earth, Emperor Zee. What are you d-d-doing here?"

"Ree-pooo-orrrt!" Emperor Zee demanded; his voice sounding like I told you it would.

"Nothing to report s-sir," Bink said shivering.

"Yooo-rrr not on vaaa-caaa-tion Beeenk. Haav yooo lo-caa-ted the Diiiig-beee orbbb?"

"Not exactly s-s-sir."

"Wherrrr'sss Maaa-rrr-teee?"

"Marrrty has abanndoned the missssion to l-l-live on Earth and eeeat tofuuu."

"Yooo telll Maaa-rrr-teee thattt hisss greeeen asssss izzzz Satuuuurn gassss. Havvv a niccccceee daaaayyy!"

Emperor Zee winked out. Just as the conversation ended, Bink was removed from the barrel, packaged, cooled very quickly to 13 degrees below zero, hardened, and shipped.

CHAPTER 17

Marty Mooncricket was wearing shades, his stovepipe hat, sipping a dirty martini, and lying on an inflatable rubber float shaped like a flying saucer in the pool at Leo's house. The repo men hadn't taken the water out of the pool yet.

I dig this planet. The Earthlings are chowderheads, but the planet itself is pretty cool. There's chocolate wine, boiled peanuts, and Ed Galloway's Totem Pole Park off of Route 66. And Earth is flat like Earthlings' heads, not square, Marty thought to himself.

Leo Sachs was watching Marty from a window as repo men worked behind him removing more of his possessions. Fran, in a bikini, came by and looked at Marty through the window with her father.

"Isn't Marty wonderful, Daddy?"

"Terrific. Doesn't he have a job or a home or some place else to go? He's always in that pool."

"I don't think they have pools where he's from."

"I thought he was from Cleveland. They don't have pools in Cleveland?"

"I'm going to change," Fran said, ignoring her father's question. She climbed the stairs pushing her way past the repo men who continued removing things from the house and property, which included Leo's chair and television this trip. Leo continued looking out the window and saw Marty go into the cabana. He grabbed his binoculars from a passing repo man and focused in on the cabana door. Marty had left it partially opened. Through the binoculars Leo saw Marty peeling off his human skin revealing his true extraterrestrial self. Leo was startled and realized that Marty was the same alien he had met before who had crashed in the

---

309

flying saucer and was on the run. Leo left the main house and crept up to the cabana where he watched little green bug-eyed Marty wringing water out of his human skin suit and then drying it using the propeller on his tushy. Once it was dry Marty slipped the human skin suit back on and straightened it out. He slipped on his shades and stovepipe hat and walked out of the cabana to find Leo standing there.

"Oh, Leo, glad I caught you. I think Fran is pretty good in the sack and I'd like to make it a permanent thing if it's cool with you."

Leo stared at Marty letting this soak in.

"Are you asking for my daughter's hand in marriage?"

"I don't just want her hand, I can do that myself. I want all of her."

"I don't think so, *Martin*. I don't approve of mixed marriages."

"She can convert," Marty pointed out. "We hit it raw anyway with Tom Bodett at the Motel 6 on Whitley. He always leaves the light on for us. What's the big deal?"

"The big deal is…I don't want my daughter married to *a creature from outer space!*"

Marty was astonished…sort of. "A *WHAT?!* Do you think I'm a creature from outer space, like your movie *The Creature from Gruesome Gulch* only from outer space and not from Gruesome Gulch?"

"I knew you before you were…human, remember? Don't forget that. I saw you take your…*costume* off…in the cabana."

"You're disgusting, Leo, watching me undress! You should be ashamed of yourself!"

"No more games, Marty. Here's the deal…if you really want to be with Fran we get that Digby orb back and you and Bink will star in *Marty and Bink and the Search for the Digby Orb* like we talked about before. Either you help me with the picture or you lose Fran and I tell the authorities how to find you and Bink. I don't want to be like this, but you can see I'm in trouble. Where is he anyway?"

Marty looked past Leo out the back window as the repo men were hoisting the flying saucer onto a flatbed truck. He darted out back and approached the supervisor.

"Not that I care, but what are you doing with that?"

"Do you believe this thing? We found it half-buried and covered with leaves in the brush back there."

"So what are you doing with it?"

"Repossession, pal. Just like the rest of the stuff. The bank wants all property of value and this looks like it could bring a few bucks. That's probably why the old man was hiding it."

"Where are you taking it?"

"Impound lot for now. The bank will probably auction it off. These movie props, especially sci-fi, are hot collector's items."

Marty watched the saucer being taken away on the flatbed and followed behind on foot slowly. As the truck went over a speedbump the license plate 'DIGBY 1' fell off and wobbled to a stop at his feet. He picked it up and looked at it sadly. It was pretty obvious that he was getting confused about his feelings. Fran came outside and put her arms around him.

"Why does Daddy look upset?"

Lost in thought he didn't hear her.

"Marty!"

"Huh? What?"

"Why is my father upset?"

"I don't know, maybe because he's losing things that are important to him."

"You're probably right. I've never seen him so depressed. They even took his movie awards to auction off. I need to get some things at the store for dinner. Come with me."

A short time later Fran and Marty were in Ralph's Supermarket shopping, which was a good reason to be there. Fran was busy squeezing lemons and thumping melons while Marty was moving through the aisles biting right through packages and eating everything he could. A clerk saw Marty eating a can of creamed corn (the can included) and confronted him.

"HEY!"

"HEY!" Marty heyed back.

"You can't eat that without paying for it!"

"I just did."

"I'll throw you out of here!" the clerk threatened.

"You're threatening me?" Marty asked, already knowing the answer. "All I get are threats on this planet."

Marty stormed up front and grabbed the store microphone.

"ATTENTION SHOPPERS! THE CLERK IN AISLE 6 NEXT TO FROZEN FOODS JUST THREATENED ME. HE'S SHORT AND UGLY AND OBVIOUSLY HAS A NAPOLEON COMPLEX. HE

ALSO HAS A STRONG DESIRE FOR ME TO GO EXTREMELY UNREASONABLE ON HIS ASS."

An assistant manager handed Marty a note which he looked at.

"SHOPPERS, FOR THE NEXT 30 MINUTES ALL CANNED PASTA OF ANY BRAND WILL BE FIVE FOR FIVE DOLLARS AND MATZO AND HALVAH ARE TWO FOR ONE. GOD KNOWS HOW LONG THEY'VE BEEN SITTING ON THESE SHELVES. MOSES PROBABLY PUT THEM THERE. THANK YOU SHOPPERS, AND NOW BACK TO OUR STORY…"

Marty returned to aisle 6 where the clerk was upset and waiting for him. Several shoppers gathered around the confrontation. The clerk snapped at Marty.

"If you don't leave this store now, I'm gonna use you for a mop!"

"Alright," Marty said pointing to the floor where the clerk was standing. "Just don't slip on that banana while you're mopping with me."

The clerk looked at the floor. "What banana? I don't see a banana."

Marty gestured and turned the clerk into a banana.

"*That* banana."

The shoppers screamed and ran for their lives. Marty reached down and picked up the banana.

"I think I'll have a banana split, a popular treat amongst Earthlings. Now, what flavor ice cream do I want?"

He opened the ice cream freezer door and something grabbed him and pulled him inside. A zeptosecond later Marty was shivering and staring at Bink who was sitting inside a "Sweet Dreams" green mint ice cream container badly bruised and freezing. Marty was ecstatic.

"BINKY BOY! What happened to you?"

"You kicked me and I was made into ice cream. That's the short version. The long version is long; you'll have to read it. Emperor Zee is on my case. We gotta find the Digby orb, Marty. That's our mission here, not screwing around with Earthling girls."

"But I love Fran, I think, maybe. She's my whole life, I think, but I could be wrong. I'd be lost without her, possibly, I'm not sure."

"Have you been watching soap operas?" Bink asked.

"Maybe. Congratulate me, we're engaged."

"Mazel tov."

Fran opened the freezer door and they made like a banana and got the hell out of there.

The next day, Leo and Fran were poolside at what was left of the house, having a heated argument.

"I don't want to hear it, Daddy!"

"Well, you're going to hear it, young lady. I'm not asking you, I'm *telling* you. Break it off with that Marty Mooncricket. I don't want you to see him anymore. I needed him to do something important for me and he didn't. That shows me how selfish he is."

"You never like anyone I bring home!"

"So far it's been a hoodlum and an alien from outer space. There has to be more on the menu. Not only is he from another planet but he's also a little nuts."

"How do you know about him?"

"Never mind, I'll make this very simple. Break it off with Mr. Mooncricket or lose your inheritance."

"I thought you were broke."

"Just do what I say."

"That's not fair."

"I didn't say it was, Franny. You need a real man. You've been around my movie monsters and space creatures since you were a little girl, so you're used to seeing them. Maybe that's the problem. A real alien literally drops out of the sky and you're engaged to him."

"I wasn't going to tell you yet, but I guess I should, we're living together part-time at the Jack Elam Hotel on Yucca Street with a bunch of old character actors in Hollywood because we were tired of paying for a room at the Motel 6 and Marty proposed and I said 'yes'. But you're right, Daddy, he's nuts. The Jack Elam Hotel is weird. It only has two windows in the whole building and they face in opposite directions."

"Marty won't turn sane the minute you get married. It will only get worse. Break it off now while you have the chance."

Later that night in room 6B of the Jack Elam Hotel, Fran Sachs was lying in bed wide-awake looking around the room in disgust. Outer space memorabilia was everywhere. Black lawn & leaf trash bags were duct-taped to the ceiling with glow-in-the-dark star stickers all over them looking like a poor man's night sky. Models and toys of spaceships, space creatures, and odd characters filled the place. Styrofoam planets hung down from the ceiling on fishing line. It was a sight to see to say the least. Marty Mooncricket was sound asleep. He was snoring up a storm and the antenna on his head was spinning slowly while stiffening now and then. He was dreaming that he was fighting off imaginary lovers and talked in his sleep. The ladies he was fighting off were well-known sci-fi movie actresses from the 1950s. Marty started to twist and turn as he fought them off.

"Stop it Anne Francis, star of *Forbidden Planet*, you'll poke my big eyes out with those things!" and "You're tickling me Beverly Garland, star of *Not of This Earth* and *It Conquered the World*…A threesome? I don't know, my fiancée might find out."

Fran had enough and nudged Marty.

"Wake up, Marty, I want to talk to you."

Marty started to stir and looked at her.

"Who the hell are you? Are you trying to seduce me too?"

"It's me, Fran Sachs, your fiancée for the next few lines of dialogue."

Marty squinted at the time on his Saturn-shaped alarm clock with the seven rings around it that clanged together when the alarm went off.

"You're not my fiancée. I could never be involved with someone who would wake me up at this ungodly hour. I have my Star Trek convention tomorrow and I need my beauty sleep. William Shatner and George Takei will be there and there's friction between them. That should be fun."

Fran was serious. "Marty, I can't marry you."

"Okay. Goodnight," he said turning over to go back to sleep. Fran shook him.

"I'm not kidding! Look at this room! This isn't the room of a mature grown man who's ready for marriage! This is the room of a deranged little boy! I can't marry you, Marty. I need a *real* man."

Marty sat up. "Well, I'm not a *real* man. I'm an alien from the planet Digby. I thought you knew that. It's not something an Earthling would easily forget."

"I'm serious, Marty. I need someone I can depend on. I want a husband who's a doctor or a lawyer or something respectable like that."

Marty reached under the bed and pulled out an inflatable sex doll.

"How about her? She's not a man, but she's a lawyer and she went to medical school for two years before she transferred to law school."

Fran knocked the sex doll away. She was mad. Fran was mad, not the sex doll, although the sex doll might have been mad too. You can never tell what emotions sex dolls are feeling. From my experience anyway…I mean…that's what I heard.

"I can't deal with you anymore, Marty. You're too weird. And you're from another planet. It's like sleeping with a big insect. It's yucky."

"An *insect?!*"

"Or a pickle. An insect or a pickle," Fran said insensitively.

"How come Earthling women always have revelations at 4:00 A.M.?" Marty said sensitively.

"This has been a long time coming, Marty."

"Oh yeah? Well I think your daddy's been dancing on your head. Give me back the ring, clean up, make me breakfast, leave money on the dresser, and get out."

"I'm not going anywhere and you're not getting the ring back," Fran made clear. "According to 'Dear Abby' if the guy breaks the engagement then the girl can keep the ring!"

"First of all, *I* didn't break the engagement, *YOU* did. And second of all and most of all, I don't give a red shift shite what 'Dear Abby' said. She didn't pay for that engagement ring, I did, and I want it back right now!"

"You didn't buy the ring, Marty. It used to be a paperboy, remember? You turned a nice kid with a paper route into an engagement ring! That's horrible!"

Marty fumed, "Quit trying to distract me. Give me back the ring!"

"NO!"

Marty grabbed her finger and tried to wrestle off the ring. Fran bit his arm and he released her. She tried to run, but he caught her, and bit down on her hand attempting to pull the ring off with his teeth. She twanged his antenna and he doubled over, grabbing her foot and tying it to the leg of the bed. He left the bedroom and returned a few moments later wearing two goldfish bowls taped together as makeshift goggles for his large bug-like eyes and menacingly holding a buzzing chainsaw. Fran screamed and FRANtically (see how I did that?) twisted off the ring. Marty shut off the chainsaw and gestured, turning the ring back into the paperboy it once was.

"Paper mister?" the paperboy asked.

Marty took a copy and looked at the headlines: "MARTIANS STILL AT LARGE!" Angry, Marty threw the newspaper at the boy, who left in a hurry. Fran was sitting on the floor in the corner, totally frazzled, panting, and pointing at Marty. She was angry too.

"My father was right about you! You're nuts!"

"*I'm* nuts?! You're the one who's been walking around with a paperboy on her finger."

"Why don't you just go to your stupid Star Trek convention now? Maybe you can steal the Enterprise and go back where you came from."

"Alright, I'll go, but not because you're telling me to, but because it was *my* idea. You don't tell me what to do, Earthling! I hope you and your father live happily ever after. Life isn't a movie that he can direct, you know."

With that classic line that I wrote, Marty stormed out. Two miles away, Leo Sachs was meeting with Conrad Quinn, the 27-year-old wunderkind chairman of Upstart Studios. Conrad Quinn was the kind of guy who had his ass kicked on a daily basis when he was young, and with good reason. Thankfully for him, daddy had money and pull. Quinn sat majestically in his massive executive chair looking down on Leo who was sitting on the other side of Quinn's tremendous desk absolutely dwarfed, which was the psychological intention. It was sad really. Leo Sachs, a man who had devoted his life to filmmaking, appeared and felt almost insignificant compared to the youthful Mr. Quinn who had total power to greenlight projects. Quinn's personal assistant/*yes*-man Owen Wixx who had plans to murder Quinn at some point, was also present. Wixx looked at Leo as though Leo was a little pathetic joke.

Quinn pulled a bottle of top shelf whiskey out of the bottom drawer of his desk, poured himself a glass, and offered some to Leo who refused. Then he tried to get something straight.

"Let me get this straight, Mr. Sachs, you want this studio to finance a movie about something that falls to Earth and two creatures from another planet try to track it down. It doesn't sound very original."

"Not original at all," Owen Wixx added. Leo looked at Wixx like he wanted to see him torn apart by wolves or by anything at all, as long as he was torn apart.

"Oh, it's very original, Mr. Quinn. There's never been a movie like it." Wixx chuckled.

(I hate Wixx more than Leo does. He's got one more line later in this scene and then I'm killing him off.)

"Mr. Sachs, do you have any idea how much money special effects on a movie like that would cost this studio?" Quinn asked in a way that was shutting Leo down.

"Not a cent," Leo answered.

"Why not?"

"Because it's all going to be real. We won't need special effects, no CGI, nothing. The meteorite is real and the creatures from another planet trying to find it are real. Remember that flying saucer that landed on the freeway? It was all over the news."

"That was a PR stunt, Mr. Sachs. You've been in this business and in this town long enough to know that. We just don't know what it was promoting yet."

"It wasn't a stunt, Mr. Quinn. I have the aliens that were in that flying saucer, and they're very real."

Wixx chuckled again and shook his head, assuring he was going to die soon.

"Uh huh, and where exactly are these aliens?"

Leo had enough. "Are you going to greenlight this picture or interrogate me?"

"You're not giving me anything substantial. You're babbling on about meteorites and monsters from outer space that you think are real. You made a lot of 'so bad they're good' movies in your time that I always enjoyed watching, but with all due respect, those days are gone. Have you ever seen *Nightmare Alley* with Tyrone Power? *That* was a great film and Edmund Goulding was a great director. He wasn't selling bad cheese."

Leo lost it. "Screw you! This isn't the only studio in this town, so quit acting so high and mighty. I don't need you, kid. I'm giving you the opportunity to back my next picture, yes or no?"

Quinn laughed, as did Wixx of course, which only upset Leo (and me) more.

"I appreciate the thought, but to be honest with you, Mr. Sachs, trying to sell a movie these days with you attached as director wouldn't exactly excite people and start a buzz. And that's what this business is all about. There's a new wave of filmmakers now. Some may have even been inspired by you, but to be straight with you, Leo Sachs doesn't have a chance these days."

"Listen smartass, I was making pictures before you were sperm. I was a legend in this town!"

"And that's the key word, Mr. Sachs, *WAS*. You're absolutely right, you *were* a legend in Hollywood, but that was a different time. Things change. Look at me, I'm 27, and I make seven figures a year." He gestured to Wixx. "That idiot does nothing but kiss my ass all day long and makes more money in a month than a working man makes in a year. No one said it was fair, Mr. Sachs. It isn't. It's obscene. But that's the world today. It's not your world anymore. Why don't you retire? Take it easy. You made a name for yourself long ago. You made your mark. People respect that. Retire and enjoy the time you have left."

"Go watch your old movies. Somebody should," Wixx added, assuring his demise.

Quinn snapped, "Shut up, Wixx!"

The comment hurt Leo deeply. He sat quietly and the jagged edge gave way to a man whose spirit was crushed.

"I can't afford to retire, Mr. Quinn. I'm broke. I need to make this picture…please."

Quinn felt bad, but still shut him down.

"I'm sorry, Mr. Sachs…Now if you'll excuse me I have another appointment."

Leo stood up, shook Quinn's hand, and walked out. Speaking of "crushed," a large block of frozen sewage fell out of an airplane passing by overhead, crashed through the roof and ceiling of Quinn's office, fell on Owen Wixx, and splattered him everywhere including all over Quinn's suit. Quinn throttled the whiskey bottle and tried to drown himself internally.

Over the next several weeks Leo had meetings with executives, producers, and VPs of Development at different studios, each one worse than the next. The last time I saw him he was leaving what looked to be a porn studio in the San Fernando Valley and he didn't look happy. Marty and Bink didn't look happy either, as they walked the streets of L.A. feeling just as upset and dejected as Leo.

"I hate this planet," Marty grumbled.

"If we find the Digby orb we can go home," Bink brought up.

"I had a chance to find out where it is and I blew it. Maybe Emperor Zee will let us come home anyway."

"I don't think so, Marty, he's mad at you. You're an alien without a planet."

Marty stopped in his tracks, suddenly struck with an idea.

"I got it Bink! I know how we can get Emperor Zee to let us come home even if we don't find the Digby orb. We forget the orb and we conquer Earth in the name of Digby! We'll be folk heroes and superstars on Digby! He'll beg us to come home!"

"What do you mean, Marty?"

"What do I mean, Marty? I mean we take over Earth like the dumbass Martians always try to do in those movies. But we're not Martians. *We* can think. So *we* can pull it off."

"THE *WHOLE* PLANET?! You and me are going to take over the whole planet?!"

"Yes…except maybe not Harrison, Arkansas. I don't want anything to do with that place."

"How can just you and me take over an entire planet?" Bink wanted to know. And to his credit it was a terrific question, Marty answered very specifically.

"Remember we won that couple's weiner eating contest at Dola Dipper's birthday party? We would each start at opposite ends of the weiner and meet in the middle. It was weird and thought provoking, but we beat Joey "Jaws" Chestnut and Black Hole Bertha! If we can do that, we can conquer this dumb rock all by ourselves. And by the way, there's a place called Weiner, Arkansas. That explains everything."

"But eating weiners is different than conquering a planet. How can we conquer Earth?"

"Two words Binky Boy: television. Earthlings watch television all the time. It's all they do. In fact, it's called 'The Idiot Box' because they're idiots. They're not as bad as Martians, but it's a nail-biter. If we can get on television, we'll be seen by zillions of Earthlings. We tell them we're taking over Earth and there's nothing they can do about it. Now let's get to a TV station and get it over with. It shouldn't take over ten minutes."

Kids in West Hollywood were glued to their television sets watching the public-access puppet program *The Franky Frog Show* which could only be seen in West Hollywood. Franky Frog was singing his signature song "Can't Be Sad on a Lily Pad" while other puppet cast members were behind him singing along. They were Maggie Mayfly, Larry Locust, Wendy Weasel, Ollie Oyster, Hazel Herring, Vinny Vulture, and Earl Earwig. Suddenly the picture on the screen became wavy. When the picture refocused, Marty and Bink were flanking Franky Frog in their original little green bug-eyed alien forms. They were wearing little trench coats and huge dark novelty shades over their big bug-like eyes. They looked like very intimidating and sinister hand puppets even though they weren't hand puppets. Marty growled, "Beat it toad," to Franky Frog while knocking him away. Marty and Bink then looked directly into the camera and addressed the viewers *Outer Limits* style.

Marty

"There's nothing wrong with your cheap television set because we're controlling what you see."

Bink

"Don't change the channel or we'll change it right back, and if you turn your TV off, we'll turn it back on. And if you unplug it, it will still be on."

Marty

"So just sit on your Earthling rumps and pay attention."

All across the 1.9 square miles of West Hollywood a few parents started paying attention to Marty and Bink's announcement to the world (i.e. West Hollywood and nowhere else). Naturally the parents assumed it was just a puppet skit on *The Franky Frog Show*. While Marty and Bink were "conquering Earth," a very distraught Leo Sachs was wandering the streets, conquering a bottle of Night Train (or was the Night Train conquering him?). He passed by Cindy Sai's house and happened to glance in the window, where he saw Marty and Bink on the 1953 Motorola. Marty addressed the audience like an alien who knew what he was here for.

"Can you say 'WORLD DOMINATION' boys and girls?"

A kid watching the show pointed to the screen and said, "I want one of those scary bug dolls, Mommy!"

"We'll see," said Mommy who was eyeing the shirtless gardener. On screen Bink pointed to Marty.

"He's Marty Mooncricket."

And then Marty pointed back to Bink.

"And he's Bink Le' Dink, and we are… (They announced together) THE BAD BOYS FROM OUTER SPACE!!! We are hereby taking over your planet Earth in the name of our planet Digby."

"It's the only square planet in the universe!" Bink added.

"Isn't he cute?" Mommy commented, now looking at the television because the shirtless gardener put his shirt back on.

"Wouldn't you rather have a Bink doll?"

Marty was serious and commanding as he looked threateningly into the camera at the viewer.

"From now on you Earthlings will abide by the following rules. You will stop saying, 'That's what I'm talkin' about' and 'Get 'er done'. You will also stop calling a cap a 'hat'. A cap is not a hat. A hat has the brim all the way around it. A cap only has the bill part in the front. Wake the hell up!"

Bink

"You will stop pressing the button on an elevator more than once when it's already been pressed."

Marty

"You will stop looking into a mailbox more than once to check if your mail has gone down into the box when you know damn well that it has."

Bink

"You will stop eating Hawaiian pizza. Pineapple does not belong on pizza! And (they announce together) NO MORE NOSE JOBS!"

Franky Frog, star of *The Franky Frog Show*, tried to crawl back on screen and Marty swatted him away. Franky's girlfriend on the show, Rhonda Rhino, saw what happened, got mad, and charged at Marty and Bink. All the puppet animals and the hands inside controlling them magically became fists and joined in thrashing Marty and Bink. Kids and parents throughout West Hollywood who were watching the beatdown all started laughing, thinking it was a fun scripted bit. It wasn't. Paula Polar Bear put her huge paw over the camera lens so the young audience couldn't witness the massacre. My guess is that their plan to conquer Earth failed. Some time later Marty and Bink (or rather, what was left of them) were sitting in Madame Wong's in their original little green bug-eyed alien form, bandaged, bruised, very drunk, and still drinking. Every scumbag, roughneck, and dreg of society in the bar just stared at them in terrified silence.

"I got one for ya, Binky Boy…How many Earthlings does it take to hang a picture?"

"I give up, Marty. How many Earthlings does it take to hang a picture?"

"Ten: one to hold the nail and 23 to push the wall!"

They both broke up laughing hysterically as the other… "customers"… gawked.

"I got one, Marty…How many Earthlings does it take to screw in a light bulb?"

"I give up Bink, how many?"

"Ten!"

They both howled with laughter and took more sips of their Roy Rogers. Marty glanced up and saw Leo stagger in.

"Don't look now, but look who's here."

Leo staggered over to their table, pulled up a chair, and sat down.

"I don't remember inviting you to sit with us," Marty sneered. "You don't want to be seen with a couple of overgrown grasshoppers from outer space, and we don't want to be seen with an undergrown doofus from Earth. Now beat it or maybe I'll have some of these classy Earthlings here beat you."

"Marty, just because I don't want you with my daughter doesn't mean I don't like you."

"Don't worry about it, we broke up. It was your doing. Don't deny it. What do you want?"

"I want to talk to both of you. I think we can help each other."

"You always say that," Bink said.

"Hear me out. Please. I don't think you guys are very happy on this planet. God knows I'm not. You need to get back to Digby and I need to make a name for myself again."

"I think you need us a lot more than we need you," Marty said.

"That's what I think too," Bink agreed.

"You may be right," Leo conceded. "Boys, making this picture *Marty and Bink and the Search for the Digby Orb* means everything to me. You're my last hope for a comeback."

Marty took a serious sip from his Roy Rogers.

"I'm not good enough for your daughter, so you're not good enough for me. Get lost."

Leo started for the door, spun around, lost his balance, fell down, got back up, and went up to the bar.

"Give me a bottle of Mad Dog to go," he told Big Mama. But Big Mama was paralyzed, just staring at Marty and Bink, so Leo reached behind the bar, took a bottle, and left. As he walked out, as broken as could be, a scruffy tattered older man who looked like he had been on the road for quite some time, and a mangy mutt entered. This man was Dusty "Duke Rook" Ketchum who studied the art of the scam under America's greatest con man, Joseph "Yellow Kid" Weil. Ketchum rode the rails with vagabonds who taught him survival through the Hobo Code and shared jail cells, showers, and secrets with the best of the worst. He bilked, swindled, and fleeced his way across the country, and here before him were two little aliens about to learn a hard lesson about life on Earth. The mangy mutt with him was the very same mutt from the greatest dog joke ever told. If you haven't heard it, and even if you have, it goes like this. A man is driving along some back roads in a rural area. He passes a little house set back some distance from the road with a sign out front that says, "TALKING DOG FOR SALE." He stops the car. He can't believe what he's seeing. He thinks about it and then drives up to the little house. He knocks on the door. A few minutes later a man who looks like he knows his way around dirt, opens the door.

"Yep?"

"Yes, hi...I saw your sign out front about a talking dog for sale. Is that a gag?"

"No, it's a dog."

"And he talks?"

"That's what the sign says, don't it? He's 'round back. Go interrogate *him* instead of me."

The man shuts the door. The other man goes around back and sees this mangy mutt lying down in a small fenced-in area. He and the dog look at each other curiously. The man approaches the dog and says, "Can you...*talk?*"

"yeah," the dog says. "It looks like you can too."

The man is stunned and doesn't know what to say next.

"Cat got your tongue?" the dog asks.

"I'm sorry. I've never met a talking dog before. This is remarkable."

"I understand," the dog says. "You see me here like this, but I've had an amazing life. I worked for the CIA as a spy for twelve years. I traveled all over the world pretending to be a guide dog or a comfort dog or just some stray hanging around top secret meetings and I would overhear top secret information that could endanger this country or our allies and I'd report back so our government or ally governments could take proper action and thwart possible and probable attacks. I flew with Special Operations Squadrons and parachuted into enemy territory to infiltrate places that humans weren't able to get to and survive. Two years ago I was sent into space to make the same space flight as Laika the Russian dog did in 1957. She was the first animal to orbit the Earth. She died in space. She's always been my hero. After that space flight I retired and came here to live. I was married for a short time to a real bitch. We had a litter of puppies that have gone out into the world and I hope they have good fulfilling lives. I haven't heard from any of them in a while, but I hope they're doing well."

"Wow! You've had a spectacular life full of adventure!"

"That I have," the dog said.

"I'll be back in a minute," the man said. He went around to the front of the house and knocked. A few minutes later the owner answered the door.

"Yep?"

"Hi. How much do you want for the talking dog?"

The owner thought a minute and said, "Five bucks."

The man was shocked. "Five bucks?! For a talking dog?! Why only five bucks?"

"Because he's a liar. He's never been out of the yard."

Well the man paid the five dollars and took the talking dog home. Long story short, the talking dog had a torrid affair with the man's wife and when the man found out about it he killed his wife and took the talking dog to an animal shelter. The talking dog had another torrid affair with the girlfriend of a rap "singer" (notice the quotation marks) called "Da Dope." His girlfriend, "Princess Pardee" worked at the animal shelter a few days a week to earn dope money. The dope helped Princess Pardee cope with Da Dope. In exchange for sexual favors PP (as I call her) "accidentally" allowed the talking dog to escape one night. He was walking along some railroad tracks just when Dusty Ketchum jumped off a freight train. They struck up a conversation and had traveled together ever since. They sat down with Marty and Bink.

"Busy table," Marty mumbled.

"Where are you guys from?" the dog asked.

"Des Moines," Marty answered, like an alien from Des Moines.

"We're really from Digby. It's square," Bink added.

Marty clamped his alien hand down over Bink's alien mouth. "Don't pay any attention to Mr. Le' Dink, here. He's a real space cadet."

He released Bink and studied the mutt intensely. Marty and the mutt sniffed each other's rears and then Marty pressed his nose up against the mutt's nose. They were nose to nose.

"Say, aren't you a dog?" Marty wanted to know.

"Yep," muttered the mutt.

"Are you a talking dog?"

"Yep."

"You can talk, but can you juggle?"

"Nope."

"I can juggle," Marty professed proudly. "And I can also talk backwards, like this: .oot sdrawrof klat nac I"

"Have you ever seen a talking dog before?" Ketchum questioned.

"Nope."

"I have," said Bink.

"You have not," Marty said.

"But I wanted to."

Ketchum started his spin. "A talking dog is worth a lot of money."

Bink frowned. "We don't have any money."

"Don't you have jobs?"

"For what?"

"To make money."

"For what?"

"So you can buy things."

"Like what?"

"Like the things people need, and want to have, for good lives on this planet."

Marty shook his head. "In case you haven't noticed, pal, we're not really from Des Moines. We're from another planet. That's why all the yahoos in this place are staring at us and wetting their pants. They're scared shitless, because they don't know what we're going to do next."

Ketchum looked around and saw that Marty wasn't kidding. He continued spinning his web.

"If you had money you could buy things like fancy cars and boats and big houses."

"With furniture?"

"Yes, with lots of furniture."

"And household appliances?" Bink asked, hoping for the best possible answer, which Dusty "Duke Rook" Ketchum was more than happy to give.

"Sure. You can buy all kinds of household appliances: washing machines, toasters, blenders, food processors, juice squeezers, whatever you want."

"*JUICE SQUEEZERS?!*"

"Sure," Ketchum smiled his smile that wouldn't win any dental awards. Bink's antenna got stiff and his propeller twirled fast lifting him up into the air. Without even looking,

Marty reached up and pulled him back down.

"Can we make money, Marty, *please?*"

"I don't think it's a good idea, Bink. It'll interfere with our mission."

"Oh please, Marty! Think of all the appliances we can buy!"

Marty conceded, "Alright, but only for a little while. We didn't come to this planet to work. Can you get us jobs, unwashed Earthling?"

Ketchum reeled them in. "As a matter of fact, this is your lucky day, fellas. A friend of mine is looking for two guys just like you to work for him."

"When you say 'just like you' you mean handsome, smart, and sexy," Marty confirmed.

"Of course," Ketchum confirmed back.

"What kind of work?" Marty wanted to know and rightfully so.

Ketchum thought for a moment. "It's in the entertainment field. You gotta have good stage presence because you'll have a big audience. You guys seem like naturals the way you attract attention."

Marty looked around at all the scumbags staring at them and agreed.

"I starred in a one man theater show about the life of Quisp, Off-Broadway," Bink proudly proclaimed.

Marty shook his head. "Yeah, six billion miles Off-Broadway and it wasn't a one man theater show, Bink. You got stuck in one of those dirty Digby glory hole booths at Madam Mancowitz's Gravitational Pull Lust Lovers Emporium and you screamed for help for twenty minutes. That's not a theater show."

Bink shrugged. Ketchum said, "Well now is your chance to star in a *real* theater show. What do you say?"

"Could we get as famous as E.T. and Barbarella?" Bink asked, hoping for the right answer.

"Much more famous," Ketchum said, making the truth his little bitch.

Bink looked at Marty who was daydreaming that he was at the Academy Awards in the audience wearing a gold sequined tux and flanked by Sigourney Weaver and William Shatner. On stage at the podium Sam Jackson was opening the envelope.

"And the motherfuckin' nominees for the Best fuckin' Actor in a starring role in Dusty "Duke Rook" Ketchum's fuckin' friend's theatrical whatever-the-fuck-it-is, are Sir Laurence Olivier, Al Pacino, Dustin Hoffman, and Marty Mooncricket, whatever the fuck that is. And the fuckin' winner is..."

"MARTY MOONCRICKET!" Bink blurted.

Marty snapped out of it.

"What?"

"Can we star in this guy's friend's show?"

"I'm offering you the world, fellas." Ketchum smiled desperately in need of a dentist.

"You mean if we work for your friend, that the world will be ours?"

"Absolutely. Don't pass it by. You may never have the chance again."

"You hear that, Marty?! We can have Earth if we star in this guy's friend's show! Emperor Zee would be so proud of us for conquering Earth that we could go back home!"

"Alright, let's do it!" Marty said stoked (whatever the hell that means). "Take a hike, Evan Teitelbaum, Marty and Bink are about to make it big!"

CHAPTER 18

The following night we're at a pathetic seedy seen-better-days carnival sideshow just outside of Pasadena. Barkers in front of exhibition booths tried to entice people in with wild tales and claims as bait for the curious. At the entrance to the freak show exhibit area was a hideous statue honoring the legendary Pig Boy, considered the world's greatest oddity, aside from that nutty Congresswoman from Georgia. There were such novelty and freak acts as "Rubber Man" who just sat there wearing a condom, "The Dog-Faced Boy" who had a face that looked like a labradoodle's ass, "Skeleton Girl" who was really just a plastic life-size Halloween prop with a cheap hooker's wig thrown on it, "The Boy Who Turns to a Duck" which was a boy sitting on a stool and next to him was a duck on a stool. Every 10 seconds the boy would turn and face the duck and then turn back and face the audience (I demanded my money back from that one), "The Bearded Fat Lady" who was a fat broad with a beard, not the most attractive thing that ever lived, and "The Geek," a real alcoholic who would bite the heads off of chickens and snakes for a bottle of booze. A very short time ago he was the young wunderkind chairman of Upstart Studios, but life happens. The exhibition booth on the far corner was obviously the big draw as there was a tremendous crowd surrounding it. Out front a sign proclaimed:

"REAL LIVE MARTIANS!
YOU WON'T BELIEVE YOUR EYES!
ENTER AT YOUR OWN RISK!"

Percy's own Barry Slinger prowled the platform at the entrance to the exhibit in his loud parakeet green striped jacket, skimmer hat, and fake handlebar mustache, speaking through his pink plastic toy megaphone.

"Ladies and Gentlemen! Boys and Girls! Locals and foreigners! Come see what your mind may not be able to grasp! Here and now, live and in person, are two very real authentic genuine Martians from the planet Mars in outer space! Mars is over 241 million miles from Earth, but these Martians are right in front of you! They're dangerous! They're mysterious! They're weird! They're real Martians! See for yourself!"

Marty and Bink were inside a 10-foot-by-10-foot round goldfish bowl. Curious Earthlings…I mean, human people, gawked and stared at them absolutely astonished. Marty was livid and glared at Bink who was happily waving to the crowd.

"Isn't this great, Marty? Show biz is my life!"

"Then you're going to have a very short career, because when these gawking idiots leave, I'm going to kill you."

A young boy standing on his father's shoulders tossed leaves and grass into the big goldfish bowl. It dropped down on Marty who looked at it and then at the kid.

"What the hell is this?"

"Food for you to eat," the kid said, meaning well.

Marty scowled. "We're not crickets, Junior."

"You look like crickets," the kid said in an attempt at suicide by alien.

"Well thanks for the leaves and grass, Earthling. Do you like chocolate pudding?"

"Sure!"

Marty did what Marty does. He gestured and turned the kid into a huge glob of chocolate pudding which flies immediately descended on. I *think* it was chocolate pudding. The crowd screamed. Several ran for their lives. The Bearded Fat Lady knocked the big goldfish bowl over, yanked Marty and Bink out of it, and sat on them.

"That boy was just trying to be nice and you killed him. So now I'm gonna make some green pancakes for me and the Geek who I have a crush on. Here's how that feels."

She rose up a few inches and then slammed back down on Marty and Bink. They both let out very muffled screams.

"Is this the Digby orb, Marty?" Bink grunted.

"No, Bink," Marty groaned. "This is the largest black hole in space and we need to get out of it because she and that Geek will eat anything, and we're next." He addressed the monstrosity sitting on them. "Tiny Earthling, wouldn't you rather eat that big glob of chocolate pudding over there?"

"That's dessert," she said, despite the hundreds of flies all over it.

The Geek looked at Marty and Bink under the Bearded Fat Lady, spit out a chicken's head, and licked his chops.

"I'll bite their Martian heads off and you can eat their bodies."

"We're not Martians," Bink whimpered again.

"Bink has an excellent point that would hold up in court. We're not Martians, so technically, morally, ethically, and legally, this is a mistake. It's a lousy way to go, being eaten by a drunken studio head turned carnival Geek and a thawed-out mammoth in drag."

Just then a group of kids from West Hollywood who happened to be wearing Marty and Bink T-shirts, toy Marty and Bink antennae on their heads, battery-operated spinning propellers on their rears, and carrying Marty and Bink lunch boxes, passed by and saw Marty and Bink trapped under the hairy fat broad. Two of them were carrying the Pig Boy statue from the entrance that they really shouldn't have been carrying. The first kid who noticed Marty and Bink pointed excitedly and yelled to the others, "IT'S MARTY AND BINK FROM THE FRANKY FROG SHOW!" Then he announced, "DON'T WORRY MARTY AND BINK, WE'LL SAVE YOU!"

The Geek snarled and lunged at the kids, but stopped snarling and lunging when he got clobbered with the Pig Boy statue. Then all the kids got on one side of the Bearded Fat Lady while Rubber Man and the Dog-Faced Boy shoved a plank of wood under her humongous heinie and pried her up as much as they could as the kids strained, groaned, and grunted tilting her a little more and pulling Marty and Bink out from under her. It was one of the greatest concerted efforts in history, and it worked, even though they all needed hernia surgery soon afterwards. If a bunch of kids and two freaks can stop a snarling geek and move a bearded fat broad enough to save the lives of two little aliens, then why can't we all just get along? Marty and Bink thanked the kids, signed autographs, posed for pictures with them, and left. They wandered aimlessly through the streets thinking about their next move.

"I hope we're getting royalties from all that merchandising," Marty said. "We're probably more popular than that Franky Frog because we have personality and no one's hand is up our ass."

Bink said, "Now that we're famous, maybe we *should* stay on Earth. We could wear sunglasses indoors like Jack Nicholson and get our star on the Walk of Fame and cruise Hollywood Boulevard on Saturday nights in a purple lowrider driving up and back on the same street 10,000 times making the car jump up and down using hydraulic suspension while accomplishing absolutely nothing other than having the cops recognize us and we could get our alien handprints and footprints in cement at the Chinese Theatre and eat at Denny's at two o'clock in the morning."

"No, Bink. Our mission is to find the Digby orb and that's exactly what we're going to do."

They wandered onto Skid Row without realizing it and approached some derelicts.

"Have any of you world-weary Earthlings seen the Digby orb? It's yay high and yay wide," Marty described, without physically demonstrating the size. There was no answer, just blank stares.

"Use the Martian Mind Melt on them," Bink suggested, "that way you'll know what's in their heads."

"Good idea, Bink, but doesn't Digby have a mind melt? Oh I forgot, Martians need to melt their tiny useless minds together to think. I'll give it a shot."

Marty attached his forehead to a derelict's forehead. He turned the derelict's right thumb up and the left one down. Marty then stood on his left leg and wound his antenna counterclockwise until he felt the tension. He then released it, like the propeller on a rubberband-powered balsa wood airplane allowing it to spin as he concentrated deeply. He reached back and gave his rear propeller a twirl. Three seconds later a crackling current of a green flash shot from Marty's antenna directly into the derelict's head. Suddenly there was a blinding burst of an orange pulsating wave sending sizzling sparks into Marty's antenna. Marty went flying and screaming in agony. He hit a wall hard and sunk to the ground in a daze. Bink rushed over to him.

"Marty! What happened?! What's wrong?!"

Marty seemed to be in shock and dazed but could talk.

"I just saw inside an Earthling's mind, Bink! It was horrible!"

"What did you see?"

"It's hard to explain. It's like a 3 pound 15 centimeter long vacuum cleaner bag full of dreck."

"Maybe the Martian Mind Melt wasn't such a great idea. Sorry, Marty."

"That's okay, Bink. You didn't know."

A derelict feeling sorry for Marty passed him a bottle, but before Marty could take it, it was snatched away and swigged by another resident of Skid Row, Leo Sachs, who had hit rock bottom. Marty looked at Leo like he was being pestered.

"Are you following us?"

"I was here first," Leo said.

"We're famous now," Bink tossed in.

Leo took a long swig from the bottle.

"That's the point, Bink; you're famous *now*, so what? You're famous in a 'What-have-you-done-lately?' town. That kind of fame doesn't last long. And when you die they say, 'I thought he died 20 years ago.' In Hollywood they bury you while you're still breathing."

Marty rubbed his head still feeling the effects of the Mind Melt and looked up at Leo.

"What happened with your movie?"

"Screw it. No one wants another picture from the late not-so-great Leo Sachs. That kid at the studio was right; it's not my world anymore."

He took another gulp.

"It's not our world either," Bink reminded him. "And by the way, Camner didn't like how that studio punk was treating you, so he turned him into a carnival geek who bites heads off of snakes, chickens, and almost Martians who aren't Martians. He's dead or unconscious now because some of our fans took him out with a statue of Pig Boy."

"Good. Other than that, this planet stinks."

"Yeah, but you got lots of broads here," Marty chimed in. "All we got on Digby is square stuff and a catapult."

Leo was plastered, but said his piece. "We're destroying ourselves while we all stand by and watch us being destroyed while we watch. This rock is nothing but wars and greed and power-hungry mad men trying to tell us how to live and what to live for."

"But you got lots of broads here," Marty pointed out again.

Leo corrected him, sort of. "Most broads in Los Angeles are men and most men are broads. Me, I was a greedy power-hungry prick with a prick. I crushed anyone who got in my way…even my own family." He grabbed the bottle from Marty and took a swallow. "And look at the great Leo Sachs now. I don't have control over anything in my life anymore, not my kid, my ex-wife, my career, not even a couple of talking grasshoppers from outer space."

"Maybe you don't have control because you *try* to control. Maybe if you didn't try to control, you would have control," Bink said philosophically as Leo, Marty, and many of the Skid Row occupants within earshot listened. "What I mean is you can try to control your own life but it shouldn't be at the expense of others. We're all different, but we all have something to offer each other and we should respect that."

They all stared at Bink, touched by his wisdom. Marty was especially moved.

"That's a great message, Bink. 'We all have something to offer each other'. I'll never forget that as long as I live. If I was reading this book and not a favorite character in it, I could stop reading right now and still think it was the greatest novel ever written. But I'm not reading it, so I won't think that. I will when I read it, but not yet."

Bink continued. "Mr. Mooncricket here has a control fetish too. I let him think he controls me because it makes him feel good, but he really doesn't control me."

Marty was absolutely devastated by this news.

"Is that true, Bink?!"

"Sure."

Marty snatched the bottle back from Leo and took some serious gulps. Leo looked at Bink.

"You mean if I teach you guys something and you teach me something, it's not so one-sided and I won't be such a bad guy."

"Something like that. Maybe. Sort of. Not really, but okay."

Leo thought a minute.

"Let's say I teach you to shine shoes just by spitting on them or I teach you that if you swallow a watermelon seed that a watermelon will grow in your stomach and people will think you're the first male pregnant alien but it's really just a watermelon."

Marty and Bink stared at Leo who said, "Now *you* teach *me* something."

Marty thought a minute just like Leo did.

"Okay. Did you know that if you bounce the top of your antenna on a girl's heaving bazoombas while you're taking one-eyed Peter to the optometrist in the dark jungle of joy that it'll drive her wild?"

"I didn't know that," Leo admitted in shame. "What if I don't have an antenna?"

"You can use a toothbrush, but it has to be hard bristle or it won't work."

"You didn't do that antenna thing to my daughter did you?"

"Heck no!" Marty lied, winking at Leo who frowned as police sirens approached.

"IT'S THE FUZZ!" Bink announced.

Several people scattered as two paddy wagons pulled up and an officer got out of a wagon and spoke through a bullhorn: "IT'S TOO CONGESTED HERE AND WE ARE GOING TO RELOCATE SOME OF YOU TO A NEW TENT CITY CAMPSITE. YOU'LL HAVE BATHROOM FACILITIES, SHOWERS AVAILABLE, AND 24-HOUR SECURITY. YOU ARE NOT BEING ARRESTED, ONLY RELOCATED, SO IF WE POINT TO YOU, GATHER YOUR PERSONAL BELONGINGS QUICKLY AND STEP INTO THE REAR OF THE WAGON WE TELL YOU TO GO TO. AGAIN, YOU ARE NOT BEING ARRESTED."

Marty, Bink, and Leo were among those selected. They entered one of the wagons as instructed and off they went. After a 45-minute ride the paddy wagons stopped not far from Four Oaks Farm in Simi Valley where the tent city was located. The wagons were relieved of their contents and drove off. Marty slipped on some cow leavings and landed tush-first on the ground. Bink slipped as well and landed tush-first on Marty who didn't appreciate it.

"This is one of my recurring nightmares other than watching a gentile playing Tevye in a stage production of *Fiddler on the Roof*. Bink, your propeller is sticking in my nasty sack and I don't swing that way. Get up!"

Bink climbed off of Marty who got up too and they slipped around until they were able to steady each other.

"Where are we, Marty?"

"From the smell and my experience here so far, I would say we're in Amou Haji, an Earthling who hasn't bathed in 60 years, or maybe Philadelphia."

Suddenly a faint humming sound came from a building situated off a private road on the opposite side of the tent city. The sound had a strange effect on Marty and Bink as some powerful force seemed to grab them. Their antennae bent sharply toward the building and it hurt plenty as they both let out a yelp. Their propellers started to twirl and they were pulled like alien paper clips to a powerful magnet toward the building as the other Skid Row residents watched in amazement, none more than Leo Sachs. The building was the Aerospace Research Facility and the "magnet" was the Digby orb, but you probably knew that, you smart cookie you. Inside the lab strange things were happening. The green glow around the orb became larger and more intense. It seemed to reach out in the direction Marty and Bink were approaching from. The hum got louder and stronger. A team of research scientists led by Dr. Arnold Kazazian, rushed into the lab, but kept their distance from the orb.

"What's happening?!" Dr. Kazazian asked. And it was an excellent question considering the situation.

Another scientist, Dr. Wayne "Pip" Puzo (an arrogant asswipe) replied, "The meteorite is going berserk. I don't know what caused it. Let's break it open and take a look."

"I wouldn't advise that right now," Dr. Kazazian cautioned.

"We're scientists," Dr. Pip Puzo said in defiance. "It's our duty to learn all we can, and the only way we can do that is by breaking it open."

The Digby orb started to spin and change colors from green to yellow to black to purple and back to green. Arrogant asswipe Dr. Pip Puzo put on blue medical gloves and protective glasses. He removed a diamond lapidary saw disc blade, a chisel, a stonemason's hammer, and a grinder from a cabinet. The orb wobbled frantically.

Dr. Kazazian was getting perturbed.

"Dr. Puzo, being a scientist doesn't give you the authority to dissect everything you don't understand, even though that's what you're renowned for. Leave the meteorite alone."

Dr. Pip Puzo (who's starting to piss me off too, and you know what that means) ignored Dr. Kazazian and moved toward the "meteorite" to cut into it. Dr. Kazazian glanced out the window and saw Marty and Bink being pulled toward the building at great speed. Marty attempted to save himself by grabbing onto a cow's tail and holding on for dear life, but the force was too strong and pulled him loose as the cow let out a very unhappy "MOOOOOOO!" Bink also attempted to fight the force by grabbing onto the teats of a cow's udder and got a face full of unpasteurized unhomogenized milk and kept on flying toward the building. Just as Dr.

Pip Puzo was about to make the initial cut, Marty and Bink rocketed toward the lab, crashed through the window, and slammed face-first into the Digby orb, scaring the hell out of Dr. Pip Puzo who backed off. Marty and Bink were both stuck on the orb, their faces plastered against it.

"I found it!" Bink announced proudly in a very muffled way because it's hard to talk with your face smashed against a large mysterious orb from outer space.

"Good work, Bink," Marty mumbled sarcastically also in a very muffled way because it's hard to talk with your face smashed against a large mysterious orb from outer space. Sergeant Dalton and other security guards rushed in and asked the famous cop question: "What's going on here?" which is sort of like the famous porn question, "What are you doing?" only different. Both stem from lack of awareness and critical thinking skills. The Digby orb stopped spinning and Marty and Bink slid off. Dr. Pip Puzo ordered the security guards to restrain them on lab gurneys with straps. He also told Sergeant Dutton that Dr. Kazazian was interfering with secret government procedures and had him restrained as well, which Sergeant Dutton apologized to Dr. Kazazian for, stating that his hands were tied as he tied Dr. Kazazian's hands. Dr. Pip Puzo looked at Marty and Bink strapped to the gurneys and said, "The meteorite can wait. Let's open these two up and see what we can learn."

To everyone's shock and amazement he skipped right over the ass probing and went right to dissection.

Marty and Bink were light-years past scared.

"Are we in trouble, Marty?" Bink asked, knowing the answer.

"Looks that way, Bink. Any affection I had for this planet is quickly dissipating."

The other scientists (a few of them extras from the Trojan Jackass scene) put on blue medical gloves, surgical masks, and prepared for the dissections of Marty and Bink who were absolutely terrified and shaking. Just as Dr. Pip Puzo (who has pushed me too far) was about to cut into Bink, the Digby orb wobbled furiously, spun like a supersonic dreidel, and projected a blazing green tractor beam that hurled those scientists about to perform and assist in the dissections, against the wall knocking them unconscious. Dr. Pip Puzo was only dazed and went outside for a moment to get some fresh air when ironically the back end of a tour bus that Mr. Percy had blown up months before (that somehow got suspended up in the sky) came crashing down on top of Dr. Pip Puzo, killing him instantly. Oh well. You get what you get. The Digby orb hummed and the straps holding Marty and Bink snapped open.

"We're free!" Bink announced just as another scientist wearing a protective mask over his face rushed in.

"I'm on the fence about that," Marty mumbled.

The scientist ordered Sergeant Dutton and the other security guards to load the "meteorite" (which had stopped its humming, spinning, and glowing show) into the Aerospace Research van since the facility was no longer safe and he would transport it and the aliens to a secret safer location. The guards did as they were instructed and the scientist, Marty, Bink, and the Digby orb took off in the van. The scientist pulled off his mask and it was (let's all say it together...) *ALLEN LIPSCHITZ*...oh...you thought it was Leo. No, I have to use Allen Lipschitz in scenes now and then because remember I told you that the casting director for this book blackmailed me and we're heading toward the end of the book, so I have to squeeze him in where I can. That said, they did pick Leo up at the tent city campsite before heading back to L.A. Allen Lipschitz glanced in the rear-view mirror and saw several government vehicles containing angry government security officers hot on their tail and closing in fast.

"They figured it out," he said like he was trying for an Academy Award. "Line?"

"We got big trouble," Marty said, glancing at my notes.

"Thanks. We got big trouble," Allen said making that method acting class pay off. The van weaved in and out of traffic with the government vehicles in hot pursuit. It was a typical chase scene, nothing you're going to call your imaginary friends about and say, "I just read the greatest chase scene ever." But then something different did happen, and you can tell your imaginary friends about this. The van ran out of gas and just as it was coming to a stop and the government boys were closing in, the Digby orb started to glow green again and hum and spin like it was trying to win The Major League Dreidel Championship. And yes, that's a real competition held at a bar on Manhattan's Lower East Side. The last winner that I know of was Pamskee Goldman who had a world record spin of 17.8 seconds. Congratulations, Pamskee! So anyway, just as the government vehicles tried to box them in, the Digby orb went nuts and the van started to rise and fly!

"WE'RE FLYING, MARTY!" Bink yelled just as the van smashed into the top of a telephone pole and fell back down to Earth with a crash.

"Not anymore," Marty pointed out.

The security officers rushed the van with guns drawn. Marty greeted them with a grin.

"I think every blockbuster novel should have a few good chase scenes, don't you?"

"That meteorite is government property," the lead officer said with about as much emotion as a brick. "Hand it over right now or you'll be cleaning toilets in San Quentin."

Marty gestured and turned all the security officers into toilet brushes.

"Who's gonna be cleaning toilets now?" he asked in a rhetorical kind of way. He turned to Leo and bit part actor Allen Lipschitz who were a little shaken up by what they just witnessed. "Me and Bink want to thank you for helping us get the Digby orb. We had a great time on your planet being attacked and chased and put on display like a couple of freaks, and almost dissected, but I think we've overstayed our welcome and it's time to go home now. We owe you. If there's anything we can do–"

Leo thought of something they could do.

"Be in my movie. It means real fame and fortune for you and a comeback for me. Don't forget what Bink said, 'We all have something to offer each other.'"

"I don't remember him saying that at all," Marty said. "Leo, you're asking us to become public property; to give up our freedom and our privacy so we can be hounded by Earthling groupie chicks day and night who will beg for our autographs and to bump nasties with us. You're asking us to have tour buses that Mr. Percy in Percy hasn't blown up yet, full of dimwitted idolizing tourists from Texarkana, Arkansas, and places like that, come by our 12 bedroom, 14 bath (even though Bink is the only one from our planet who uses the bathroom to…adjust his antenna) mansion in Beverly Hills just to catch a glimpse of us or go through our garbage. You're asking us to have our faces plastered all over the place, like on coffee cups and billboards like Nick Nero before what happened to him happened to him."

"We already got our faces on T-shirts and lunch boxes from *The Franky Frog Show*," Bink mentioned. "Maybe we could have a sandwich named after us: 'The Marty and Bink Sandwich' with bologna, cheese, tongue, and a whole lot of ham, the taste is out of this world!" he giggled as Marty ignored him and continued.

"The paparazzi will be everywhere. They'll be jumping out of the bushes and hiding in the toilet and waiting for us and following us and more groupies will show up and the *National Enquirer* will have scandalous articles about us: "Marty and Bink Search for Intelligent Life on Earth and Find Nothing", "Marty and Bink Caught in Love Triangle with Yield Sign"-

Bink jumped in. "Marty and Bink Caught in Love Octagon with Stop Sign."

Marty ignored him.

"And we'll have to go to all those wild Hollywood parties and dance like Fred and Ginger."

"I can dance like Ginger," Bink said proudly.

"No you can't."

"But I want to."

Leo pushed...a little. "So what's your answer, guys? Do I make you world famous stars, or do you want to stay recognized only in West Hollyood which is 1.9 square miles where you'll only be known to some kids and a few adults who think you're hand puppets."

"Leo, the last time we tried show biz on this planet we ended up in a fish bowl at a carnival freak show. I had higher aspirations for myself."

"You were conned, Marty, and you know it. I'm talking about a real picture and real show business. You'll hobnob with real stars and you'll be stars too."

Marty got very serious. "Like Judy Jetson?"

"Sure," Leo said, not sure who Judy Jetson was. Marty and Bink looked at each other as their antennae sprang up and erect. Marty threw in a condition.

"If you give Allen Lipschitz a bit part, we'll do it."

"Done," Leo promised with a grin.

Bit part actor Allen Lipschitz was thrilled that he was going to get another bit part and he thanked them all. He didn't thank me who created his ass, but at least he thanked them.

Leo was very happy. "Now we need a producer. Elliott told me that there's a new producer in Hollywood who's looking for offbeat projects. I'll have him set up a meeting."

Three days later, Leo, Marty, and Bink stood in front of the new producer's door reading two signs. One said:

"MADAM MANCOWITZ PRODUCTIONS
(part-time visionary, clothing alterations,
fortunes told, curses cast and lifted)"

The other said:

"I'D TURN BACK IF I WERE YOU!"

They looked at each other.

"You don't need to make a comeback," Marty tried explaining to Leo because he was more than a little overly concerned about entering that office. "You're world famous as the King of Schlock."

"Yeah, but I'm broke," Leo reminded him. He opened the creaking door cautiously and saw the old swamp witch looking exactly like an old swamp witch should look, sitting at her desk stirring a desktop cauldron. There were cobwebs everywhere, a few bats hanging around, and vile vials of various potions and lotions.

"Come in children," she beckoned, "and tell me who you are."

"I'm Leo Sachs, the director," said Leo Sachs, the director. "My agent Elliott Fineberg arranged for me to pitch my next picture to you."

"Oh yes, Elliott Fineberg, the persistent putz. And who is with you, dear?"

Bink pointed to Marty. "He's Marty Mooncricket."

Marty pointed to Bink. "And he's Bink Le' Dink and we are... (all together now) *THE BAD BOYS FROM OUTER SPACE!*"

Leo took the wheel. "They're from the planet Digby which they tell me is the only square planet in the universe. They came to Earth to search for a special kind of meteorite that apparently has strange powers. We found it and it's in our possession. The picture I want to make is based on their story. It's called *Marty and Bink and the Search for the Digby Orb*."

"Clever title. Do you have a screenplay to show me?"

"Not yet. Bink here is writing it."

Marty looked at Bink, "Since when?"

Bink shrugged. "Since now, I guess. I found out about it when you did."

"I couldn't read it anyway, my dear. I'm blind as a coal miner with no eyes trying to eat in that Blackout Dining in the Dark restaurant in Las Vegas where you eat in pitch black darkness and they don't tell you what you ate until after you ate it. But sight is subjective. There are many

340

people with perfect vision who can't see a thing. Will there be roles for my unfaithful husband Frank's skeleton and his unfaithful dog Scooter? You know I stopped feeding those two bastards 37 years ago."

"Sure," Leo assured her, not really sure himself.

"And will there be a bit part for Allen Lipschitz?"

"Absolutely! I already spoke to him about it."

"Very good. Alright my children, I will produce your movie. Let us toast our agreement with my very special creation 'Madam Mancowitz's Meshugana Moonshine.'"

She ladled her concoction from her desktop cauldron into those cheap red plastic recyclable cups that all the sluts drink from in every single orgy film ever made...I'm told. She handed the slut cups to Leo, Marty, and Bink with dead-on accuracy like she knew exactly where they were, which was a neat trick for a blind swamp witch turned movie producer. They raised their cheap red slut cups and Leo made the toast.

"Here's to *Marty and Bink and the Search for the Digby Orb*, a Leo Sachs film of a Madam Mancowitz Production starring Marty and Bink as Marty and Bink, salute!"

The three of them drank and then they tried to open their mouths to talk and couldn't. For the same solution that kept Nick Nero from removing the *Creature from Gruesome Gulch* costume, had sealed their lips. And you know what that was. They dropped their cups, panicked, and tried desperately to unlock their lips, but it was impossible.

"Don't worry, children," Madam Mancowitz said soothingly, "some aliens and schlock directors can't hold their Meshugana Moonshine. I'll have the new Mafia don, Izzy Neroni, meet you on the set in the next scene. She'll know what to do."

Madam Mancowitz's maid came in, saw the red slut cups on the floor, and announced that she wasn't picking them up, adding, "I'm a maid, not a housekeeper."

Two weeks later we're on the set of *Marty and Bink and the Search for the Digby Orb*. More specifically we're at Quality Studios 5628 ½ Santa Monica Boulevard where Ed Wood shot most of *Plan 9 From Outer Space*. Things were hectic as they usually are on film sets. Lights, cameras, and cables were being moved and adjusted, people with script copies, clipboards, and walkie-talkies were running around. Aston, the director's assistant from the Barstow shoot was there to help Leo (If I didn't kill him off. I don't remember if I did or not.) Allen Lipschitz was rehearsing his line. Inside the makeup trailer, makeup girl Britney Calhoun was applying green touch-up powder to Marty and Bink as the most powerful chick in organized crime, Izzy Neroni, was having them sip the antidote to Madam Mancowitz's Meshugana Moonshine of Datu Puti vinegar, solvent-based degreaser, and refined pomace olive oil mixed using 33 1/3 percent of each, through very thin bendable plastic straws from cheap red plastic recyclable slut cups. Not that this is important, because it isn't, but you should know in case you're ever asked, that Britney Calhoun learned her craft studying paint-by-number kits and never got her GED because she was always screwing around with the guidance counselors when she should have been in class. Marty and Bink, having gone full Hollywood, were wearing satin robes, ascots, and shades. Leo had already had his antidote and could talk again. He came in to check on his stars. Marty finished the antidote and was now able to talk too. He wasn't happy.

"Leo, our trailer faces a brick wall. We want a view of the girls' shower."

"I'll tell Aston, if he wasn't killed off earlier. If he's alive he'll take care of it. Just so you understand the filmmaking process, we don't shoot the picture in order. It's put together in the editing room. So we'll start toward the end and work backwards."

Marty looked at Bink. "Earthlings are nuts."

"Have either of you had any acting experience?"

Marty nodded. "I said 'I love you' in the heat of passion about 25 million times and didn't really mean it. Does that count?"

"That's good enough. Now here's the story that Bink wrote. A meteorite with strange powers falls to Earth and you guys are trying to find it. If you don't find it you can't go home to Mars."

Marty looked at Bink, "Very original. Why are we from Mars? What's with Earthlings and Mars? There are other planets, you know. Earthlings are obsessed with Mars. They don't understand that (to paraphrase psychotherapist Michael Tuch) if the Milky Way was an Earthling, Mars would be the rectum."

"I had to change it a little to protect the innocent," Bink explained.

"And why is it called the Digby orb if we're from Mars?" Marty asked. It was an excellent question that I was wondering myself.

"I'm a writer," Bink answered. "Writers can do anything we want. That's why they call it 'writing' and not 'wronging'."

Marty understood...sort of. "Alright, I'll stoop to play a Martian, but only to prove what a great actor I am and that nothing is beneath me. I'm the Dustin Hoffman of Digby."

The scene was set up for a rehearsal and blocking. Aston, if he wasn't killed off earlier, got everyone in their positions. Leo handed Marty and Bink their script pages for the scene and gave them direction. "Alright boys, in this scene you found the Digby orb and you're going to put it in the van. Then you'll drive the van to your flying saucer, hook the Digby orb up to the saucer, and head back to Mars with the orb in tow."

"Intense. What's my motivation?" Marty asked like a true method actor.

Leo thought for a moment and said, "Two nights in the Snooty Fox Motor Inn on Western Avenue with Judy Jetson and a can of bed bug repellent."

"I'm ready for my close-up, Mr. DeMille."

"Alright, let's run through the dialogue that Bink wrote. We're on scene 59. We'll do a take with the cameras rolling. Go ahead Marty, your line."

Marty read from the script. "Is this the meteorite, Your Highness?"

He scowled at Bink who read his lines in return.

"No, you idiot, this is a fat broad. You are so dumb I can't believe it. How do you remember how to breathe when you wake up in the morning?"

Marty read his response lines through clenched alien teeth.

"I'm sorry for being so dumb. I wish I was as smart and as handsome and as wonderful as you...Your Highness."

"Well, you're not. You're a jerk. And furthermore your apologies mean nothing. Now let's put the Digby orb in the van and get out of here before the evil Earthlings catch up to us."

Marty looked up from the script. "Are you kidding with this dreck?"

"You're an actor, so act!" Leo urged. "Now roll the orb into the van. I want looks of desperation because you have to leave quickly, combined with elation because you found the thing, combined with aggravation because even though you're rolling the orb, you're getting a hernia because it's heavy."

They rolled the orb into the van.

"Good. Now, look off into the distance. You see the evil Earthlings coming to get you!"

They did as directed with ridiculous expressions of surprise on their faces. Suddenly their expressions became real as Marty and Bink saw

Aerospace guards, operatives, and government officials surrounding the set and coming toward them. Leo hadn't noticed and continued directing.

"Now jump in the van and drive a few feet off the set so my cinematographer can work out the camera angles."

Marty and Bink jumped in the van. The suits gave chase with guns drawn. Marty was at the wheel and Bink was on the floorboard working the pedals.

"FLOOR IT, BINK!"

Bink slammed down on the accelerator and the van sped away from the set. Leo chased the van yelling, "CUT! CUT! STOP!" Bink slammed on the brakes and Leo jumped in.

"What the hell are you guys doing?! I said a *few feet* off the set!"

"Take a look!" Marty said as he turned Leo's head in the direction of their pursuers. There was a hail of gunfire, Bink mashed the gas, and the van sped away.

It was just after midnight outside the city impound yard when the van silently rolled to a stop. Marty and Bink slipped on black ballerina onesies that they had accidentally taken from two little girls leaving their ballet class two days before. It was very similar to when they ambushed those Girl Scouts for their uniforms and cookies several scenes back. In fact, they were the same little girls who would be in deep therapy for decades. Now keep in mind that I don't condone the way they ambush little girls. I think it's terrible. But in great literature the characters take on a life of their own and the author just sort of sits there and watches. There's very little I can do at this point. Marty and Bink then brought out some black Kiwi shoe polish and smeared it on each other's faces. When they were done they marveled at each other.

"Bink, you look like Al Jolson!" Marty marveled.

"So do you, Marty!" Bink…marveled back. "We're the Jolson Twins!"

They both got down on one knee and sang "Toot Toot Tootsie." Leo interrupted them.

"Would you mind telling me what you're doing?"

Marty explained. "This is our clandestine operation scene. We're wearing black and in blackface so no one will see us. The Outlaws of Asteroid #9 taught us how to do this. Me and Bink will find the saucer. You stay here and watch the Digby orb so it doesn't escape. Do you think you can handle that? Relax Leo; you're too uptight all the time. That's why you Earthlings have ulcers and prostate problems."

With that, Marty and Bink spun their propellers and flew over the wall of the impound yard. Dogs started barking. Marty and Bink climbed over and around cars and trucks, ducking from passing lights.

"Do you see it?" Marty whispered.

Bink looked around. "Not yet. How do you know it's here?"

"Because when Earthlings don't know where to put things, they put them here." Marty explained.

Bink saw a radiator to a 1970 Chevy Impala and his antenna stiffened. He approached it lovingly and embraced it.

"I'm in love, Marty!"

"Not now, Bink!" Marty said firmly. "Find the saucer. We gotta try to fix it and get outta here."

"Can I marry this radiator if I find the saucer?" Bink asked like an alien smitten by a radiator from a 1970 Impala.

"With my blessings," Marty replied.

"Will you be my best man?"

"I'm touched, Bink. Of course I'll be your best man."

"And will you throw me a bachelor party with strippers and cheap red recyclable plastic cups and a dancing bear?"

"Sure. Now find the saucer."

Bink concentrated very intensely. His antenna started to bend and point and tick like a Geiger counter. As Bink moved in the direction his antenna was pointing him to, the ticking got faster and louder until finally he came upon the flying saucer which was parked between the Scooby-Doo Mystery Machine which had strange smoke pouring out every time the door opened, and Katy Perry's VW Jetta.

"I FOUND IT, MARTY! HERE IT IS!" Bink yelled to Marty who was 18 inches away from him. Suddenly lights flashed on, dogs barked like mad, and Aerospace guards, impound guards, operatives, and government officials stormed toward the two little aliens. Helicopters appeared seemingly out of nowhere and hovered above with searchlights criss-crossing the impound yard.

"BINK, LET'S SCRAM!" Marty yelled to Bink who was the same 18 inches away from Marty. Bink started running as fast as his little alien legs could go, stopped, went back for the 1970 Impala radiator, and headed toward the van. He tossed the radiator over the wall to Marty who calmly stepped aside and let it drop. Bink spun his propeller and flew over the wall. He saw the radiator on the ground as he slowly touched down next to it. He looked at Marty, horrified.

"You killed her!"

"It was a suicide, Bink. She jumped. I couldn't stop her. It's just as well; she wasn't your type anyway. But *these* are much easier to carry." He showed Bink two United Pacific SHC01-15 15" Chrome 3 Bar Fiesta Style hubcaps and smiled. "They're sisters...twins. They'll do anything you want."

Bink was thrilled as he embraced the hubcaps.

"Thanks, Marty. You're swell!"

"I know," Marty agreed. "Now let's blow this joint."

They jumped into the van and sped away just as the guards, dogs, and company all jumped the wall. The guards pulled out their guns and shot out the rear tires of the van which collapsed and fishtailed with sparks flying everywhere. The rear doors to the van flew open and the Digby orb popped out and rolled down the street. Marty, Leo, and Bink jumped out of the van and chased it.

"IT'S GETTING AWAY!" Bink panted.

"I CAN SEE THAT. NICE WORK, LEO, I'M SURE GLAD YOU DIDN'T LET THE ORB ESCAPE!" Marty panted.

"IT'S NOT MY FAULT!" Leo panted more than Marty and Bink were panting.

"MARTY, WHY ARE WE RUNNING AND PANTING IF WE CAN SORT OF FLY, IN A WAY, BUT NOT GREAT?" Bink wanted to know.

"GOOD POINT, BINK, LET'S DO IT!"

They twirled each other's propellers to get started and each grabbed Leo under an armpit lifting him into the air with them. Under his weight they could only fly about four feet off the ground and were actually dragging him.

"Lose the beer belly, Leo," Marty complained. "I'm getting another hernia. All I get from this planet is inguinal hernias and the clap."

As they chased after the Digby orb, they heard more gunshots and bullets whizzed by their heads. Marty glanced back and saw their pursuers gaining on them. He wasn't happy.

"This planet bites," Marty mumbled under his breath but loud enough so he could hear it. They chased the Digby orb through the streets, alleys, and sewer systems of the city. As we have previously witnessed, the orb did seem to have a mind of its own at times, which kicked into high gear during this wild pursuit which was exactly like that great chase scene in *Bullitt* with Steve McQueen, except it was completely different. The Digby orb seemed to veer away from potentially dangerous situations like oncoming traffic, roadblocks, marriage (I kid!), and strip clubs, when one runs out of "Do you like my dancing?" tip money ten minutes after getting there. The orb took a few peculiar twists and turns and ultimately popped up and into the backseat of a "juiced all around" purple lowrider that was parked in front of the building that was the Lincoln Savings and Loan in 1985 which is where I met and befriended vertically challenged actor Billy Curtis who you might know as Clint Eastwood's sidekick Mordecai in *High Plains Drifter* or the Martian in *Angry Red Planet* or the little version of The Thing in *The Thing* starring the big version of The Thing, James Arness of *Gunsmoke* fame. Billy also played Mayor McCheese in McDonald's commercials and the hero in the all-midget western *The Terror of Tiny Town* the cast of which was the Singer Midgets that played the Munchkins in *The Wizard of Oz*. Billy was thrown off the set several times for making passes at Judy Garland who would say to him, "Mother wouldn't approve." Marty, Leo, and Bink arrived at the lowrider with not a moment to spare and their pursuers right on their tails. Marty popped the hood.

"We gotta hotwire this rig quick," Marty said panickingly ("panickingly"?). "Bink put your left tongue on the orb."

Bink did so and the orb started to glow green and spin counterclockwise causing Bink to quiver.

"Leo, hold Bink's middle birdie finger with one hand and my middle birdie finger with the other hand while I touch the negative battery post with my right tongue."

They all did as Marty instructed and shook like mad as the Digby orb spun faster and faster, its green glow growing stronger with each spin. Like an inferno of electrical current, a zillion volts (alright, not a zillion, but a lot) zapped through them all causing their skeletons to flash like flashing skeletons. The guards, operatives, dogs, and government officials arrived on the scene and dove for cover as the lowrider started up with the power of a GE9X high-bypass turbofan jet engine with a takeoff thrust of 110,000 lbf (pound force) which is so powerful that it's more powerful than the other ones that aren't as powerful. It's also 13 feet in diameter which would have been too big for the lowrider, so what Marty did was pretty smart. He put the same power of the GE9X into the existing engine. Marty pulled his right tongue loose from the battery and jumped into the driver's seat. Bink hit the floorboard, and Leo fell into the backseat next to the Digby orb.

"NOW, BINK!" Marty yelled.

Bink slammed down on the accelerator and they took off burning tracks in the street a foot deep. The lowrider literally rocketed down the street and was going so fast that it used the street as a runway and took off into the night sky with those on the ground watching in amazement. Higher and higher the purple lowrider soared, eventually breaking through the Earth's atmosphere and entering outer space. Marty and Bink were finally heading home.

Chapter 19

Marty set the lowrider on cruise control as they headed for Digby. He put his feet up on the dashboard under the dangling fuzzy dice and pulled out a copy of *Detective Magazine* with Sheldon Danger on the cover and thumbed through it. Bink looked at his twin hubcaps and his antenna started to stiffen.

"I have to go to the bathroom," Bink announced.

"No, you don't, you horny disgusting little green alien you," Marty replied without looking up from the magazine.

"I CAN'T BREATHE!" Leo gasped. "THERE'S NO OXYGEN HERE!"

"Quit complaining and enjoy the ride," Marty said. "Look at all those beautiful stars and planets and just pretend you can breathe."

"I can't wait to get home," Bink said to no one in particular.

"Me too," Marty said to no one in particular too.

"There's so much to do there," Bink replied to no one in particular.

"Yeah," Marty responded to no one in particular too.

"What could Leo do there?" Bink asked sort of rhetorically to no one in particular again.

"I don't know. Maybe he could sell patio furniture," suggested Marty to no one in particular but hoping Bink would hear it.

"I guess we're heroes now because we found the orb and saved Digby," Bink guessed.

"I guess so," Marty guessed back.

"They'll probably have a parade for us and put our pictures on postage stamps and cereal boxes and name a pizza after us," Bink hoped. He stopped hoping and looked at one of the hubcap sisters. "She sure is a looker. Thanks for giving her to me, Marty. You want her sister? Two broads at one time is too distracting, especially twins. You don't know who's doing what where how and why. You take her sister."

"Okay, but only for a night. Marty Mooncricket is a lone wolf in the desert of love." Marty glanced at the sister hubcap, saw his reflection, and winked with his big bug-like eye. Suddenly his reflection got wavy and then the not-so-attracive face of Emperor Zee appeared. Marty was so startled that he almost ran into the ZX-12 as The Outlaws of Asteroid #9 cruised by searching for loose star maidens that they wouldn't have to pay.

"You're a lousy driver, Mooncricket," Emperor Zee pointed out.

"Your face scared the muffins outta me Sir. Almost no disrespect intended."

"REPORT!" Emperor Zee demanded in an unnecessarily loud voice that no self-respecting hubcap would use.

Marty cringed. "We're on our way home with the Digby orb right now."

"Nevermind," Emperor Zee said.

Marty pulled Bink off the gas pedal.

"What? Nevermind what?"

"You can come home, but you don't have to bring the rock."

"*THE ROCK?!*"

Emperor Zee laughed. "The Digby orb is really just a rock."

Marty pushed Bink down hard on the brake pedal and the lowrider came to a screeching stop in outer space. Marty was fuming.

"You mean to tell me that all this was for nothing?!"

"No, no, this was a test," Emperor Zee said sort of toying with the truth.

"*A TEST?!*" Marty growled. He shook his antenna angrily at Emperor Zee, "*TEST THIS! You made us risk our rumps for a ROCK?!*"

"In case we're ever attacked by Earth I need to know who's loyal to Digby."

"Earthlings are too busy attacking each other; they don't have time to attack us. You're a real schmecklehead, sir. Disrespect intended."

Marty turned the purple lowrider around. It was an illegal U-turn, but no one saw him.

"What are you doing, Mooncricket?" Emperor Zee asked. It was similar to the famous porno question when the older woman walks into the room and sees a young couple banging their brains out and has no idea what they're doing.

"What does it look like I'm doing, Emperor Schmecklehead? I'm heading back to Tinseltown. Bink and I have a movie to star in. You can read about us in the National Enquirer. If you're ever in the neighborhood drop by and I'll have my bodyguards throw you off a roof. Chow."

With that he tossed the hubcap out into space and watched it float away and get pulverized by passing space debris. Bink was horrified.

"You killed her!"

"It was a suicide, Bink. She was jealous of how you looked at her twin sister."

Marty and Bink slipped on their Hollywood shades and headed back to Earth making the lowrider hop up and down all the way. Bink looked in the backseat.

"I think Leo's dead, Marty. He hasn't had any oxygen for over four hours and he's stiff, blue, and bloated. He doesn't move except when the car bounces up and down."

"He's not dead, Bink. He's in a state of temporary unoxygenated animated somewhat reverse anhydrobiosis dormant cataleptic deferred stupified slumber. An astrophysicist at Syracuse discovered that oxygen particles cling to stardust, so just reach out and grab some and put it in his mouth and that'll hold him until we get to Earth. The somewhat great Leo Sachs has a blockbuster movie to make starring me, you, and the Digby orb!"

Hearing that, the Digby orb spun in its seat with excitement and flashed brilliant colors as the lowrider bounced up and down toward Hollywood.

The grand premiere of Leo Sach's new motion picture *Marty and Bink and the Search for the Digby Orb* was quite a spectacle. Held at Mann's Chinese Theater, not too far from the Jack Elam Hotel, the movie drew big crowds as word spread that no special effects or costumes were used and that Marty and Bink were the real deal, making it the first science fiction film of its kind. Instead of a red carpet, a green glowing carpet led into the theater. Searchlights criss-crossed the night sky to let everyone know that this was something very special. The courtyard of the theater, and Hollywood Boulevard right out front, was jammed with cheering fans and Hollywood hucksters hawking Marty and Bink merchandise from "I Dig

Digby" T-shirts to bug-eyed alien novelty eyeglasses. Several rented ride-share limousines were dropping off low budget B movie quasi-celebrities such as the late Jeff Morrow, the late Whit Bissell, the late Hazel Court, the late Arthur Franz, the late Faith Domergue, and the late Nick Nero (but he was just late). Inside the theater lobby, Leo, Marty, and Bink, all wearing glowing green tuxedoes were greeting the quasi-celebrities and special guests. The Digby orb, wearing a gold sequin tuxedo, was on a special pedestal in the center of the lobby being interviewed by reporters and not answering. Doris was there with her new husband and daughter Fran. Ushers were handing out gaudy lighted antennae for patrons to wear on their heads during the screening. The quasi-celebrities and guests put on the antennae and made lousy jokes about them. Marty and Bink glanced at each other, unamused. Leo saw that they were disturbed by this and tried to play it down.

"It's Hollywood hype, boys. Don't be upset."

"Who's upset?" Marty asked, upset. "This is just another example of why Earth is the laughingstock of the entire universe. Your species is nuts."

"You'll get no argument from me. Speaking of nuts-"

Doris approached Leo with her new husband on her arm.

"Congratulations, Leo."

"Thank you, Doris."

"Leo, this is Henry Barnes, my new husband."

Leo and Henry shook hands warmly.

"I heard you remarried, Doris. You have my sympathy for your misfortune, Henry."

They both laughed. Doris wasn't amused. Henry stopped laughing.

"It's a pleasure to meet you, Leo," Henry said. "I've enjoyed your work for many years."

"Thank you. I think you'll like what you see tonight too. There's never been a picture like it. What kind of business are you in, Henry?"

"I manufacture rope. Our motto is 'If you're at the end of your rope, we'll sell you another one.'"

"Very clever, a rope's gonna come in handy married to her."

Doris pulled Henry away. She wasn't amused. They passed by Elliott Fineberg who was talking to Bink.

"I'm serious, Bink. I can definitely see you doing television commercials when you're not making movies. I see you as the live version of Quisp, only with talent. You have one of those great character faces that casting directors love. I'll represent you. We can write up the contract on a napkin right now. I'll get my usual 90 percent and you can have 10 to do whatever you want with."

Doris stormed back to Leo who was talking to Nero who was long unstuck from the Creature costume. She interrupted their conversation.

"How come the same time I remarry you make it big again?"

"I planned it, Doris. Now I have lots of money and I don't have to pay you a dime."

Doris looked around. "Lots of names here. I guess they still remember the late great Leo Sachs."

Marty moved behind Doris and slapped her on the tush. She let out a yelp, spun around, and glared at him. He quickly pointed to Nero who looked down at them both and scowled, ending it right there. Marty eased away and bumped into Fran.

"Hello Marty," she said warmly.

"Good evening," he said coldly.

"I thought the government was after you and Bink. What happened?"

"Are you asking because you care or for the benefit of the reader of the greatest novel ever written?"

"Both."

"Me and Bink are famous celebrities now. They can't touch famous celebrities because we're famous celebrities and they can't touch famous celebrities."

"That's not true, they can arrest you," Fran said.

"Well they won't, because every time I see one I just turn them into phallic symbols. You see that guy in the black suit over there eating the hot dog? He's here to arrest us after the movie. But he won't, because six-foot rubber dildos can't arrest anything."

Marty gestured and turned Mr. Black Suit into a six-foot rubber dildo. A few people screamed, but most just gathered around to look on admiringly. This was Hollywood, so they all liked what they saw for different reasons. Marty blew on his finger like it was a six-shooter. Several people applauded him and he bowed.

"I've missed you," Fran admitted.

"Of course," Marty replied. "Once you go alien you can't go back again."

"Are you seeing anyone?" Fran asked.

"I'm dating thousands of broads with holes in them, but no one in particular. What about you, as if I care."

"I've dated a little," Fran said, "but no one really does to me what you do."

Marty pondered. "I thought you needed a *real* man, not a big insect or a pickle, as you so eloquently put it, as I recall."

"I'm sorry about that, Marty. My father didn't want me seeing you."

"I know, so what makes you think he's changed his mind?"

Leo overheard the conversation and stepped into it.

"I'm not thrilled about having green grandchildren, Marty, but you're okay."

"So are you, Leo, for an Earthling anyway."

Most of the monsters and some of the odder characters in this book such as The Evil One, the Cosmos Command, the Qudrags, the Festersmits, the Moola Boola Agboos, Madam Mancowitz's maid, all the Titans and Greek gods aside from Mercury and Hercules, the Flookies, the Percy comic, the Seething Aardsnarks, the Gray Gilfs, the Yoobs, and several others were CGI (computer-generated imagery) as we say in the biz. Just before the film was to start, many of the actors who portrayed some of your favorite characters in this book piled in to see *Marty and Bink and the Search for the Digby Orb* since many were curious about the mysterious orb that kept flying through their scenes. And many had parts in Leo's earlier films when they were starting out. I honestly don't remember the names of the actors because none of them will go very far, but the characters they portrayed will stay with me and most of you for a very long time. This novel had a cast of thousands and there were many extras and bit parts, so not everyone could fit into Mann's Chinese Theater which has a seating capacity of 932. Therefore I will only list some of the characters that did show up and were permitted to watch the film in the theater: Rollo Starguy, Sluggo, Alfie, Big Al, King Creole, Helen Rothenstein of Troy, Madam Mancowitz, the evil dwarfs, the stripper, Manny "The Wrench" Sanchez, Sheldon Danger, Maximus Moore, Uncle Buddy, Stanley "Squirm" Jerkins, Mad Dog Leibowitz, Zelda Borealis, Mr. Green Jeans, Sam and Midge Benowitz, Chester "the Man in the Moon" Flemlock, King Tyndareus, Irma Finkelstein, Aunt Goldie, The Chinaman, Big Mama, Fred and Ginger Tanaka, The Fat Man, Old Man Perkins, Emperor Zee, Lana Holliday, Ivan Kash, Milo Mabbitt, the deranged killer, Dweezle Dwindle, the Seven Member Quartet, Dusty "Duke Rook" Ketchum, the repo men, Dr. Arnold Kazazian, Owen Wixx, Don Neroni, Angelo, Toto, Izzy, the boy who wanted to date Molly, and many more. An usher whispered in Leo's ear and Leo announced to those in the lobby, "ALRIGHT EVERYONE INSIDE! IT'S SHOWTIME!" The actor who played Mercury (out of costume) ran into the theater, purposely tripped, and landed on his keister to everyone's delight. The actor who played Hercules helped him up and they both laughed. Everyone filed into the theater. Many couples went in arm in arm including Marty and Fran.

Bink looked at his hubcap, "Looks like it's you and me, Gorgeous."

The actor who played Private Detective Maximus Moore walked up with a box of popcorn and said, "You can sit next to me Bink." They entered the theater which was buzzing with anticipation and excitement. The sight of 932 people wearing gaudy lighted jiggling Marty and Bink antennae was ridiculous, but expected. While the opening credits rolled, a strange sound was coming from the Digby orb in the lobby. The orb started to wobble violently and then bizarre sounds came from it. Horrible sounds. Sounds like fingernails on a blackboard (yes, like what Captain Quint did in *Jaws* to get the attention of the what-to-do-about-the-shark committee), like rats chewing on tin foil, and perhaps the most horrible sound of all, side 2 of *The Plastic Ono Band – Live Peace in Toronto* 1969 where Yoko Ono just screams for 17 minutes and 38 seconds straight. A burst of glorious green light surrounded the Digby orb and with one final spin it cracked open and out oozed glowing green albumen (the white in a chicken egg), a green yoke, the inner and outer membranes, blood spots, the chalazae (twisted strands that anchor the yoke), the vitelline yolk membrane (which protects the yoke and keeps it separate from the egg "white"/green), the germinal disc (a tiny white, but in this case, green dot on the yolk) and a pair of big bug-like eyes and a tiny antenna and propeller that slithered down to the lobby floor. It was sad. It was disgusting. It was both sad and disgusting at the same time. I guess all that zigzagging through the universe, rolling down streets, and bouncing around in a van and a lowrider was just too much to take and the poor little alien embryo never had a chance. I would prefer to end with something more upbeat and hopeful, but I can't think of anything.

FIN

ABOUT THE AUTHOR

Howard Camner is the author of 22 books including the Pulitzer Prize nominated <u>Poems from the Mud Room</u>, the acclaimed autobiography <u>Turbulence at 67 Inches</u>, and the self-help humor book <u>Happy Birthday to...*Who?* (The Definitive No Holds Barred Father's Guide to Surviving Kids' Birthday Parties)</u> as well as having published in numerous national and international journals and anthologies. His books and sound recordings of his work are housed in prominent literary archives worldwide including historical archives in the United States and royal collections in Great Britain. He was a founding member of New York's Literary Outlaws and the West End Poetry Troupe. National libraries housing his work include Spain, Japan, China, Greece, Russia, India, Ireland, and France. He was named "Best Poet" in the New Times "Best of Miami" edition of 2007 and was inducted into the MDC Hall of Fame for Literary Arts in 2014. His comedy play *Flaming Floss* was featured at the Edward Albee Last Frontier Theatre Conference in 2003. His original feature film screenplay *Duck Duck Goose* was placed in the archives of the Academy of Motion Picture Arts and Sciences and his 1980s comedy cable talk show *Life is a Four Letter Word* is housed in the Library of American Broadcasting / Paley Center for Media in New York, the Barco Cable Television Archives, and the UCLA Film & Television Archive. Camner received the Albert Nelson Marquis Lifetime Achievement Award for Literary Arts in 2018. Homebase is with his family in Miami. Most of the writing gets done at his singlewide lake mansion in Interlachen, Florida.

CPSIA information can be obtained
at www.ICGtesting.com
Printed in the USA
LVHW111928021121
702258LV00011B/221/J